Under Renovation

STEPHANIE HADDAD

Cover design by Anna Pearlman

Copyright © 2020 EM.press Books

All rights reserved.

ISBN: 9798665592299

Also available from
STEPHANIE HADDAD

A PREVIOUS ENGAGEMENT

LOVE REGIFTED

LOVE UNLISTED

SOCIALLY AWKWARD

--

MY LIFE IN YOGA PANTS:
An Essay Collection

OTHER KINDS OF LOVE
A Short Story Collection

For my theatre family.

CHAPTER ONE

"I'm not breaking up with your girlfriend for you, Shawn."

"I didn't say *for* me. I said *help* me. That's different, Quinn," he said, leaning forlornly on the bar counter.

My twin brother is a confident, carefree man, with a long and complicated dating history. He definitely knows how attractive he is and how easily it can get him into trouble. Shawn's carefully tousled hair and "twinkling eyes," as I'd heard them described, have always earned him plenty of attention. We have the same auburn hair and hazel eyes, but Shawn had gotten a few extra benefits from the gene pool and not just the extra height. He'd also inherited Mom's winning smile and Dad's natural charisma—which made him truly charming. Still, even with his good looks, Shawn wasn't exactly a *player* in the negative sense. He just hated commitment.

It was bizarre to see him practically begging for help with anything, especially a dating problem. Something as straightforward as breaking up with a woman shouldn't be an issue for him. *So why this time?*

If this had been any other kind of request, I would've already said yes. Shawn and I have always looked out for each other—I'd often covered for him to sneak out at night; he'd taken the heat for a lamp I broke playing soccer in the house. We might not always get along, but we'd hide a body for each other, no questions asked. There's just one forbidden area: romance. We do not get involved in each other's dating lives. Ever. It's too messy.

It was just a regular Monday night at our Uncle Charlie's bar, where Shawn worked as the Assistant Manager and I helped out a few times a week. Sure, the bar had emptied early that night, just like every night since the laundromat next door closed, but that didn't make it okay to argue there.

"You know I can't help. Leave me out of it," I said, elbowing him out of my way. "Do we have to talk about this now? Here?"

"Yes," he said flatly. "It's literally the only time I can get your attention these days."

"I know, I know…" I agreed. We lived together, but our schedules were so opposite that we were rarely home at the same time. Shawn liked to blame me for keeping myself so busy all the time. He wasn't exactly wrong about that, but I didn't see the problem.

I pushed past him as I finished disinfecting the cherrywood bar counter, which formed a U in the back corner of the bar. I stepped through the swinging half-door into the main seating area and wiped down the rickety chairs and three small, wobbly tables.

Sorry Charlie's was a cozy neighborhood sports bar that had once been a popular hangout, but it was showing its age after nearly 25 years in business. Uncle Charlie used to dream of turning this place into a real restaurant, but now, he was focused on keeping the doors open.

"I've never asked you to get involved before, but I need your help this time. This one's different, okay?" he said, pouring me a gin and tonic. *Bribery.*

"How?" I frowned at him.

Shawn placed my drink on the counter, but I pretended not to notice.

"Well, you're partially responsible for this one."

"Excuse me?"

I finished the tables and returned to the counter to wipe down the bar stools. I cleaned off the fingerprints from the black leather, worn thin in some places, torn in others. With my job completed, I tossed the dirty rag into the bucket of pungent, lemon-scented cleaner. I put my hands on my hips and glowered at my brother.

"First of all," he began, crossing his arms. "I met her *because* of you. I only went to that Christmas charity ball because you dragged me."

"I shouldn't *have* to drag you. Both of us are supposed to be at the foundation's events, not just me."

"Second, *you* introduced us. I wasn't even looking for a girlfriend," he continued, ignoring me. He wiped his hands on the wrinkled, stained apron around his waist. "Then suddenly you're standing there with Gina, who's wearing this *insane* dress. Honestly, any straight man alive wouldn't be able to—"

"Pause," I warned him. I breathed deeply to collect myself. "I introduced you to one of the foundation's new employees and now I'm a matchmaker?"

"And you're terrible at it," he said firmly, as though this was perfectly logical. I picked up my drink and held it in front of him, narrowing my eyes. He muttered an apology and dropped ice cubes into it. I took a drink. For his safety.

"To be clear," I continued. "Did I also force you to hook up with her in the coat check? And put her number in your phone?"

"Okay, that's fair," Shawn said with a grimace. He picked up a bottle of glass cleaner and sprayed down the empty glass shelves along the wall. I watched him wipe them down and realign the alcohol bottles with the labels all facing out, the way I liked them.

"Anything else you're pinning on me?"

"Yeah, actually," Shawn said, frowning. "Was there something you maybe failed to mention? A detail that might've been of some importance to me?"

I shook my head, staring blankly at him. I twirled my glass around and listened to the ice cubes clink.

"Gina has a kid, Quinn. And you knew."

I paused, with my drink halfway to my lips. Of course, I knew about Gina's son Dylan. She was my employee.

"Let's say I did, theoretically," I said. "What's the problem?"

"A kid, Quinn. An actual child."

"Yes, a small human. So?"

"We've been dating for three months and I *just* found out—*by accident!* Why didn't you tell me? You had to know that it would freak me out."

"Because it's none of my business, Shawn," I scowled, taking another drink. He didn't like my answer, but he didn't argue. "And how was I supposed to know that Gina hadn't already told you?"

"But why wouldn't she tell me?"

"Probably because she's worried about us having this exact conversation."

"*The kid* isn't the problem. Although," he said, contemplatively. "I can see why you'd assume that about me. It's me, Quinn. *I'm* the problem. What if she expects me to be a father figure to him somewhere far, *far* down the road? I am the *last* person any kid wants for a step-dad."

"Agreed." I was impressed with his level of self-awareness. I took another sip of my drink and sat down on my favorite stool. "Were you planning to get that far down the road?"

"I don't know! Maybe? But I can't now, it would be a disaster," he said, exasperated. "And if I know *now* that it won't work out, shouldn't I tell her before things get serious? I don't want to waste her time if she's looking for something that I can't give her—right?"

"That's... shockingly responsible of you, Shawn," I said, impressed.

"Yeah, I don't like it," he frowned. "Because this woman is hot and *incredible* in—"

"Boundaries," I warned.

"The kitchen. What did you think I was going to say?" he said with a perfect deadpan. Only his smirk gave him away.

"Look, I realize this isn't the best situation, but you need to talk to her yourself. Just be honest about it. Tell her exactly what you told me—maybe without the kitchen part."

I tipped back the end of my drink and placed the empty glass on the counter. I picked up the duster and walked to the far wall to clean the photo frames and sports memorabilia. The oldest photo, a snapshot of Dad and Uncle Charlie on opening day of the bar, needed a new frame. I'd only been seven, but I could remember that day so well. The bar had been packed, Dad had been beaming, Shawn and I had greeted people at the door—until Mom had dragged us home for bedtime. We'd had so much fun that day. Dad had arranged balloons all over the place. He'd brought them all home for Shawn and me when it was over. If you looked closely at the photo, you could see them in the background.

Shawn was quiet for a while. The clinking of glass bottles was the only sound in the bar, until I finished dusting and returned to the counter. We made eye contact and he groaned loudly.

"Quinn, please. I have no idea what I'm supposed to say. Will you at least write me a script?"

"I'm going to get some work done in the back now," I said, crossing my arms. "Maybe you can take this quiet time to write your own damn script. You're a big boy. I believe in you."

He stuck his tongue out at me. And okay, I did the same back at him. Even at 32 years old, there's something about a sibling that brings out the childishness in you.

In the back room, alone and surrounded by nostalgia, I took a deep breath. My dad and my uncle had managed *Sorry Charlie's* together until my parents died seven years ago. Uncle Charlie had handled the bar's operations and Dad, an investment banker, had fronted the money and managed all the finances; they were a perfect team.

Shawn and I had basically grown up in this bar. I'd often done my homework on milk crates in the backroom. Shawn preferred hiding underneath the bar to play his Gameboy, which drove Dad absolutely nuts.

Already exhausted, I dropped into the old, squeaky chair in the office and sighed. I didn't know where to begin. Papers cluttered the desk in all directions, even on top of the keyboard—receipts, sales reports, scraps of paper, and bank deposit slips. Sometimes, Uncle Charlie would paperclip them to each other in chronological order, but that was rare. I scooped everything up and shoved it into the empty file sorter.

I turned on the computer—a relic that needed replacing—and started with the top of the pile. I made some decent headway on a stack of bank deposit slips before Uncle Charlie entered from the stockroom. He was lanky thin and about as tall as Shawn, with an angular face and a wrinkled forehead. The dim overhead lighting shone off his bald head. His black shirt was pristinely ironed, and his waist-tied apron was a bright, bleached white. He was a near replica of my Dad, his older brother, just without hair.

By now, Uncle Charlie was older than Dad would ever be.

He carried a creased multi-page bill of lading that listed everything on today's shipment. Not paying attention, he dropped the whole thing onto the keyboard and inadvertently typed about 100 letter M's into my spreadsheet.

"Shipment's checked in. Everything's there for a change." He bent over and picked up some paper scraps from the floor. "Heard you bickering out there. Shawn having another lady problem?"

I shrugged. "Something like that."

"Hey," Shawn said. The kitchen door swung back and forth behind him. He scowled at me. "Now you're getting Charlie involved?"

Uncle Charlie gave him a look. "Who's watching the bar?"

"It's 9 o'clock. We're closed." Shawn placed the drying rack on the counter. The day's empty glasses clinked together.

I checked the time on the computer screen which was ten minutes behind—and would remain ten minutes behind until the computer croaked, no matter how much I fought with it. Stubborn as Uncle Charlie. I yawned, rising from the chair, and shoved the stack of file folders into my tote bag. *There, portable paperwork.* After putting on my jacket, I hefted the bag onto my shoulder, and gave my uncle a kiss on the cheek.

"Time for me to go home, gentlemen. Early day tomorrow. You gonna be okay with him on your own?"

Uncle Charlie smiled.

"I repeat…" Shawn said, miffed. "Hey!"

"Oh, Quinnie," said Uncle Charlie. "If it's not too much trouble, could you help me file my taxes again?"

"Already on it." I pointed to the papers exploding from my bag, a weak smile plastered across my face.

For a while after Dad died, Charlie had kept an accountant on staff, but when business started suffering, he'd let him go. I'd jumped in to help him stay on top of the finances, just until things got better, but strictly as a volunteer. Shawn's salary was his only income, and the foundation paid me enough, so I refused anything from Uncle Charlie.

"Thank you, sweetheart. You've always been the smart

one," Uncle Charlie said with a proud smile.

Shawn scoffed. With a wink at my brother, I headed for the door.

"See you at home," I called to him over my shoulder. "And you can put my drink on *your* tab."

A short drive later, I pulled into the driveway of our childhood home, a white two-story Colonial with black shutters. Shawn and I had inherited the house when Mom and Dad died. They'd bought the property and helped design the house long before Shawn and I were even a thought. Much to the construction crew's chagrin, they'd insisted on literally laying the foundation of their new home. That's how one of Mom's gardening gloves had become encased in the concrete of the basement floor.

While workers built the house, Mom had created a gorgeous garden in our front yard. Once she'd decided I was old enough, she'd taught me how to do some of the smaller jobs and our annual Save the Garden weekend became one of my favorite traditions. Every year, I'd learn something new—how to revive dying plants, what time of day to water the garden, how to properly prune rose bushes. We'd weed, trim the hedges, dump huge bags of soil to create raised flower beds, and plant new tulip bulbs. Mom would let me pick out which flowers we planted around the tree in the front yard. The purple petunias had always been her favorite.

Walking up to the bright yellow door, I dodged the overgrown hedges, carefully navigated the uneven walkway, and trotted up the concrete steps. The garden, her pride and joy, was now in complete disarray. She would've wanted me to maintain it. I'd promised myself that I would. So, I made my annual pledge to get control of it by summertime. I knew exactly what to do; I just needed to find two or three consecutive days off to do it properly.

As usual, I found my ancient fawn-colored Great Dane, Franklin, sitting patiently in the hallway, wagging his tail. He barked his greeting and nudged me in the hip to go out. I dropped my things, grabbed a flashlight, clipped on his leash, and headed out for our nightly stroll.

"No pulling tonight, Frankie," I warned him. Walking a 180-pound dog who liked to chase squirrels was dangerous for anyone—even worse for little me. After a decade of walking this route, I knew where the trouble spots were, but I still had to remind him not to accidentally kill me.

I inhaled the clean, fresh air deeply through my nose and exhaled from the mouth, meditating while Franklin led me around the block. The stillness, the quiet, the moment of just being. My favorite part of the day. By the time we were home, I couldn't stop yawning.

I propped open my agenda on the bathroom counter—I'd always preferred physical planners to digital calendars—and scanned the pages while I brushed my teeth. Line by line, item by item, homing in on the most important tasks I needed to accomplish. Then, as I flossed, washed my face, tweezed a few stray eyebrow hairs, and poked at a zit forming on my chin, I brainstormed any items I might've missed. Like the clean towels in the dryer downstairs.

I left the bathroom, tweezers still on the counter, and hopped down to the basement to collect them. Franklin laid across my neatly-made bed while I sang songs and folded the towels. He rested his chin on the pile of washcloths and watched me with his big brown eyes. His ears twitched whenever I sang one of his favorites. He was a big fan of showtunes, especially *Wicked*.

The laundry was done and put away. My nighttime routine had been completed. I'd mostly finished prepping for tomorrow. I grabbed my agenda from the bathroom, doubled back to put the tweezers away, and finally tucked myself into bed with the agenda spread open on my lap. One more scan. Without this crucial step every night, the next day could easily be a disaster. I couldn't miss a thing. I needed to prioritize every task. I couldn't drop a ball somewhere and let someone down—people counted on me.

I yawned, just as I remembered that I hadn't prepared a craft project for this Friday's story time at the library. I reached into my messy bun for my pen to jot that down, then scribbled a few last tiny reminders on my to-do list. I tossed the pen and the agenda on my nightstand and turned off the light, double checked that my alarm was set properly, and started up the rain sounds app on my phone.

    I was officially tired enough to sleep.

CHAPTER TWO

In the morning, I arrived at the Mara Davis Foundation with three stacked trays of coffee and a bag of scones. I'd started this Tuesday morning tradition when I took over as president after Dad died. I struggled to push open the big glass doors with my hip, then just barely averted disaster on the freshly buffed floor. As I passed the receptionist's desk, where Janet had been watching me the entire time, I muttered a *good morning* and handed her the medium coffee, hot, with milk and sugar.

I walked swiftly through my delivery route, handing out the orders I'd memorized long ago. A large, black hazelnut coffee went to Julia in marketing. I left a coffee with cream, no sugar, and one shot of espresso for Danny, our event planner. Tim and Tom, the identical twin brothers who worked in IT, were grateful for the pair of medium regular coffees with cream and sugar. Bradley, who headed up our annual charity walk, preferred hot tea with honey. Gina was out, so I skipped Human Resources.

Finally, I made a quick swing through accounting, where I dropped off Jeanne's dark roast and Minnie's decaf latte with soy milk. They were lovely women who loved to gab about their cats, but honestly, my schedule was too tight today. Maybe next Tuesday.

I brought Leah's extra-large iced mocha, and the bag of scones to the breakroom. By the time I arrived, my coffee was lukewarm. Gross.

"Every single time," I muttered. While my coffee rotated happily inside the microwave, I arranged the scones onto a paper plate with napkins stacked neatly beside it. Leah Lancaster, the foundation's CEO, arrived right on time to start our day together with caffeine and breakfast pastries.

She picked up a blueberry scone and set it delicately on a

napkin as she slid into a chair. Leah broke the scone into small pieces, careful to keep the crumbs over the napkin, and then ate them one at a time. The microwave dinged, and I sat down with my coffee and an orange-cranberry scone.

"Thanks for breakfast, *Mom*," said Leah, smirking. "You know, as much as I appreciate Quinn the Caffeine Fairy, it's probably time to take things down a notch. Seven years of Tuesdays is a lot."

"Are you complaining?"

"As an employee, I wish every day were Tuesday," she said, twirling the straw in her cup. "But as your friend…"

"I know, I know."

"You *are* allowed to come to work without catering."

"Yeah, but caffeine improves productivity. That's science."

"Is it?" She sighed. "You know we get *paid*, right? These people could buy their own coffees."

"Maybe I just like to share," I retorted.

We've had the same conversation every week for years. It had become a part of the tradition. After she gave up, we parted ways to get to work. I stopped outside my office to check the mail stuffed into my wall file—mostly junk, as usual. When I turned the corner and spotted *Shawn* sitting behind my desk, I nearly walked right back out.

"Hey, Quinn."

He spun the chair around, wearing an unzipped hoodie, a faded Dave Matthews Band t-shirt, a pair of loose-fitting jeans, and a pair of battered Vans. His hair was a tousled mess, and the smile on his face was troublesome. Looking at him and then at me—in a black pencil skirt, pale pink blouse, and heels, with my hair in a French twist—said it all.

"Why are you in my office?"

"*Our* office… We're co-presidents, remember?"

My lips pursed. "Weird. It doesn't look like your name's on that door."

"It's implied."

"Look, Shawn, Gina's not in today, so if that's why you're here, you're out of luck."

"Who said anything about her?"

"Don't lie. I'm not in the mood for this today." Not that I was *ever* in the mood.

"Calm down, okay? You've got *Resting Crisis Face*. You know, the face you had for most of high school. Didn't someone have a senior quote about it in the yearbook?"

"Yeah..." I said, putting a hand on my hip. "You."

Shawn laughed, sitting with his feet propped on my desk, crossed at the ankle. I wanted to tip the chair backwards and watch him tumble to the floor, but I controlled myself.

"What are you doing here?" I sighed.

He yawned, stretching his arms above his head, then reached for the water bottle on my desk. He took a long swig, nearly draining its contents.

"Got anything to eat?"

I pinched the bridge of my nose to fight my impending headache. "I'll ask one more time. What are you even doing here?"

Shawn shrugged his shoulders and finished the water.

"Come on, I have work to do."

"I'm sure you do." He yawned again, picking at the label on the water bottle.

"What's that supposed to mean?" I snapped.

"For the millionth time, you don't do anything here."

My eyes narrowed. *Here we go again.*

Shawn had always insisted we weren't needed at the Mara Davis Foundation, which Dad had established fifteen years ago in his sister's honor. To me, inheriting the role of co-presidents meant we should do our best to fill his shoes. But because the foundation had been staffed and successful before Dad died, Shawn claimed we were useless figureheads.

"Look, one of us has three meetings before 2pm and the other hasn't combed their hair today. Can you just go home? Please?"

"Which one am I?"

"I *will* punch you, Shawn William Davis."

"Can I stay if I promise to go to the meetings?"

"If you're saying you want to work here, I've got plenty for you to do."

He frowned. "You're not the boss of me."

I stuck my tongue out at him, right as Leah walked through the open door, carrying a manila envelope, stuffed to the brim. She seemed amused and totally unfazed by our childish behavior—which probably wasn't a great indicator of my professionalism.

"Thanks for coming in, Shawn," she said.

"Sure thing, Leah," he smiled, putting his feet back on the floor. Leah Lancaster is the kind of woman who commands a room just by standing still. Even Shawn paid attention when she spoke.

"This will be quick, I promise," Leah said. "I need both of you to sign the budget proposal for next year."

"Already? It's April, Leah." I blinked, then turned on Shawn. "Why didn't you just tell me why you were here?"

Leah pulled the paperwork out of the envelope and dropped it with a thud, scattering some of the mail on my desk. The empty water bottle fell to the floor, its torn label flapping on the way down. She showed us where to sign or initial and explained what the budget entailed. Shawn scrawled a lazy signature on the correct lines and handed the sheets to me. Even though it wasn't necessary, I read through each page from top to bottom, still standing, still holding a cold cup of coffee.

"Stop pretending you know what you're doing, Quinn," my brother laughed, getting to his feet. He had never been a fan of hanging out at the foundation. He picked up the bottle on the floor and tossed it into the bin. "Okay if I take off?"

Leah nodded and dismissed him. I mumbled a goodbye, still flipping through the paperwork. It wasn't that I didn't trust Leah to propose the budget. She'd worked her way up from intern to CEO here. She was as dedicated to this company and its success as I was. Mostly, I was looking for typos. It's hard to shut off English Major Quinn.

When he was halfway out the door, I called after him.

"I left scones in the breakroom, if you want one."

Moments later, Shawn ran from the breakroom past my office, Rocky Balboa style, with a scone in his mouth. Leah laughed, dropping her super-business persona, which she only did with me.

"That was… odd."

"What can I say?" I shrugged. "He's an odd guy."

"But so nice to look at," she smirked.

My nose wrinkled. "Eww, Leah."

CHAPTER THREE

After I left the foundation for the day, I changed into my comfy clothes and joined my best friend Faith in the high school auditorium for another afternoon of drama camp. She'd established the Middlesex Drama Cares after-school program five years ago and I'd become Technical Director Quinn. I spent a few afternoons a week and Saturday mornings here with Faith, a small army of children between the ages of five and twelve, and a pair of teenage volunteers—Faith's daughter Abby and her on-again-off-again boyfriend Will.

"Okay, everybody, let's take it from the end of the dance number. Lilly, you're downstage left by this point. Yup that's it! And I need the rest of the chorus out here for the final pose at the end of the song. Come back, girls!"

Faith's patience seemed abnormally thin. Her strawberry blonde hair was pulled into a messy bun and frizzing on the sides. She was squinting like she had a headache, leaning forward on her elbows on the lid of the piano. She watched the kids with a half-scowl on her face. Her daughter Abby, a near replica of her with dark hair, sat in the front row, giggling with Will. Faith turned around and shushed her, then returned her attention to the stage.

"Am I still over here?" asked Harry Jackson, who was very talented but so confused, so often. He was playing Don Lockwood in our production of *Singin' in the Rain*, alongside Lilly Evans as Kathy Seldon, and Oliver Miller as Cosmo Brown. The musical was our big season finale, scheduled for the end of June, right when school let out for summer.

"Yes, perfect. Don't forget to cross before you say the line, okay?" Faith replied, watching the other kids return to their places. She blew a stray hair out of her eyes. "Take it from, 'I just had to tell you…'"

Faith ran the kids through the song a few times then asked Abby and Will to lead the kids in a few theater games. She flopped into the chair next to mine and the hinges of the seat creaked. The auditorium had been renovated about ten years ago with the money my parents had donated, and even then, the swing-bottom seats still squeaked.

"How goes?" she asked, leaning over to peer at the notes I'd been taking in my script. "Are those the light cues? That seems like a lot."

"That's just act one."

"Oh my god, Q, I'm sorry."

"Not your problem," I said, pushing her off my arm. "You have the vision. I make it happen. That's how this works."

"Promise you'll tell me when I get outta control, okay?"

"You've been out of control since we were students in this building," I laughed.

I spent the last thirty minutes of rehearsal scanning the pages of act two. When I heard Abby nearing the end of Simon Says, I nudged Faith in the arm. She stirred, blinking a few times.

"Wake up, lazy."

"I wasn't sleeping."

"Sure, just thinking really hard?"

"You try teaching kindergarten all day and we'll see how perky you are at 5pm."

"Come on, old woman," I poked her again, then stood up. *Creak.* "I'm not getting these kids out of here by myself."

When the game ended, the kids erupted into conversation and laughter, pushing each other to get to their belongings. Some of the younger kids showed off Pokémon cards to each other. A few of the older kids tapped away on their smartphones. We helped them into jackets, put backpacks on their shoulders, and brought them all outside. Faith paraded the bus riders around to the side lot and I stayed with the kids getting picked up at the front entrance.

One by one, kids hopped into cars and waved goodbye, until just Oliver Miller remained. He'd brought a note saying his dad would pick him up, but I was starting to get concerned there was a mix-up. Oliver stood next to me, zipped up in his bright green jacket, chattering away about the show. He didn't seem concerned.

Just as I scrolled through my contacts to call his dad, a blue sedan turned into a front-row parking spot.

"There he is, Miss Quinn!" Oliver exclaimed. The car door opened, and a man emerged, just in time to catch Oliver in his arms.

Normally, I'd introduce myself to a new parent. Oliver had just signed up a few months ago and I hadn't had an opportunity to meet Mr. Miller yet. Still, it didn't seem right to interrupt them as Oliver gabbed away, with his dad's undivided attention. I felt like a total creep just standing there, watching them, so I turned to head back into the building.

"Miss Quinn! Come meet my DAD!"

Well, okay fine. I slipped my phone into my pocket and walked toward them.

"Quinn Davis. I'm the program tech director. From what I hear, you're Oliver's dad."

"Theo Miller. It's nice to finally meet you," he said with proud amusement, as we shook hands. His palm was warm and his grip firm. "Oliver has been talking about you nonstop. He was just telling me that you're the nicest person *ever*."

"Oh, really?" I laughed nervously. *Why was I nervous?*

Maybe because I was checking him out—and *hello,* hot stuff. Theo Miller is reasonably tall, with an athletic build, and a casual, confident posture. He's probably early to mid-30s, around my age, with an easy smile on his face. He wore jeans, a light blue button-up shirt with the top button undone, a brown leather jacket, and a pair of trainers. Theo had an easy, relaxed smile that lit up his dark, chocolatey-brown eyes. I could have stared into them for a good long while. And okay, I wanted to run my fingers through his thick, dark hair. Like, just for a second.

"I apologize for being so late," he said, shoving his hands into the pockets of his jeans. "Halfway here, I realized that I didn't have your phone number."

"That's an easy fix. I'll text you. Just save my number." Still smiling, I reached into my back pocket for my smartphone and swiped across the screen to open my contacts.

His phone buzzed in his pocket. "You have my number?"

"I have all the parents' contact information... For emergencies—nothing creepy." *Stop it.* "Definitely not for personal stuff or whatever."

Theo made eye contact but didn't say anything.

By now, Oliver had climbed into the back of the car and dropped his backpack into one seat. In the other, apparently, he found a surprise.

"Oh awesome!!" He ran back over to us, triumphantly presenting a red cardboard box with yellow handles. "It's a HAPPY MEAL, Miss Quinn."

"Oh, how fun! Did you get a toy?"

He tore open the box and frantically dug through it, pausing to shove a handful of fries into his mouth, before resuming his attack.

"I found it!" He held up the plastic-wrapped toy in victory. "It's a Pokémon!"

"You must think I'm a terrible parent," Theo shook his head, his face flushed. "I'm late, I don't know how to reach you, and now I'm feeding my child a box of junk food with a toy inside. Terrible parent."

"That all depends."

"On...?"

"Whether you let him open the toy *before* or *after* he eats all of his dinner." When our eyes met and he realized I was joking, some of the nervous tension ebbed. His shoulders lowered slowly. "I mean, if you let him open it before, then you're a *cool* terrible parent."

Thankfully, Theo laughed. And sure enough, when Oliver brought him the toy, Theo ripped it open and handed back a small plastic monster.

"Eat your food, don't just run around playing with Charmander. And don't spill your milk in the car please!"

Oliver skipped off toward the car again and Theo watched until he was safely back inside.

"What's a—"

"Charmander?" He asked. I nodded. "Orange baby lizard

thing with fire powers."

"Oh. Sure. Makes sense."

"Honestly, the only thing Oliver talks about more than Pokémon is how much fun he has at theater camp, especially with you."

"Really?" I thought I might be blushing. "I'm so glad."

"I'm happy we found your program. I never got the chance to try theater in school, so I didn't know how to get him started. His teacher told me about Drama Cares."

"What stopped you from getting involved?"

"Soccer took up too much time. I don't think I could've managed both at once."

"That's fair. I *did* do both at once," I said with a laugh. "I stuck to the technical stuff though, which was easier to do around my soccer schedule. Rehearsals were always at the same time as practice, but I could squeeze my tech duties into the off-times."

"What kinds of stuff?"

"I've tried all of it at some point or another. Mostly set building, but I've worked on lighting, sound, props... I was an excellent stage manager," I said with a laugh. Actors feared me and my clipboard. "Once and only once, I made costumes. After I accidentally sewed the arm holes shut on a bunch of princess gowns, they sent me away with a hot glue gun and fake gems to put on plastic tiaras."

"I can't see myself being good at that either," he admitted with a smile. After a moment of thought, he continued. "Maybe I'll give it a try someday, when Oliver's older and I won't need a sitter."

Oh...

Then a lightbulb went off.

"You know," I began slowly, suddenly nervous to talk to this man. "If you really want to give it a try, Mr. Miller—"

"Theo."

"Right, Theo. I could use some help backstage. And you won't need a sitter because you'll be *with* Oliver." And me. I was so damn proud of myself. "I'd love to have you—I mean, your hands. Like, you know, have you as a second pair of hands. But only if you have the time for it, of course."

I was no longer so damn proud of myself.

"I would *love* that," he replied. He had the most adorable smile on his face. "It's perfect. Thank you!"

We picked a few Saturdays for him to volunteer and he typed them all into his smartphone calendar. It would be great to have some help, which was, of course, my primary reason for asking him. But now I could see him regularly… and I did not hate that at all.

"Awesome," he said when he finished. "I can't wait."

"Yeah, this is great," I said. "It was, uh, nice meeting you."

"You too, Miss Quinn."

"Just Quinn's fine," I smiled.

"Right, Quinn." He offered a parting handshake. This time, his hand lingered just a bit too long. "And thank you for all you've done for Oliver. He's had a rough time adjusting since we moved here in January. I've never seen him so happy about anything."

"It's my pleasure. You have an amazing little boy. I'm so glad you found us."

We stood there looking at each other for a minute, trapped inside this uncomfortable silence. *Should I say something? Does he want to say something? Should I just walk over and run my hands through his hair anyway?*

"Dad! I'm done! Can we go home now?" Oliver's voice popped the bubble around us. Theo blinked. I exhaled. "Bye, Miss Quinn!"

"I'll see you Saturday," I said.

He nodded and then walked back to the car. I watched until he'd pulled out of the parking lot and turned down the street. Faith cleared her throat behind me, and when I turned around, she was staring at me with her hands on her hips. *How long has she been standing there?*

"What the hell are you still doing here? Go home, Q."

That's an excellent question because he's definitely wearing a wedding ring.

CHAPTER FOUR

On Wednesdays, I snuggle puppies—and clean kennels, but mostly I snuggle puppies. I'll be honest, I often prefer the company of dogs to that of humans. Sitting on the floor of the pet shelter with puppies all over me is my happy place. It's like therapy, without the copay, and with the added feeling that I've done something good for animal-kind.

That day, I was enjoying the vicious attack of two rescued goldendoodles, a squishy pug, a little corgi with stubby legs, and a fluffy collie mix who'd just been separated from his mother. Some of the puppies I played with at my last visit had since been adopted, which always makes my heart happy.

The collie mix, whom I'd quickly named Percival, playfully bit the end of my thumb. I faked a tiny yelp and he cocked his head to the side, perplexed. *Humans don't make puppy sounds.* I could melt from the cuteness.

"Oh, I like you, Percy," I said, holding his little face in my hands. "You're gonna be a playful guy and have fun with lots of kiddos."

"I can't adopt him out yet," said Mary Beth, the shelter's manager. She and I were in the same high school class and had volunteered here together for years. When the previous manager retired a few years ago, Mary Beth had taken the job. "He still needs all of his vaccines and everything before he can leave. You'll have plenty of Wednesdays to play together."

"It will be the highlight of my week," I said, scratching his head.

"Alright, spill. What's the scoop outside of the shelter walls these days?"

"Still not getting out much?"

"You know me," she admitted. "I'll take a night on the

couch with Netflix and my cats over almost anything else. Doesn't mean I can't live a romantic life vicariously through you, right?"

"See, you're making the mistake of assuming *I* have a romantic life," I laughed. One of the goldendoodles tackled the other and bit his ear. I picked up the assaulted puppy and scratched his head. Percy got jealous and pounced on my hand. "I mostly go from Charlie's bar to the foundation to the theater and back again. With a pit stop here for snuggles."

"No sexy bar patrons?"

"I spend most of my time in the back office. And Shawn's not exactly willing to scope out guys for me."

"No hot, young donors to the foundation?"

I laughed. "Not exactly our typical demographic."

"Pfft," she scoffed, then laughed. "You're right. You gotta get out more, too."

Mary Beth returned her attention to cleaning the windows and dusting the ledges, leaving me to enjoy the sounds of playful puppy growls. But not for long.

"Hey, Quinn," she said, hesitating. "How's Shawn?"

Like most of the girls, and some of the guys, in our high school, Mary Beth had a crush on my brother. Shawn dated for fun, not for commitment, so he had lots of dates, but not a lot of girlfriends. To be fair, most of the girls just wanted to make out with a hot guy or take him to prom. And Shawn does clean up nicely.

For Mary Beth, however, there had always been more to it. According to her, their hands had touched one day during a lab experiment in chemistry class—and instantly, she knew. Like a bolt of electricity shot through her body. She'd never worked up the nerve to approach him, but still pined for him. He probably had no idea.

"He's the same old Shawn," I shrugged. "You should swing by the bar some time and say hi."

"I'm sorry. I know I ask about him every time I see you," she added. "I wish I'd been braver in high school."

"I'm telling you, just drop in and talk to him."

She nodded. She wanted to. She wouldn't.

Before I knew it, it was time to put the puppies back and clean up the empty kennels, including the one Franklin had inhabited, a decade ago. It's a stinky, dirty job, but I didn't mind doing it after so many years. Long ago, I'd developed my own cleaning routine, which cut the time in half. With my jobs all done for the day, I gathered my things, checked my phone for any messages, and adjusted my ponytail.

"Thanks for your help today," she said, same as every Wednesday. "See you next week!"

"Yeah, sure thing." I waved as I stepped through the door.

Outside, the wind whipped my hair around and my jacket flew open. When I shifted to zip it up, one strap of my tattered tote bag tore at the seam. It was hanging by a thread now and badly needed repairs.

Mom had given me the tote bag years ago as a birthday gift. She'd been tired of watching me carry around a battered old purse I'd bought at a consignment shop. It was an ugly mustard colored designer-brand bag from three or four seasons previous, but it had enough pockets to fit everything I needed.

Every time Mom saw it, she'd said, "Quinn, it's time for that to go."

"I'm not spending tons of money on a stupid bag, Mom," I'd argued, wrinkling my nose. I had rent and utilities to pay and textbooks to buy. My part-time job at the campus bookstore paid minimum wage and only saved me 10% on those textbooks. English lit majors need *a lot* of books. Pricey handbags hadn't been not high on my list of priorities.

Tired of arguing, mom had finally taken matters into her own hands. For my birthday that fall, she'd driven to my dorm at Yale with a container of cupcakes and a single gift—a pale green, floral tote bag with shoulder straps and lots of pockets. It was magically bigger on the inside, with plenty of room for my anthologies and novels, notebooks, play scripts, and soccer cleats. It was perfect.

Obviously, a bag like that can never be retired. It must be fixed. *Duct tape.* Techies can fix anything with duct tape.

A sudden boom of thunder rumbled, and a flash of lightning streaked across the sky. Dark clouds rolled in and poured rain onto the city, while I sprinted to my car. By the time I made it, I was drenched, and the bag was soaked, which threatened its integrity even more. Safely inside the car, rain pounding away on the windshield and roof, I closed my eyes and took a deep breath. I wrung my hair out and dried off with the emergency towel I keep in the backseat. That helped. As the burst of adrenaline ran the rest of its course through my body, I felt the hot tears in the corners of my eyes. I'd let myself reminisce a tad too much.

Instead of dwelling on anything, though, I dried my eyes with a tissue and cleared my throat. There were three hours to kill before Charlie was expecting me at the bar. *What can I do next?* I could bring Faith a coffee and check-in on rehearsal—but she'd reprimand me for spending too much time in the theater on my afternoons off. I could head to the office and come up with an excuse to talk to Leah, but no, I'd see her tomorrow morning. Plus, given my emotional state, sitting behind my desk in a room full of reminders of my parents didn't seem like a wise choice. I could go back inside and play with more puppies, but I'd finished my work for the day, so I'd just be chatting more with Mary Beth about Shawn. I could just go to the bar early, but Uncle Charlie would make a fuss about it. All the paperwork I needed was at home anyhow. I could go home to take Franklin for a walk, but he wouldn't want to walk in the pouring rain any more than I did. And since Shawn was probably at the bar too, I wouldn't have any company at home.

Who else might need me right now? Where can I go? I reviewed all the other places I've volunteered, but most of those places needed to be scheduled, like Toddler Story Time at the library, a shift at the food pantry, or a visit at the senior center. So now what?

Maybe techies can't fix *everything* with duct tape.

It made the most sense to stop at home for a few hours. Between Uncle Charlie's taxes, baking cookies for the youth center bake sale, making dinner, checking on Franklin, and doing some light chores, I could be plenty useful—and busy.

It wasn't pouring when I arrived at the house, but I hurried to the porch anyhow. I swung the door open, eager for dry clothes and a hot cup of tea. When Franklin wasn't waiting for me at the door, though, I forgot all about those things. I stepped into the foyer, checked behind the door, and poked my head into the dining room. No Franklin. I called out his name a few times, my voice fraying at the edges.

After the third time, I heard the jingle of the tags on his collar. As soon as I saw Franklin, I knew he wasn't feeling well. He grimaced as he lumbered toward me, but his tail wagged. *My sweet boy.* I walked forward to save him some steps and scratched behind his ears. He paused, closing his eyes, blissfully content. I squeezed my eyes shut in relief, then concentrated on breathing deeply and exhaling all the panic from my body. My heart rate slowed. Still concerned, I squatted down to his eye level and took his sweet, graying face in my hands.

"Ohhh, what's wrong, baby boy? You okay?" I knew he wasn't *totally* okay, but he licked my cheek to try to convince me. "You're alright, aren't you? Come on, let's go out."

Even though it had stopped raining, he was in no shape for a walk. Instead, I let him out the sliding door of the kitchen into the fenced backyard. Shawn had recently mowed, so Franklin could wander about freely without fighting through weeds and tall blades of grass. The front yard and the garden were a mess, but we tried to keep the backyard usable at least. Soon, it would be warm enough to have dinner on the patio, maybe light up that old firepit my parents installed many summers ago. I couldn't remember the last time I'd been able to relax like that.

The afternoon passed easily as I puttered around, talking to Franklin about everything I was doing. When I left, he was sleeping peacefully, cookies were cooling on the counter, dinner was in the fridge for later, the kitchen was swept and mopped, and the living room was vacuumed. I even had time to put clean sheets on my bed.

Time flies if you stay busy enough not to think about it.

Keeping myself occupied helped Thursday fly right by as well. I followed my routine from the foundation to rehearsal, then stayed up late to finish Charlie's personal taxes. Those were much easier to do than the business taxes for the bar. Every time I looked at that paperwork, my eyes crossed.

Friday began, as usual, with a busy schedule of volunteering shifts. I read two books about panda bears for Toddler Story Time at the library, dropped six dozen cookies off at the youth center, and visited the retirement home to play chess with a couple of the residents.

Before long, it was time to get dressed up for the foundation's monthly cocktail party. Technically, both Davis kids should've attended. Shawn had wriggled his way out of tonight's duties once again, but working with Charlie was a good excuse, so I didn't give him hell about it. That left all the schmoozing up to me. I dug out my favorite black dress from the back of the closet, shoved my feet into a pair of Mom's strappy heels, and turned on Business Quinn mode. The dress, the smile, the handshakes, the small talk. Representing my parents' legacy was my biggest, most important job.

Then it was Saturday, the day I'd been waiting for… Theo Miller's first day of theater.

CHAPTER FIVE

Nearly giddy with anticipation, I briefly wondered *how wrong* it was to be super attracted to another woman's husband. Obviously, it would be wrong to act on it, but it's just a crush, right? It wouldn't hurt anyone. And hadn't he said something about needing a sitter for Oliver? Perhaps he was a single parent... who wears a wedding ring. *Come on, Quinn.*

I was proud of myself for not stalking him on social media though, no matter how badly I'd wanted to. Seeing family pics of him and his wife would ruin my harmless crush immediately. I'd also probably say something dumb and give myself away, like "where were you staying when you went to Mexico last summer? I'm thinking of taking a trip." As Faith has often said, I have *no chill* when it comes to guys.

Theo and Oliver arrived on time, holding hands while the little Miller gave his dad a full tour. Side by side, Oliver looked like his tiny clone, right down to the dimples.

"Here's the audience, Dad. All the seats are here for the people when they watch the shows. And that's the stage, plus the curtains. There's a rope that *closes* the curtains if you pull on it. Miss Quinn said I can try it when I get a little older—maybe next year! Dad, can I come back here next year?"

"One thing at a time, Ollie," Theo said, hiding a laugh. They'd wandered close to the piano, where I stood flipping through my notes, and Theo smiled to greet me. "How do we know Miss Quinn will take you back in a year?"

"But he's such an excellent tour guide," I said. "I couldn't possibly let him get away."

"Miss Quinn!" Oliver is possibly the happiest, most

excitable child I've ever known. "This is my dad!"

"Yes, we met on Tuesday, remember?" I made eye contact with Theo, who seemed equally amused. "I'm so happy you're both here! Shall we get to work, gentlemen?"

The best way to get a newbie acclimated to the tech life is with a power drill. Theo said he'd be more comfortable trying out tech stuff, but I had no idea if he was the handy type. *If he isn't, he will be by the time I've finished with him.* Oliver joined the other kids for a vocal warmup with Faith, while I led Theo to the workshop backstage.

"The next thing on my to-do list is a second staircase. It needs to match this one." I kicked the first one with the toe of my shoe. "Well, it's only three steps, so I guess you can't call it a whole *case* of stairs, but you get what I'm saying."

"I can do that," he said, encouraged. Theo headed right for the two-by-fours stacked in the corner and plugged in the power drill nearby. He sat down on the floor and started laying out the materials, ready to go. *It seems I won't be teaching much today.* After a moment of silently staring at him, I realized he was looking at me for something. He held out a hand, palm up. "Okay, I'm ready. Screw me."

"I'm sorry... what?"

"Screws? Can I have some please?" he repeated, opening and closing his hand. When he looked up at me, his eyes were wide, and his face was a vibrant shade of red. And so was mine, I knew it. After another pause, he recovered. "Sorry, it's a joke the guys have on the jobsites. But I can see—I hope you weren't—"

"Oh! Got it!" I punctuated the words with a strained laugh. I grabbed the box from the counter and handed it over. "It's fine. You should hear some of the stuff theater people say to each other. I think you're gonna fit right in."

"Thanks, Miss Quinn."

"Just Quinn," I reminded him.

"Right, Oliver's not here."

I picked up a second drill and sat on the floor nearby, in front of my own project, but couldn't focus right away. I admired him working, fully concentrating, hands steady. A man using power tools is... hot? I let my mind wander to, uh... places. Theo raised his head and we made eye contact. *Busted.*

I blurted the first words that came to mind. "You clearly don't need my supervision."

"No," he said with a shrug. "But I enjoy your company."

"That's good," I said with a smile. "Because you're stuck with me all day."

"Eh, it's not so bad," he teased. "What are you working on?"

"This bad boy right here," I pointed to the upside down 4x4 platform in front of me. "Needs some legs before we can use it. This will go on the stage—with the stairs on either side so the kids can get up and down. We'll need two more of these to make the whole thing."

Theo noticed the drill in my hand and slid the box of screws across the dusty floor in my direction.

"So, Theo," I began nervously. "What do you do for work?"

"I'm a project manager," he said. *Whirrrrr.*

"Is that like a contractor?"

"I work *with* contractors, but it's a different thing," he explained. "Basically, I manage the entire construction project from beginning to end. So, I work with the client, the architect, and the different kinds of contractors to make sure everything gets done right, on time, and within the budget."

"That's... cool. I mean, it sounds like it could be interesting."

"It's a lot like what you do here, to be honest. Instead of a construction job, it's a show. And you're managing all these tech projects, making sure it all gets done."

"Maybe, but it's Faith's program. I just volunteer."

"I think that would technically make her your client," he said with a grin. "Somebody's gotta make sure the kids have a floor for tap dancing."

"I guess that makes you one of *my* contractors..."

He laughed, lining up the top of the second stair. Theo was working quickly—I was impressed.

"So where are you guys from? You said you just moved here, right?"

"Yeah, Oliver and I moved from Chicago in January. I grew up a few towns over from here, but I got married and stayed in

Illinois after college," he paused. *Whirrrrr.* "The company I work for opened a Boston location and they offered me a promotion if I transferred."

"So here you are."

"So here I am. It made sense to come home," he said, eyes still on the drill. "Since it was just the two of us, I wanted Oliver to have more family around. My parents are still living in the house where I grew up. I bought a house here though, didn't want to be *too close* to Mom and Dad."

"Sure," I said, trying to focus on my job. Let's review... only he and Oliver moved to Boston, to be closer to family. Where was his wife? Were they separated? He wouldn't move so far away from his son's mother if it were temporary. So maybe divorced? But then, he probably wouldn't still have a wedding ring on. Was she in the military and deployed somewhere? The ring made more sense if that were true, but why would someone move in the middle of their spouse's tour?

Faith often criticized me for being too nosy, so I decided to just drop it. Something was not lining up, but it was none of my business. *Time for a subject change...*

"So, what do you do for fun?" I asked.

"Let's see... cooking, going to the movies on rainy days, hiking with Ollie... I also enjoy crossword puzzles and long walks on the beach." He looked up, finally, and we smiled at each other. "Is my interview over now?"

"What can I say? You're more interesting than I am."

"I doubt that," he said with a grin. "What does the talented *Miss Quinn* do outside the theater?"

"Lots of stuff," I hesitated, searching for a concise way to explain it all. I gave up. "It's... complicated."

"Okay...?" Theo pulled the first staircase toward him and tried to tighten some of the screws, but they were perfect, obviously. No adjustments required. Satisfied, he moved closer to me.

"Mostly, I'm just the president of a charity foundation."

"*Just?*" he said, handing me a couple screws to finish the second leg. "That sounds like a big deal."

I shrugged. "It's only a few days a week, plus events."

"And? I sense the list goes on…"

"I help out at my uncle's bar a couple times a week."

"You're a bartender?"

"Me?" I couldn't help it, I laughed. I could only imagine Shawn and Charlie letting me pour drinks. They don't even let me mix *my own* drinks. That's on par with letting Charlie file his own taxes. "No, back office stuff, mostly accounting. I started helping him when…" *Nope.* "A while ago."

"Charity president, theater director, private accountant." He counted it all out on his fingers. "Any other pursuits?"

"Volunteering, here and there," I added. "I spend most of my free time at the animal shelter, the library, and the senior center. And I like to help out with the soccer team fundraisers when I can."

"Wow," he said, with a playful smirk on his face. "It's just too bad you don't have enough to keep you busy."

"I'm sure I could find some room on my calendar somewhere…" I countered. That was a little more forward than I'd planned on being, but the more I talked to him, the braver I got. "If I needed to."

He raised his eyebrow at me with the hint of a smile on his lips. And in that moment, I realized two things. One, that he was absolutely, totally, devastatingly handsome. Two, that he seemed reasonably receptive to the idea of spending time with me on purpose.

"Alright," I said, switching gears. For my own safety. "There are two legs left to attach to this platform. You've got a drill; I've got a drill. I'll race you."

"Are you sure that's a good idea?" he asked, with that charming expression still on his face.

"Scared, Miller?"

"Okay fine," he smirked, narrowing his eyes. It was kinda sexy. No, it was *a lot* sexy. "You're on."

"Ready?" He nodded. "Set?" He focused on his hands, lining up the drill and the screw. "Go!"

I worked quickly, driving two screws into one side of the platform, straight into the leg. Then I scooted around and did the same thing to the other side. I should've set a timer for myself. I might've broken my previous record.

"Done!" I shouted, putting my hands up. And just a split second after me, Theo did the same. "Oooh, so close! Sorry, Miller."

He scowled. "That was definitely a tie. And even if you *were* a second faster than me, which you *weren't,"* he said, with mock defensiveness. I tilted my head. "It's only because your hands are so little. Easier to move around the tight spots."

"Don't hate the player," I said defiantly. Standing up, I placed two hands beneath one side of the platform. "Can you help me flip this thing?"

Theo got up, grabbed the side opposite me, and we turned it over. Then I climbed on top of it, about a foot from the floor, and jumped up and down a couple times.

"I like to test these out before a bunch of kids dance on them."

"Solid plan."

Riding that wave of boldness, bolstered by the adrenaline of competition, I forgot to be nervous. I extended a hand to Theo and said, "Get up here."

And he did.

"Look how confident I am in your carpentry skills," he said, then stomped his feet. "Seems as sturdy as my corner."

"Yeah, yeah," I laughed, then performed a perfect time-step over his side. Ten years of tap dance lessons, all preparing me for that moment... "It'll do."

"Show off."

I laughed and swatted him on the arm—which was precisely the moment my adrenaline dissipated. Physical contact was just a tad too far under the circumstances—wasn't it? Theo grabbed his arm, feigning injury, and stepped toward me.

"Ouch, Miss Quinn..." he said, trying not to laugh.

"If that hurt," I said, boldly looking him in the eye. "Then you don't wanna see my right hook."

He smiled, and the mood suddenly shifted. We both seemed to realize how close together we were, just inches away. My heart pounded. More adrenaline, *right?* Nothing to do with his eyes. I desperately wanted to ask about his wife. She wasn't around—

where was she? And is it okay to be staring at him like this?

"Well," I said, blinking. The reminder was sobering. "We still need two more of these. No racing this time. I don't want to embarrass you twice in one day. You'd never come back."

He nodded, laughing, but didn't speak again for a while. It also took us an extra minute to climb down.

CHAPTER SIX

On the way home, I played the *Singin' in the Rain* soundtrack in the car, hoping I'd be too occupied to obsessively pick apart every moment with Theo. It didn't work. Mixed messages could be dangerous, so I thought it wisest to let this go. But the only *no* message I'd received was the ring itself. Everything he said and did looked a lot like *yes*. I was going to drive myself nuts.

At home, Shawn was snoring on the couch after a long night at the bar. The TV was still on, but Netflix was asking if he'd like to continue watching *The Great British Baking Show,* so he'd probably been napping for a while.

Franklin clambered to his feet with a grunt when he heard me come in, so I nixed our walk and let him out in the backyard. I sat out on the porch while he sniffed around, paused to stretch, and sniffed around some more. I missed our walks, but maybe giving him enough time to rest and recuperate would mean we could go back out there soon.

Even though Shawn had mowed the grass, the backyard still needed help. The fence could use a sanding and a new coat of white paint. The weather had chipped away at the paint in an uneven pattern, like an abstract work of art. Dad had a weed whacker somewhere in the garage, so it would be easy to tackle the tall grass and weeds near the perimeter. A huge oak tree filled the far-left corner of the yard, with a broken wooden swing dangling from the lowest branch. I'd spent so many summers reading in that swing, my feet swaying as I gently drifted back and forth. Sometimes Shawn would run up behind and push me, startling me enough to drop the book into the dirt. I'd yell, mom would peek out the kitchen window, and Shawn would hold up his hands, claiming his innocence.

Once the chill of the air sank in, I called Franklin back into the house and gave him a treat. I turned on the tea kettle, prepped a cup and tea bag, and debated making a cup for Shawn too. I crept back into the living room, switched off the TV, and waited to see if he stirred. He mumbled something and rolled over onto his back. He cracked one eye open, saw me, and grunted, *Go away.*

Okay, no tea. When he's grumpy, I don't mess with him. We'd either end up in a heated argument or a food fight, depending on which buttons I decided to push. No thanks.

When Shawn and I were kids, things were so much easier. We'd looked so alike, Mom said, that people thought we were identical until she started dressing us differently. Then everyone said we were the *boy version* and *girl version* of the same kid. We hated that.

As we grew older, the differences had emerged. Shawn had a huge growth spurt in eighth grade, leaving me several inches behind. I dyed my hair "blonde" in high school and it was never really returned to its natural color. We got braces together, but Shawn was *horrible* about caring for them. When the braces came off, my teeth were perfectly straight; Shawn's front teeth were just *slightly* askew, and he had several cavities. The orthodontist refused to try again.

In our teen years, things had become more complicated. We'd kept our distance from each other—at least, as distant as twins could be in a small-town high school with only 500 students. The school administrators wisely placed us in separate homerooms every year, but that didn't stop the teachers from constantly comparing us.

"Your brother has such a natural talent for chemistry," they told me, a girl who would rather read anything—even Charles Dickens—than touch any chemicals. Shawn went all the way up to A.P. Chemistry and aced the test; I just picked the smartest kid in my class to be my lab partner and tried to survive the year with both eyebrows and all my fingers intact.

"What are you afraid will happen to your fingers?" Shawn had asked once, after he'd spent two hours helping me study for the final.

"Have you even *heard* of hydrochloric acid?" I'd said,

horrified. "I like being alive!"

Shawn had laughed hysterically.

"You science people are weirdos."

Meanwhile, Shawn heard all about my soccer skills. "Your sister had a great game last night! What a goal," they would tell him. Shawn might've thrown the game-winning curveball from the pitcher's mound more than once, but I enjoyed running circles around him on the soccer field. He's still never stolen a ball from me.

We were different, but we never faltered in supporting each other. Shawn had gotten detention for beating up the kid who spread nasty rumors about me. I protected him in my own way, too, usually from gossipy girls. During one soccer practice, I'd overheard two girls badmouthing Shawn. I "slipped" and kicked the ball right at them.

"Dammit, Quinn!" Shirley Johnson had yelled. "You could've taken my head off!"

"If I wanted to take your head off, I would have," I'd replied, jogging by to retrieve the ball. "Now, stop talking about my brother and maybe I'll mind my own business."

Ohh, to be sixteen again. Wouldn't it be nice to solve problems with a good instep kick or two?

Problems like Uncle Charlie's taxes.

With my cup of tea, I sorted the paperwork into categories on the table: bills, sales reports, receipts, deposit slips. I wanted to bang my forehead on the table, but there wasn't time for that. The tax deadline loomed just over a week away.

Franklin meandered over, sat beside my chair, and rested his chin on my knee. This was his polite way of saying he had to go out. I stapled together a pile of invoices and he nudged me with his head to remind me that he was there. I paused to scratch behind his ears, and he squinted in pure bliss. When I stopped, his eyes popped open and his chin rested on my knee again.

"Hang on, buddy," I said to him. "I'm almost done with this."

He nudged again.

"Okay, okay. I'll take a break." I scooped up the papers and moved the pile into one corner of the table. I let Franklin out the sliding door and took my empty cup to the sink, where a stack of dirty dishes awaited me. Obviously, that must be handled before I could do anything else. *Obviously.* I unloaded the dishwasher, put the clean dishes away, then reloaded it with whatever would fit. Then one cleaning task led straight into another, and before long, I was scrubbing the pots from last night's dinner and wiping down the counter.

I placed a clean pot on top of another in the dishrack, but it slipped and clanged to the floor. Shawn, always a light sleeper, woke instantly.

"You okay in there?" he called from the living room.

"Fine. Sorry!"

"Want a hand?"

"Uhh... sure. Thanks."

He entered the kitchen in pajama pants and a t-shirt, stretching and yawning, and picked up a dish towel. I washed, he dried. I stacked the pots and he put them away. He squirted detergent into the compartment inside the dishwasher, placed the last few forks in the basket, and pressed the start button. I scrubbed the table and countertops while Shawn swept the floor. In under ten minutes, we'd cleaned the whole kitchen—as a team. That hadn't happened in so long. It made me smile.

"That wasn't so bad," I said, stepping back to admire our work.

"We are well trained," he said with a smile. "All those nights Dad would send us in here to clean up after dinner?"

"The cook doesn't clean!" My Dad impression had grown rusty. "I tried to sneak out to do *homework* every time. I'd rather write a lab report than dry 75 forks."

He shook his head. "Those never-ending forks. How?"

We shared a laugh, standing together, and I was suddenly overwhelmed with sorrow. Seven—almost eight—years seemed like a long time, but how much time does it take to get over losing your parents?

"I miss them, Shawn." I could feel a rogue tear sliding down my cheek. "How have we made it this long alone? It's not supposed to be like this."

My brother pulled me in for a hug, squeezing hard enough to

crack my back—which I didn't realize I'd needed so badly. He sniffled but kept his head over my shoulder, where I couldn't see the tears that I felt dampening my shirt. It was the first time in years that we'd had a moment like this. And it didn't last long.

"Okay, Quinnie Poo," he teased, releasing me. "Those taxes aren't going to do themselves."

"Go take a shower," I replied, putting my hands on my hips. "You smell like whiskey and stale cologne. You're gross."

"No, *you're* gross."

I balled up the damp dish towel on the counter and tossed it at his face. It missed by a good six inches, but we both laughed about it anyway. After all, I was *not* the All-Star pitcher in the family.

"Fine," he yelled, walking toward the stairs. "I'm going, I'm going."

Later, I hitched a ride with Shawn to the bar, hoping to find some missing paperwork to finish the business taxes. I climbed into the passenger side and paper bags from Dunkin crinkled under my feet. My brother caught the judgmental look on my face.

"Don't you dare say a word," he said, narrowing his eyes. "I'll clean when I feel like it."

"As long as the bags are empty, I don't care."

Of course, within seconds, I'd balled up all the bags and shoved them inside the biggest bag.

"You're a mess," he said, as he turned the key in the ignition and backed out of the driveway.

"No, *you're* the mess. I'm the cleaning crew."

Faith texted while we were on our way over. Abby was out on a date with Will and Faith was *bored*. She demanded Shawn have a martini ready when she got there.

With Will? They're back together again?

I guess so...

How do we feel about this?

Eh... they're 15, they'll figure it out.... Right?

So, extra olives in that martini? lol

Extra olives. EXTRA. No joke. I want all of them.

Not long after we arrived, Faith sauntered up to the bar counter and perched on her favorite stool: third from the wall on the left side. Right next to my favorite stool, with the letter Q that I'd cut into the leather. I'd lost scissor privileges for two weeks, but the stool was officially mine forever.

"How's your new best friend?" Faith teased. She took a sip of her martini—my brother's specialty. Shawn had even given her *four* olives. "Oliver's dad, huh? He's pretty."

"Theo," I replied, careful not to catch her eye. *If I look over here at this coaster, she won't be able to read my facial expression.*

"*Ohhhhh, Quinn.* That bad, huh?"

"What?"

"You're crushing on him super hard. I don't blame you."

"I am not. And even if I was, which I'm *not*, so what? Crushes are harmless," I looked away and took a drink. "Besides, he might be married. I don't know what's going on there."

"Are you sure?"

"Wedding ring." I held up my left hand and wiggled my fingers. "That's usually what that means."

"Well, Theo is the only one on any of the paperwork—no Mom anywhere. And Oliver's grandma is the only emergency contact. Don't give up on him yet."

"He talks about everything like it's just him and Oliver. I just don't get the ring though. What divorced man keeps his wedding ring on?"

"I don't know, people do weird things," she shrugged. "Don't start judging him already. Maybe he didn't want to get divorced. Maybe she left him."

"How is that better?" I groaned in frustration.

Fortunately for me, Shawn picked that precise moment to sidle over to us.

"Hey, ladies."

"Don't do that," said Faith, wrinkling her nose. "Don't say

ladies. It's creepy."

"I've missed you, Faith," he grinned. "Nice necklace."

"What do you want, Shawn?" she groaned.

"Why do you immediately assume I want something? Can't I just compliment a nice piece of jewelry?"

"I bought this at TJ Maxx for $15, Shawn. It is *not* a nice piece of jewelry." Faith lifted the pendant to show him.

"Yikes," he said, leaning back. "Learn to take a compliment."

"Quit it, guys."

"He started it," Faith said, poking him in the shoulder. His expression turned to mock outrage.

"What do you want, Shawn?" I asked, sighing.

"I want to talk to Faith…" he said, dismissively. "She might be more helpful than you."

She crossed her arms, suspicious. *This should be fun.*

"You're a single mom—"

"Thanks for the reminder," she said, pulling an olive off the cocktail sword.

Shawn explained his Gina situation and Faith listened attentively, chewing on the olive. When he got to the end, her eyes were wide.

"Tell her the truth," she said simply.

"I don't want to make her feel bad about her kid or something…" he said, concerned.

"Oh, she won't. She might hate *you* though."

"That's fair," he sighed. Then he turned to me, his eyes pleading. "Can you please help me with a script?"

I shook my head one more time.

"Fine, Quinn. I'll remember this the next time you ask me for ice in your drink." He picked up my gin and tonic, finished it, then walked off. Unbelievable.

CHAPTER SEVEN

On Monday afternoon, I strolled into the bar victoriously, with every single dollar accounted for on Charlie's taxes. It had been a stressful year for sure, as evidenced by the huge drop in revenue around the time the laundromat closed next door. I never realized how much business we were getting from people waiting for their clothes to dry. There were several regulars who'd just disappeared without a trace. Without a reason to come down here, I guess they weren't loyal after all.

"Hey, Uncle Charlie," I said when I spotted him in the office. "I brought all your paperwork back. Let's get those taxes filed."

The back office remained a mess with no counter space, so I brought my tote bag—still duct-taped within an inch of its life—out to the bar and placed it on the counter where I could spread out. I set up my laptop and pulled out the folders containing the neatly reorganized paperwork. Charlie picked them up and skimmed their contents.

"You're the best, kiddo." He gave me a broad grin. "What would I do without you?"

I walked him through page by page and explained what he was paying in taxes on the bar. He made a face but nodded along. Once we were done with that, I picked up the second folder and we did the same thing with his personal taxes.

"Is that number right?" Uncle Charlie had gotten to the bottom of the form and his refund. He took the pair of glasses from his shirt pocket and perched them on the end of his nose, squinting. "That seems a little larger than usual…"

"It's correct, don't worry. I ran the numbers like five times," I said, smiling. "Remember, you took a pay cut last year to help keep the bar afloat. If we can get business to trend upward this year, maybe you can give yourself a raise next year. You've earned it, Uncle Charlie."

"For what? I live here, day and night. If my house weren't paid for, I'd probably sell it and sleep in the backroom."

I forced a laugh, but the mental image of Uncle Charlie sleeping under the desk back there was all too real.

"Listen, what I wanted to talk to you about," he said, picking up a towel from the bin of clean rags. While he spoke, he wiped our fingerprints from the shiny bar top. "As soon as I can manage it, I've decided to hire an accountant again. You don't need to be chasing after an old man for bank receipts for the rest of your life or at least the rest of *mine*."

"Don't be silly," I said slowly. Unless there was mystery money hidden in a floorboard, the bar couldn't afford it. "I've never minded it. Dad did it, I can do it. Things are tight—I'd rather you spent it on something else that I *can't* do."

"Quinnie, your dad was my business partner. He got paid to do this work, and you're volunteering your precious time to do it."

"I don't mind—"

"Now come on," he scolded me. "You're young, you shouldn't be hanging around in here. You could go back to school, sweetheart, pick up where you left off."

"I told you, I'm not going back to school," I said, getting frustrated. How many times did I need to go round and round about this? "I'm working at the foundation now—that's good enough for me. And I don't mind helping you."

"Well, I *do* mind. I've been leaning on you too much. It's not right."

"Shawn helps too."

"Shawn gets *paid*. He works here, on the books," he said, turning to me. "You've been volunteering all this time, just like you do with everything else. You keep giving away all your time, what's left for you?"

I couldn't give him an answer. Because I didn't have one.

"Anyway," he said, shifting tones. "That's not a problem for today. We've already gotten my taxes done, so there's nothing to discuss until next year. Okay?"

Just like Dad, when Uncle Charlie said *okay* like that, the conversation was over.

After my morning coffee and scone with Leah on Tuesday morning, I was having trouble focusing on the huge to-do list I'd written so neatly in my agenda.

A stack of papers needed sorting, but instead, I was staring at the bookshelf. I'd changed a lot of things in dad's office, but the bookshelf remained untouched: Dad's awards on the top shelf; the books he'd read while establishing the foundation fifteen years ago on the second; a gallery of family photos. Shawn and I were the stars in almost every single one.

The most important photo was of Dad, Uncle Charlie, and their younger sister Mara, a victim of cystic fibrosis at age eight. Back then, the treatments had been limited, and the disease wasn't well understood. Mara was the whole reason this foundation existed; her memory was the force that drove my dad to make a difference in the lives of other affected children.

The photos on the walls told the story of the foundation's history, a trail of Dad's successes. There, he was posted with presidents, governors, senators, billionaires, and of course, several of the children his foundation had helped.

Dad had been a financial analyst for nearly thirty years when he died. People had trusted him, and he'd changed their lives. When Shawn and I were born, Dad had taken a big leap and left the investment firm to become an independent consultant.

The decision turned out to be a smart move for him, and for the well-being of our family. Dad didn't want to miss a moment of our lives, so he built his work schedule around our games, performances, and birthdays. He was the super fan with his face painted in school colors, shouting "GO DAVIS!" from the stands. He was famous on the Yale field.

Dad made sure our family was provided for: Shawn and I had successful college funds, the house was paid for, and their retirement fund was secure. Dad always believed that people who had enough should help those in need, and his personal tragedy had led him here. In its first decade, the Mara Davis Foundation had raised millions to fund the research and treatment of cystic fibrosis.

When he died, Dad's incredible legacy needed to be preserved. There was so much more that he could've accomplished. Someone needed to continue his work. A Davis needed to keep it going. That was why I'd stepped into this office and dedicated myself to the foundation's success.

Much to the chagrin of my uncle, brother, and best friend, I'd left grad school to begin my new career as foundation president. I'd set aside my own plans to teach, because through the foundation, I was *saving lives*.

"Quinn," Uncle Charlie had said. "Your parents wouldn't expect you to do this. They invested in *your* future as much as that foundation."

"You don't even know what you're doing," Shawn had grumbled. "Why didn't you just throw your money at something and run?"

"Like you did?" I'd replied, perhaps too harshly.

"You have no idea what you're talking about," he'd snapped. We'd stayed close and leaned on each other for the first six months after the accident, but somewhere along the way, things had started to break down. "Stop pretending you're important. They don't need you."

"Mind your own business, Shawn. No one asked you."

"Take your own advice," Shawn had said coldly. "Mind *your* own business and leave this one alone."

But what else could I do now that they were gone?

When Leah made her way into my office, that day, she found me with my head in my hands.

"You...okay?" she asked, hesitating.

My head snapped up. I was *mortified*.

"Yes, sorry. I'm good." She didn't look like she believed me, but she didn't challenge me either. I pinched the bridge of my nose. *Shake it off.* "What's going on?"

"Lou Prescott just emailed me about the catering for the gala. He wants an extra $15 per plate."

"What is wrong with that guy?" I asked.

Leah heaved a deep sigh and dropped into one of the black

leather chairs facing my desk, her favorite one.

"It's too late to get a new caterer, but never again. I'll tell Danny to find a better company next year."

"How can I help? Want me to call him?"

"I can handle it. Permission to destroy him?"

"Have I ever tried to stop you?"

When I smiled, the vague pain in my head became a low-key throb. I did not want to go to rehearsal this afternoon with a headache. Again. That had been a particularly horrible day. I rifled through my desk drawer for my emergency bottle of acetaminophen. I tipped the bottle into my hand to extract one dose, plus an extra pill for good measure.

"All good in the hood, Quinn?"

"Just a headache... can you get addicted to Tylenol?"

Leah frowned. "That's not a thing."

"So what are you going to tell Lou?"

"We're going to negotiate our way back down to the original price, obviously."

Leah never ceased to amaze me—she was always so calm and confident, while also tearing someone apart. If I could figure out how to channel my energy like that, I'd be unstoppable. I was just grateful that Leah was on my side.

"Can you also solve world hunger?" I asked, only half-joking.

She leaned back in the chair and crossed one leg over the other. "If I had a big enough fundraiser, I'm sure I could pull something off."

CHAPTER EIGHT

At rehearsal that afternoon, Oliver arrived with another note saying his dad would pick him up. I didn't hate that. I'd replayed every moment of our day together over and over so many times, like a favorite song. The idea of seeing him again made me all warm and tingly. Crushes are the worst.

Focus, Quinn. I had a lot of work to get done and Faith needed my help. We blocked the last three scenes, then ran through the big number at the end of act one. Only two kids had forgotten the choreography, which was amazing. I became so wrapped up in how proud I was that I'd almost forgotten about Theo. Almost.

Dismissal time arrived, so it was time to put on jackets and backpacks, track down water bottles and snack wrappers, and organize kids into lines. I zipped up a few backpacks and then gave six-year-old Megan extra help turning her coat sleeves inside-in. On rainy days, the parents often came inside to pick up the kiddos, so I kept everyone inside the auditorium until they left one by one. Oliver was waiting patiently beside me the entire time, so quietly that I didn't notice him at first.

"Miss Quinn," he said, thoughtfully. "Are you a mom?"

"What?" *How's that for a conversation starter?* "Oh. No, sweetie. I have a doggie but no kids."

"I think you should be a mom," Oliver said, as though he'd given this matter a lot of thought. "You're nice and you're a good listener. And you bake cookies sometimes, which is probably the best thing moms do."

"What about your mom?" I asked, before immediately regretting it. I hadn't intended to put this on Oliver. It was just a reflex. I would've asked any kid that question whether I'd met his attractive, possibly single dad or not.

"She's in heaven, Miss Quinn," he said, shrugging his little shoulders. "Daddy says you can't mail cookies and stuff from there."

Oh.

That was a punch in the gut. Not ever, in any way at all, had I thought about *that* as a possibility. Thinking about those words, which just dropped right out of his mouth as a fact, Theo wearing his ring made a lot more sense. In fact, assuming he was a widower should've probably been at the top of the list of possibilities. I recovered as quickly as I could.

"I bet your dad makes cookies. That must be fun."

"Un-uh. He made a cake one time and it got all stuck inside the pan," he said, frowning. "It smelled gross in the house for a while. I can't remember if my mommy made cookies, but Grandma does. Chocolate chip."

"My favorite."

"Me too!" He beamed from ear to ear. Then Oliver, somehow satisfied with this interchange, followed me to collect my own things. I was bent over, stuffing things into my tote bag, when I heard Theo's soft, deep voice behind me. My stomach flip-flopped. I nearly fell over.

I heard the impact of Oliver greeting his dad with a hug.

"I was talking to Miss Quinn, Dad."

"Oh yeah?"

I turned around and there he was. Theo smiled, clearly amused. He wore a pair of jeans, a t-shirt from a 10k race, and that brown leather jacket. Casual, relaxed, and still so neat and put-together. When I wear jeans and a t-shirt, I look like a hungover Medusa. It's not pretty. It wasn't something Theo should ever, ever see either. *Mental note: throw away all t-shirts. Except tech shirts.* I would permit myself to retain solid black t-shirts only.

I wasn't ready for the squishy, nauseous feeling I got when I made eye contact with Theo. Oliver's words echoed in my mind as I looked at him now. Magically, all our interactions had a new meaning. That flirting and goofing around felt more like the start of… something? *Talking to him is already hard enough.*

"Hey, stranger," I said, cringing. *So corny. I rest my case.*

"So, Miss Quinn, where have you been all my life?" *This* is what he says? *He's making fun of me, isn't he?*

"Waiting for you." *Oh my god, Quinn. Shut. Up.*

He laughed kindly, and I felt like I'd been set up.

But I can't just leave well enough alone, so I kept going. "I mean, not waiting too long. But at least for the past few minutes, right here. Not that you're late. No, I mean, just... You asked."

I tried to cover up my verbal explosion with a laugh, but I was... unsuccessful. From behind me, I heard Abby ask, *Mom, what's wrong with Auntie Quinn?*

"Oh, hey Theo," said Faith, coming to my rescue. She walked over to join us. "Is this woman bothering you?"

Traitor.

"Not at all," he said smoothly. "In fact, she's quite entertaining."

Everyone paused for a second before Faith got us back on track.

"I think I'm all set here," she said, turning to me. She gave me a *look*. "Abby and Will can help me lock up."

"You sure?" I asked anyway.

"Yeah, I'm fine," Faith promised. She added a wink. With my back turned to Theo, I mouthed a silent *thank you* and made a mental note to bring her a fruit basket someday in appreciation.

"I'll walk you out, guys," I said to the Millers, keeping my voice steady and calm. Theo seemed pleased. Oliver cheered.

Outside, the rain had stopped, but the chill of spring hit me with a powerful gust of wind. In my rush, I'd forgotten to put on my jacket, which was slung over my arm, under that wonky strap of my tote bag. *I'll be fine. I don't need it.* A second wind whipped my hair into my face, a few strands stuck to my lips, and I changed my mind. The bag, however, was filled to the brim with the day's accessories and some stuff that had probably been in there for months, easily. I shifted things around slowly, carefully, just enough to wiggle my jacket free, but the duct tape failed. Everything tumbled to the ground.

Frozen in horror, I watched tampons scatter across the parking lot. The sheet music sailed into a puddle. My cosmetic bag rolled underneath Theo's car. Everything was everywhere. I sighed, closing my eyes, mortified. As soon as I recovered, I started gathering whatever items I could, but my dignity was not among them.

Almost immediately, both Oliver and Theo sprang into action. Theo gingerly took my jacket from me, the only thing still in my hands, and held it out while I slipped my arms into the sleeves. Oliver brought over an armful of my belongings. I held the tote bag open and he dropped them all inside. The sheet music was dead on arrival and my sunglasses had cracked, but everything else seemed okay. Theo knelt on the pavement and retrieved the cosmetics bag under his car. He helped me round up all the tampons, which I tried to pretend were lollipops, so I wouldn't crawl into a hole to die.

"Thanks," I said quietly, fighting my embarrassment. "I thought the duct tape was gonna hold this thing together."

"Our pleasure. But it might be time for a new bag," Theo replied kindly, before turning back to Oliver. "Car's unlocked, buddy. Go ahead and climb in and get all buckled up. I'll be right there."

Oliver skipped toward the car, wearing a big smile on his face. Halfway there, he suddenly stopped, turned, and ran at me full speed with his arms outstretched. The impact of that hug nearly toppled me to the ground. A stray tampon popped out of the bag and rolled across the pavement.

"Goodbye, Miss Quinn!"

"Oh," I said, startled. *This is new. And unexpected.* "What a good hugger you are!"

And then Oliver was safely in the car. Theo seemed amused, with a faint smile on his face.

"You've got yourself a number one fan," he said, after a silent pause. I swallowed hard and then shrugged my shoulders casually. Like this stuff happens to me all the time.

"Soooooo..." I tried to steer the conversation elsewhere, but I couldn't think of one single innocuous topic. I refused to talk about the weather. Theo did not help, just standing there with his hands in his pockets. And then a lightbulb went on. "You'll be here Saturday?"

"Absolutely. Painting clothes this time, right?"

"Yes, that's great. Definitely have clothes on..." I froze. "For painting. Painting clothes."

Again, I got that raised eyebrow and half-smile, an expression I understood to mean, *you're a hot mess and I'm trying not to laugh at you.*

A muffled giggle behind me turned into a cough. *Faith's behind me, isn't she?*

Theo said his goodbye and trotted off to his car. I closed my eyes tightly, dreading the look I expected to see on Faith's face when I turned around.

"Can I help you?" I scowled at her.

"Honestly," she said, fighting off another laugh. She picked up the rogue tampon and tossed it at me. It bounced off my forehead and into the puddle. "I think you're the one who needs help."

Shawn was sitting in the kitchen when I got home from the animal shelter on Wednesday, and he looked happier than he had in days—since this whole Gina nonsense had begun, now that I thought about it.

"Oh hey! You're home!"

I gave him a smile and greeted Franklin when he trotted over. He looked okay today, not as happy as Shawn, but much better than he had lately. I reached for his leash, but Shawn stopped me.

"I already walked him today," he said. I gave him a skeptical look. "Not the whole neighborhood, don't worry. We just went around the block. I hope that's okay."

"Yeah," I said, surprised. *Shawn never walks the dog.* I gave Franklin a good scratch behind the ears. "Thanks."

"Hungry?"

"Yeah. I'm starving."

Shawn took two plates out of the dishwasher and handed one to me. He reached into the fridge and pulled out the supplies for ham and cheese sandwiches.

I grabbed the bread, a knife, and a bag of potato chips from the pantry.

"Are you ready to be proud?" he asked, spreading mustard on a slice of bread.

"Of your sandwich-making skills?"

He gave me a look. I laughed at him.

"No," he said, after a pause. He tore open the bag of chips and poured a few onto each of our plates. "I, Shawn Davis, have successfully dumped my girlfriend... live and in person."

I hesitated, hoping there was more to the story before I reacted. We both sat down at the table—I took a bite of my sandwich.

"Isn't that great?" He leaned back in his chair with a proud smile on his face. "All. By. Myself."

"Wow, that's... so... grown up, Shawn." I shoved an entire chip in my mouth, chewed, and swallowed while I figured out what to say. "And how did this occur? I'd like to know *how* proud I should be first."

"Gina came into the bar to see me. She was mad that I was ignoring her calls this week."

"Losing points here, Shawny."

"But instead of blowing her off," he said carefully, clearly afraid I would take Gina's side. "I asked Uncle Charlie to cover me at the bar for a few minutes and I walked her outside to talk."

"Okay, getting better."

He seemed relieved, shoving the last few chips into his mouth.

"Right?" he said, proudly, with his mouth full. Shawn rinsed the crumbs from his plate and placed it in the sink. Then he leaned back on the kitchen counter with his arms crossed over his chest.

Chewing, I waved my hand to encourage him to keep talking.

"So, we go outside and sit on that bench in the park around back. And she's all, 'I don't think you're taking this seriously, Shawn' so I'm like, 'I do take you seriously but I can't be a stepdad' so she said, 'You should never be a stepdad because you're a child,' and I'm like, 'Fine, break up with me then' and that was it."

I coughed. "To be clear, she broke up with you?"

"No, I was honest and that made her want to break up with me, but since I'm the one who started it, I'll take the win."

"Sure."

"Proud of me?"

"Brimming with pride."

"Quinn. Are you being sarcastic?"

"Nooo, of course not." I shook my head, equal parts amused and disturbed. Then I took the last bite of my sandwich.

"Yes, you are."

I shrugged, handing him my empty plate.

"Come on, Franklin. Let's go outside. Uncle Shawn needs to do some self-reflection before he goes to work tonight."

The dog trotted slowly behind me, motivated by the magic word: *outside*. My brother watched me leave with a scowl on his face.

CHAPTER NINE

Even in ratty old clothes, Theo looked good. *How is he even a real person?* His paint clothes consisted of a faded old Radiohead t-shirt and a pair of beaten up jeans. Still neat, trim, fit, and effortless.

"I've been meaning to ask you," he said, as we walked to the workshop. "The plaque out front, the last name of the donors who renovated the theater is Davis. Any relation?"

"My parents." My heart thudded in my chest. *Was he going to ask about them?* I hadn't considered what would happen if he did, but I didn't want to steer the conversation toward death.

"That's cool," he said, genuinely. "Did you go to high school here?"

"This is the very theater where I constructed a six-foot tall storybook out of plywood, twenty rolls of duct tape, and a lot of paint. I mean, *a lot* of paint."

"Impressive."

"Why thank you," I said with a grin. "If you walk down the hallway to the bathroom, there's a wall of pictures from past shows. You better believe it's up there."

He laid down the cloth, careful to cover as much floorspace as possible. Not that this workshop floor was pristine, but I tried to maintain some semblance of cleanliness.

"What are we painting today?"

I walked over to the wall, where I'd stacked several 4' by 8' wooden frames covered in canvas.

"These things are called flats. Basically, they're panels that we'll hang next to each other to create the background on stage."

"Are those ocean waves painted on them?"

"We did *The Little Mermaid* last year. This is my finest 3am creation right here," I said proudly. "But we're going to need several coats over these dark blue waves. I hope we're *not* here until 3am this time."

"There are worse places to be." Theo helped me lay the flats down on the floor and picked up a paint roller.

"Wait and see what happens when I breathe in too many paint fumes. You may change your mind." Just for good measure, I cracked open the tiny window of the workshop.

"That sounds entertaining," he said, smirking. "I don't see any downsides."

"Paint Fume Quinn is a lot like Drunk Quinn, but with more clothes on." I was so focused on painting that I sort of forgot who I was talking to... "Oh my god, that's a horrible thing to say to a parent."

Flirting or not, I should at least *try* to be *a little* professional. I cleared my throat, desperate to keep my eyes averted. At the sound of his poorly concealed chuckle, I felt compelled to backpedal.

"Sorry. I didn't mean—" I stammered. "That's not an accurate—"

He laughed louder.

I took a deep breath and finally looked at him. "You must think I'm a mess."

He grinned. Then turned his attention back to the flat he was painting. Slow, metered, even movements of the roller, up and down, along the canvas of the flat. It was mesmerizing.

"You keep looking at me, Davis," he said with a wry smile, eyes still on his work. "And I'm going to finish painting my flat first."

I scoffed. But I didn't speak again until I was halfway done and confident that I could beat him. He was still ahead, but only slightly.

"During our junior year," I began, still concentrating on my work. "Faith and I got into huge trouble because of some flats."

"Do tell." He kept painting and didn't look up. My plan to distract him and take the lead wasn't working.

"I was stage managing the spring show—*Grease,* Faith was playing Rizzo—and she stayed after rehearsal to help paint the flats. She was in the middle of a bad breakup, so she let out some stress by painting some very not-nice things about her boyfriend on the flats. We had a good laugh about it because, you know, Paint Fume Quinn."

"With all her clothes."

"Correct," I said, in stride. "Anyway, we had a great time, and then painted over them with the lockers of Rydell High School. We managed to get them finished *and* hang them that night, but we neglected to make sure the paint had *covered* the words…"

"No," he gasped. "What did they say?"

"Some unflattering comments about Geoff's… you know…" I decided to leave out the part about discovering Abby was on the way.

He laughed, and then I laughed, and it seemed we'd made an agreement not to discuss my unprofessionalism.

"Were your breakups that dramatic?"

"Me? Nah," I said with a shrug. "Faith had enough drama for both of us. There was one guy I dated for most of senior year, but nothing else notable. Most of the time I was too busy for a boyfriend, so I didn't date much. Not much has changed."

"Why not?"

"I'm surprised at you, Mr. Miller. That's a nosy question," I said playfully. I didn't want to tell him that I hadn't met a man worth making time for. I especially didn't want to explain how hard it was to form new relationships after my parents died.

"Apologies," he said, playing along. "I'm a nosy guy."

"If you must know, I'm still waiting for my brave, handsome prince to rescue me from the witch who kidnapped and imprisoned me in a tall tower and feeds me poisoned apples. I've also been cursed to become an ogre at night. There's a spinning wheel in there too somewhere. Maybe a dragon. And the only thing that can save me is True Love's Kiss."

I paused, turning pink. He lifted one corner of his mouth.

"How's that for relationship drama?" I said, recovering.

"Does your nose grow when you lie?" he asked, then poked the tip of my nose with his index finger, covered in white paint. The motion startled us both. After a moment, he started to apologize. I was more interested in revenge, so I took my paint roller, fully loaded with the same paint, and dragged it down the front of his shirt. Scoffing loudly in mock offense, he wiped the paint away and flicked it at me.

"Don't start a fight you can't finish, Miller," I laughed, climbing to my feet. "You don't want to do this."

"Maybe I do," he said, standing up.

I held the roller in front of me and stepped toward him, but my foot slipped on the tarp and I *fell* toward him instead. The roller flew from my hand, landing on the small area of floor that was not covered by a tarp. My whole life flashed before my eyes. And the next thing I knew, I was in Theo's arms.

He helped me get back up on my feet, still holding me around the waist, and once again, we found ourselves face to face, with mere inches between our lips... I mean, us.

"Hi." He cracked a smile but, thankfully, did not laugh. He also did not let go.

"Hi." My knees nearly buckled beneath me. "Thanks."

"You're welcome." *Oh god, just lean in, Quinn.* "I had to protect the flat I just finished painting, after all."

"Huh?" I said, sad when he finally released me.

"Look down."

Sure enough, Theo had finished painting his entire flat, and won the race.

"I believe the score is now one-to-one, *Davis."*

CHAPTER TEN

A new month brought with it another cocktail party, so I spent most of my week rounding up all my energy to put on another dress and turn on Business Quinn mode. Once again, Shawn was off the hook, because helping Charlie was more important than schmoozing. It would've been nice to have someone loom threateningly to thwart old men telling me how beautiful I was, but at least I had Leah to commiserate with me. Plus, plenty of champagne and a Lyft to get me home safely.

I limped into the house on sore feet, eager for Franklin snuggles and bedtime. But the hallway was empty when I opened the door. I called his name and listened for his jingling tags, but still nothing, so I began to panic. I dropped my bag in the hallway, kicked off my shoes, left the door still open with my keys sticking out of the lock, and searched the house room by room to find him. I forgot that my feet hurt.

"Franklin!" In the kitchen, I found a full water bowl and untouched food dish.

"Frankie! Come here, boy!" In the living room, his favorite spot on the couch sat empty.

"Franklin! Come on, buddy! Frankie!" I bolted up the stairs, trying to keep my cool on the edge of a meltdown. *Where is my dog?*

"Good boy, Frankie. Where are you?" My bedroom was empty.

"Franklin!" Shawn's bedroom was empty.

The door of my parents' bedroom always stayed closed. I didn't bother to check in there.

I popped my head into the bathroom and peeked behind the shower curtain, though I didn't expect to find my Great Dane in a bubble bath. I couldn't leave any stone unturned.

He's a 180-pound dog, where could he be? I hadn't lost him in the house like this since he was a puppy and he would hide under... *I know where he is!*

"Franklin! I'm coming!" I called, running down the stairs at full speed, completely unconcerned for my own safety.

"Oh, sweetie. There you are!" I said in my calmest voice.

He'd been hiding under the dining room table, that favorite hiding spot of his puppyhood. It had always been a safe zone for him. He'd wiggled his way underneath and laid out flat. I had to pull out all the chairs to clear enough exit space and then I nudged him out of there. Reluctantly, he emerged, limping, and wincing in pain. It was the worst I'd seen him.

My poor, good boy was in pain and I didn't know what to do about it. I sat on the floor with him and made my best attempt at a visual check, but nothing was obviously wrong.

The truth was, Franklin was old. I'm not an idiot. I take Frankie to the vet twice a year, keep him up to date on his shots, buy him fancy dog food with whole-grain, all-natural ingredients. Probably better than the food I made for *myself*. I'd been doing my best to make this dog immortal and he'd already lumbered past the life expectancy of his breed. He was the best dog who ever walked the earth. I couldn't imagine my life without him.

After a few uncertain steps, Franklin slid back down to the floor. He looked tired, possibly lethargic, and I'd never been more scared in my life. Despite it all, I kept my voice calm and steady, stroking his head gently.

"It's okay, sweetie," I said slowly.

He lowered his head to the floor, rolling slightly to his side, looking for belly rubs. I obliged, and he closed his eyes in contentment—or as contently as possible given the pain. When he finally fell asleep, sprawled out in the middle of the living room rug, I hopped to my feet and dug around my purse until I found my cell phone.

I dialed the vet's emergency number.

"Dr. Russo, it's Quinn Davis."

"Oh, hi Quinn! What's wrong?"

I explained how I'd found Franklin, what he was doing, and did a physical exam with the vet's guidance. It woke him up but didn't seem to cause any serious discomfort. He wiggled a bit when I touched his hip, but not in pain. I gave Dr. Russo a full report and he exhaled a long breath.

"Is he lethargic? Has he eaten or had any water today?"

"He just seems tired, like he's just too sore to move. It doesn't look like he's had anything to eat or drink today—his bowls look untouched."

"Any idea how long he might've been stuck there?"

"I don't know. I wasn't home much today..." I began, trying not to panic. *Had he been there all day? Wait...* "Shawn was here until the afternoon, though, and he would've called if Franklin was like this. He wouldn't just leave him."

"Okay, Quinn," he said, taking time to choose words. "A lot of dogs start developing arthritis around Franklin's age, if not sooner. If he's in the middle of a bad bout, he'll bounce back soon. He's going to move a little slower, though, and you might have to shorten your walks with him. Give him some aspirin now, and let's see how he's doing tomorrow. If he isn't any better, or you think the pain is getting more serious, call me back as soon as you can. Okay?"

"He's okay for now?"

"I don't think you need to rush him in here. For now, let's see if some little lifestyle changes help get him moving around again. You can give him aspirin up to three times a day—if it seems to be working. If not, there are other ways we can manage his arthritis."

"Thanks, Dr. Russo," I said, taking a deep breath. I needed to slow my racing heart.

Within minutes, I'd traveled to the nearest pharmacy and stocked up on enough aspirin to last at least a year. At home, I dosed out the right amount and got him to swallow it with a spoon of peanut butter. Franklin had never given me trouble about taking meds. We'd always just trusted each other.

"There, buddy," I tried to sound reassuring and curled up on the floor next to him, using a couch pillow and a small throw blanket to get cozy. The stress knocked me out cold, and I dreamed about little baby Franklin.

My parents hadn't even wanted a dog, but Franklin wasn't

just any dog. A little over ten years ago, just after I'd graduated from Yale and moved back home, I saw a post Mary Beth had put up on social media. Three one-day-old puppies that had arrived at the animal shelter when their mother had died. It broke my heart.

I called her immediately and volunteered to come back to the animal shelter and help. We had to bottle feed the puppies and sterilize everything constantly. Without the antibodies they should've gotten from their mother's milk, they were susceptible to every germ and speck of bacteria. Most dogs in these circumstances wouldn't survive. The female puppy died on the second day and I cried for hours.

After that, I stayed late every night, just sitting with those two little puppies, and willing them to live. I fed them and sang them songs. Benjamin would lay still and listen, pricking an ear up every so often, but Franklin always crawled into my lap and stared up at me when I sang. They both pulled through perfectly healthy and Benjamin got adopted almost immediately when they were old enough.

Franklin, though, was special. I'd begged the manager to put him on hold for me. There was a connection between me and that dog unlike anything I'd felt before. It sounded silly to say that out loud back then, but the manager understood and gave me some time to convince my parents.

Mom and Dad were not "pet people," as I was often reminded. And Faith was still living in the house with baby Abby too, so it was easy to argue that the house was already full.

Somehow, after a week of pleading, they agreed to visit the animal shelter and meet him. Of course, the second they saw him, they fell in love. This big awkward puppy with giant ears, so gentle and full of love. Mom said later that they'd agreed because of how we looked at each other. They understood.

I woke up around 2am when Franklin licked straight across my forehead, his version of a *thank you.* I opened my eyes to see him standing over me, wagging his tail. I pulled myself to my feet, celebrated with many head scratches and saying lots of excited things—*what a good boy!*

Franklin had grown from silly puppy to sweet elderly dog in the blink of an eye. When I headed for the kitchen that night, guided by one hungry stomach, Frankie padded slowly behind me. I opened the fridge and dug out some leftovers, he headed for his water dish and crunched a few bites of his kibble from the bowl. Together, we ate in silence, probably equally relieved.

Shawn came home shortly afterward and was surprised to find us both awake.

"Did the cocktail party run late?" he asked. I hadn't realized I was still wearing my dress.

Even though he looked exhausted, he sat down at the table with me and stayed awake while I told him the story. Franklin sat patiently on the floor next to him, with a paw on his knee. He wanted attention.

"Oh, poor Frankie," he said in his Uncle Shawn voice, scratching behind Franklin's ears. His tail swiped across the floor, wagging happily. Shawn turned to me. "You must be exhausted, Quinnie."

"That cocktail party was a doozy. I was already wiped before I got home," I groaned. Suddenly, I yawned, stretching my arms above my head. "I'm just glad he's okay and I can get some sleep."

"Same here. We were weirdly busy tonight—everyone decided to watch the Celtics game at Charlie's. I don't hate that, but ugh... I'm tired," he said, then returned the yawn.

"Can you hand me my phone?" He turned and grabbed it from the counter nearby. "I need to cancel tech tomorrow, which sucks, but I'm not leaving him alone."

"Don't," said Shawn, putting the phone on the table. "Get some sleep and go to tech. I'm off tomorrow—a miracle, I know. I'll stay with Frankie, okay?"

"Really?" I said, my eyes growing wide. Shawn's always pitched in to help care for Franklin, but he'd never expressly volunteered to dog-sit. "That would be so great. *Thank you.*"

"Stop acting surprised," he said, laughing. "Go clean the mascara off your face and go to bed. You look like a raccoon."

I punched Shawn in the arm on my way by, but I smiled the whole way to the bathroom.

CHAPTER ELEVEN

On day three of Theo's new theater career, we hung lights. The high school auditorium had plenty of stage lights already, but we'd asked to replace some of the older ones and now I had to put the new ones up. At least I had an extra pair of hands strong enough to lift this stuff. I could do it, but not alone. And I couldn't imagine trying to get Abby up on the ladder with a twenty-pound piece of equipment.

Faith brought the kids to the cafeteria to play theater games. They'd been working so hard during rehearsals that they deserved some fun. It also kept them off the stage while Theo and I worked.

"Ever hung stage lights before?" I asked, slipping on my work gloves. Because nothing says *ouch* like touching hot metal.

He shook his head. "I'm sure that's not a thing that contractors normally do."

"Not a contractor," he said, with a faint smile.

"Right, sorry," I said. *Noted.*

"But you're right. This will be a first for me."

"And how are you with ladders?"

"Afraid of heights?" Theo asked, a faint smile on his lips. "The Indominable Miss Quinn has fears?"

"Indominable, huh?" I smiled back. "And how would you know?"

His mouth dropped open just a tiny bit. *This is fun.*

"Here, take this," I said as I tossed him a wrapped bundle of cables. He caught it, then stood awkwardly still, looking at it. "We're gonna need to run that from the tech booth back there, which is a mega tripping hazard. Don't let me forget to tape it down when we're all done."

"Should I…"

"Just drop it downstage right for now. I just want to get everything sorted first." With my back turned, busy digging through the rest of the wires and tools, I could almost hear him frowning in confusion. I stood up and looked over my shoulder at him. Yup. I pointed. "Right there."

"Sorry," Theo said under his breath.

"Don't worry about it," I said, crossing to him. "It's my fault. We've spent all this time in the workshop, you've never had the chance to be on the stage. And I've never given you a proper tour."

Theo stepped back and gestured with both arms toward me, standing center stage, "Take it away, Miss Quinn."

"Okie dokie," I began, facing straight out to the audience. "We say Stage Right and Stage Left to indicate which side of the stage we're entering, exiting, etc. The directions are from the perspective of the *actor*. So, if you're standing here..."

Theo moved back to centerstage, right next to me. His arm brushed mine and the warm tingling was back.

"This is stage right," I said, moving my arm to the right. "Downstage means *toward* the audience, and Upstage means..."

"Toward the back?"

"Exactly, which makes more sense when you're facing the stage, in my opinion." I hopped down and turned around, waving for him to join me. "Come here, I'll show you."

Theo joined me, concentration on his face. It was like I could see him processing and storing it in a mental database.

"In ancient theater times, the stage was tilted toward the audience, so *downstage* meant the actors were actually moving down—and vice versa." I waved my arms around to demonstrate.

"That sounds terrifying and dangerous."

I shrugged. "People have done scarier things in the name of theater. Next lesson?"

"So far so good."

"Now, the *really* confusing stuff is that the Stage Right and Stage Left are backwards for the audience." I pointed to my left. "That's Stage Right. Seems basic enough, but when you're up and down on stage and off doing tech stuff, it's easy to get turned around. You can also just say *House Left* and *House Right* when you're out here."

"Stage Right is House Left?"

"Correct. You're a quick study, Miller."

He shrugged. "I've got a good teacher. She's very engaging."

"Okay," I said with a mischievous smile. "Quiz time. Take me to Stage Left."

Theo took two steps to his left, paused, then he pointed to the right and made a clicking sound.

"Got it. Now, follow me. We can save the rest of the tour for another tech day." *Of which, I hope there will be many.*

Back on the stage, I braved the ladder to show him what we were doing. I took a deep breath before gripping the sides, white-knuckled, and walking up. Theo held it steady for me with this nervous expression on his face. *Was he worried about me?* Up at the top, I closed my eyes and tried not to look down.

Stage lights are giant, heavy monsters. When he handed me one to demonstrate, he was even more concerned.

"This thing is half your size... are you sure you're okay?"

"I'm not *that* little. Now pass me the lantern already." Resting it on top of the ladder, I showed him the clamp, the yoke, and the cable, so he could take directions. And then I hefted that thing up there and hooked it up. "We'll focus them later. Let's just get them all up for now."

Theo practically picked me up off the ladder and put me back on the stage. He climbed up and made me hand him the lights. You'd never know he hadn't done this before.

For a while, we worked quietly together, with only my directions interrupting the silence. It was nice to be teaching him something new, instead of building and painting. This was a theater-specific task, something only I would teach him. My mind raced with ideas for future lessons. Of course, I didn't know if he *wanted* to learn it all, but I hoped he did.

"Record time," I said, when we'd finished.

I walked down the aisle taping the cables down while Theo folded up the ladder and returned it to the storage closet. He came back with the push broom—without being asked—and swept the stage while I wrapped up the extra cables.

And now, nothing to do but wait for the kids... Theo sat in the front row and stretched his legs out. I sat on the edge of the stage, facing him.

"Thanks for helping me with that," I began, searching for an easy topic. "I asked Shawn to help me last time and it was a disaster... let's just say he's not exactly trustworthy with ladders."

"Shawn?"

"My brother, what more do you need to know?"

"I'd love to meet the brother who torments Miss Quinn," he grinned. Theo adjusted his position, bending his knees and leaning toward me.

"No, thanks. He's *a lot* to take in. And what about you? Brothers, sisters?"

"Only child," he answered. "I was raised with so many cousins, I guess my parents decided I didn't need any siblings."

"And how'd that go?"

"Having three older cousins was dangerous. I learned how to swim when they threw me into the deep end of my grandma's pool. I learned how to play goalie by having a soccer ball kicked repeatedly at my face," Theo said, touching his head. "But I got pretty good at it."

"I can see how that might toughen someone up."

"Something like that."

I reached into the cooler next to me and pulled out two water bottles. I offered one to Theo, who took it with a quiet *thanks,* and cracked the other one open. After a quick gulp, I decided to brag a little bit.

"Well, you're talking to the three-year high school district MVP."

Theo looked impressed. "What position did you play?"

"Center forward." I lowered my brow in playful seriousness. "And I would *smoke* you."

"I don't know about that," he frowned. "I was the starting goalie on the varsity team from sophomore to senior year."

"College too?"

He nodded. "Two-time champion team. All-star both junior and senior year. You?"

"Full ride to Yale, Ivy League Rookie of the Week seven times. I still hold the record for most points scored by a single player."

"I'm sorry, but you wouldn't get a single one past me, no matter how hard you tried."

"That sounds like a challenge, Miller," I smirked, playing it cool. I don't know how bragging about our soccer careers had turned into some weird form of flirting, but I liked it a little too much. "Do you still play? There's an adult league here in the fall. You should join us."

Faith entered the auditorium with a procession of tired children who were ready to go home. As soon as Oliver spotted his dad, he bolted down the aisle to the stage. Theo stood up and caught him, something I'd learned was routine for them, with a big grin on his face.

"Hey, Oliver," he said, crouching down. "Miss Quinn was just telling me about how she plays soccer."

Oliver's eyes grew wide as he looked up at me. "Really? Awesome! I'm so good at soccer, you gotta come see me play! Will you? Please, Miss Quinn?"

"Oh really?" I looked at Theo, who was grinning mischievously. "Yes, Oliver. I would *love* to come to your soccer game."

"The kiddie league season starts at the end of May, so you'll have some time to practice," he said, then added a wink. "It's on, Davis."

CHAPTER TWELVE

Faith showed up at my door later that night, bearing gifts of dinner and wine. Abby was having a sleepover party with some of her friends and Faith was bored. When Abby was younger, Faith had always been desperate to get some time for herself. But now that she had a teenager with an active social life, Faith seemed to get lonely, quickly.

"I needed to get out of the house," she said. The cork of the wine bottle popped, and a glass of wine appeared before my very eyes. "And I didn't want to drink alone. Plus, we never see each other anymore."

"Um, I see you almost every day."

"But when was the last time we went out somewhere? I'm *bored.*"

"You rang?" Shawn said, poking his head through the kitchen doorway. I sighed audibly, tipping my head back in exasperation.

"Never, ever tell Shawn that you're bored on a Saturday night."

"To be fair," Shawn grinned evilly. "If you hate fun, you should never say that to me at any time, ever."

"Yes, the King of Fun." I groaned.

And then Faith did something completely bizarre—she handed her phone to Shawn.

"Do it," she said.

"FINALLY!"

"What are you doing?" I asked, already concerned for my phone's safety.

They both ignored me. A couple of taps to start the download and Shawn passed it back to Faith.

"Now just open the app and fill in the info," he explained.

"It's going to ask you for your credit card information, but it won't charge anything until after the 30-day trial is over. Just go ahead and put it in there."

"This is a scam to steal my credit card, isn't it?" Faith said, frowning at the phone screen.

"Please," he replied. "I doubt there's an available balance, Faith."

He was likely not wrong. Faith has a serious weakness for designer scarves. She didn't argue.

"What. Are. You. Doing?" My curiosity was piqued. And I walked right into his trap. Instead of answering, Shawn picked up my phone from the table. "Oh no you don't."

I reached for it, but Shawn brushed my hand away and stepped back far enough that I couldn't reach him. Unless I climbed over the table and lunged at him, which I briefly considered.

In silence, Shawn tapped away on my phone. Faith cleared her throat, pretending to be fully engrossed in her phone screen. And then months of badgering comments came back to me.

"Oh, no no noooo," I said, grabbing Faith's phone from her hand. Sure enough, there on the screen was the profile creator for *LoveMatch.com.* "Whyyyy?"

Shawn was standing there, looking victorious. He held out his hand, presenting my phone to me, with the same page loaded on the screen.

"Fill it out, Quinnie," he demanded, and by the look in his eyes, he wasn't budging. "*Or I will.* And before you ask, I'm paying for it. That's how dedicated I am to your happiness."

"I'm not doing this. I don't want to *date.*" I scowled, crossing my arms. He tucked the phone between my arms, then opened the dishwasher and started unloading the clean dishes. A classic Mom move. There would be no arguing. *Fine.* I started with my name and worked through each section in silence.

"Do I need to put my *real* birth year on this?" Faith said, looking at me.

"Come on, Faith, you don't want a relationship to begin with lies," said my brother with an air of wisdom suddenly about him. Shawn carried the glasses over to their respective cabinet, arranging them on the shelf one by one. "And for *the love of god,* please disclose that you have a child."

Faith looked over at me, stunned. She pointed a finger at him. "Who the hell is this guy?"

I turned toward Shawn, who'd made his way back to us. "What exactly do you mean by *relationship?* This is for hook-ups, isn't it?"

Faith coughed to disguise a laugh and turned her attention back toward the phone screen.

"Not that I'm looking for hook-ups or anything."

She coughed again, but Shawn and I ignored her.

"Do you think I would set *you* up on a hook-up site?" Shawn said. "You're all about commitments and shit like that."

"You're so romantic, Shawn," said Faith, without looking up this time. She was typing away in the text box for *Your Interests,* mumbling to herself.

"What are you lying about now?" I said, leaning over her shoulder. "Horror movies—true. Disco—also true. Crochet?"

She shrugged. "I'm interested in *learning* to crochet. That counts."

"The history of the guillotine?" I struggled not to laugh. Shawn did laugh. "Come on, Faith."

"Go ahead and check my Google searches."

"I'm good, thanks. I'm sure that list will thin the herd for you."

"That's the goal," she smiled widely. "What are you putting on yours?"

"Mostly basic stuff," I said, racking my brain for things I like. I handed her my phone with what I'd come up with so far. "Nothing about 18th century execution methods."

"Let's see... Your interests include classic literature, dogs, chess, theater, soccer..." She trailed off, then paused for a moment. "Sorry, I fell asleep reading that."

"Long walks on the beach?" Shawn suggested, only partially kidding. "Pina coladas?"

"I hate pina coladas." I made a face. Coconut cream is the devil's mixer. "Do I *need* to put an alcohol preference on this? Doesn't that make me sound like a lush?"

Shawn leaned forward and refilled my wine glass.

"Nah, you can probably leave that out." Faith put my phone down on the table and typed quickly on her own screen. I heard her mumble *martinis* as she typed.

"I think you're getting the hang of this," said Shawn, picking up my phone and tucking it *back* into my crossed arms. "My work here is done, *ladies*."

"I am not going to give you the satisfaction of reacting to that anymore," Faith said.

"What? *Ladies?*"

Faith twitched.

"Shawn, I don't even *want* to do this," I said, putting the phone down. "Not only do I have *zero* time for dating, but I have *zero* interest in dealing with relationship drama right now."

"And when was the last time you had a date?"

"Why does that matter?" I snapped. "Not everyone needs a revolving door to their bedroom."

"Ouch," he said, feigning offense. He picked up my phone, opened my hand, and placed it on my palm. "I just want to help."

"What happened to boundaries?"

"Ah, this is the loophole," he said, clearly prepared for this question. "This isn't about a specific relationship, so why would there be any boundaries?"

"Cut it out, guys. This is for fun, Q. Just do it. Now... what did you put for *Describe your perfect partner?*"

"Regular stuff," I said nonchalantly. I picked up my phone and unlocked the screen, handed it back to her. "Nothing exciting."

"Eyes: brown, Hair: dark brown, Height: between 5'10" and 6', Personality: confident but not arrogant, good sense of humor, kind heart..." she read, droning on. "Interests/activities: soccer, theater, loves dogs... construction?"

"Like building sets and stuff," I said, shrugging. "I hate doing that alone."

"Basically, Theo," she said, fighting a laugh. Shawn busied himself by wiping down the countertops, letting us argue it out. "You've just described Theo."

"No, I didn't!" I snatched the phone out of her hand.

"Wait... who is Theo?" Shawn turned around; he couldn't resist. Faith's eyes grew wide with excitement.

"Nobody," I replied quickly.

"Oh, he's somebody," Faith said, amused. "Just look at her face. She hasn't mentioned him?"

"Why would I mention a drama kid's parent to *Shawn*?"

Shawn shook his head, ignoring me. Faith barreled on.

"Theo is a *hot dad.*"

"Of course, he is."

"What's that supposed to mean, Shawn?" My voice went up an octave. Still, they ignored me.

"But Q is freaked out about pursuing anything."

"Because he wears a *wedding ring*," I interjected.

That got my brother's attention. "A wedding ring? Faith, how do you—"

Faith held up her hand to stop him mid-sentence. "Riddle me this, Shawny: all the paperwork is in his name. He and his son moved from Chicago—alone, no wife—to be close to family."

"And?" Shawn asked, scowling.

"Okay, fine. Oliver told me his mom lives in heaven. I think she died. But Theo hasn't said a word, so I don't think I'm supposed to know that." I typed away, hiding my hot, probably red, face.

Faith smacked me. "You didn't tell me that!"

"Why does it matter? Keeping the *ring* on seems to indicate that he's not dating," I frowned.

"Okay," said Shawn, after a beat. "Am I canceling this membership then?"

"No!" I said too quickly. "I mean, yes. Just cancel it please. I don't want—"

"Because of Theo?" he asked, innocently. "Yes, cancel, because of Theo?"

"No! Don't cancel—"

"Keep the membership. Got it." My brother gave me a thumbs up.

I have been set up.

Faith laughed so hard she cried. Eventually, she calmed down enough to finish her profile while I still typed away. Not five minutes after Faith hit *save*, her app alerted her to a message.

"Wow, that was fast," she said, reading. "He's a European history professor who DJs on Fridays at that disco club downtown."

"No shit," said Shawn, craning his neck to see.

"But could he possibly live up to Faith's impossible male standards?" I asked, mockery in my voice. She flipped the phone around to me, where a green-eyed, dark-haired, tan, physically fit man stared back. "I'm sorry, no. There's no way that's a real picture of this guy. That has to be a model."

Faith checked his profile again. "It's both, Q. He was a model for ten years to pay off his student debt."

"That's not a real person," Shawn chimed in.

"No one pays off student debt in ten years," I added. Faith rolled her eyes at me.

"Okay, fine. I guess I must swipe right so I can meet him and see for myself. He invited me to drop by the club next Friday to watch him DJ."

"That's... weird."

"Not weird enough for me to say no," she smirked. "So who's coming with me?"

I sighed. "Take Shawn. He's a better wing-man."

"As exciting as it is to watch someone DJ, I'll be working," Shawn said, tipping the end of the wine into our glasses.

"Oh, too bad, guess I have to bring Q with me," Faith said. "Remember how I said we need to get out more?"

"Scoping out dates for you is not as enticing as you'd think."

"Honestly," she said, musing. "I can't think of a better excuse. I won't go alone, and I'll have you to protect me. And you can go just to have fun, no date. It's the perfect plan."

I grimaced at her, not convinced.

"Fine. I'll have my own private disco adventure—to a club which may or may not be a safe place to meet a stranger—specifically to meet a stranger whom I may or may not want to date—who may or may not also be a serial killer."

"It's good to see Faith's melodrama isn't fading with age," said Shawn, sitting down in the chair next to Faith. She flicked his arm. He swatted at her hand.

"I could go alone without getting murdered," Faith said, a little huffy now. "I'm an adult."

"On paper," said Shawn. Faith punched him in the arm. He winced in pain, rubbing at the spot with his other hand. "You're so violent."

"Sorry," said Faith, grinning innocently. "Gotta practice my self-defense in case this guy really is a serial killer."

"Fine, I'll go," I relented. "But you'll owe me."

I'm going to regret this.

CHAPTER THIRTEEN

"Wow," said Leah, stepping into my office. She crossed the floor and parked herself in her favorite leather chair. "You're here early."

"And so are you."

"I'm *always* here early," she replied.

I shrugged. "I've got stuff to do."

"Okay, President Davis, what's on your schedule?"

I opened my weekly agenda and scanned my to-do list for the day. "Looks like a list of phone calls to past donors and a lunch date with Marie."

"The hotel manager?"

"Yeah, she's easier to deal with in person, because I'm not convinced she reads her emails," I said. "That's about it though. Anything I can do for you? I'll need to leave here at two o'clock to run to the hardware store before rehearsal this afternoon, and then drop the cookies off for the high school soccer team's bake sale—but I should have plenty of time. If you're overloaded with planning the gala, I can take something off your plate."

"I don't think I'm the one who's overloaded," she said, frowning. "How are you squeezing all that in?"

I shrugged. "That's why I'm here early. Happy to help."

"It's okay, I've got this one," Leah said, turning for the door. She stopped. "I'm proud of you for not catering today."

"Huh?"

"No Tuesday coffee delivery. This is groundbreaking."

"Uh oh…" I checked the time on my laptop screen—yup, late. I grabbed my jacket, nearly knocking over the coat rack, and headed for the door. "I'll be back in twenty minutes."

Any time I disrupt my routine the slightest bit, even if it's to improve efficiency, my internal clock gets all screwy. And a ball gets dropped. *But there's still time to catch this ball!*

"Purse!" Leah called after me. I doubled back for it and saw the frown on her face. "I thought we were making progress."

I grinned sheepishly. "Traditions are important, Leah."

Thirty minutes later, I'd delivered the coffees and scones and returned to my desk. Except for a few stray hairs sticking to my forehead, it was like I'd never left. With a deep, centering breath, I opened my agenda. A note on that day's square pointed to a to-do list I'd scrawled onto an extra-large Post-It note. In addition to what I'd rattled off to Leah, I had a few more errands I'd forgotten about: picking up my dresses from the cleaners, buying dog food for Franklin, stopping at the post office to mail the care packages to the troops.

Two and a half hours until lunch. If I can get through my work here, I can leave at noon for lunch, then run all the errands before I'm needed at the theater. Perfect.

Time to buckle down and start hacking away at the list. During the next few hours, I used my special time-management system, which I called *running on timers*—breaking the day into twenty-minute intervals and alternating between tasks. Twenty minutes to check and reply to emails. Twenty minutes to update the Drama Cares expense sheet. Stretch break. Twenty minutes to call and thank past donors. Twenty minutes to confirm the rentals with the costume shop. Coffee break. Item after item, crossed off the list. The secret to my productivity.

With ten minutes to spare, I shut down my laptop, packed up my things, checked in with Leah, and climbed into my car. Whew.

There were lots of new puppy friends for me to snuggle on Wednesday. They were all different from last week's puppies, except for Percy, who was still not healthy enough for adoption. I met a little dalmatian with floppy black ears, a pair of orange Pomeranians, a pug named Duke, and a chocolate lab who barked at my shoes for a solid five minutes.

"Where are all my friends from last week? Big rush on puppies?" I asked, holding Percy on my lap. He wiggled around until he could lick my chin.

"Mother's Day," said Mary Beth, who was busying herself with the weekly dusting. "Apparently, families like to give their mothers one more thing to take care of to commemorate this Hallmark holiday."

I laughed half-heartedly, mostly to be polite. And a sudden realization hit Mary Beth. Hard.

"Oh my god, I'm so sorry. That was insensitive." She dropped the duster and took a step toward the corral. "I'm sure this is a hard time to get through without your mom."

"It's okay," I said, smiling weakly. I scratched Percy's head, looking away from Mary Beth. "You can't control when pets get adopted. It's great that they're getting homes."

Mary Beth paused, taking time to choose her next words.

"How long has it—"

"Eight years, next month." My answer was queued up and ready. Percival tried biting me a couple times, because he still thought it was funny for humans to make puppy sounds.

"Really?" she said, surprised. "It feels like less than that. I can't even imagine what you and Shawn have been through."

I shrugged. *What even is time anyhow?* I sat and stroked the little furry head of the Pomeranian named Brandy. She closed her eyes, panting, and soaked up every minute of the attention. Her brother Bernie nudged my other hand impatiently, looking for similar treatment. He got some scratches too, of course.

"How are you doing?"

"I'm okay," I finally said. "It's mostly just weird, and the realization that it's been *so* long is upsetting."

"How so?"

"Sometimes it feels like a million years, and other times it feels like a couple of weeks, but it never hurts any less."

"How's Shawn doing?" she asked. There was more concern in her voice than curiosity.

"He's hanging in there," I answered. "I know it's still tough for him too, but he's not the most emotional guy. We don't talk about them a lot."

"One day, he's going to impress you," she said, picking up the pug and giving him a squeeze. Duke licked the side of her face and she smiled. "There's more under the surface there. You'll see it someday."

"You seem awfully sure about that," I said, lightly.

"I'm good at reading people," she said with a shrug. "And I spent a lot of time trying to read Shawn back in the day."

"Just come by the bar already and say hi. You never know what'll happen."

I went straight to the bar from the animal shelter, motivated and energized by all the tasks I'd been *slaying* lately. It just felt like the right day to finally clean that office properly.

"Hey, Uncle Charlie!"

He stood at the sink, washing glasses by hand, and listening to sports talk radio. We hadn't been able to replace the dishwasher yet, so this had become a routine activity. Sometimes, I thought he might prefer it that way. I grabbed a dishtowel from the rack and headed over to give him a hand.

"Oh hi, Quinnie." He kissed me on the cheek, then handed me a glass to dry. "Thank you."

He passed me the clean glasses one by one and we worked in silence. Wipe, swipe, repeat. Wipe, swipe, repeat. Someone on the radio ranted about the Red Sox blown lead over the Yankees. Some outfielder missed an easy catch, a relief pitcher lost his focus, blah blah blah... It amazed me how many people had opinions on things they couldn't do themselves.

"Doin' okay?" he asked. "You're awful quiet today."

"Same old, same old," I answered. Dad's favorite response earned a fond smile from my uncle. "And what about you?"

He grunted a noncommittal reply. Typical.

"Been thinkin' about that refund I'm gettin' and what to do with it," he said, eyes on the sink.

"Are you finally going to take a vacation?"

"That's the thing... need to tell ya somethin' and I don't want you to be upset."

My heart rate shot up instantly. "Are you okay, Uncle

Charlie? Is there something... wrong?"

He made a *tsk* sound at me, frowning.

"Just because I'm old, you think I'm dyin' now? No, nothing's wrong," he frowned. "But I know how you are."

"And how am I?"

He tilted his head at me.

"Don't you try to argue with me," he said, a warning look in his eyes. He handed me the last glass and turned off the water. "But I want to use the money to renovate the bar."

My mouth dropped open, with arguments queued up and ready. Uncle Charlie raised a hand, still not finished.

"Thought real hard and my mind's made up," he said firmly. "So instead of arguing, why not help me get started?"

"Why?" I blurted out the question. He considered me for a moment. "Not to make an argument, just so I understand."

"The bar's doin' bad, Quinnie. But you know that."

"Maybe things will turn around soon," I replied, forcing a smile. I put the last glass on the drying rack.

"Been on this rollercoaster for 25 years and every time things go up, the peak's lower than last time. Gotta break the cycle. Puttin' money into renovations now might give us a shot at getting things right again."

The logic seemed sound. If anyone knew this bar, it was Charlie. But was it the best option? Charlie was getting older and the business was getting tougher.

"Maybe it's time to sell—"

"Don't you dare say that, young lady." Uncle Charlie frowned. "I told you we're not arguing about it. "Right now, the only thing I want is to start planning. Can you help me with that?"

I nodded. Charlie's check wasn't nearly big enough for the work this place needed. A bandage on a gaping wound.

"Oh hey," said Shawn. "What are you doing here? You're early."

He strolled in from the bar, a towel over one shoulder, carrying a couple empty boxes from the last shipment. Charlie disappeared into the office and Shawn picked up the rack of clean glasses. I followed him out front.

"Can we... talk?" I asked, hesitantly. He walked behind the

bar and I walked around to sit on my favorite stool. "We may have a problem."

"Oh, the refund thing? I know." Shawn placed the crate on the counter and wiped his hands on the towel.

"You... know? Why didn't you tell me?"

"Cool it, Quinn," he said, placing the glasses neatly on one shelf, sliding each one into nice, neat rows. A few times, he stopped to clean a spot from one of the glasses.

"Why didn't you tell me?"

"He just told me last night," he said defensively. When the last glass had been placed, he kicked the crate under the sink and out of the way. "When did I have time to tell you? You were sleeping when I got home. I was sleeping when you left this morning."

"Were you at least planning to tell me? Because it doesn't seem like you are the least bit concerned," I said, anxiety rising. "What are we going to do about this?"

"Quinn..."

"We need to fix this."

"Okay, hold on there," said Shawn, hands on his hips. His eyes were fixed on me. "First of all, the bar belongs to Charlie, not us. Second, Charlie is perfectly capable of making decisions. If this is how he wants to spend his money, that's his choice. You and I may not agree with him, but—"

"Agree?" I interrupted. "It's a horrible idea. He doesn't think he deserves anything for himself."

"In his mind, this *is* doing something for himself."

"It isn't though. His whole life is this bar—he should be taking time to relax," I said. "His check isn't big enough to do a full renovation. He's not thinking right about this, Shawn. I don't want him to waste his money."

"You gotta stop, okay? You can't micromanage everything. That's not your job."

"No one else seems interested in being the responsible one."

"Seriously," he said, shaking his head. "Cut it out."

"If you want to let him waste his money, then—"

"Quinn!" Shawn said sharply, slamming his palm on the counter. "Can you just give me a *chance* to work this out?"

I blinked, stunned. "Fine. You fix this one."

"You and your crusade to *fix* everything is getting out of hand…" he said, trailing off as he walked to the backroom.

Shawn had better know what he was doing.

CHAPTER FOURTEEN

At home, Franklin was waiting patiently at the door for me for the first time all week.

Dr. Russo said moderate walking would be good for him, and that it could prevent his joints from getting inflamed and causing him so much pain. He advised some slight modifications, like shortening the walk and taking breaks. I needed the walk just as much as Frankie's joints, if not more. I could manage that.

Leash in hand, I led the way to our new route, about two-thirds of the original trail. Franklin trotted alongside me gingerly, but without pain, and he was just so darn happy. He stretched his neck out and sniffed the air in all directions. *Freedom.*

"We both needed the fresh air, huh?"

A couple blocks from the house, I stopped to let Franklin inspect a hydrant and checked my phone while I waited. No missed calls, no urgent emails. There was just one message—Theo, it seemed, needed some help.

> How exactly does one "run lines" for a play? Asking for a son...

> Ask Oliver to recite his lines without looking at the script

That was an easy one. I resumed my leisurely walk with Franklin, with a vague smile on my face. I imagined Theo and Oliver flipping through the script together, looking for the highlights that marked his lines.

> Um okay but how tho?

> You read his cue lines, then he recites his line to you

> Uhhh cue line...?

The line another actor says before his. I'll get you a glossary

Smart

Halfway through the walk, I sat down on the sidewalk in front of Mrs. Johnson's house and let Franklin flop down across her lawn. Break time.

He says he has to be off-book? Does that mean everything has to be memorized?

I'm gonna make you *write* the glossary. You're brilliant.

Wait. Oliver says you throw the script away?!

I laughed out loud at that, probably more than I should have. Sitting on my neighbor's lawn with my giant dog as the sun went down, laughing all by myself. Franklin lifted his head and his ears twitched at the sound.

Ohh nooo! He can keep it, just can't use it onstage.

What a relief. He stopped crying.

He was crying?

Nah, just wanted you to feel guilty for a second

Feel free to order your own glossary.

Franklin had propped his head on my knee, scrutinizing me. I took a picture of him with his eyebrow raised and texted it to Theo.

Even Franklin is judging you

But look at that face, I can't even be mad

"See, Frankie? I think you'll be good friends."

That Thursday was our last rehearsal before Mother's Day, and the kids were gloating about the crafts they'd made. Sandy was giving her mom a popsicle-stick birdhouse she'd painted with purple hearts. Mark bragged about his macaroni self-portrait; he just knew Mom would hang on the wall in a big, pretty frame. Cammie had turned her school picture into an ornament to hang on her Mom's desk at work.

Oliver was hunched over a book in the far corner of the auditorium. I hadn't seen him turn a single page. He was trying to look like he wanted to be left alone, but he needed someone to talk to. I headed up the aisle and dropped into the chair next to him. His Batman book was upside down.

"Hey, buddy," I said softly, wrapping my arm around his shoulder. "Are you okay?"

Oliver let out a sudden, loud sob that caught the attention of a nearby group of kids, having their snacks a few rows up. Oliver hid his face in his book again, embarrassed, until they turned away. His tears fell silently after that.

"Miss Quinn, I miss my mommy," he sniffled.

It absolutely shattered my heart. This had to be a heart-wrenching weekend for them. It was hard for me, but I was a grown woman. Oliver must've been in unimaginable pain. He was so small and so young. He *needed* his mommy. He deserved to have her back.

"Do you want to talk about her?" My smile felt strained.

He thought for a moment, wiping a tear from his cheek with the cuff of his sweatshirt sleeve.

"I only remember a couple things. She had pretty, brown hair. And she sang songs all the time. Her favorite color was green, like me." His voice cracked.

"Let's get some water and have a snack, okay?"

I stood up from my seat and took his hand. We walked slowly out the front door. I got him a juice box from my emergency snack basket, then brought him to one of the benches by the soccer field and sat down.

Oliver climbed onto the bench next to me and wrapped his arms around my neck. I held him tightly. I wasn't sure why it made *me* feel better to comfort this little guy with big brown eyes, messy hair, and dimples in his cheeks. My heart was broken for Oliver and Theo. I just wanted to hug them both tightly and make it better. I had an idea.

After rehearsal, Theo was one of the last parents to arrive—as usual. I was beginning to think he did it on purpose so we could talk. He pulled into his usual parking spot and hopped out, an ear-to-ear grin on his face. If he was as upset about Mother's Day as his son was, it didn't show. Although, if I were a widowed parent at this time of year, I would overcompensate too.

"Hey!" He said to me, as Oliver tackled him around the legs. He paused for only a moment to absorb the impact, then continued to speak. "Was this monster good for you today?"

"A perfect angel, as usual." I smiled at Oliver, who looked up at me without letting go of his dad's jeans.

"You must be seeing a different child, then." Theo answered playfully. Oliver giggled, pressing his face into Theo's leg. I just wanted to keep the smiles on their handsome faces.

"Hey, um... If you guys are free Sunday, I've got a couple of free passes to the zoo. Would you like to join me?"

Oliver looked up at his dad, eyes wide, and Theo looked down at him, beaming. Knowing he'd won, Oliver's smile spread wider.

"That sounds great," Theo said. "But that's Mother's Day. Are you sure—"

"Totally fine. I'd love a nice Sunday adventure." I had to shut that down quickly. A story about another dead mother wouldn't improve things.

"Okay then. Oliver and I are visiting my mom in the morning, but we can meet you there around lunchtime..."

"Perfect. Shall I pack a picnic lunch?"

"Can you bring grapes?" Oliver finally let go of Theo. He practically jumped up and down when I nodded.

"It's a date," Theo said, then got that back-pedaling look on his face. "I mean... It's a..."

"I know what you meant," I said with a smile. It felt good to end the day on such a positive note, but I also felt like I needed to be real with Theo. "Can I talk to you for a minute?"

"Sure," Theo said. "Get in the car, Ollie. Be right there."

Oliver skipped over to the car and climbed into his seat. Once he was settled, Theo turned back to me.

"I just—um, I wanted to let you know that Oliver let me know…" I tried and failed to say this as matter-of-factly as possible. I told Professional Quinn to sit down and let Normal Quinn talk for a second. "Oliver told me about his mother."

Theo's face transformed before my eyes. His carefree, easy smile fell, and his eyes grew bigger. I could tell that it was more sadness than surprise, more acceptance than anger. He let out a deep sigh.

"I'm so sorry, I didn't want to bring it up—"

"No, it's okay. I'm glad he told you," he said, recovering. "Especially since I didn't tell you myself."

"I understand why you wouldn't," I said with much more empathy than he could know. "He had a tough day today, with all the other kids talking about Mother's Day gifts."

"He seems okay now," Theo said, checking on him over his shoulder. He had that *Batman* book out again, right side up this time, and smiled widely. "Thank you."

I shrugged like it was no big deal, but to me, it was. If I could turn the day—maybe the weekend—around for Oliver, it would make my own weekend a whole lot brighter too.

"Thanks, Quinn," Theo said, with a genuine smile. "It's weird, but I'm really relieved that you know now."

Oh, so am I.

CHAPTER FIFTEEN

A disco club is an interesting place. It wasn't very different from a regular nightclub, but it had been a long time since I'd visited any club. The disco music pumping from the speakers didn't have that heavy, pulsing, floor-shaking bass like techno music. A real-life disco ball spun from the ceiling, scattering colorful lights everywhere. The bar was crowded with people dressed in the clothing of various decades, especially the 70s. So much white polyester. I would've felt out of place in my dress if not for the other half of the group, more modernly attired. There were plenty of sequin dresses like Faith's too.

"How have I never been here before?" she asked, awestruck, over the sounds of Donna Summer.

Faith dragged me up to the bar and ordered me something blue, which was delicious and a bit heavy-handed on the alcohol. We spent a few minutes wandering around, careful not to crash into any of the couples spinning around the dance floor. Eventually, we made it to the stage at the back of the room, where the fantasy man stood, in real life, an actual human being after all. I fought the urge to hold his picture up next to him, in awe that a man turned out to be as attractive as he promised. Faith, from the look of her, was struck by a similar thought. He wore a horrendous wide-collared, reflective white shirt, unbuttoned to his mid-chest—and yet, it was working for him.

I elbowed Faith in the ribs. Without taking her eyes off him, she leaned over to my ear.

"This guy is amazing and terrifying."

"In a serial-killer kind of way?"

"More like a can-I-speak-words-with-him kind of way."

Her DJ date looked in our direction, found Faith in the crowd, and gave her a sexy wink, with one corner of his mouth turned up. The lighting was too erratic for me to tell if there were sparks flying, but I could sense the tension in the air.

"Holy moly, Faith."

They weren't breaking eye contact. I was impressed that he could still work like that, eyes away from the turntable, not focused on his hands. The intense staring contest made me feel like a spectator—which was exactly what was supposed to happen. Neither of us really believed Faith was going to get axe-murdered today; she just wanted to get me out of my house. But I was growing overwhelmed by it all. Faith could read it all over my face. Sensory overload.

"I'm okay if you want to get some air."

"I'm not ditching you."

"No, I'm *releasing* you," she said with a grin. "Go get some air. Meet me out front in two hours. Okay?"

"Thank you for not forcing me to be the third wheel."

She shrugged. "I'm a good friend."

I downed the rest of my drink, placed the glass on a nearby table, and headed for the door. I passed nimbly through the chaos of the dance floor and the crowd at the bar. The bouncer held open the door for me, with a nod and a smile as I walked past him. Once the air hit me, I breathed deeply. *Clean, outdoor air.* There'd been so much perfume and cologne in there, it was an incredible relief.

The weather was so perfect that it seemed wrong not to stay outside for at least a little bit. I picked a direction and started walking along the sidewalk in the sexy black dress and heels Faith made me wear. I'd insisted on bringing my little cropped cardigan, despite her protests, so I was prepared for a nice evening stroll.

At a leisurely pace, I could take it all in—the people, the sights, the sounds, the smells. Along both sides of the street, diners sat outside at black, wrought iron tables, tucked between velvet ropes and restaurant façades. Suddenly starving, I stopped to scan the menu at the nearest restaurant. And then I heard someone call my name.

"Quinn!" Theo shouted, startling a few nearby diners. Including the woman sitting across from him at a table for two.

Oblivious to the look of shock on her face, he stood up and waved me over to them. He was wearing a tie, a foreign look for him. Then I remembered what *I* was wearing...

I looked around for a safe path to him. I could easily imagine myself tripping over the velvet rope, maybe twisting my ankle in these shoes, falling onto a nearby table, sending diners scrambling, and humiliating myself in front of this gorgeous man. Nope. If he couldn't catch me, what was the point?

The host unclipped the rope, and I wove through a cluster of small tables toward Theo and company. My heart pounded louder with every step closer. And then there I was, face to face with Theo, completely unsure what to do. A handshake? Too business-y. A high-five? A first bump? Weird. A hug? Are we at *hugging* yet?

Instead, Theo greeted me with a gentle touch on my arm and a wide smile.

"You look amazing, Quinn," he said. I blinked. *So do you...* "What are you doing here?"

"Playing wingman for Faith, but she set me free. I really hate clubs."

He stared at me like he was seeing me for the first time. With these heels on, I was a lot closer to his height than usual. Maybe it was messing with him.

His companion cleared her throat and Theo snapped out of his trance. He turned to the blonde woman with curly hair and big, stunning chandelier earrings. If this were a different situation, I would've asked where she got them.

"Carol, this is my son's drama teacher," he said.

"Nice to meet you." She shook my hand, but she *did not* think it was nice to meet me at all. Her thin lips made a straight line on her face.

"A persistent mutual friend set us up. So here I am," he explained with a shrug.

"Great! Well, I don't want to interrupt," I said. My palms felt sweaty and tingly. "It was nice to meet you, Carol."

"No, wait." Theo pulled an empty chair from a nearby table and dragged it behind me. "Have a seat with us."

Carol's eyes grew wide. Stunned, I dropped into the chair

with a thud. He pushed me in closer to the table despite my half-hearted protests: *No, no I can't possibly. I don't want to interrupt you. Honestly, I should be getting back to Faith.* None of those did any good because they were all lies.

"Your timing is perfect," he said. "I was just telling Carol about Oliver."

"Oh?" *A topic I could handle.* "He's a wonderful little guy. Very talented."

Carol remained silent. And we all know what happens when Quinn faces silence...

"He's so kind, too. Oliver is always one of the first kids to help out and he works so hard. We've just loved having him around, my partner and I—not my *partner* partner. For the theater program. Not like *that*. Not that there's anything—I just, not me. I like men."

An uncomfortable pause followed. Theo leaned back and crossed his arms. *Was he smirking?*

"He only started a couple months ago, but he's just a natural," I rambled. "Honestly, Theo, next time you're volunteering, we can sneak into the audience to watch his big solo."

"You volunteer there?" Carol interrupted, turning to Theo

"He's my newest stagehand," I beamed. "He's been helping me with set construction. We've spent a lot of time backstage, you know, doing stuff."

Theo coughed. I realized how bad that sounded.

"But, not stuff like *that*, I mean building stuff and painting and... Where was I going with this?" I blinked a few times, desperate for a way out. My eyes flickered to Theo, who was just staring at me with... that sexy raised eyebrow look with the half-smile. Not helping. Annnndddd I kept going...

"Anyway, Oliver is wonderful—is that where we were? And Carol, he's such a handsome little guy, too."

"That's nice."

"Just like his dad," I added, in a face-palm kind of moment. Too flustered to backpedal, I froze in place while the heat of my embarrassment melted my face.

"Well," Theo said suddenly, startling me. Took him long

enough. "This is fun."

"If you'll excuse me," she said, standing. "I need to visit the restroom."

Theo and I watched in silence as she picked up her purse and walked away.

"Oh god, I'm so sorry."

"For what?"

"Ruining your date," I said, dropping my forehead onto my crossed arms. "What a jerk."

He laughed. He actually *laughed.* "You're not a jerk."

"I just embarrassed myself."

"You did. And it was wonderful."

I lifted my head and scowled at him.

"Your awkwardness just saved me from the most boring, horrible date of my life."

"Blind dates are the worst."

"My cousin Josh has been on my back about getting out there and dating again," he said, pausing. "He said it had been *long enough.* I finally gave in, but I regretted it as soon as I let him set it up. I've been dreading this night all week."

"I'm sorry."

He shrugged, catching my eye. "I'm suddenly feeling much better about it."

Oh.

"What are the odds she's coming back?" I asked.

"Zero. She just walked down the sidewalk behind you."

I tried, like a little bit, to hide my smile. Couldn't do it.

"Will you have dinner with me, Quinn Davis?" asked Theo, also unable to hide his grin. "It's the least I can do after that heroic rescue."

I checked the time on my cell phone and slid it back into my purse. I still had about 90 minutes before Faith was expecting me back at the club.

"I have some time to kill."

Beaming, he leaned forward conspiratorially. "Quick... Italian or Mexican."

"What?"

"Pick one. Italian food or Mexican food?"

"Mexican."

"Done," Theo said, then he waved to the server.

"What are you doing?" I asked.

"Exactly what it looks like," he grinned. "Getting out of here and bringing you to that taco place three blocks up the street."

"This is... strange."

"I'm a strange guy," he said, smiling again.

Once the entrees were packed up and the bill was paid, Theo stood up and led the way out of the courtyard. After about ten seconds of walking, I felt that familiar urge to fill the silence.

"You know, it was rude to set me up like that. I should be very angry."

"I panicked," he shrugged. "But you didn't have to try so hard. You being there, dressed like *this,* was probably enough. You didn't need to drag my good looks into it."

"I guess I panicked too."

"We make the perfect pair." The instant the words were out of his mouth, our eyes met. "Not that this is a date. I mean, it could be if you wanted, and I'd be okay with it, because... But that's not why I..."

I waited in silence, truly amused. Somehow, his frantic babbling calmed my nerves. It was adorable. We started walking again, but only made it a few blocks before he spoke.

"I don't want you to think I just assume every attractive woman I meet wants to date me. But you were here and I... This doesn't have to be a date. We can just have a parent-teacher meeting. With tacos."

"Tell me more about how long it's been since you've been on a date," I teased. "Because you're doing great."

He laughed weakly and I almost felt like I was torturing him. I hadn't prepared myself for anything like this tonight and it was all happening so fast.

"So... yes to the dinner? Or no to the date? Or..." he trailed off, turning his attention across the street. "Hang on a sec."

I stopped walking and watched Theo cross the street toward a man sitting on the ground. He crouched down to him and they exchanged a few words, then a smile, and Theo handed him the to-go boxes. Theo reached into his pocket and handed the man a fork.

Okay, that was... something. When he strolled back over, hands free, I didn't know what to say.

"Do you know that guy?"

"No, but he looked hungry," he said, shaking his head. Then he grinned brightly at me. "Besides, I'm not going to eat that food—I'm having tacos."

"Did you steal a fork?"

"Do you think a place like that gives out plastic forks?"

I laughed, shaking my head. "Very clever, Robin Hood."

"Now," he said, a new wave of confidence in his expression. "Let's just call this a *maybe* date and get some food. I think we're far too hungry for that kind of pressure right now. What do you think?"

I didn't answer right away, letting my brain process his words. I've never been a fan of *maybe*. If I insisted that we call this a date, things would change, right? Would it be better? Or would it just get weird? If I chose *maybe* that left things open—no one was committing to anything.

"I think I can get behind that," I said with a grin. *Why not?*

"See? I knew my night was turning around." Beaming, he took my hand in his—sending a rush of warm tingling through my body—and led me up the street toward the tacos.

As we walked, I imagined we *were* on a date. But not a first date. Rather, as a couple, comfortable in each other's company, spending our time together, away from everything else. Now that I knew this could've been a date, that fantasy seemed a lot more realistic.

CHAPTER SIXTEEN

Faith was waiting for me, head down, typing on her phone. She had a business card in her other hand, like she was adding someone to her contacts.

"He gave you his card?" I asked, amused.

"Weird, right?" she said, still typing with her thumb. "But not a serial killer. At least, I don't think so."

When Theo and I laughed, she looked up, startled.

"Mr. Miller, to what do I owe the pleasure? Quinn didn't mention she'd have company." She fixed her eyes on me.

"She stumbled upon me up the street, trapped in a disastrous blind date. What a rescue," he told her.

"You guys want to grab something to eat?"

"We ate," Theo and I replied in unison. *Oh god, please don't make this weird, Faith.* I stared back at her.

"Interesting," she said, trying hard not to explode with questions. "Shall I leave you alone on your date or..."

"I should get back home and relieve the babysitter, I'm already out later than I said I'd be." He sounded disappointed.

Faith watched silently as Theo and I did another dance of Handshake, Hug, or High-Five. He touched my arm again when he said goodbye, but I went for it. I hugged him—as my heart raced. Every bit of me felt warm and tingly. After the briefest pause, he pulled me in a little closer—just a teeny bit.

"Thank you, Quinn," Theo said near my ear. "You saved my night."

"No problem at all," I said, as the hug ended. Even then, we stood close together. I felt remarkably calm given the emotions swirling around my brain. "See you Sunday, right?"

He winked, nodded at Faith, and gave us both a wave before crossing the street on the way back to the restaurant.

My best friend waited until he was out of earshot before she spoke.

"It seems we both have stories."

I looped my arm through hers and we started walking up the street. "I'm sure yours is more entertaining."

"Not really. I mean, he's pretty much as advertised. Maybe a little egotistical, but definitely interested."

"You gonna call him?"

"Maybe. I don't know."

I stopped and faced her, hands on my hips. "Faith Anderson, what's going on?"

She exhaled, searching for words.

"I am a single mom with a teenage daughter. I teach kindergarten and run an after-school drama camp. My favorite food is mashed potatoes. I own *reading glasses*. I bake *for fun*. My feet hurt in these heels, my head hurts from that music, and this tiny purse does not contain any Advil," she said abruptly. "I do *not* belong here."

"Mister Disco DJ... not the one?'

"This is not my life anymore." She said, pouting. "Am I in crisis? Is this what that's supposed to feel like?"

"Ask my *Resting Crisis Face.*"

"How is that any different from your normal face?"

I smacked her arm. Faith laughed and started walking again, dragging me along. I stole a glance in the direction Theo had walked off... just in case I could still see him.

On the first Mother's Day after Abby was born, Mom and I had taken Faith out for the afternoon. In the early years, when Abby was too small to join us, she'd stayed at home with Dad. Our annual date became a tradition. The three of us would have lunch together in the city and get pedicures at the salon across the street. Mom was alive for seven of those Mother's Days. And that last year, we'd let Abby tag along with us. Mom called us the Fabulous Four and bragged all day about her daughters and beautiful granddaughter to everyone she saw. Faith had spent most of the day near happy tears, Abby had asked for each of her toenails to be painted a different color, and I'd taken pictures everywhere.

Mom and Dad died a month later. Even if I'd known it would be Mom's last Mother's Day, I wouldn't have changed a thing. It was a perfect day.

To Mom, Faith was a second daughter and Abby was her grandchild. My parents had welcomed Faith into our home when her own parents tossed her out for getting pregnant at 17 years old. When I told my parents, Mom sprang into action. No questions, no judgment—my parents welcomed her into our home. Practically overnight, Mom's home office became Faith's bedroom, complete with a crib and everything she needed. My dad helped Faith pack up at her parents' house and move in with us. Now a teenager, Abby had never met her real grandparents. Mom and Dad were all she'd known. Shawn was her only uncle. I was her only aunt.

When I went away to school, Faith stayed with my parents, growing closer to them with every passing year. Once I'd graduated and moved home, Faith had decided that she and Abby should find their own place, a small apartment on the other side of town. She wanted her daughter to have her own bedroom and more space to have playdates. Once again, Dad helped Faith pack her things and move on to a new stage in her life. Mom cried. The house was too quiet without giggles, too empty without a highchair and toys, too neat and clean. Mom insisted Faith and Abby visit every weekend. She'd loved them so, so much.

After Mom and Dad were gone, we moved our lunch and pedicure date to the Saturday before Mother's Day. This year, however, Faith wanted to change up the plan. She texted first thing in the morning.

> I'm an old woman and half-dead from last night. Can we do an at-home thing instead?

> Of course – be here in an hour

Shawn helped me pull together a breakfast buffet—pancakes, bacon, scrambled eggs, fresh fruit, toast, and hash browns—with time to spare and not a single argument. I was impressed with us.

Faith was also impressed when she and Abby arrived moments later. Franklin was ecstatic to see them and nearly toppled Abby to the floor in all his excitement. She giggled, scratching his head, and it warmed my heart. Shawn gave Faith a kiss on the cheek and a bouquet of fresh flowers—*aww*—and then greeted his niece with their secret handshake.

He stayed for breakfast too, which was a nice bonus to our day. It was nice to just hang out together as a family. We didn't do that enough these days. Then, for his final trick, Shawn made mimosas appear from thin air.

"I didn't even know we had champagne," I said, as he placed glasses in front of Faith and me.

"Hey!" said Abby. "Can I have one? Pleeeease, Uncle Shawn?"

Before Faith could answer her, Shawn turned around and placed an identical glass in front of Abby. She was delighted, I was amused, and Faith was not having it.

"Shawn, come on," she grumbled. "She's fifteen."

"*You* come on," he said. "Drink it, Abby. What's in that?"

She took a big sip through the straw and her face fell. "Just orange juice."

Shawn held his hands out—*See?* And Faith apologized. Abby, however, pouted for the rest of breakfast.

As my brother and I cleaned up the dishes, Abby and Faith transformed the kitchen table into a nail salon. Faith had brought a large container of nail supplies, but I insisted on contributing. She was, however, not happy about what I had to offer.

"Some of these nail polishes are from high school, aren't they?" she said.

"Don't you judge me," I feigned outrage.

The bottles clinked together as Faith moved things around and got organized. Abby, well-trained by her mother, was rifling through the container for the right tools. I casually picked up a nail file and started to round off the corner of my thumbnail.

"Um, no," Faith chided, taking the file from my hand. "First, remove that chipped polish."

I stuck out my tongue at her but did as I was told. Faith had flawless nails every day of her life, so I didn't think it was prudent to argue. Abby handed me the nail polish remover and some cotton balls, and I got to work.

"Hey, Auntie," Abby said politely. "Do you want some help?"

"Why?" I looked up at her open hand, waiting for me to hand over a cotton ball. It was already dyed a pale pink from the polish I'd been swiping at. "Am I already doing this wrong?"

Faith and Abby exchanged a glance and I gave up. And while my niece took over my manicure, I was subjected to her mother's nagging.

"Okay, I smell nail polish. Time to go," Shawn said, grinning. He'd changed into his black shirt, neatly ironed, and held an apron in his hand. He gave us all kisses on the cheek, leaving Faith for last. "Happy Mother's Day, weirdo."

After he left, Faith decided to turn on me. "So, have you heard from Theo?" Faith grinned, thrilled to have a captive audience.

"Since twelve hours ago?" I frowned. "No."

"Is that Oliver's dad?" Abby asked, looking up from my nails. "He's nice."

I wrinkled my nose at the strong scent of acetone, growing stronger with every swipe of the cotton ball.

"It's possible that I *maybe* might have invited them out to the zoo tomorrow."

Faith put down the cuticle pusher and glared at me. "Do you tell me *anything* anymore?"

"Should I?" I tossed a stained cotton ball at her. Abby sent me to the sink to wash the polish remover off my hands, and placed nail tools on my mat.

"I put them in order for you, Auntie, so just work your way from left to right. File, cuticle pusher, buffer." Abby was beaming. *This kid.*

"We need to make sure her nails are perfect, so she looks good on her date."

"It's not a *date*," I groaned.

"It is."

"It's *not* a date. Oliver is going too."

"What do you think, Abby?" asked Faith. Her nails shone with the clear polish she was applying. "Auntie asked a man she is interested in to go out somewhere with her for the day."

"Sounds like a date." My traitorous niece grinned.

"Isn't that wrong, though?" I asked, skeptically.

"How?" Faith sighed, placed the cuticle pusher on the table, and folded her hands neatly.

"You know…"

"No, I don't." She waited for me to speak. I stared at her. "Why is it wrong?"

"He's one of the parents…"

Abby started filing the rough corners of my nails to round them out. I watched her do this for a while, avoiding eye contact with Faith.

"We don't have rules against that, so what's the real issue?" Faith picked out a color and rolled the bottle between her palms.

I exhaled loudly. Abby held up two polish options for me, two similar shades of purple. I pointed to the one without glitter.

"Does it seem like I'm… uh…" I watched Abby file a jagged edge of my nail while I searched for a way to phrase my thoughts. "Playing mom for a day?"

"Eww, no way," Abby jumped in. "It's not, like, brunch or something."

"See? Even the kid agrees."

"Kid?" Abby was outraged. "I'm fifteen, Mom."

"You heard what I said," Faith replied. Abby scowled, but kept painting my nails, slow and steady. "*You* know you're not playing Mom. And Theo could absolutely say no if he thought it was creepy."

"I'm just afraid it looks like I'm trying to steal a family. Maybe?"

"Your mind goes to demented places, Q."

This time, I picked up the *bag* of cotton balls and threw the whole thing at her.

CHAPTER SEVENTEEN

The zoo was packed with families on Mother's Day, which might have bothered me if I hadn't had the company I did. Theo and Oliver didn't seem affected either, given the smiles on their faces as we sat together on my picnic blanket, sharing lunch. Oliver was tossing grapes for Theo to catch in his mouth, but they were laughing so hard that his tosses were too wild for Theo to get anywhere near them.

"Okay," Theo said, as their laughter subsided. "If we want Miss Quinn to be impressed, we need to concentrate. Ready? Focus... and go!"

Oliver twirled a grape between his fingers, squinting one eye closed like a sharpshooter in a battlefield, took aim, and launched it into the air. As though in slow motion, the grape arced across the length of the blanket and straight down. Theo adjusted slightly and caught it.

I erupted in applause. "That was AMAZING!"

Oliver's giggles returned. "We did it!"

"Well, Miss Quinn," said Theo, after eating the grape. "Are you impressed?"

"Of course! Who wouldn't be?"

"Why thank you. We've been practicing that for literally years. Kid's got a good arm, huh?"

"One of his many talents," I added. Oliver beamed. "Excellent work, sir."

"Thanks, Miss Quinn! It's your turn!"

"Oh, I don't think that's a good idea. I'm a pro. I wouldn't want to show you up." I leaned back on my palms, getting ready just in case they were serious. I'd spent many lazy summer days doing silly things like this with Faith, Shawn, and a couple of the neighborhood kids. I had always been the best at this game, even when we had to use popcorn.

"Oliver, I think that was a challenge." Theo said, wearing that mischievous grin.

Eyes narrowed, Oliver grabbed a new handful of grapes and took aim. After the first grape went wildly off course, Oliver's giggles returned. It bounced off my forehead. A second grape zoomed past my ear. There was no chance of catching these grapes, but the poor kid couldn't control his infectious laughter. I bit my lip to stop myself from joining him. *I have grapes to catch, after all. This is serious business.*

"Oliver, pal," Theo interrupted. He grabbed the last bunch of grapes from the container and plucked a few from the stem. "I think we're going to need to give Miss Quinn a fair shot at this, don't you?"

Oliver nodded, nearly wheezing with laughter.

"You ready?" Theo asked. I sat up a little straighter and we made eye contact. Instead of trying not to laugh, I was suddenly trying to calm my racing heart. When I was ready, I gave him a nod.

The next thing I knew, a little green grape arced beautifully upward and fell at exactly the right angle, almost dead center. Nearly perfect. I caught it with ease, between my teeth, just like the old days. Oliver cheered. Theo shot me a look that was both impressed and…

Ohhhhh.

Basically, he was looking at me exactly the way I looked at him—when I thought he couldn't see me. Without Oliver with us, this most certainly would've become a real date very quickly.

After lunch, we were back on the trail, watching Oliver skip from one animal exhibit to the next.

"A TOUCAN! DAD, IT'S A TOUCAN."

He ran up ahead of us most of the time but waited for us to catch up whenever he stopped at an enclosure. He read all the little signs about the animals and even sounded out the harder words on his own. Trailing behind him, Theo and I had settled into a companionable silence and the shared joy of watching this child lose his mind over an anteater.

On our way to the llamas, my hand accidentally brushed

Theo's and my whole arm suddenly tingled, like the nerves were waking up. We'd drifted closer together while we'd been walking and when our arms brushed against each other again, he took my hand and interlaced our fingers. So cozy and warm, so intimate—like a little secret between us. I didn't think I'd ever been turned on by holding hands... in a zoo?

"Quinn," said Theo, in a low, quiet tone. "Thank you for today. I haven't seen him this happy since we moved. Hell, I haven't seen him this happy for a long time."

"My pleasure. This is the best zoo trip I've had in ages."

"It's been hard on him. Us..." Theo trailed off and I felt his body tense. Our eyes remained straight ahead, both of us watching Oliver skip around the monkey enclosure.

"I can't even imagine." *I mean, I definitely could imagine.* But I didn't want to talk about my Mom, and by then, the time to bring it up had come and gone. "Can I ask a nosy question?"

"Anything," he said, squeezing my hand.

"How long has she been—"

"Four years and three months," he answered quickly. He queued that answer up just like I always did. "A few weeks before Oliver turned three."

More than half of Oliver's life.

After that, when there wasn't anything else to say, our comfortable silence returned. When Oliver rejoined us, excited to share what he'd learned about giraffes, Theo released my hand. It was probably better if Oliver didn't start asking questions about that anyhow.

Even so, everything was completely different now.

CHAPTER EIGHTEEN

Tuesday's pickup time followed a familiar pattern. Oliver and I waited in front of the building while all the other kids jumped into their cars. At least the spring days were growing longer, so we still had some daylight before the sun would set. When we were alone, Oliver shrugged his backpack on and gave me a thoughtful look.

"Miss Quinn," he said, after a moment of contemplation. "I think my dad has a crush on you."

Oh, okay then.

"I want you to be good friends because I love you both so much."

I still couldn't say anything, so I just let him keep going.

"I mean, you don't have to love each other," he continued. "You can if you want to... I decided that it's okay. But only if you decide that it's okay too. Do you want me to tell my dad?"

Theo's car pulled up and Oliver was too excited to wait for an answer. He skipped to the car and I followed him automatically, my brain screaming the whole way.

Why is it screaming? Because acting natural after this man's tiny clone dropped a bomb on you is impossible. That, plus everything that happened over the weekend, I couldn't look Theo straight in the eye without changing color. Not that it stopped me. His eyes are amazing.

"Go ahead and get in the car, Ollie," Theo said, after he'd squeezed the little boy tightly. "I'll just be a sec, okay?"

"Wait! I have to ask Miss Quinn something first." And then he rushed back to me and waved for me to bend down so he could whisper into my ear. "Is it okay if I tell him?"

"If that's what you want to do," I whispered back. I gave him a hug. "Now get in the car."

Theo waited for Oliver to climb in and turned back to me. His jaw was stiff with determination.

"Quinn, I need to say something."

"I'm.... uh... I'm listening?"

"I just had the best weekend I've had in a *very* long time. And somehow, I managed to mess it up."

"Um... how?"

"I wanted to tell you—or ask you, really—I wanted to just come out and say it to you. And then I chickened out."

I opened my mouth to respond, but he kept talking.

"I like you, Quinn. I *really* like you," he said, working himself up to it. To his credit, he didn't falter again. "And a *maybe* date wasn't good enough. Can we do this the right way? Would you have dinner with me on Friday?"

"Yes," I said, hiding my elation. Maybe. "Let's do this the right way."

"Oh, thank god," Theo whispered. His smile was broad and brilliant, awash with relief. "I don't know what I would've done if you said no. Of course, if you change your mind..."

"I'm not going to change my mind."

We stood there facing each other for an awkward minute or so. Was hugging a thing that we could do, with Oliver right there? Should I wave?

Do not wave, Quinn.

"I'll see you soon," I said, still frozen in place.

"Yeah, goodnight."

Finally, when Oliver called to him from the car, Theo was able to turn away. Poor little kiddo was probably bursting at the seams to talk to his dad—especially after watching the two of us talking.

Things would get a whole lot easier for both of us if he would just kiss me already.

On Wednesday night, Faith, Abby, and I had promised to give Charlie and Shawn a hand with a few things at the bar. We entered through the back door to the stockroom, where my brother stood, surrounded by several stacks of boxes. Everything had been pulled from the shelves onto the floor, in the middle of the stockroom. We had to scoot around the perimeter of the room to get to him.

"Hello, ladies," said Shawn. His shirt was ironed, his apron was spotless, and he was holding a clipboard. *A clipboard.*

"Again, eww." Faith stuck out her tongue.

"I know, I know. I can't help it," he said with a chuckle. He nodded to Abby. "Hey, favorite niece."

"Hi, favorite uncle," she laughed. They took a minute for their secret handshake, then Abby threw her arms around him for a hug.

"Okay, so what are we doing?" I asked warily.

Shawn turned the clipboard around to show us a bulleted list. *A list.* "There are a few small tasks you can do if you're not up for the heavy lifting, but the basic idea is to reorganize the stockroom shelves to be more practical. Uncle Charlie's been digging through stock to get to the staple items—it doesn't make sense. And he's gonna hurt himself."

"Where *is* Uncle Charlie?" Faith asked, looking around the tiny room—like he could be trapped beneath furniture or boxes.

"Out front," Shawn answered in a low voice. "I gave him some small jobs to keep him occupied and safely out of the way."

"Clever," I said, impressed. "We don't need him to get crushed under a box of tequila."

"Just specifically tequila?" Shawn said, trying not to laugh.

"Shut up."

"Okay, okay, let's get started," he said, handing us each a sheet of paper.

"Quinn, most of your list is stuff out front," he instructed. "We need some of the frames replaced, some reorganizing behind the counter, stuff like that. And you're in charge of keeping Charlie busy."

"I'm in the fridge?" Faith asked, her eyebrows high.

"We need to pull out anything that's past the expiration date and everything needs a good wipe down. I'll send Abby in with the label maker so we can get it all back in order, too."

"You're lucky I brought my jacket, Shawn," Faith answered, eyes lowered.

"I get to play with the label maker?" Abby seemed excited about this.

"Yes, ma'am. I'm going to have you do some stuff back here with me, too. I need some extra help for sure. Look at this mess."

"Wow, you've really spent some time on this..."

"Try not to look too surprised, Quinnie," he said, with a hint of pride. "Contrary to popular belief, I am not an idiot. Just help me out and don't give me any lip."

One of my jobs was to sort through the bar towels and throw away the ratty ones. Uncle Charlie did *not* like to waste "perfectly good" things. But Shawn was determined, evidently, to get this place updated. He'd handed me a basket full of new towels— *Washed and dried at home*, he said—and told me to fold and restock the drawers. All of this, I had to do discreetly because Charlie was sitting across from me, polishing the taps.

"Been keeping me busy all afternoon," Charlie said, amused. "Like he forgets who's boss around here."

"I'm glad he's stepping up," I replied. "We're all a team."

"Since your dad... passed," he said carefully. "Things haven't been the same in this place."

"Of course, it never will. But Shawn and I are more than capable of picking up where he left off."

Mid-fold, my phone buzzed on the counter. And the name on the screen sent tingles all over.

"Hey Theo," I answered quickly, startling my poor uncle.

Charlie dropped the coasters he was organizing on the counter. I pressed the phone to my ear and went outside to talk privately. The weather was beautiful, but the street was empty of foot traffic. The closed laundromat loomed next door—an eyesore that was standing between us and the main road. And in my opinion, the roadblock between customers and the bar's success.

"Hello," he said cheerfully.

"What's up?" *Do not blurt out random things.*

"Listen," he cleared his throat. *He's nervous. It's adorable.* "About Friday...."

He trailed off and a lump formed in my throat. *Is he canceling?*

"Are we still on?"

"Oh. Yeah, of course," he quickly reassured me. I exhaled audibly. *So much for playing it cool.* "I just wanted to ask, uh… if you have… any food allergies?"

I blinked a few times before I could fully process it.

"No." *That's all I got. Sorry.*

"Great! I didn't want to take you someplace with food you're allergic to. I have a cousin who is allergic to fish and a blind date took her to a sushi restaurant… so that went poorly. I don't want any disasters. Or epi pens."

"Thank you for thinking about that. I'm happy to say that I'll put anything in my mouth." Pause. Cue embarrassed expression and more blushing. "Food, I mean."

"Uh… cool."

Oh, this will be fun…

CHAPTER NINETEEN

Going into work early was possibly my best idea ever and I'd incorporated it into most days at the foundation. Uninterrupted, I made it all the way through my inbox, carefully responding to every email. Then I sifted my way through the mail and papers stuffed into the plastic wall file outside my office. There was a folder full of drafted grant letters for me to edit and approve; a stack of mail the width of my wrist; and a few inter-office memos from various departments regarding various mundane things. "A kindly reminder to eat ONLY your own food from the breakroom" and stuff like that. But the silence didn't last for long.

"Why are you here so early?" asked Leah. "Again?"

Her voice startled me, and I knocked several envelopes to the floor. With a smirk on her face, Leah crossed the room and slipped into her favorite chair.

"Early mornings are *my* time to be alone and hide at my desk," she said.

"Although, I'll note that you're currently at *my desk*," I said flatly.

"Touché." She laughed and took a sip of coffee. Then she shifted in her chair, crossing her legs. Serious Business Leah mode. "Have you ever thought about taking some time off?"

"From here?"

"From everywhere," she replied, waving her right hand in a big circle. "All of your places."

I sat with her words for a moment, flipping through the mental rolodex of my responsibilities. Impossible. Who would fill all my shoes and wear all my hats?

"I can't do that," I said with finality. "Besides, I don't think I need to. Everything's fine. All the work gets done."

"But how are *you?*"

"I'm fine," I said, surprised. *Did I not seem fine?* "Where is this coming from?"

Leah didn't respond, and apparently decided to let it go. She leaned forward and grabbed a handful of envelopes from the top of the mail pile on my desk. She tore open a couple of the letters, scanned them briefly, and tossed them into the trash.

"So much junk mail," she observed. "Why do you need an invitation to refinance your home?"

"You can't imagine the stuff that turns up here."

Without looking up, she spoke, "Need any help with the grant letters today?"

"Nah, I can manage them. I'm flying through them now that Toni's got the hang of it. She's a quick study, by the way. I like her. I should get her coffee order for next week..."

"Hmm," Leah frowned. "Job applications?"

"I've skimmed them already." I pointed to a folder on the end of the desk. She grabbed it and started flipping through. "Those are the decent ones."

"Quinn," she said, finally looking up. "You do know that these are things I can do, right?"

"Of course," I answered, meeting her eyes.

"And they are part of *my* job, right?"

"Sure."

"So... would you mind if I take *all* of them, please?"

"Uhh, sure. Okay," I answered, a bit stunned. I reached into the file sorter and pulled out a second folder, stuffed with rejections.

"Thanks," she said, standing. "I'll check in later, okay?"

I managed to squeeze in a few rounds of timers before my next distraction arrived. I set the timer for twenty minutes to complete one task, twenty minutes for the next, and so on... Slowly, I chipped away at my to-do list. I needed that structure if I actually wanted to get anything done that day.

"Hey, Quinn," Shawn said, with a rap on the open door. His voice startled me. I didn't even hear him walk in. When I looked up, he seemed... odd. He was wearing a button-down shirt, for starters, and his face was clean shaven. His hair was tamed, not flopping everywhere in its usual fashion. Shawn looked professional.

Mouth agape, I had no words.

"Do you have a sec? I need to talk."

"Shawn, what's—"

Suddenly, Janet's nasally voice travelled into the room through my phone speaker. "Neil Taylor's here to see you."

"Relax," Shawn said, correctly reading the concern on my face. "He probably just wants to chat."

Leah came around the corner with a puzzled look. "Did Neil schedule with you? Oh hey, Shawn."

"I'm sorry, Shawn. I don't have time right now," I said, earnestly. "I have no idea what Neil wants, but I have to—"

"Real advice this time," he pleaded, holding up his hands in surrender. "It's about the bar."

"Now's not the time, Shawn."

"Okay, so *when* is the time?" He asked, an unreadable expression on his face.

"Look, I can only deal with one thing at a time—I can't do this now. Besides, you asked me to let you handle that. So handle it, okay?"

"If you'd listen to me for five seconds—"

"No," I groaned, ready to tear my hair out. "I'm here right now, not at the bar. I can't do *everything*. Maybe you could pick up the slack for a change?"

His expression turned icy cold. "I'll see you at home."

"Shawn, what—" I stopped immediately and forced a smile. "Neil! Hi!"

Neil Taylor swooped into my office with a big smile on his tanned face. He shook everyone's hands and took a seat—in Leah's favorite chair. Frowning, she stepped over to the other chair and sat down. Shawn stayed still, but his expression had also shifted to fake pleasantness.

A long-time friend of my parents, Neil had been a big supporter when I became president, pushing back against the board members who didn't like the idea. He was one of the wealthiest people in New England, but you'd never know it. Although Neil perpetually looked like he'd stepped off a cruise ship—rested, smiling, happy to be wherever he was—he was just a regular guy. The neighbor who mows his own lawn, babysits his own grandkids, shops for his khakis at the mall. Aside from galas and big events, he wore casual business attire. Hardly ever a suit jacket, never a tie. There was a picture of him with my parents on the bookshelf behind him. And yes, they were all on a cruise ship.

"Quinn, Shawn, how've you been? I know I say this every time, but it's just uncanny how much you look like your parents. More and more every day." Neil looked wistful for the briefest moment. "Still miss 'em. All the time."

"What brings you in, Neil? So good to see you," I said.

"Just in the neighborhood," he smiled. "Thought I might check in on the team. All good for the board meeting next week?"

"All set," Leah chimed in. "I'd be happy to get the—"

"Nah, there will be plenty of time for that at the meeting." Neil rested one foot on his opposite knee, leaning back. He looked over to Shawn and me, still standing as though Neil had hit *pause* when he walked in. "I have to hand it to you two. Everything you've done, just astounding. You've helped this place grow more and more every single year. Your parents would be proud."

"Thanks, Neil," Shawn answered. "But Quinn's the one working her ass off in here."

"Well," said Neil, "Thank you, Quinn, for all you're doing."

Was that it? Nothing earth-shattering. Just a friendly visit, nice words to say. I was relieved to know that nothing catastrophic had happened. And okay, I was amazed at Shawn. Neil shook Leah's hand, then gave me and Shawn each a hug.

"Oh, one last thing," Neil added, turning at the door. "I've been thinking a lot about where we're heading, and I think we should have a check-in. I've got some new ideas. I'm hoping we can break out of the bubble we're in—there's more opportunity out there for new donors. Can you put together something for me? Maybe two weeks?"

Leah and I looked at each other.

"Sure, Neil," she replied quickly. "I'll get the team together. We've got a new hire who might have some fresh ideas."

"Shouldn't be a problem. Janet should be able to schedule us in a couple weeks," I agreed.

"Great! I'll see you at the meeting," Neil promised as he headed for the door. "Let me know if you need anything. And Shawn, let's get in a round of golf sometime."

The idea of Shawn playing golf was laughable, but I wasn't even in the mood to enjoy it. Neither was Shawn, given the look on his face.

"Hang on, Neil. I was just leaving," Shawn said, glaring at me. "I'll walk you out."

CHAPTER TWENTY

On our first official date, Theo was nervous. He arrived at my house four minutes early and didn't do much talking for the entire twelve-minute drive. Things got a little easier once we sat down, thankfully, and he found his confidence again.

"How's Franklin?" *Great start.* I'd only mentioned him a couple times—I was impressed.

"He's just the best dog on the planet, basically."

"I always wanted a dog. My wife was allergic," he explained, and then a shadow of *something* crossed his face. "Plus, our apartment just wasn't big enough and then when Oliver came along, we didn't want to raise him *and* a puppy at the same time."

"Yeah, I can see that being a challenge," I smiled. "Franklin had a lot of training to do before he understood the power of his own size. He weighs more than I do so it was sort of important."

"Any other pets?"

"Aside from Goldie the Goldfish, nope. Shawn had this little newt for a while," I paused. "But he should not be left in charge of another being's life."

"Killed it, huh?"

"It wasn't pretty." I sighed, remembering the little body floating in the water. "He didn't mean to hurt it, he just never paid attention to it. He'd forget to feed it, then try to make up for it later with extra snacks... The lizard murder was accidental."

"Yeah, my baby frogs had a hard life, too. But so far, I've managed to keep Oliver alive by myself," he admitted. "People change."

"You know... it's nice to be on a not-first date."

"Technically, it—"

"*Technically,* sure. But we've already gotten to know so

much about each other that it's not as stressful."

"Yeah, you're right," he shrugged. "We've already covered the major stuff. What have we missed?"

"I already know *everything*. You might be surprised to know how much Oliver has spilled about you."

"Let's not talk about Oliver tonight," he said, with a half-smile on his lips.

I froze, not sure what to say.

"Truth is," he explained, very matter of fact. "Thinking about each other as Oliver's Dad and Miss Quinn changes… *this*. We spend a lot of time talking about him, but I want to get to know each other as two single adults sharing a bottle of wine and a reasonably awkward conversation."

I hadn't expected him to say that, but I was surprisingly relieved. I wanted to date Theo, not Oliver's dad. There was already something there, and it just needed some room to grow. It was amazing that he felt it too.

"I agree," I said thoughtfully, processing all of that. "I'll admit though, that this is a first for me."

He swallowed. "Same."

"I think we can handle it." I reached across the table and placed my hand in his. He squeezed it and smiled. "Even the awkward part. We have incredible potential there."

"Thanks, Quinn."

"Now… as far as the incessant questions go, Miller," I shifted tone, aiming for that playfulness I loved so much. "You can't turn around and say that I talked the whole night."

"Wouldn't dream of it," he said. Then he slipped right back into reporter mode. "Tell me about your brother."

"Twin brother. Shawn."

"Interesting." He paused, grinning mischievously. "I've never had dinner with a twin before."

"Your flirting hasn't improved."

He sighed. "Can I say I'm out of practice?"

"I'd like to say I'm out of practice, too, but I'm just terrible at talking to attractive men…"

I froze. He raised his eyebrows.

"See? Maybe we should give up on flirting."

"Is witty banter okay?" he asked.

"I can do that. Latent sarcasm?"

"What? I couldn't possibly manage sarcasm..." He rolled his eyes. We both laughed easily, finally relaxed. Theo raised his wine glass and clinked it against mine. "To normal conversations."

I tipped back my wine and—oops—drank it all. His glass, however, remained half-full. *Does he now think I'm a drunk?* No, because he'd already poured me a refill from the chilled bottle on the table. Theo sensed my silent turmoil and smiled.

"Faith warned me that you have a deep love of Riesling."

That took a moment to process. "She... what?"

"Relax," he reassured me. "I'm driving."

Theo parked in front of my house and walked me to the door, hand-in-hand, in a comfortable, easy silence. I guided him around the tripping hazards of the walkway. It used to be flat and smooth, but over the years, it had become wonky and cracked. Mom used to plant marigolds along the sides of the stones every spring. Some of them still struggled to bloom every year; the stubborn resilience of nature never failed to impress me. It all made me incredibly self-conscious as we walked.

"Thanks for walking me up," I said. "I'm sorry about dragging you through the jungle. I've been meaning to get out here and take care of it, but..."

I gestured around me and shrugged.

"Why not hire landscapers?"

"I can do it," I replied, maybe a tad defensively. "I'm perfectly capable, just busy."

"I have plenty of people I can send out here to help you get it under control," he offered. "Then you can focus on maintenance."

"I don't want to waste the money. Like I said," I smiled weakly. "I've got hands. I can do it."

We'd reached the front porch and he dropped the conversation. I climbed to the top step, key in hand. He stood with one foot on the second step and one on the third, leaning on the railing. Franklin started barking at the jingle of my keys.

"Would you like to meet him?" I asked, looking at Theo's

wide eyes. "He's very friendly."

"Absolutely," said Theo. "Why else would I come here?"

I smirked at him.

When the door opened, my beautiful boy was sitting nice and straight, his tail wagging. You'd never know he'd been in too much pain to walk just a couple weeks before. One step in the door and I had a pair of paws on my shoulders. He licked my face first, then turned to look at Theo. Dropping back down to the floor, he barked a few times, a deep, low rumbling sound that terrified most small creatures.

Theo, on the other hand, was beaming from ear to ear.

"He's beautiful," he said in true admiration. And then his voice changed octaves: "Aren't you a beautiful boy? Who's a good dog?"

Once I'd clipped on his leash, I walked Franklin outside and down the porch. Theo stepped aside to give Franklin a wide berth. He started sniffing the air around my date skeptically, but when Theo held out a hand, palm up, Franklin relaxed. After a moment, and a quick look at me for approval, he licked Theo's hand.

"You officially have permission to pet him."

Very slowly, Theo stroked Franklin's head until the big pooch's tail was wagging again. He took a step forward and licked Theo right across the face.

"Come on, boys," I announced, gripping Franklin's leash tightly. "It's time for a walk."

"Me too?"

"Yes, you too." I returned Theo's broad smile and took his hand. The dog nosed Theo in the thigh. "In fact, Franklin demands it."

"Who can refuse this big goofy boy?"

Franklin and I fell into step easily as we gave my date a full neighborhood tour.

I told him about some of my neighbors who'd run from this pocket of suburbia as soon as high school was over. I'd always planned to do the same, but… that didn't happen.

"I think it's nice here," Theo said thoughtfully.

"Yeah, me too." My reply surprised me a little bit. Until

then, it had just made sense that Shawn and I kept a house without a mortgage, which was too good a deal to pass up. But maybe my sentimentalism was a factor after all. "Ooh! And that red house over there? That's where Muriel Baker lived, our resident old woman."

"Scary?"

"No, she was awesome," I laughed again. "She gave out full-size candy bars at Halloween. On the Fourth of July, she made sure to buy enough sparklers for every kid in the neighborhood. She used to pay Shawn and his friends $5 each to hang her Christmas lights."

"Not you?"

"Remember that fear of ladders?"

"Right, Miss Quinn's biggest foe."

"Anyway," I said, playfully nudging him with my elbow. "When she died a couple years ago, there was a line around the block at her wake. She was a pretty cool lady."

"Damn. I wish I'd had a nice old lady in my neighborhood. Ours chased us off her lawn with a broom."

"That's too bad," I sighed. "I can't imagine Mrs. Baker being mean to anyone. She was just the sweetest person."

Franklin started to slow down. Break time.

"Do you mind if we pause for a few minutes and let Frankie rest? He's been having a hard time with his arthritis," I said, as Franklin plopped onto the Thompson's lawn, sending dandelion fuzz in all directions.

"I don't mind at all." Theo sat down on the grass next to Franklin and stretched his legs out in front of him, leaning back on his hands. Like he was just taking it all in.

I dropped down next to them, assessing how much space should be between us—not too close and not too far. I found the "just right" spot and leaned back alongside him. The sun had dried up yesterday's rain, so the ground was dry, but a chill had arrived with the night air. I straightened up, pulling my thin cardigan sweater a little tighter around me, and crossed my arms. I tried to be subtle; I was afraid he'd try to rush me home if he knew I was cold. Despite my efforts, he noticed. In a moment, he'd pulled off his leather jacket, and wrapped it around my shoulders.

"Better?" Theo asked, pulling me closer to him. I closed my eyes and I rested my head on his shoulder. *This is nice.* "Don't get too attached though. That's my favorite jacket."

"Nope, it's mine now." Smiling, I nudged him gently. My smile grew wider at the sound of his laughter. Then suddenly, he kissed my forehead. A familiar, sweet kiss that silenced us both. We sat frozen for a moment. Did Theo worry that he went too far—that it was an intimacy we hadn't shared yet? And I was sitting beside him, wondering if he'd fallen into an old habit and the kiss was meant for someone else.

There was no way to have that conversation without melting into a puddle of humiliation and sliding into the gutter across the street. *Time for a subject change.*

"As you can see, I live in a terrifyingly dangerous neighborhood," I said suddenly.

He exhaled, relaxing. "It's always the quiet ones."

"If I were going to break into a house, I'd look for a place like this, far from a police station where no one pays attention to anything."

Franklin slowly climbed to his feet, ready to go home. Theo stood up briskly and wiped the loose grass clippings from his pants. All clean, he reached out and helped pull me up, face to face again, with his jacket around me like a cocoon.

"Very clever." Our eyes locked and he took my hand. Instantly, all was forgotten. "In fact, you'd make the perfect criminal. Small, unassuming, probably stealthy when needed, definitely too pretty to be evil."

"Oh, really?"

"At first glance, no one would ever think you robbed banks or stole cars," he mused.

"Excellent," I grinned. "My plan is working."

"I wouldn't be surprised if I saw your face on a Most Wanted poster."

Back at the house, Franklin crossed the lawn and sat on the steps, waiting patiently for his treat. I unlocked the door, unfastened the leash, and let him inside, tossing a biscuit to him from the box on the shelf. Satisfied, he trotted off toward the living room and I heard the thud as he laid down in his dog bed. There was an awkward pause then, with me halfway across the threshold into my house—am I going in or out? Did Theo have any expectations? More importantly, did I?

Frozen there, I only moved when Theo began to talk. He was still standing on the steps, leaning back against the railing, with his hands in his pockets. When he didn't make a move to follow me into the house, I pulled the door mostly closed behind me and handed him his jacket. He slung it over the railing next to him.

"This was fun, Quinn. I needed a good night out... not that I, I mean... with good company, not just any night out. I can go to a movie for a night out, but by myself that's boring, so I just..."

"You're impossible," I said, amused. *The longer we stand here, the more he'll babble.* "And you should stop talking right now."

"Why? All I'm saying is..."

I decided not to let him finish. I took a step forward and kissed him. Just a little ice-breaker kind of kiss. A *let's-see-what-happens* kind of kiss. Then came the silent pause and the paralysis. I'd caught him off guard. Even though it wasn't the most passionate kiss, there was a warm, tingly feeling to it. He must've felt it too. Face to face, gazing at each other, the tension crackled between us like one of Mrs. Baker's famous Fourth of July sparklers.

Theo put his hands on my waist and leaned in for another kiss. This one was less like an ice breaker and more like diving into the deep end of the pool. My hands moved along his chest, past his pounding heart, and then over his shoulders. I wrapped my arms around his neck as he tightened his around my waist.

"Six weeks," he whispered.

"Huh?"

"I've wanted to do that for six weeks."

"Then shut up and do it again."

I felt Theo's laugh in his chest just before he did, indeed, kiss me again. This time slower, more intense, the kind that just melts your insides. He held me so tightly and with so much desire that I wished we'd gone inside. Just as I finished that thought, I noticed we'd migrated a step or two toward the door. *Am I moving backward or is he moving forward? Both, I think.* Either way, the moment my back touched the door, I learned that it hadn't latched closed.

The door swung open, and we both lost our balance. I tipped backwards, certain that I was about to get a concussion, when Theo smoothly caught the doorframe, without breaking us apart. Dipped back on his arm, not concussed, hovering above the floor, I leaned back from the kiss and looked into his eyes.

"Nice save, Miller." My voice was low, breathy. "You're very graceful for a goalie."

"Are you seriously taunting the man who just saved your life?"

"Is this better?" I kissed him again as he pulled me back onto my feet. "We're a mess."

"A beautiful mess," he said, resting his forehead on mine.

"Thank you for walking with me."

With a sweet little kiss on my nose, Theo unwrapped his arms and set me free. I stood on the porch, watching him hop down the front steps and stroll up the walkway. Then he stopped abruptly and turned around. My stomach flip-flopped. *He's coming back.*

Theo hopped back up the stairs and took me in his arms again—eye to eye, lips just an inch from mine.

"Forgot my jacket," he whispered. Theo reached around to pick it up off the railing. I leaned forward and kissed him one more time, sweet and gentle.

"You did that on purpose," I said with a smile. He gave me that scandalous raised eyebrow and then let me go.

"See you tomorrow?" he asked. I nodded. And then he left for real.

I sat on the top step for a while, breathing deeply to slow my heart to a normal pace as I processed the evening's events. I've been on dates. I've had boyfriends. I've had many first kisses. Theo could've been just another name on a list, but now, Theo *was* the list.

Why on earth did I let him go home?

CHAPTER TWENTY-ONE

Just as I stepped out of the shower the next morning, my phone buzzed with a text from Theo, looking for a coffee order. *Bonus points.* I had never in my life turned down a chance for coffee, why start then?

When I pulled into the parking lot, I was surprised to see his car already there. Not just on time, early. He was sitting on the hood, holding a pair of coffees. Of all the weird things to give a woman that warm, tingly feeling...

"Where's Oliver?" I asked, closing the car door behind me. And the first two words I'd spoken to him violated the no-Oliver dating agreement. Oops.

"He's inside, helping Miss Faith turn on lights. She insisted she needed a helper for that difficult task. I think she's just scared of the theater ghost." He smiled, offering one coffee with his outstretched hand. "Or kindly giving me the chance to do this."

Theo hopped off the hood of his car, wrapped his free hand around my back, and pulled me toward him for a kiss. Warm and sweet and so tender.

"I'll get her a fruit basket to say thank you," I said breathlessly, and then kissed him again. "We should get inside before we're discovered by other parents."

I stepped back, reluctantly, but Theo tightened his arm and pulled me in again.

"One more."

Then one more became two more and would have been three more if I let it. I placed a finger over his lips, and he gave me the most knee-weakening, mischievous smile I'd ever seen.

Ohhhh, it was hard to walk away from that.

"Come on," I reprimanded half-heartedly. "I need to pretend I'm professional now."

He laughed but let me go this time. "Afraid the other dads will be jealous?"

"No," I answered. I laced my fingers between his and tugged him toward the building. "But I am positive the moms will be."

Inside, Faith was waiting for me with an expression that said, *I hope you used your time wisely.* I winked. *You can thank me later,* said her smirk. But I could tell she was proud of herself.

"Come on, Theo," I called, walking down the aisle. I'd let go of his hand when we stepped into the building. It was time to activate Professional Quinn and leave Lusty, Enamored Quinn outside. "We're going to make it rain onstage today."

"We're... what?"

I laughed. Faith laughed.

"You have no idea what you're in for," she warned.

"It's okay, I'm game," he said as he reached the end of the aisle. He took a sip of coffee, set it down on the stage, and draped his jacket on a seat in the front row. Once he was done preparing himself, he gave me a sly grin. "I like it when Miss Quinn bosses me around."

Faith raised one eyebrow, but kept her mouth shut about whatever she was thinking.

"Best of luck," she said instead. "I bet Quinn she couldn't pull this off."

"Oh yes I can." I bragged. She'd only agreed to do *Singin' in the Rain* after I'd drawn her a blueprint of the "rain machine" I'd insisted I could build. "Hold my coffee."

Three hours later, my clothes were damp, Theo's clothes were damp, and Faith was chiding me for the puddle of water on the floor, but a mini irrigation system stretched from stage right to stage left. I stood at the edge of the stage, admiring my work—*our* work—but nervous for this test run.

"Okay, turn it on!"

Backstage, Theo flipped the switch on the pump, sending water up through the hose and across the ceiling. There was a pause, when nothing happened, and the only sound was the quiet whirring of the pump. And then, a perfect cascade of water rained down into the trough on stage, which funneled water back into the system.

The kids cheered. Theo cheered. Leo the janitor popped in to see what was happening, and he cheered. Even Faith cheered.

"I told you we didn't need a plumber!" I said to Theo, as he joined me downstage. "Just a regular contractor, I guess."

"Still not a contractor."

"Eh..." I shrugged, tilting my hand back and forth. *So-so.* He laughed.

"Okay... You were right. I never should've doubted you."

I paused. *Did I hear him correctly?*

"Was that an apology? I didn't catch an *I'm sorry* in there anywhere..."

He chuckled and leaned over to whisper in my ear. "I'll give you a proper apology later."

And now I have goosebumps. *How am I supposed to focus like this?*

Saying goodbye to this jaw-droppingly handsome heartthrob of a man in front of his son, other children, and parents, was impossible. When dismissal time arrived, Theo offered to clean up the mess we'd made. He packed up the tools, carried everything back to the workshop, and disconnected the pump. Safety first, et cetera.

I helped pack up the kids—shoes and jackets, bags, and accessories—returning an occasional comic book, hair elastic, or water bottle to its owner. Once they were ready, Faith lined them all up at the door for pickup. I climbed back up on stage and picked up the mop I'd left leaning against the wall.

"Hey, I'll take it from here," I said, as I spotted Theo coming out of the workshop. "Oliver's waiting to leave."

"Hi, dad!" Oliver called, waving from the front row. He was sitting patiently, reading another one of his Batman books. Once Theo waved back to him, Oliver returned to reading.

"Come on, buddy. Do you need to use the bathroom before we go?" Theo asked. Oliver nodded. "Hurry up!"

Oliver skipped toward the boys' room while Theo collected his things. There we were, alone in this huge auditorium, me mopping the floor, Theo zipping up a backpack. But again, it was *impossible* to say a proper goodbye under those circumstances.

The two of us were kind of awkwardly frozen. *Are we back to Handshake, Hug, or High-five now?* We couldn't get caught, especially not by Oliver. Obviously, Theo wanted to talk to his son if and when the time came. There wasn't anything we could do now.

Basically, these were the thoughts our eyes screamed at each other while we stood there. It was painful.

Oliver returned, cheerfully yelling, "I'm ready now!"

"Well..." said Theo. "I guess it's—"

"Yeah, thanks for your help today," I said with a strained smile.

"Always a pleasure." He winked.

"Dad, can we have pizza for dinner?" Oliver said suddenly. He was waiting on the floor, jacket on, watching us. "Miss Quinn, do you want to come over for dinner? Dad, can she?"

I blinked, taken aback. "Oh, I can't, sweetie. I need to help my uncle tonight. Maybe another time."

"Pleeeeeease, dad!"

"You heard Miss Quinn. She can't tonight," he answered, more amused than surprised. "Maybe sometime this week though?"

"Pleeeeeease, Miss Quinn! You can see my Pokémon cards and play a game with me."

"Sure, Oliver. That sounds fun," I smiled, my mind spinning. Not able to look at Theo, I picked up the bucket and gripped the mop handle tightly. "Gentlemen, it's time for me to finish cleaning. Thanks again for your help today."

I offered a weak smile, then decided to turn my back and just start walking toward the janitor's closet down the hall. Behind me, I heard Faith return and start chatting with the Millers. As soon as they were gone, I expected she'd be on my heels, nagging me to tell her everything. I wrung out the mop tightly, then dumped the dirty water into the utility sink. I heard footsteps coming down the hallway, just as I was returning the mop to the rack. The door creaked open.

"No, Faith," I groaned. "I'm not doing this, we're not in high school. The only thing I will say is, yes, he's a good kisser. And that's all I'm telling you."

"Well, that's good news," said the voice behind me, which did not belong to Faith. I squeezed my eyes shut, totally humiliated... again. Once I was brave enough, I turned around to see Theo with his back against the closed door. The janitor's closet is not a big room, so I should've sensed it was *not* Faith behind me. I deserved every bit of my embarrassment for being so carelessly unobservant.

I could barely make eye contact. And when I did, I felt my face change color. Theo, however, seemed pleased with himself.

"I love a positive review, now and then." He laughed. And then I laughed. The way his eyes came alive when he laughed—it was just... *ugh*. Especially when he was only four feet away. Theo gently touched my arm and pulled me toward him, but I resisted.

"I'm so glad that my humiliation brings you joy," I said, using snark to recover what was left of my dignity. "What are you doing back here anyhow?"

"Faith sent me," he shrugged. "She stayed with Oliver, told me to check on you. She said you'd need help back here."

"I'm clearly fine," I retorted, with extra snark. "And now you're in my way."

"As I recall," he said. This time, I let him pull me against his chest. "I owe you an apology."

Softly, he tilted my chin up and leaned down until our lips met. My mind went blank. I forgot I was in a supply closet that smelled like disinfectant. I didn't think about the single bulb on the ceiling, with the chain clinking as it swayed back and forth. And I was not worried at all about the grime on my clothes or the wet strands of hair stuck to my neck.

Because when Theo kissed me, it was just him and me. The only scent was his skin, the only sound was our breathing, and the only sensations I felt were the warmth of his lips and the heat of his body.

His hand slid into my hair, as he left a trail of kisses along my jaw and down my neck. I heard a little gasp of surprise, which turned out to be mine. I desperately hoped he'd keep going, but he stopped at the collar of my shirt and returned to my lips. My disappointment was only momentary, though, because I could feel his hands on my back, moving along the skin beneath my damp shirt, and that was even *better.*

Steadying myself, I stepped backwards and bumped right into one of the utility shelves. Several bottles of cleaner crashed to the floor, one of them cracked and started leaking blue fluid in all directions. Another bottle took down a bucket on its way to the floor. It made a loud crash on impact and rolled over to the corner where the brooms were stacked, knocking one over. The handle crashed down on just the right spot to turn on the finicky cold-water tap.

Ohhhh my god.

I'm not sure if I only *thought* that or said it out loud, but I can say for sure that we'd very abruptly cooled off. And while I scrambled to locate the crate of rags, Theo laughed so hard there were tears in his eyes. I tossed a rag in his direction, hitting him right in the face.

"Help me clean this up," I said, fighting my own laughter. "This is 50% your fault."

"You know," Theo said, sopping up the spilled cleaning fluid with the rag. "It's probably for the best, because I don't think I could've stopped on my own."

"Oh, really?" I struggled to keep the disappointment from my voice.

"Really." Finished, he tossed the rag into the utility sink and moved the empty bucket back to its place on the shelf. He stepped around the other fallen bottles and took me in his arms. "What is it about you that makes me act like a teenager?"

I shrugged and leaned my head on his chest.

"You are not the kind of woman who should be making out in a supply closet."

"You might be surprised." My voice was muffled against the fabric of his shirt. He chuckled. I lifted my head to look him in the eye, wearing a sly grin on my face. He kissed me one more time and then stepped back.

"If I don't leave right now…" He trailed off and I resisted my urge to stop him. "I'm sure Oliver's bothering Faith to come find me."

"Yeah, probably," I agreed, although I knew Faith wouldn't let that happen. Just like I knew she'd be grilling me for information after *this*. "I'll finish the clean-up. You go take him home."

He nodded and stepped toward the door. With his hand on the knob, he turned back to me.

"Tuesday…" he hesitated. "Would you… uh… What Oliver said about dinner, would you… Pizza?"

"Are you asking me over for pizza on Tuesday night?"

He nodded, grinning nervously. I think he might have been holding his breath. *What happened to the confident man who just put his hands up my shirt in this little closet?* I didn't answer right away, instead busying myself with picking up the spray bottles.

"I'll be there," I replied, amused by the differences in these two versions of Theo. It was oddly arousing to know I could make someone so nervous.

His parting smile was equal parts relief and happiness.

"Now go home, before I change my mind," I said, sternly. I pointed a spray bottle at him with my finger on the trigger. He blew me a kiss and closed the door behind himself.

I was right, of course. Faith bolted down the hall and opened the closet door the second the Millers were gone. She stuck her head in and didn't bother with hellos.

"Oh my god," she said dramatically. "What was going on back here?"

"Come on," I replied, with my hands on my hips, still clutching a bottle of spray cleaner with one hand. "You sent him back here. You *know* what happened."

"All I *know* is that he was gone for a long time. Oliver and I played at least ten rounds of *I Spy*. And then we heard this huge crash. I thought one of you *died.*"

"Surprise! We're both alive." I rolled my eyes at her, placing the bottles back on the shelf. I leaned the broom back against the wall and drained the sink. She watched me with her mouth hanging open.

"What *happened* back here?"

I shrugged. It was fun to torture Faith. "Just knocked over some stuff. No big deal."

She regarded me for a moment, eyes narrowed, trying to read me. Finally, she just shook her head.

"This is worse than the time I found you in here with Christian Douglas. And *he* walked out covered in mop water."

"Let's go home, Faith." I bit the inside of my cheek so I wouldn't laugh while I shut the light off and dragged her back to the auditorium. *Not* telling Faith was way too fun.

CHAPTER TWENTY-TWO

At the board meeting, Leah and I presented the foundation's first quarter numbers. It was all very boring and uneventful. As someone who'd once planned to be an English teacher, the business-y words and numbers were just not my strong point. Could I present? Sure. Did I understand what they meant? Totally. Would I rather have written an essay about the foundation's success and future direction? Definitely.

When the meeting ended, I got another hug and a glowing review from Neil. While his gushing over my successes did make me feel good about my work, I knew I owed much of that to Leah. It just seemed to matter to Neil that his support was behind a *Davis*—it didn't matter which one. The way he reminisced and made such a fuss that we looked like Mom and Dad, the way he would say over and over how proud he was of his decision to become the Chairman of the Board and back the cause that mattered to his dearest friend Bill Davis.

It was a lot. And I didn't know how to handle that.

But I should've passed the credit onto Leah. *I am a terrible person.*

Theo and Oliver lived in a little blue house with perfectly trimmed hedges all along the front and a brick porch leading to the front door. The driveway had been recently decorated with chalk art in Oliver's unsteady, crooked handwriting. I carefully avoided parking on the rainbow he'd drawn and the dragon that lived beneath it.

Pizza night at the Millers was not delivery. Instead, Theo and Oliver had made dough from scratch.

"Miss Quinn, I decorated this one for you!" Oliver proudly

presented a pizza with pepperoni slices in a heart. Theo shook his head, amused.

"That looks delicious!" I declared. "Thank you, Oliver."

Having dinner with Theo and Oliver was a strange experience. My brain wasn't sure where to categorize it. Was this a date? Was I just hanging out with friends? When Oliver was there, were we Theo and Quinn or Oliver's Dad and Miss Quinn?

While Theo cleaned up after dinner, Oliver sat me down with a box of Pokémon cards and walked me through his favorites, show-and-tell style.

"This one does 300 damage! And his health points are so high, it's like, almost impossible to beat him. And look at this one—he's my favorite."

It was adorable but very confusing.

"There'll be a quiz later, Miss Quinn, I hope you're taking notes." Theo said, very seriously. He barely fought off his laughter. "You should teach her how to play the game, Ollie."

At that, Oliver's eyes lit up. He scurried away, his feet pounding up the stairs, followed by the sound of a door opening. As he ran back down, he shouted.

"I have the mat, Miss Quinn! We can play now!"

"What's the mat for?" I asked Theo. He was drying dishes and, to be honest, I'd prefer to be doing that to learning this... but the kiddo was *so* excited.

"Hell, if I know," he laughed. "You're in for a treat."

It took Oliver over twenty minutes to explain the game, with lots of starts and stops.

"Wait, hold on," he said, more than a few times. "I can't remember what this does. I need the book."

Just then, an alarm went off on Theo's phone.

"Nooooo!" Oliver whined. "Five more minutes? We didn't even play yet!"

"Time for bed, Oliver," said Theo in his dad voice, which is a thing I never thought I'd find attractive.

"Just one game?"

Theo frowned. Oliver dropped his arms and shoulders in disappointment.

"It's already past your bedtime. And it's a school night," he reprimanded, still in that firm parental tone. "You can play another time."

"Can Miss Quinn sleep over?"

Theo looked at me and I could barely maintain eye contact. I was blushing again, and Theo was speechless.

"Sorry, buddy. I gotta go home and take care of my doggie."

"You have a dog? What kind? Can I meet him?" Oliver leapt at the opportunity for another distraction.

"Come on. Say goodbye to Miss Quinn." Theo tried to push through the awkwardness. I couldn't look at him, afraid I'd giggle. "Get upstairs, I'll be right up."

Oliver pouted and whined some form of objection.

"Oliver..."

With that, he threw his head back and sighed deeply. Oliver wandered off like that, through the living room and to the staircase. He trudged halfway up the stairs, before pausing with a realization. He turned on his heel and hopped back down, skipping the last stair altogether.

Oliver ran at me, full speed, with his arms outstretched. "Goodnight, Miss Quinn! I LOVE YOU."

Theo cleared his throat. Was Oliver picking up on what was happening between his dad and me? Kids aren't idiots.

If anything, I was the idiot, because I hadn't considered how much work it might take to acclimate Oliver to a new dynamic. How would he feel if things got serious? When people get involved with a single parent, obviously talking to the kids was an important milestone. But with Oliver, it hadn't been that obvious—we already knew each other, loved each other, apparently. That didn't automatically mean he'd be okay with me becoming a part of the family. Sure, he'd said it was okay if his dad and I loved each other... but he's seven.

Then, just as quickly, Oliver skipped off toward the stairs.

"Just so you know, I haven't... um... talked to him about anything yet," said Theo, nervously. He had, of course, already spent time considering that. "I mean... I don't want to assume that you... I wouldn't do that without talking to you first. If you think we should tell him, I will. But if that's not something you're ready for, then... Why don't I just wait?"

I smiled, biting my lip.

"What?"

"It's cute when you ramble like that."

He grinned, sheepishly.

"Let's wait for now." That was a whole different kind of pressure I wasn't prepared to manage just yet.

"Well," he said abruptly. "I'd better go up and make sure he brushes ALL of his teeth and not just the four in the front."

"Okay, I should probably…" *What should I probably?* Stay? Was that a good idea? "Get home to walk Franklin."

"Sure, no problem." Theo looked crestfallen.

"Sorry. Next time?"

Over his shoulder, Theo yelled, "I'll be up in two minutes. You'd better have your pajamas on!" Then he turned to me and whispered, "Come on, I'll walk you out."

As I put on my jacket, I was having second thoughts.

"I wish I could stay for a bit. I just don't think it's a great idea if Oliver doesn't—"

"You're right," he agreed. "Not yet."

Theo pulled me close to him and I rested my head on his shoulder, lost in the feeling of his arms around me and the smell of his cologne, mixed with fabric softener and just a hint of tomato sauce. Handsome, strong, emotional, *and* domesticated. He kissed me tenderly on the forehead.

"I'm glad you came for dinner, sweetheart."

We stared at each other oddly for a moment.

"No to *sweetheart?*"

I wrinkled my nose. He laughed.

"Goodnight, Quinn," Theo sighed, placing a surprisingly chaste kiss on my lips. I applauded his restraint. And for the entire car ride home, I lamented how responsible we were being.

"Come on, Frankie," I said sweetly to my darling baby boy. "Mommy needs to walk some stuff off."

Franklin wagged his tail eagerly as I clipped the leash onto his collar. I grabbed the flashlight, locked the door, and started down the usual path. The fresh air, the sound of crickets in mid-spring, the quiet padding of Franklin's paws on the sidewalk, the stillness of the trees on a gorgeous wind-less evening. It was hard to think about anything negative.

I much preferred the fantasy of walking around the neighborhood with Theo again. But how would this work? When could we see each other? We'd never have time alone, not at rehearsals for sure, but also not at home, with Oliver around. Until he knew, we'd need to be extra careful.

My phone buzzed with a text from Theo.

> Why did I let you leave?

Franklin slowed his pace, so we stopped to let him rest. Sitting on Mrs. Greene's lawn together, nearly the same height, I held him to me, petting his back. As I sat there, considering the words on my phone screen, I decided to answer him.

> Why did I leave?

There was an unspoken agreement between us that we would make this work... somehow. Pickup times were the most frustrating. I once thought the tension would break once we'd kissed, but that backfired. Hard. In fact, it took such extreme measures to resist that we avoided all close contact.

Theo would arrive amidst the other parents and Oliver would hop to the car. No face-to-face interaction. Usually Theo waved and gave me a wink. And then, he'd text me a corny pick-up line.

> Are you a parking ticket? You've got FINE written all over you.
>
> Did it hurt when you fell from heaven?
>
> Something's wrong with my eyes. I can't take them off you.
>
> Gotta find my library card, cuz I am totally checking you out.

I kinda loved it.

After one such dismissal, we spent an extra amount of time staring at each other across the parking lot before he finally climbed into the car. This was turning out to be one of the strangest relationships I'd ever had. Normally, you have a boyfriend and you see each other at scheduled times. You go out, do something together, have sleepovers—ahem. But with Theo, we saw each other constantly and couldn't do much about it. You want to make out with your boyfriend? Cool, make plans. If I want to do that with Theo, we needed to hide. Of course, we couldn't keep our hands off each other when we *did* get the chance.

No wonder I was standing there like an idiot, watching them drive off, genuinely considering how bad it would be to jump in my car and follow him home. And of course, Faith found me out there. I think she'd come to expect it now, because she'd brought all my stuff out of the auditorium and locked the doors while I stood there. Again, like an idiot.

"Get in the car," she said sharply. "I need breadsticks."

CHAPTER TWENTY-THREE

"Since when do you eat at chain restaurants?" I asked, wrinkling my nose at the mushroom ravioli the server put in front of her. The spaghetti and meatballs on my plate was more my speed—simple, classic, a well-rounded meal... Something like that.

"Are you kidding? I love it here." Faith made a show of unfolding her green cloth napkin and placing it gingerly on her lap. She smiled demurely at the server. I swear she batted her eyelashes. "Thank you so much, Roy."

I stared, waiting for her to look at me. My silence got her attention.

"Okay, fine," she leaned over and pulled her phone from her purse. After a few swipes across the screen, she held it out for me. I took the phone from her, squinting at the photo of a man with dark hair, glasses, and...

"Faith," I snapped. "Is this our server?"

"Maybe." She shrugged, keeping her eyes carefully averted. When I cleared my throat to get her attention—and an explanation—she fessed up. "I thought I could scope him out, and get your opinion, all at the same time. After the DJ thing..."

"No luck there?"

"As I said, that's not my world anymore." She scrunched up her nose. "I called him, we talked for about ten minutes, nine of which were about being a DJ. I... can't."

I scrolled through Roy's profile. A restaurant server, working his way to a doctorate in psychiatry, owns two cats named Sigmund and Carl, spends his free time waterskiing and playing beach volleyball, and loves going to the movies. Specifically, horror movies. When I looked up, Faith was staring at me, eager for my reaction.

"Good, right?" she said, once she'd run out of patience.

"Isn't he just... everything? And now that I've met him, and I know he's a real person..."

"I don't love the ulterior motive here," I grumbled, handing the phone back to her.

"Even if I'm buying? Even with unlimited breadsticks?" She held up the empty basket, a sheepish grin on her face. "We can have Roy refill it."

I ignored her. "But I do applaud your due diligence. Just try to stop drooling. It's embarrassing."

"Look, you help me with my man problem, and I will help you with yours," she smiled mischievously.

"For the last time, I don't *have* a problem."

"But..." she prompted, drumming her fingertips on the table. "Go ahead and say it."

"But this is so frustrating," I sighed. *Might as well say it.* "I feel so... trapped? Like we're stuck on opposite sides of glass. I see him all the time and we can't touch each other."

"See? I knew you had a problem." She smirked with her water glass halfway to her mouth.

"Oliver doesn't know about us, so we can't even relax at his house. And if we want to go out or go to my house, he needs a sitter," I said, stabbing a meatball with my fork. "That makes it sound like I resent him for having a kid—and I absolutely don't. I love Oliver. But I'm starting to be afraid of getting too involved with him. And I like him too much to stay level-headed here...."

Faith waited, expecting me to continue. I did.

"Not to mention what happens when we tell Oliver—if he ever decides to do that. It would make things infinitely more serious, because now there's a child invested in this relationship too. This is uncharted territory for me. Plus, he's a widower—"

"For four years, not four days."

"Granted." I lowered my head with a sigh of frustration. "There are just so many *extra* things to deal with here. It's... terrifying. Is it even *okay* to get serious with him right now? Are there rules about this?"

Suddenly, Roy and his doctoral studies waltzed back to the table to refill our water glasses. Faith held her glass up for him to refill. I mumbled my thanks politely, but she was not going to let him get away.

"Excuse me, Roy. We need a man's opinion here," she began. I kicked her under the table. She ignored me. "How long would you say is an appropriate amount of time to mourn your partner's death before seeing someone new?"

"Umm..." *Poor Roy. Poor, sweet Roy. He doesn't have a chance.* He thought for a moment, put the water pitcher down, and slid into the bench next to me. "I don't normally go into my work here in the restaurant, but if you really want to know... Spousal grief management and survivor's guilt is a common area of study in psychiatry. I'm working on my doctorate in a similar area."

"Hmm..." said Faith, clearly enamored. "I knew you looked like an expert."

He beamed. Faith swooned. I ignored them.

"And...?"

"It's fascinating," he continued, turning to me. Every study shows similar results. Women, on average, wait eight years to start dating again."

"Eight *years?"* I was crestfallen. That's a long time. Theo was only halfway there.

"For women," he added, clearing his throat. "To answer your friend's—"

"Faith." I interrupted. It seemed like the thing to do now that she'd thrown a psychiatric doctoral candidate at me—for research purposes. I supposed I could give her an assist with him. He seemed nice.

"To answer Faith's question," Roy said, turning back to her. She smiled, still completely silent. "The average waiting period for men is closer to three years. Especially if there are young children involved."

"Three years? To date?"

"No, to marry. In some cases, it's only months before they start dating again," he frowned. "By three years, they've usually dated, proposed, and walked down the aisle. Others wait a lot longer to get their lives in order. Maybe some men think they can't heal alone. Who knows?"

"Thank you, Roy," Faith said, after she had clearly collected her senses. "You've been *very* helpful."

"You're welcome," he smiled and got to his feet, grabbed the pitcher, and walked back toward the bar. Sure enough, after a few steps away, he turned back to look at Faith one more time.

"What the hell was that?"

"I think that was the most epic two birds I've ever killed with one stone," Faith said smugly. "He has officially passed the screening test. And he used his magical mind powers to put *your* bonkers brain to rest, didn't he?"

"That felt more like a well-coordinated attack." I squinted at her, scrutinizing every micro-expression. "Did you set this up?"

"Sometimes the only way to get to you," she smiled angelically. "Is through well-documented research and facts. I almost asked him to write a paper."

I blinked a few times, just stunned.

"Abby and I came here last night and met him. It was *her* idea to get his help," she said, proudly. "Not only was he willing to help out, but he is totally okay with me having *a teenage daughter.*"

"That's awesome, but…"

"But everything he said was based on actual research. That part was true," she grinned. "Even Abby agrees that you should go for it. In her words, 'He's cute, for an old guy.' Isn't she a delight?"

I did not, 100% did *not* want to condone her behavior. Meddling, sneakiness, manipulation… but she cared a lot about this. Evidently. Plus, it did help.

I nodded, selecting another breadstick. I focused on chewing for a while, but I couldn't quiet down my brain.

"Why can't he just be divorced like everyone else?"

"Is that *better?*"

"I don't know, but this sucks," I groaned. "I mean, how does this work? It's hard enough to date when you're not being compared to another woman."

"He's not going to compare you." She grabbed another breadstick and twirled it in the marinara sauce before lifting it to her mouth. She continued, while chewing. "He is *always* going to love her. But you're not replacing her. You couldn't, even if that was your end goal." Faith took another bite. "It's up to him whether he's ready or not."

"Yes, however, I need to decide if *I* can be okay with that. What if I'm there all the time, surrounded by pictures of her, listening to stories about her... It's weird, right?"

"This is real life, not that book *Rebecca*," she interrupted. "You're not marrying some weird, way-too-old millionaire with a first wife who died under mysterious, sinister circumstances. You're not inheriting a closet full of her clothing and a creepy old woman who brushes your hair at bedtime every night."

"Eww."

"Literature in the 1930s was a strange and exciting landscape," she recited, with a very bad impression of my voice. "I've heard you say that at least 9,000 times. You are not a gothic romance heroine."

"Back to the point, professor?"

"You're never going to step into her shoes—figuratively, and especially not literally. You are *never* going to make Theo and Oliver forget about her. She's gone and will forever be frozen in time as the young mother who died." She pointed the remainder of her breadstick right at me. "You need to be okay with that. But is it any different from you moving on after your parents' deaths?"

"Um. Yeah," I said, curtly. "Way different."

"I don't think so."

"I'm not out looking for other parents. I'm just me, remembering how much we loved each other, and trying to do my best to move on."

"Loss is loss," she said, breadstick down on her plate. "You've lost different things, but you've both lost *important* things. Instead of worrying about this stuff, just listen when he opens up. Ask about the pictures of her. Let them keep her in their memories. You're an addition to their lives, not a replacement."

I sighed deeply, letting it all sink in. Faith laughed suddenly.

"God, can you imagine the crisis you'll have when he asks you to marry him?"

I threw the last bite of my breadstick at her.

CHAPTER TWENTY-FOUR

After that, I tried to put all that doubt aside and just focus on what was developing between us. Roy had helped, as much as I didn't want to admit it. So, all the fun I was having with this possible-new-relationship with Theo started to bleed into other areas of my average day. One such Wednesday morning, I did a lot of happy cleaning around the house, bothering Shawn with my "incessant humming."

"Are you dating this guy now?" he asked, rubbing the sleep from his eyes. I stopped humming and turned to him. "Don't act so shocked... Faith told me."

"What the—"

"Faith tells me stuff," he yawned. "She's basically my sister too."

"But she doesn't need to tell you about Theo."

"She does when I text her to ask why you're so... perky."

"Fine," I scowled at him. But then realization hit. "I don't know if we're dating, actually. We haven't talked about it yet."

"Should I cancel that dating app account?"

"Oh, I already canceled that," I said, moving clean silverware from the dishwasher to the drawer. "The day after we made it."

He scowled at me this time.

"Why do I help you?"

I grinned innocently. "I think I'm doing okay on my own, Shawny."

Before he took a shower, I made sure to hum as much as possible. And I made him fold all the towels the way I liked them folded, so they fit in the linen closet better. He grumbled but he did it.

In the interest of new beginnings, I thought I could extend an olive branch to my brother. I was still feeling guilty about shutting him down the other day, and we'd done a good job of ignoring each other since. When he came downstairs, dressed and ready for work, I stopped him.

"Hey," I said suddenly. "I'm sorry about last week. I really didn't mean to shut you down."

"Didn't mean to? Or didn't mean to do it so harshly?"

"Okay, that's fair," I said, wrapping up the cord to the vacuum. "You didn't deserve what I said."

"Duh."

"Anyway," I said, getting back on track. I wheeled the vacuum back to the closet and closed the door. "I'm sorry. And I want to help you. What did you want to talk about?"

"It's fine now," he said, shrugging. "I handled it. We can talk about it later at the bar. I've gotta leave early for some errands."

I nodded, my mind flipping through possibilities, and let him go. I could wait until later. Once the entire house was clean from top to bottom, I headed to the bar. Motivation and optimism oozed from my pores. I was ready to clean that office, finally.

"Hey, Uncle Charlie!" I breezed into the bar and found him at the counter, looking through a stack of papers. He was concentrating and didn't hear me, so when I sat in my favorite stool, I startled him.

"Oh hi, Quinnie." He gave me a warm smile, creasing his eyes at the corner.

I leaned over the bar and gave him a kiss on the cheek.

"How's tricks?" I asked. Dad used to say that all the time.

Before Charlie could answer, my brother walked through the swinging door and joined us. He smiled, like I hadn't just spent the morning tormenting him with early 90s Mariah Carey hits.

"What's on the to-do list today, boys?"

"Probably should talk first," Charlie suggested. "What d'ya think, Shawn?"

I looked back and forth between them, trying to read either of their expressions without success. Whatever it was, I suddenly felt very good about sitting down.

"Come on, guys, what's up?"

Uncle Charlie cleared his throat. "Numbers aren't good. Don't know if we'll recover this time."

"Yeah, I've noticed," I said, sadly. *I just filed all the taxes, remember?* "But we've had struggles before. So, what's the plan?"

"Unless we do something big, we might not be able to keep the doors open," Charlie sighed.

That was a gut-punch.

"Why didn't you mention this when we talked about renovating? I don't get it. How did things change this much so quickly?"

"Your dad used to say I was optimistic to a fault..." he said with a frown. *Yeah, I could relate to that.* "And it took Shawn to get me to face reality."

"Shawn?"

"Come on, don't look so surprised." Shawn grumbled, crossing his arms over his chest. "Stuff happens around here when you're out saving the world."

"What's that supposed mean?"

"Enough, you two," Charlie raised a hand and we both snapped our mouths shut. "Gettin' tired of your bickering."

Shawn and I mumbled apologies and Uncle Charlie kept talking. "Shawn priced it all out and showed me how much we'd need, realistically, to update this place the way I wanted. My refund wouldn't even cover half of it. Just can't make it work."

"So... we're closing the bar?" Maybe there was a little more panic in there than I intended, but this was not lining up with the good day I'd been having. This was a big problem.

"Didn't say that." Charlie shook his head. "Don't be jumping to conclusions, okay?"

"What is it, then?"

"Shawn is going to take care of it."

Umm, huh? I looked at Shawn, but he was too busy picking at a loose thread on his sleeve.

"He's purchasing half of the business. We're going to use the funds to make the renovations we need."

"Shawn... what?" My head snapped from Charlie to my brother and back. Charlie was beaming, Shawn was still fighting that one thread. *I have no words. How does Shawn have money for this? What is happening?*

After a stretch of silence, Shawn finally looked up. He stared at me, expressionless, daring me to finish my thought. I felt compelled.

"Shawn, that's—wow, I didn't... it's—"

"Good?" Shawn asked, flatly.

"This is all so... wow," I said lamely. *What else was I supposed to say?*

"We're also going to hire another bartender and a bus boy. That should give me more time to create the appetizer menu." Charlie's wearing the biggest smile I've ever seen on his face, big forehead wrinkles and everything.

"Wait, wait. Appetizers?"

"I always wanted to offer more than dry pretzels—like french fries, hot pretzels with mustard, chicken wings..." said my uncle. "Your dad and I used to dream up things we could put on the menu with clever little names. I found a list of them on an old bar napkin a week or so ago. After that, how could I not?"

"So, you and Shawn are—" *What? Taking over? Partnering up? Leaving me out of it. Is Shawn replacing Dad?*

"I've asked him to become half-owner of the bar. We're signing paperwork later this week." He was still beaming. When he saw my face, though, the smile faltered. "Quinnie? You okay?"

"Yeah," I said, biting my lip. "This is great, guys. Seems like you've got a handle on things. When do renovations start?"

"Soon, but we haven't hired anyone yet," Shawn answered, finally speaking up. "We're going to get a few quotes first. Know anyone?"

I squinted at him. *Is he for real?*

"Quinnie," Uncle Charlie said softly. He picked up my hand from the bar. "It's time to start thinking about the future of this place. Shawn needs a path and I need help. It's the—"

"And what am I supposed to do?"

"Uh, obviously you're still going to help out whenever you stop by. Nothing changes," Shawn said, trying to sound upbeat. "It's not like I'm kicking you out."

"There's gonna be a new accountant, right? Plus, two new staff members. It sounds like you'll have enough hands."

"Isn't that great?" asked Uncle Charlie, with a great big grin on his face.

So great.

After rehearsal the next night, Faith sensed my distress and dragged me back to her house. It helped that Abby was out at a study group and she didn't want to be alone, but I pretended not to notice. It only took one glass of wine before she got the brunt of my complaining about my brother, my uncle, and the wrongs they were inflicting upon me.

"Don't you *hate* doing his accounting?" She poured me a second glass almost right away.

"It's literally the worst thing ever," I said, downtrodden. "But it was *my thing*. And it's not just that. It's everything else I do. They won't need me anymore."

"Part of you has got to be relieved here, Q. Think of all the free time you'll have if someone else takes over all those little jobs you hate."

"I don't *hate* them..." *I do hate free time, though.* I took a not-so-small sip.

"You'd rather spend fifteen hours a week cleaning up after Charlie and Shawn than do *anything* else?"

Not willing to answer that honestly, I picked a cucumber slice out of my salad.

"I don't know why you can't see what's going on here... and why it bothers you."

"Please, enlighten me." I drained my wine glass, holding it straight up in the air to shake free that last drop in the bottom. *This is not juice, Quinn.*

"Easy, kid." Faith moved the bottle to the other side of the table. "You know you *should* be happy but you're not and you don't know why. You've got this weird disconnect that started after... you know."

I reached for the bottle; she put her hand on it.

"Not everyone needs you all the time. In fact, it's good when they don't."

"But if they don't, what happens to *me?*"

"You get to have healthy relationships free of dependency. Doesn't that sound nice?" She said this as she lifted the bottle and poured a refill for both of us. "Like this wine here. You don't *need* it, because I have plenty of other drinks in my kitchen to choose from. It doesn't *need* you because I could drink it and it would still fulfill its purpose. But you still like each other, so here we are."

"I don't think that makes sense, Faith."

"Finish that glass, then reassess," she said firmly. "But then you gotta stop, because that's the end of the Riesling."

CHAPTER TWENTY-FIVE

Theo was late for pick-up again and it was just Oliver and me standing together in front of the building. Even Faith had gone home, tossing one last smirk at me as she walked to her car.

"Keep it together there, Miss Quinn."

"Mind your business, Miss Faith," I called back.

She laughed again. The amusement she took from my dating life was both infuriating and endearing. Mostly, I just feigned irritation and objection, but in reality, it made me weirdly happy. She knew I liked it, but I'd never admit it.

"Miss Quinn?" Oliver said quietly.

"What's up, Oliver?" I bent down to his eye level. His little nose was running, remnants of a cold that was going around the camp. I grabbed a tissue from my pocket and swiped his nose quickly. It made him smile. "You okay?"

"Yeah," he said. "I like standing here with you."

"I do too, buddy."

"Miss Quinn?" His face was pinched in thought. I waited quietly to let him sort things out. "Do you like my dad?"

Oh, uh...

"Your dad?" I tried to play this off with surprise. I was not surprised. I was, however, surprised that I didn't know what to say. I'd been expecting this. I'd even thought up some possible answers to this question when the time arrived. *Of course, we're friends!* Or *Yes, he's very nice.* Or even *What do you mean? Like, how?*

As my brain spun through these options, I realized Oliver was eager for a reply. A boy who wanted to hear an answer he desperately needed. But, strangely, I couldn't tell if he wanted me to say yes and admit my feelings for his dad or, alternatively, deny everything and reassure him that I didn't want to be his new mommy.

"Well, Oliver," I said, struggling. If I couldn't answer it, why not make it more awkward... "Does your dad like me?"

Kill. Me. Now.

Oliver's face broke into a big, beautiful grin. Somehow, I'd nailed it with my reply. *He's happy at the possibility that I might like his dad. This is good... yes?*

"Yeah," he said shyly. "He said he was going to talk to you when he came to pick me up. I think he wants to ask you to come visit our house again."

Oh, okay then. As if on cue, Theo's car turned into the parking lot. Oliver jumped up and down, while I became a nervous mess. If he'd been talking to his son about me, enough for Oliver to pick up on something, I'd better be prepared to field related questions.

The car parked, Theo climbed out, Oliver ran over and tackled him with a hug. When Theo pointed toward the backseat, Oliver cheered. There was a fresh Happy Meal in there, so he climbed in swiftly and shut the door. Once Theo had Oliver settled in, he finally turned his attention to me. Looking into my eyes, his smile was radiant.

"Worst dad ever," I said, hands on my hips.

"Guilty." He laughed, walking towards me. "Sorry I'm late."

"It's okay," I said.

"No, it's not," he said, shaking his head.

"I don't mind. Oliver and I have wonderful conversations out here," I said, with a smirk on my face. The little boy's words were ringing in my ears.

"Listen," Theo said. He always said this before something important, I had learned. "If you're free this weekend..."

"I am."

"Excellent. I'm cooking dinner on Friday night," he said definitively. "And you're coming over."

"Can I bring something? Maybe dessert for the little guy?"

"Absolutely not."

"Says the man who just brought his son a Happy Meal. Are you cutting desserts from poor Oliver's Friday nights?"

"Of course not," he said. "Do you think I'm some kind of

monster?"

"What kind of monster are we talking about?" I smirked.

He gave me a devilish grin, then walked back to the car. *Oh, well then.*

It had been over a week since I found out Shawn was becoming Charlie's partner. Even longer since I'd sort of attacked him in my office. It was getting harder to compartmentalize. So maybe I'd been avoiding my brother—again. Not that it was particularly hard. I was the early bird and Shawn was the night owl. Mom had always said it drove her nuts when we were little, because one of us was always awake. Now, the way things were working out for us, it felt like one of us was always asleep.

On that Wednesday morning, I knew what I needed to do. Determined to make things right, I woke up earlier than usual and set to work on an old family remedy.

"Apology Pie?" Shawn said. The delicious scent of cherries and apples wafting through the kitchen had drawn him out of bed and into the kitchen. "At this time of day?"

"You know I do my best work in the morning," I said with a smile. "Even baking."

"You're nuts."

"Yes, but also, I'm sorry. I've been kind of a jerk lately."

He dropped into a chair at the table, blinking away the bleariness in his eyes, and pointed toward the coffee machine. A freshly brewed pot of dark roast sat untouched—mostly because I'd forgotten about it—and I poured two cups for us. Still hot.

"I'm proud of you for stepping up to help Charlie. Sorry I kinda freaked out," I began, sitting down across from him. He shrugged and took a sip of coffee. Apparently, he didn't have anything to say yet. "I just don't understand why you didn't tell me about the bar, Shawn. Why'd you leave me in the dark on this one? You could've said something when he told me about the refund check. If you'd even mentioned a plan, I could have relaxed."

"Would you have trusted me if I said, *Hang on, Quinn. I have a plan?*"

He had me there.

"Besides, I didn't know what to do at first. I'd approached him about it before, but Charlie's always been too proud to entertain a conversation about it—you know how he is."

I nodded.

"I had the rest of my college fund that I never used, just sitting there, and I didn't want to rush into anything." He shrugged again. "It seemed like a good time to go for it. I had actual ideas. He listened to me. It feels nice to be listened to."

Ouch.

"And trusted."

"So why not clue me in?"

"I tried. That day I came to the office for advice... that's why." He took a sip of coffee and stared me down. "I couldn't wait for you to give me your attention. I had to do it on my own."

"And I thought we cleared this up already. I apologized, Shawn!"

"Yeah, too late."

Given his narrowed eyes, it was hard to ignore that little stab of guilt. But it's not like that was the only time we'd seen each other over the past couple of weeks. I wasn't about to let him put me on the ropes like that.

"Now it's *my* fault that I didn't know what was going on? You could've tried again. Couldn't you see that I was busy that day? I can't just drop everything any time you..."

"Not even for your brother."

Again, ouch.

"Not even when he tells you he needs help. And it's important."

"Shawn, come on. This is a lot for me to handle, okay? I've been a part of this too, just as long as you have."

"But this isn't *your job*. I'm the one who works at the bar," he said, putting down the mug. He pointed to himself. "I'm the one who chose to help him, while you ran away to save the foundation. What are you saving, exactly? They're fine without you. Charlie's been struggling and all you do is show up to shred papers and file taxes."

"Now that you're hiring all your own staff," I said, my tone turning cold. *This was not how this was supposed to go.* "You've taken away what little I do around there. You've taken it all on your shoulders."

"You're always going on about Dad's legacy and how noble you are for saving the foundation," he said bitterly. "You want me to play my part? Well, here I am."

"You're just making decisions on your own, taking everything away from me."

"How do you figure that?" He sounded offended. I didn't want to fight, but I couldn't hide how I felt. "You still have a zillion things going on in your life. Don't you want me to have something of my own?"

"The bar isn't yours. It's Charlie's. And it was Dad's."

"Quinn, I'm *buying* half of it," he said, nearly shouting.

I winced.

"It's still Charlie's. And the money I'm investing technically *was Dad's*. Don't you think he would want this? How about sharing some responsibility for a change?"

"Just have some pie, Shawn. I'm taking a shower."

At the end of the day, I found the pie on the counter. Untouched.

CHAPTER TWENTY-SIX

I rang the doorbell, then listened to the sound of frantic, little footsteps and a voice yelling. *I'll get it!* The door flew open.

"Miss Quinn!!" shouted Oliver, with the biggest grin on his face. He bounced up and down a few times and stepped out onto the porch, throwing his arms around my waist. "Dad!! It's Miss Quinn."

As Theo's footsteps approached, I could hear him say, "Let her *in* the door, Ollie!"

But Oliver found another reason to be excited. "She has COOKIES, Dad! Can I have some, Miss Quinn?"

"Later, Ollie," said Theo, coming into view. "Dinner first. Now get out of her way so she can get through the door."

Oliver pretended to be utterly distraught, tromping off down the hall. Theo took the plate of cookies from me, a playful frown on his face.

"I told you not to bring anything."

"I know, but I accidentally baked too many cookies for the soccer team's bake sale..." I shrugged.

"Accidentally?" he asked, skeptically.

"Oops," I smiled. "And Oliver told me his favorite cookies are chocolate chip. He also said you can't bake to save your life."

"Oh, did he?" Theo looked at Oliver, who was smiling ear to ear. "It's probably for the best. All I have for dessert is ice cream."

"Sorry, all I heard was *chocolate chip cookie ice cream sandwiches* just then."

"We *are* a good team."

Dinner was spaghetti with homemade meatballs, freshly baked bread, and a salad made from his mother's vegetable garden. *Who is this guy?* Oliver sat at the table quietly and ate every bite, motivated by the prospect of dessert. His feet didn't quite reach the floor. They swung freely beneath the table.

"Oliver, please don't eat with your whole face. Miss Quinn will think I haven't taught you any table manners."

"This food is amazing... I can hardly blame him."

"Thanks," Theo smiled at me from across the table, just the slightest tinge of red colored his face. "I don't get many opportunities to cook for other people."

"If you need a volunteer," I said, then took my last bite. "I'm your gal."

Once all three of us were done, I picked up the plates and forks, ignoring Theo's protests, and rinsed them off in the sink. On autopilot, I opened the dishwasher. Theo reached for the handle at the same time and his hand rested on mine.

"You don't have to clean my kitchen," he said, grimacing.

I pushed his hand away and loaded the dishes into the empty rack. He closed the door. We exchanged a look that I couldn't decipher. My look said *Don't be ridiculous, let me help.* And his said... something different.

Ice cream sandwiches were made, and once again, Oliver walked away wearing most of it on himself. His face, hands, sleeves, and the collar of his shirt were a sticky mess of melted vanilla ice cream and cookie crumbs. Theo shook his head, trying not to laugh.

"Alright, monster, it's bedtime."

"Nooooo!" Oliver whined. You would've thought someone had tossed his Pokémon cards into a fire.

"Quit whining and say goodnight to Miss Quinn."

Oliver dragged his feet over to me. I bent down for a hug and he kissed me on the cheek, leaving a spot of sticky, melted ice cream.

"Night, Miss Quinn. I love you."

Again. I don't hate that.

"You too, buddy," I squeezed him tightly to my chest. In seconds, Theo had a wet paper towel in hand and wiped away the ice cream spot on my cheek. I smiled at him, touched. But now that the bedtime routine had started, I didn't want to wait awkwardly downstairs just to say goodbye when he returned.

"I'll just be—"

"Stay," he said, touching my arm gently. I stared into his eyes, which seemed to affect him. "I mean if you'd like to have a drink. No... pressure... if you need get out of here. I totally understand, no problem. It's up to you. I..."

A thump came from upstairs. Theo sighed.

"I'll be back in a minute."

He paused, frustrated, unsure how to explain the tortured look on his face. When someone looks at you like that, you don't leave. Instead, I sat back down at the table and scrolled through my social media feeds while I waited. Theo took the stairs two at a time. A quiet squabble about pajamas followed, and Theo was the winner. A dresser drawer opened and shut, followed by the sound of a seven-year-old saying, *I can do it myself!*

When I finally heard Theo's shoes heading back down the stairs, my nervousness returned. The anticipation of being alone with him. The prospect of being near him, that warm and tingly feeling I felt when we were close.

Theo returned to the kitchen.

"Hi," he said, with a mischievous smile. Miss Quinn and Oliver's Dad have checked out for the night and the Oliver rule was back in effect. Suddenly, there was an open bottle of white wine and two glasses in his hand.

"Come on," he said. "We're not sitting at the kitchen table."

I climbed to my feet and followed him. Theo walked to the couch and sat, patting the seat next to him. I tried to relax a little, because if we were both nervous, who knew what might happen? I sank into the couch, curling my feet up under me, and watched him pour the wine into the glasses.

He cleared his throat but didn't say anything. He handed me a glass, kept one for himself, then leaned back into the couch and, hesitantly, put his arm around me. There was a peaceful smile on Theo's face, once he'd settled his nerves.

I, however, was not peaceful. With my head on his shoulder and his arm around me, the quiet tension was nearly unbearable. Nothing could happen, not with Oliver in the house. Theo knew it. I knew it. *Neither of us was happy about it.*

I took a drink.

"Thank you for dinner," I tried to find the right tone and change the subject, but suddenly found myself in small-talk territory. "I love spending time with you guys..."

"But...?"

"Huh?" I blinked, not sure how to respond.

"There's always a *but* when someone starts a sentence like that and trails off. Like you're working up to it. What were you going to say?"

"There's no but," I started, with no destination in mind. I watched Theo turn his gaze down to his wine glass, swirling it around. "This is... nice. Us. Together like this. It's confusing though. At the risk of sounding forward and ridiculous, and possibly embarrassing myself, are we... is this...?*"*

He blinked, expressionless. I took another drink. A big one. *Hold your breath and jump, Quinn.*

"Are we dating?"

Realization dawned on Theo, who immediately clammed up. It shouldn't have been *that* surprising. Every time we were together, and *alone,* our hands were all over each other. Last time I was here, we talked about whether to tell Oliver or not—I mean, we'd ultimately decided to wait, but if the topic had been on his mind since then, he might already think we were dating. *Right?*

"Are we?" Theo asked, then sighed. "It's been too long, Quinn, and I forget how to do all the steps. When do you decide that you're *seeing someone* and not just hooking up in supply closets?"

I laughed and took another drink. "You're asking the wrong person."

"I don't exactly know what happens next." His eyebrows pulled together. "I haven't dated in years. My wife and I were..."

He trailed off and I realized he couldn't find the words he needed.

"Together for a long time?" I asked, tossing out a metaphorical lifeline. He nodded silently.

We sat quietly together for a long time, just breathing in the same space. I didn't know what to say next, but when I tried to put myself in his position, I knew what I'd need. Permission.

"It's okay to talk about her."

He exhaled. "I'm sorry. I'm sure this isn't what you want to talk about right now."

"I repeat, it's okay." I smiled weakly, trying to read his emotions. I stroked his cheek and tucked a strand of hair behind his ear. "Tell me how you met."

His countenance relaxed and I knew we were in safe territory again. The tension in his body ebbed, and he started to talk. They'd both been dragged to a frat party by their respective friends. Theo's friend Tony wanted to hook up with her friend Michelle, leaving the two of them alone on the porch outside.

"I don't know why we didn't just leave, it's not like Tony and Michelle were coming out of that bedroom any time soon. Jane and I just sat there on the porch steps, bored, with nothing else to do but chat with each other. The party was loud and full of obnoxious drunk college kids. You know how that goes, right?"

"Oh, I do," I agreed, thinking back to that one dorm party sophomore year. There was a bathtub full of sangria, for starters, and a whole group of table-dancing drunk girls. They broke the coffee table and nearly destroyed the kitchen table too. Campus police showed up and made my roommate drain the bathtub. I shuddered at the memory.

"I would've been on that porch too," I added.

"Exactly." He exhaled, grinning. "I hope I'm not boring you."

"No, please, keep going. I love hearing meet-cute stories."

Theo and his wife, Jane, were together for the rest of college, got engaged a few years after graduating and married at 25.

"A year later, Oliver was born. She was the most amazing mother. She loved every minute of the late-night feedings, diaper changes, tantrums... I used to joke with her that she couldn't possibly enjoy the teenage years. She would laugh and tease me that she'd still be better at parenting than me. But then, she was gone. I'll never know how she..."

That was as far as we could get that night. His posture had changed to one of defeat. He stared down at his shoes, with the leather slightly cracked from wear. He was tired, a single dad doing his very best to be both parents for his son. He'd never wanted to do this alone. You plan a life with someone and then, they're just gone. Sometimes, when my thoughts got dark, I was grateful that my mom and dad went together—they wouldn't have wanted to be separated by death. It hurt twice as much for us, but they didn't suffer this kind of grief. Just the way Theo looked when he talked about Jane was proof of how painful it was.

I wanted to say something, but what? I reached out slowly and placed my hand on his. He lifted it to his lips and kissed it gently.

"Thank you," he uttered, without looking up. "It's good to talk about her..."

He moved his arm around my waist, and I settled my head on his shoulder. Theo sniffled once, then wiped his eyes with the palm of his other hand.

"Especially with you." A pause. He cleared his throat. I lifted my head from his shoulder and looked into his eyes. "I'm screwing this up, aren't I?"

"I think we've established that neither of us knows what's supposed to happen next."

"That's true," he said, thoughtfully. "It's not like either of us have exactly had *this* kind of relationship before. Is there a rule book?"

"Nah, we'll be fine. We can just make up our own rules."

"Which means, I can decide for myself when I'm *seeing someone* and not just hooking up in supply closets?"

"That logic tracks, yes."

"Great," said Theo, leaning back into the impression of the couch cushion. "That's settled then."

I blinked, expecting more. He just sat there, drinking his wine, staring off into the distance. I stared at *him*. After a few moments, he turned to me and feigned surprise.

"Oh, did you need something?"

I frowned. "Don't be a jerk."

"Oh!" he said, as realization dawned. Or rather, as he pretended that realization dawned. "Did you want to know what I decided?"

"Can one of our new rules be good communication?"

He laughed, then straightened up and turned to me. "Quinn

Davis, will you be my girlfriend?"

I almost, very nearly almost, snorted. I bit down hard on my cheek to stop my laughter. I took a moment, had another sip of wine, and then made serious eye contact with him.

"Theo Miller, you are so cheesy it hurts," I said, a complete deadpan. When he smiled, blushing, I continued, "But yes, I guess I will be your girlfriend."

"You guess," he mumbled, shaking his head. He took the wine glass from my hand, placed it on a coaster, and wrapped his arms around me. And then we seemed to pick up where we left off the last time that we trashed the supply closet: hands in my hair, his lips on mine, warm hands on skin. My senses were alive, but only Theo existed.

I was utterly overwhelmed. And then suddenly aware that this was a terrible idea.

"Wait, wait," I said, as his hand slipped into my bra. *Oh my god.* "We can't."

Theo stopped abruptly, a look of quiet panic on his face. "What? What's wrong?"

"I'm gonna break a rule here, but what about Oliver?"

"You're right." He shook his head and sat back into the cushion. "This is too fast anyway, right?"

"I mean, I didn't say *that...*" I grinned, blushing. "Maybe just not when he's upstairs."

"I'm sorry, Quinn. It's embarrassing how irresponsible I behave when I'm with you."

"It upsets me terribly," I said with a laugh. I leaned forward for another kiss, intending it to be much less passionate, but that was evidently not possible. In seconds, he was holding me again, with a hand beneath my shirt. When I felt the overwhelming urge to climb onto his lap, I broke away from the kiss.

"I think now is a good time for me to go home." I said, with just a tinge of disappointment.

"Yeah," he said, eyes on those shoes again. "I'm sorry."

"Come on. Walk me out." I stood up reluctantly from the couch and pulled him to his feet.

Theo followed me to the door and held my jacket open so I could slip my arms into the sleeves. He picked up my tote bag, now 52% duct tape and 48% cotton, and frowned at me. At first, he held it up by the straps to put on my shoulder, then thought better about it, and put the whole thing in my arms like a bucket.

"I don't trust that thing."

"That's fair." *And I don't trust myself.*

Of course, now that my arms were full, I was somewhat encumbered—and less available to be taken into another's arms. Perhaps that was on purpose. Theo opened the door for me and stepped back.

"Thanks," I said automatically. "I'll see you soon."

"Yes, ma'am." He smiled, just standing there holding the doorknob. "Oh! Almost forgot—I wanted to ask you something."

"Yeah?" I turned back to him. *Too quickly. Cool it, Quinn.*

"Do you think All-Star Soccer Quinn would be interested in a pick-up game? Oliver's kiddie league starts on Sunday and an old buddy of mine wants to put together an adult game after the kids play."

Do not look too excited.

"I promised him I'd ask you."

"That sounds… kinda awesome."

"Excellent," he said, grinning. "I may have been bragging about you…"

"Sight unseen? That's a big risk, Miller. You should make sure to put me on the other team."

"So you can kick the ball at my face?"

"You can't even be sure I really played."

"Sure, I can. I googled you." He winked.

"Creepy."

"Don't make me look like an idiot, okay?" he teased.

"Oh, I won't. At least, not by failing to live up to your expectations. You *will* look like an idiot when I destroy you."

"Big promises," he said with a laugh. He leaned forward to give me a quick, sweet goodbye kiss. "Goodnight, pumpkin."

I frowned.

"Is that a *no* to pumpkin?"

I nodded. "Most definitely."

He laughed and stole one last kiss. "Text me when you get home?"

I nodded, feeling my face warm. As I walked to the car, I took a deep breath and filled my lungs with crisp, spring evening air. Fresh and clean, full of beginnings. And all I could think about was how nice it was when someone cared for your safety like that.

CHAPTER TWENTY-SEVEN

It was perfect soccer weather. Sunny sky, light breeze, warm enough for shorts but cool enough to avoid heatstroke. I tossed some extra clothes, a water bottle, and my cleats into my tote bag, tied my unruly hair into a messy bun, and then headed out in my athletic clothes. If Theo can still find me attractive like this, it must be the real deal.

When I arrived at the park, the lot was practically filled with minivans and SUVs, lots of them with bumper stickers about soccer stars, dancers, honor-roll students, and the like. I squeezed my little car into a spot and trampled through the dirt parking lot toward the make-shift stadium of lawn chairs and picnic blankets. I spotted Theo talking on the sideline with an older blonde woman. With Oliver hugging her so tightly around the waist, I could only assume it was his grandmother.

I wove through the crowd until I reached them. Oliver, adorable in his little white and green soccer uniform, spotted me first and shouted, "Miss Quinn!" loud enough to startle several people nearby. It certainly got Theo's attention and when our eyes connected, we both realized the same unfortunate thing.

Oliver doesn't know about us.

"Mom, this is Quinn." But he was a little late on the introduction. She'd already wrapped her arms around me. Her embrace was warm and loving, the perfect "mom" hug, and I didn't want her to let go. Eventually she did, then placed her hands on my shoulders to look me up and down, smiling ear to ear.

"It's so good to meet you, Mrs. Miller, I—"

"There'll be none of that," she said kindly. "Call me Lisa."

"It's great to meet you, Lisa," I said with a smile. It seemed, to me at least, that *she* knew about us.

Still, there stood Theo, completely at a loss with how to greet me. *Hug, Handshake, or High-five?*

The kids' game wasn't very long—since those little legs can only run for so much time—and it was a fascinating mess of grass stains, tears, and chaos. Oliver, however, had a blast. He stayed alert and focused, so determined to make the big play of the game. At this age, they didn't assign official positions, so the kids sort of ran amok, sometimes rotating through various spots.

"I hate to say this, Miller," I whispered. *This kid is serious about soccer.* I can respect that. "But Oliver has future *forward* written all over him. I could see him as a midfielder too. Look at those sprints."

Theo raised an eyebrow at me. "Give him time. He's got goalie in his DNA."

Lisa Miller had joined a friend who was sitting a few blankets over from us, leaving us quite alone and extremely frustrated. Even seated at a respectable distance in two matching lawn chairs, Theo and I were having a hard time staying focused. My fingers twitched on the arm rest, eager for Theo's hand. Next to me, Theo cheered Oliver on, one kick at a time, but he wasn't wholly committed. If Oliver knew about us and we could sit close and whisper in each other's ears, would it be better? Probably not.

Somehow, we survived.

After the game, Oliver was flushed, sweaty, and in need of a bath. Theo hugged him close all the same, gushing about how well he played, and promising they would practice more goal kicks before next week's game.

"Maybe Miss Quinn can help you with that," Theo smiled, stealing a glance at me.

Lisa swooped in with a friendly smile and a light scent of perfume, fussing about how proud she was. Then, she turned to Theo.

"Why don't I take the little soccer star back to our house? I can give him a bath, put him in some clean clothes. You can play your game and come back for dinner after. Sound good?"

"That's great, Mom," he said, hugging her. "Thanks."

She looked from Theo to me and back. He smiled at me, eager for my response.

"Oh, Lisa, thank you," I replied, politely. "But I can't impose like th—"

"Nonsense," she interrupted. "You're coming for dinner, sweetheart."

"Oh... uh, okay. Thank you," I blinked a few times and I realized Theo had his mother's smile.

Oliver gave us both hugs and skipped away holding grandma's hand, singing loudly the whole way. Theo watched after them, a quiet, wistful look in his eyes. He was just absolutely enamored with his little boy. My heart squeezed.

Theo caught me looking at him. *Busted.*

"Well, now that they're gone, I can finally do this," he said, grinning. He took me in his arms and greeted me properly—with a short, but dizzying kiss. In public. Even after realizing that, however, I wasn't bothered by it. If there were other parents watching and judging, I didn't notice. And if I'm being honest, I didn't care. He stopped abruptly and stared into my eyes.

"Hey, doll face," he said playfully.

"Oh, that's interesting," I said, leaning in. "I had no idea I was dating a 1920s mobster."

"I mean, I *could* be, if—"

"That's a hard pass, Al Capone."

"Fine," Theo laughed. "Let's go play some soccer."

"Last chance, Miller. You sure you want to do this?"

Theo answered me with a look that made my insides tingle. We trotted off across the field, where I discovered that I would be the *only* woman playing in this game. They certainly weren't soccer stars, but every single one of them was bigger than me. I'd played against some *very* large women in college, but they didn't compare to these guys.

"Davis? Is that you?"

I spun around to see a familiar face walking up behind me, also wearing shorts and soccer cleats.

"Matt?" I smiled. I ignored the look on Theo's face. "Wow, it's great to see you!"

Matthew Bowen had grown older in the decade since I'd last seen him. His brown hair had begun graying at the temples, a few fine lines were etched near his eyes. But they still sparkled that brilliant, ocean blue. Mom had kept tabs on him for a while after the breakup, through gossip and the newspaper—he was a police officer in town, had gotten married, and had two sons. He still looked incredibly hot, but the good news was, it did *not* affect me the way it used to. That was a door I was happy to keep closed. Still, it was nice to see him. Dumping me did not make him a bad guy.

"Are you playing with us?" He looked around at the group, and evidently drew the same conclusion I had—if one of these guys wanted to break my leg, he easily could.

Like Theo would let that happen. Annnnddd... that was a thought I had. Interesting.

"Yeah, looks like it." I smiled, hiding the inkling of terror building inside me. "Theo, this is an old friend from high school. We were in the same class. He played on the boys' team, and everyone at school wanted..." *Us to hook up.* But I can't say THAT. *And we did.* I can't say THAT either.

Theo's expression as he sized up this situation was fascinating. I almost felt like I was torturing him. I didn't know my former high-school sweetheart would be there. That's not my fault.

"Matt, this is my..." *My what? Don't mess this up... Theo is literally right there and if you pick the wrong word...* When I looked at him, it made sense. "My boyfriend, Theo."

Theo winked at me. *Whew.*

Matt smiled and offered a handshake, which Theo accepted. They exchanged pleasantries. All was well. That little blip of jealousy in Theo's eyes was gone, but I knew what I saw.

Theo's friend Owen had coordinated the meet-up, so we let him pick teams and get the game going. He picked Theo and me to be on his team, along with a lanky thin man named Pete with ginger hair and glasses. It looked like our head-to-head match-up would have to wait. For once, though, the forces of our competitive natures would combine.

Matt had apparently been assigned to cover me, which I didn't think Theo appreciated. It was a relief for me, though, because I knew he wouldn't hurt me, and I already knew where Matt's weak spots were. For example, I knew that he couldn't defend against back kicks. So, when he'd been all over me, blocking every pass for about half the field, I stopped abruptly and passed the ball backwards to my new pal Owen.

Luckily, Owen was great at receiving. He also recognized that I was faster than him and would send the ball downfield for me. We worked out a good strategy quickly, and eventually, Pete caught on to it.

After my second goal, Owen called a water break. Sweaty, out of breath, but feeling very much alive, I jogged back to Theo. He handed me my water bottle and I drank about half of it without breathing.

Theo, on the other hand, didn't seem to sweaty or overheated at all.

"You're making my job too easy," he said, laughing lightly. "I can't impress you with my skills unless you let them try to score."

I glared at him. "That is *my* ball and I will not let anyone take it without kicking at them." *Personal motto.*

"You're terrifying." A corner of his mouth lifted in a half-smile. "In the sexiest way possible."

Owen blew the whistle to resume play. With a wink at Theo, I dropped my water bottle on the sidelines and trotted into position.

So, okay, I was getting tired halfway through the second period. *I'm only human.* Unfortunately for me, Matt knew that when I get tired, my dribbling gets sloppy. Around midfield, as I turned my body away and shifted directions, he snagged the ball with the toe of his cleat and swiftly passed it to his teammate—Brian?

With one jolt of energy, Brian accelerated down the field toward the goal. He was carrying the ball much farther out in front of him than he probably should. It was going too fast, he lost his momentum, and the ball got away. Matt was there, though, and quickly reeled it in. Owen charged on him and Matt passed the ball to Brian right through Owen's legs. Once I'd assessed the situation, watching three men fighting for the ball in Theo's territory, I jogged slowly to the center of the field. Theo saw me.

When Matt finally got the ball back and took a shot at the

goal, Theo got his chance to impress me. Matt feinted to the right and bent the ball around to the back-left corner. Theo was all over it. He read the kick perfectly and got one glove behind it—and he caught it, mid-air, before he hit the ground. When he hopped up, we made eye contact for one split second, and he punted the ball. It sailed over the field in a beautiful arc, directly to me. I bounced it off the inside of my knee, absorbing some of that heat with a smack, and dropped the ball to the grass. With a few quick moves around the other team's defender, I had a clear shot at the goal. I dribbled to a stop, heading toward the right corner, flipped the ball around my right foot, and aimed straight for the center.

Goal.

The powerhouse team of Davis and Miller had made its official debut.

After the game, which we won 3-0, the players said their goodbyes, exchanged a few "good game" comments, and left the field. On his way out, Matt stopped to say goodbye to Theo and me.

"You still got it, Davis," he said with a wide smile. "I've missed getting my ass kicked by you."

"Good to see you too, Matt," I said. Theo coughed. I nearly snorted.

"Take care," said Matt. "It was nice to meet you, Theo. Good game today. Keep an eye on this one. She's trouble."

He was laughing, Theo was not. And then we were alone again, just the two of us, sitting on the grass in silence.

"I could've blocked that kick, by the way," he said quietly.

"The center shot? Pfft."

"That guy had no idea what he was doing."

"Are you saying that I only scored three goals because he was a terrible goalie?"

Theo grinned. I jumped to my feet and nudged his leg with my toe.

"Get up, Miller. Let's see you block the shot."

CHAPTER TWENTY-EIGHT

Everyone had cleared off the field and out of the parking lot, but we had a goal and a soccer ball. It was time to settle this.

"Five shots," I said. "Best of. Winner gets a foot massage."

"I'll take that bet," said Theo, taking his place in the goal. He shrugged. "Either way, that's a win for me."

I rolled my eyes, settling into place with the ball. I lined it up, walked back two steps and one to the side. I made eye contact with Theo and he nodded. *Ready.*

Kick one was the same shot Matt had *attempted* against Theo during the game. Except, I kicked it properly and it bent right around him and into the left corner.

Davis 1 – Miller 0

"Alright, alright," he said. He brushed off the grass on his shorts and got back into place. "Consider that a freebie."

Kick two was a floater, right up inside the goal. It bumped the post and dropped straight down. Most of the time, this shot fooled the goalie. They'd jump to block it over the top, while the ball just rolled into the goal unnoticed. *Theo,* on the other hand, saw what I was doing. Instead of jumping, he slid under the ball and caught it.

"Nice read," I said. "No one's ever stopped that one before. I'm impressed."

He accepted the compliment with a sly grin and tossed the ball back.

Davis 1 – Miller 1

Kick three was a basic goal kick, off the instep, that skidded right into the left corner of the goal. Theo read it correctly, but just couldn't get the angle right. The ball bounced off his glove, so he *nearly* stopped it. But physics said the ball would roll backwards into the goal—so it did.

Understandably, Theo was pissed about that one.

Davis 2 – Miller 1

"This is it," I said, challenging him. "I score, I win. You block, we go to a fifth kick."

He nodded.

Kick four needed to be big. And I needed to prove that he *couldn't* block my center shot. *This could be it.* I had to modify it a bit as a penalty kick, since I couldn't build up the same amount of speed. I lined up with the ball, jogged up with a feint to the right, flipped it around my foot, and fired a goal kick dead center. Theo stepped right in front of it and caught it.

Okay, so he *can* block that shot.

Davis 2 – Miller 2

"All tied up... Davis," Theo taunted.

Kick five. *Ohhhh boy.* I had no choice, I needed to use my secret weapon. I didn't want to have to do it, but I couldn't let him win. I lined up with the shot while he settled into place. I hesitated, glaring at him. He stayed loose, swaying back and forth.

Getting my head back in the game, I took a long, deep breath. And then I launched off my back foot, speeding toward the ball. But just before I kicked it, I shifted my weight, and kicked with my *left* foot, into the goal.

Theo would've made a great save with one hand if I hadn't switched feet. But I had switched feet, so that ball went in like a bullet into a completely different spot than he expected.

And slammed right into his ribs as he soared through the air. The ball fell dead at the goal line. The goalie fell—hopefully not dead—clutching his side. *Ohhh nooo.*

Davis 2 – Miller 3, plus injury

"Oh my god, Theo! Are you okay?" I ran straight to the goal and dropped to the ground. "Did I murder you?"

He wheezed and laughed at the same time. Not great.

"Can you breathe okay?"

"I'm pretty sure—" He inhaled, wincing slightly. "I won."

"Yes," I replied. "Is that really—you're hurt, Theo, and that's what—"

"Worth it." And then he winked.

"You're unbelievable," I said, shaking my head. But okay, he was just as competitive as I was. It was incredibly hot.

I got him to his feet and gave him acetaminophen and an ice pack from my first aid kit. It didn't look too bad, but he'd be feeling it for a few days. He insisted he could drive, but I made sure to follow closely behind him the whole way.

Theo's parents lived just over the town line, so it was a short drive. I parked alongside the curb behind him, in front of a brick-faced Colonial. Black shutters, white trim, window boxes full of daisies, a cobblestone walkway, a small front porch with wrought iron handrails, and a *Welcome to our Home* sign. The house was situated in the middle of a neighborhood of similar homes, vast green suburban lawns, and beautiful poplar trees blooming in every direction.

I hopped out of the car quickly, hoping to prevent Theo from carrying his own stuff into the house. I slung my bag over my shoulder and then plucked his bag out of his backseat. For once, Theo did not argue with me.

Oliver ran down the front porch steps toward us. His little legs sprinted across the lush green lawn as he yelled *Dad!* and *Miss Quinn!* at the top of his lungs. Theo crouched down and caught him on instinct, which was not wise.

Ooooof. Theo tried to play it off as a joke—*oh, Oliver! You're so strong!* But the pain was all over his face. *Oh, what have I done?*

"Let's get inside and find you a new ice pack…"

"Good idea," he said with a wince. He took my hand in his on the injured side, then placed his other hand over his bruised ribs.

I spotted Lisa on the porch. She waved us in and handed her son an ice pack when he stepped into the hallway. Puzzled, Theo accepted it from her and placed it gingerly over the bruise. He started to speak but she interrupted him.

"I saw you holding your ribs outside," she said, matter-of-factly.

"Thanks, Mom." He gave her a kiss on the cheek but opted out of the hug.

"What happened to you?"

"I underestimated the power of Quinn's chip shot."

I bit my lip so I wouldn't laugh. Lisa gave me a little wink.

"Now go upstairs and change your clothes, you're covered in grass and dirt, Theodore," she scolded him, playfully.

"Mom," he said sharply.

"Sorry, sorry. *Theo*," she corrected herself. I tried not to laugh. "Your father will be home in about half an hour."

He started for the staircase, then turned back for me.

"Come on," he said. "You can get changed in the bathroom."

With us settled, Lisa returned to bustling about the kitchen to prepare for dinner. Oliver had climbed onto a stool at the island in the center of the kitchen, with a collection of coloring books and crayons strewn across the counter. As he concentrated on staying in the lines, he hummed a song from the musical. Lisa began to sing along.

Seriously, how could I *not* love this woman?

Theo grabbed my hand and tugged me up the stairs, until we reached the door at the end of the hall.

"My room," he said, opening the door. "There's a door to the bathroom through here, so we can both get changed."

Theo's room looked like that of a college student home for the summer. Blackout curtains, rock band posters, a Playstation connected to the TV, a desk covered in trophies and old textbooks.

"Bathroom's right through that door. I'll change in here," he said, then hesitated. "Actually, now that we've had some ice on it, can you take another look… you're trained for that, right?"

"I wouldn't say First Aid/CPR certification qualifies one to diagnose a broken rib. Is there an x-ray machine nearby?"

He laughed, wincing slightly as he carefully took his shirt off.

Just, took it off. Just... no shirt. Hi.

Once I pulled myself together, ignoring the fact that I was running my fingers over Theo's bare skin, I found a way to focus *medically*. The left side of his rib cage was starting to bruise, but not excessively. He was breathing normally, although he would twitch every few breaths. Nothing suggested we should rush to an emergency room.

"Any shortness of breath, lightheadedness, dizziness, headache?" I asked. He shook his head. "That's good, but you'll have to keep an eye out for those things in the next day or two. And if the pain gets worse, you should get it checked."

"Thank you," he said sweetly, maybe a little relieved too. He kissed me tenderly and—okay, I couldn't help myself—I ran my hands up his bare chest and over his strong shoulders. Theo didn't flinch.

"You know," I said, inches from his lips. I nodded toward the band posters on the wall—Weezer, They Might Be Giants, Ben Folds Five. "I've never dated a geek rock fan before."

"In my defense..." he began, relaxing his shoulders. "No, I have no defense."

"I appreciate your honesty," I said, leaning in. "I'll make an exception... this time."

"This 'hot girl seduces the nerdy kid' thing is working, Quinn." His lips hovered so close to mine. I was dying from the anticipation, desperate for his kiss.

"Shut up, nerd," I said with a half-smile.

And then his kiss came suddenly, somehow taking me by surprise. He wound his arms tightly around me, then let out a tiny cry of pain. I stopped, pulling back.

"It's fine," he whispered. "Worth it."

Just as he returned to kissing the living daylights out of me, the front door opened downstairs and a man's voice called out a hello. Theo pulled away, startled. His dad was home. It was time for dinner. And we needed to cool off immediately.

"Oh no, your dad's home!" I couldn't help but laugh. "It's

just like being seventeen again."

"No, it's not," he said, kissing my nose. "If we were seventeen, we'd be in the back of my parents' Toyota in the school parking lot. Completely alone in the dark. No one around. No one to interrupt us."

"Oh god, I wish we were seventeen."

He laughed, gave me one more kiss, his heart pounding near mine, then released me. "Come on, time to get downstairs."

"Aww," I pouted. "Does that mean you need to put a shirt on?"

Then he gave me that smoldering look with the eyebrow and the half-smile... whatever that was. It needed a name. He needed to trademark it. Theo disappeared into his adjoining bathroom with clean clothes. I rifled through the duffle bag I'd been lugging around to see what I'd brought. Jeans, a v-neck t-shirt, emergency back-up makeup, hairbrush. I could make it work.

In minutes, Theo returned, wearing a pale blue polo shirt and jeans, free of dirt and grass, every hair in place. First, I wanted to take it all off him. Next, I just admired his effortless ability to look so good. It made my heart stop beating every time.

How did I end up with this guy?

Theo wrapped his arms around my waist and gave me one more kiss.

"Do you want me to wait for you to change?"

"No," I said, shaking my head. "Go say hi to your dad. I'll be down once I don't look like a swamp creature."

"I think you look beautiful." He smiled, his lips still so close. "Hot girl?"

I shook my head, amused. "Only if I can call you Theodore."

His eyes narrowed.

"You'll get it. Someday. Now *go.*"

Theo moved aside so I could get into the bathroom and promised to see me downstairs. I smiled and waved him away. Finally alone, I looked at myself in the mirror, cheeks flushed, ponytail crooked, a tremendous smile on my face.

After looking at Theo, it was obvious to me that my first outfit was not nice enough. Even in jeans, he looked dressed up. *How?* I dug through my bag again and found my favorite sundress—pale green with light blue and yellow flowers, something that Audrey Hepburn might've worn on her yacht. At least, that's what Faith said when I bought it.

It only took a few minutes to wash my face, add some easy natural makeup, and get my hair under control. I was so eager to get downstairs and see him again that I flew through the steps. Oliver's excitement echoed up the stairs, just before the *oof* of a grandfather being tackled around the waist.

I heard Theo's and his dad's voices greeting one another.

"Don't hug him so tightly, Henry!" Lisa cried. "He bruised his ribs. Theo, where is your ice pack?"

Lisa's footsteps travelled back to the kitchen.

"Did big, tough Oliver do this to you?" said Henry Miller. His grandson giggled.

"No, I played a pick-up game this afternoon," Theo said gruffly.

"Quinn got him," Lisa said, amused. Something that sounded like an ice pack crinkled and I heard Theo mumble a thank you.

"Really?" said Henry, also amused.

"Luckily, we played on the same team. She scored three goals on the other guy," Theo answered, with a touch of pride in his voice. *Was Theo bragging about me?* "But then she took some penalty kicks on me after everyone left. We went two and two, but the last save got me good."

The ice pack crinkled, and I could imagine poor Theo's grimace as he adjusted it against his side. I started climbing down the stairs quietly, not wanting to interrupt.

"Sounds like a hell of a competitor," his dad replied.

"I'd say you should play her sometime... but she's terrifying. Definitely put her on your own team."

I suspected that Theo heard me on the stairs because he spoke louder and more playfully, as though he wanted me to overhear. As I descended the stairs, I could see Henry Miller, and was struck by how much he looked like Theo. In fact, looking at the three of them all together was like watching an age progression, live and in person. It was uncanny.

"What position?" Henry asked Theo.

"Center Forward," I said, arriving at the landing. They all turned at the sound of my voice, but it was Theo's eyes I found. His eyes widened and his mouth dropped open, just a tiny little bit. It would've been imperceptible if I wasn't watching him so closely.

"Must have a dangerous goal kick," Henry said, grinning widely. "If you're scoring on this guy and leaving bruises behind."

"I'm not convinced he didn't *let* me score..." A lie. Of course, he didn't.

"I doubt that. He's way too competitive to ease up on anyone. Not even his own dad." So, the soccer stuff ran in the family—I could see pick-up games at family parties and holiday gatherings. That would be fun. *Quinn, for real, calm down.*

"It's true," Theo added. He seemed to be breathing a little easier now. He winked at me. "It took great sacrifice to stop her."

Before I could reply, Lisa nudged me toward her husband. I offered a handshake and started to introduce myself, but Theo's dad had already pulled me into a warm embrace. *This family just loves hugs.* It was nice to be hugged and welcomed like that, but it also brought back a flood of emotions I was afraid I couldn't hide. Determined not to cry, I forced a big smile.

"The famous Miss Quinn." He stepped back and regarded me with a wistful expression on his face. "Oliver has been talking about you since he started your program. It's wonderful to meet you."

Henry ruffled his grandson's hair and Oliver giggled again. Then the little boy, bless him, took me by the hand. "She's the best teacher I ever had." His expression was so full of love and happiness that my heart nearly burst.

"Enough chatting. Time to eat," Lisa said, ushering everyone ahead of her into the dining room. I was the last to walk through the door and she hooked her arm through mine. Lisa hung back a moment and leaned toward my ear. "I'm so happy you're here, Quinn."

"Thanks for inviting me. It's nice to meet you both."

"I've heard so much about you from the two of them; I can't tell you how much happier they've been since Oliver joined your program."

"Oh, well, I—" *No pressure.*

"And Theo just goes on and on about you…" Lisa beamed. "It's such a relief to know there's someone who cares for them."

"I… he does?"

"I feel a lot better about us going away to Cabo this summer, knowing you'll be here for them," she said wistfully. "I realize that makes me sound a little cuckoo, but it's been just Henry and me since they moved home. Things have been so hard on Theo…"

She trailed off, her voice thick. Overcome, I hugged her. For a split second, I thought about how it had felt to hug my own mom. I couldn't remember.

"I can imagine it's been hard for all of you." I tried to keep my tone even.

The hug didn't last more than a few seconds, but it felt like we'd shifted somewhere new. I could imagine someday telling Lisa about my parents. Someday, but not now. Not when we were supposed to be enjoying a day together. Tears and fun rarely occur simultaneously.

Once I was seated, with Theo on one side and Oliver on the other, Theo squeezed my hand beneath the table and smiled.

CHAPTER TWENTY-NINE

"Okay, spill," Faith said suddenly. "You've barely said two words about Theo, and I don't like it."

Sometimes, Faith drives me nuts. Especially when she corners me and makes me *talk* about stuff. But I tolerate it because I know she's coming from a place of love. She also tends to be right about a lot of things—I'll just never admit it.

When Faith held me captive after rehearsal and shoved me into the high school costume closet, under the guise of locating props for the show, I didn't fight her off. Still, I kept my clipboard close by as a defensive weapon just in case.

Faith dug deep into a bin of hats and accessories, searching for various costume pieces. The high school drama club had so much stuff here, we barely ever bought anything. With all the time that would take her, Faith had the perfect opportunity to cross-examine me.

I was stuck in the back, searching the storage shelves for props. The sound of her voice startled me.

"Nosy much?" I asked, eyes on the prop shelves.

"Maybe I just want to share in your joy…" she trailed off. I scoffed. "What? I care about your happiness."

"Things are going well. Everything's fine." I dragged the step stool out of the corner and climbed up to reach the top shelf—covered in about a decade's worth of dust. I sneezed.

"*Everything's fine?* What the hell does that mean?" She tossed aside a handful of baseball caps and kept hunting.

"What do you want to know? What kind of underwear he wears?"

"That's a *great* place to start."

"*I* don't even know what kind of underwear he wears."

"I don't believe that for a second," she said, dismissively.

"You practically have sex with your eyes every time you're near each other."

I blushed, grateful she couldn't see my face. Having tasks to stay occupied makes these Faith conversations much easier.

"I told you, having Oliver around is *really* hampering whatever action I'd be getting under different circumstances. The eyes are about as close as we get most of the time."

"That's tragic," she sighed. "I'm sure you can work around it. Somehow?"

She extracted a boa from the bin of hats and accessories, then wrapped it around her neck.

"Hey... would Lina Lamott wear this, d'ya think?"

"Yup, put it in the costume box please."

"Do you at least talk to each other? Have you talked about the wife stuff? I know how worried you were about—"

"He's told me a little bit about her, but she doesn't come up often. Which I guess is good?"

"Yeah, daily chats about her would be a big red flag." Faith laughed. "But you can't ignore her either—that's not healthy."

I retrieved a set of plastic champagne flutes from the shelf and checked off another thing from my list. When I turned back to Faith, she was still wearing the emerald green boa and had added a glittering, golden fascinator to her head. Just casually hanging out in costume pieces.

"You don't have to *wear* them out of here, Faith."

She ignored me.

"What happened when you told him about your parents? I'm sure that was tough."

"We have—I haven't—it's been..."

"You haven't told him yet?" Faith stopped again, this time climbing to her feet. I tried not to *physically* shrink away from her. Thankfully, with the boa and headpiece, plus the rhinestone glasses she'd just put on, Faith was much harder to take seriously.

"No, why would I?"

She scoffed, taking a few steps closer to me. She slid the sunglasses onto her head. "For starters, he'll eventually notice you haven't got any parents."

"He hasn't asked me, so I haven't *lied* to him," I said

defensively. "He doesn't need to know that they're dead. They could be in Florida or something."

Faith scoffed. "Sin of omission, Quinn. That's a thing."

"Look, maybe I don't want to get into that stuff with him."

"You mean, like how he was telling you about his dead wife?"

"That's different... that's relationship-specific."

"Q, you're so dense sometimes, I want to scream. Stop avoiding it. That helps no one. If you're getting serious, he needs you to open up too."

"Who says we're serious?"

"Do you see this vase?" She held up an ancient-looking blue monstrosity. "I will smash it over your effing head."

"I don't want this relationship to be any more complicated than it already is. Maybe we're just..."

"Hooking up? How many times has that gotten you into trouble?"

"Ummm..." I had to think for a minute. *Christian, Rob, and Matt in high school. Lucas in college. Does James count? Nah.* "Four? But this is different." I deliberately shoved the memory of that be-my-girlfriend conversation out of my mind. That was silly. I was swept up in it. Okay, I'll admit it—I liked it. But I'm not stupid. This can't go on forever.

"That's bullshit. Theo is not a no-strings kind of guy. This is the first time he's dated since his wife died. Do you think he's looking for a *hook-up*? Based on how the guy looks at you, there is nothing *not* serious about this."

"Maybe we have too many strings," I sighed heavily. "If I tell him about Mom and Dad, that's gonna change things. All the strings could get tangled."

"I think it's time to let go of that analogy..."

"Fine. I just don't want him to worry about me. I have a whole team of people doing that. And he's got plenty of his own grief to work through... Can't I just have this *one* thing?"

"No! Dammit, Q." She waved the vase. "I'll do it, I swear."

I took the vase out of her hand and set it on the shelf.

"I never thought I'd say this but take Shawn's advice. Don't start the relationship without honesty," she said. Faith adjusted the boa around her neck and gave me a pointed look. "He needs to know. *You* need to tell him. There's no way this ends well if you don't."

CHAPTER THIRTY

On the same morning that I threw away Shawn's untouched Apology Pie, I baked a second one for Theo. It had been a couple days since the rib bruising, and while he swore up and down that I didn't need to apologize, I still felt bad. Sometimes Apology Pie is more for the person baking it than the one receiving it. And who cares? Everyone gets to eat the pie, so there's no downside.

I felt bad that I'd botched my apology to Shawn. That pie just sat there all week, ignored by my brother, and lamented by me. Poor pie. We'd been sure to steer clear of each other for the past few days because we were both too stubborn to be the one to talk first. I'd made the last attempt, so it was his turn. And I'm sure he probably believed I should apologize again since the first one flopped.

Having a sibling is exhausting.

I texted Theo in the early afternoon, hoping he'd be home that evening. This second Apology Pie had a much better chance at success. He replied to me with lightning speed, to invite me to make tacos with him and Oliver. Fine by me.

Oliver answered the door again, exhilarated. It was unclear whether he was more excited about me or the pie. The jumping and hugging almost knocked the pie right out of my hands.

"Careful, buddy, or no one's eating any pie..." I said, patiently.

"Can I have some?" he pleaded.

"Is that how we ask for something?" said Theo.

"Please can I have some pie now, Miss Quinn?"

"That's up to your dad," I replied. I'm not breaking any rules, not even in the name of Apology Pie.

"Pleeeeeease, Dad?" Oliver turned on him, pleading desperately.

"Fine, fine," Theo laughed quietly. "After dinner. Now let Miss Quinn through the door."

Theo took the plastic wrap off the pie and inhaled the delicious scent. He gave me a questioning look.

"Apology Pie," I said, blushing. "Mom's specialty, for emergencies. She once baked it for my dad when she'd backed the car into a tree..."

Theo smiled. "And what's the apology for?"

"Nearly breaking your ribs..."

"Once again... that was my own fault," he said. His tone became playful. "Not that I don't ... You know what, I'm *terribly angry* and if I don't eat this pie, I will *never* forgive you..."

I grinned. "Apology Pie heals all wounds."

"It's perfect. I'm better already."

After dinner, I insisted on cleaning up, but allowed him to cut and plate three slices of pie—the smallest one for Oliver. Within minutes, the little guy was covered in cherry filling, a vibrant red ring around his mouth. Theo chuckled. Oliver smiled wide, then shoved the last forkful into his mouth. He mumbled something around the pie in his mouth, that sounded like an enthusiastic thank you.

The nightly bedtime routine began with me washing all the pie filling off Oliver's face before he said his goodnight to me. Once he was all clean, I bent down for my hug and my *I love you, Miss Quinn*, but he found a new way to surprise us.

"Miss Quinn," he said thoughtfully. "Will you tuck me in?"

I wanted to say yes, but I hesitated. *How did Theo feel about this?* I looked at him for a reaction. His face was neutral, eerily so.

"Go brush your teeth, Ollie," Theo cut in, sensing my hesitation. "Just give us a minute, okay?"

Looking disappointed, Oliver trudged up the stairs. Once he was out of earshot, Theo turned to me.

"I'm sorry he keeps putting you on the spot," he said, frowning. "You don't need to tuck him in if you're not comfortable."

"I'd love to," I said. "I just didn't want to say yes without your permission."

"Okay, here's a new rule—you have permission to care for Oliver at any time. Would that make you feel better?" he said, smiling kindly. "He loves you. I don't have a problem with you tucking him in or holding his hand or anything. Ollie has his own relationship with you."

"Then that's settled," I said, smiling.

I followed Theo upstairs to Oliver's bedroom, decorated with various Pokémon. He wore a set of dragon pajamas and brushed his teeth lazily while reading an open picture book on the dresser. When I walked in, he took the toothbrush out of his mouth and smiled.

"Miss Quinn! This is my room!" Toothpaste covered both corners of his mouth and dribbled down his chin.

"I see that!"

"Come on, Ollie, you're gonna get toothpaste all over your pajamas..." said Theo, trying to hide a laugh. He shooed Oliver into the bathroom, took the toothbrush from him, and scrubbed the teeth in the back. Oliver rinsed and spit and Theo handed him a towel to wipe his face. "Did you go to the bathroom already?"

Oliver nodded, rubbing one eye with the palm of a hand. *Tired little guy.* Theo, once again, shooed him back across the hall and into his room. Oliver climbed into the bed but pushed his dad's hands away.

"I want Miss Quinn to do the covers!"

"Okay, okay," Theo said with a smile. He gave Oliver a hug and a kiss on the top of his head, then turned to me. "He's all yours."

We traded places and I tucked the covers around Oliver. I leaned in to give Oliver a kiss, but he threw his arms around my neck and squeezed.

"Don't go yet, Miss Quinn," he said, yawning. "Can you tell me a story?"

"What kind of story?"

"A happy one."

"Once upon a time," I began, smoothing his hair out of his eyes. "There was a little boy named Oliver, who lived in a house with his secret friend Pikachu. They played outside every day. They liked to draw on the sidewalk and play tag. When it rained, they jumped in puddles with their boots on and when it was sunny, they sat on the porch and blew bubbles all day. When they were done playing, Oliver would feel exhausted, so he would get cozy and fall fast asleep."

"Miss Quinn," he giggled. "That's silly."

"Time for bed, buddy," I said, tucking the covers around him. I walked toward the door and noticed Theo wasn't standing in the doorway anymore. *When had he left?* Craning my neck down the hallway, I switched the light off.

"Wait! Can you... will you..." Oliver's little voice asked.

"What is it?"

"Can you sing me a song?"

I nodded, smiling sweetly. I wondered if Theo sang to him every night.

"Can you sing *Somewhere over the Rainbow?*"

I scanned my brain for the lyrics, making sure I didn't promise something I couldn't deliver. Mental images of black-and-white Judy Garland became clearer and I figured I'd do my best.

Oliver turned onto his side, snuggling into the pillow, and held my hand while I sang. Before I finished, his eyelids fluttered closed and his breathing slowed to a smoother rhythm. I waited to be sure he was sleeping, then tiptoed out of the room and closed the door.

Theo was still missing. I hadn't heard the stairs creak, so he hadn't gone downstairs. He must be upstairs somewhere. I passed the bathroom and peeked into a spare bedroom. A third door turned out to be a hall closet filled with winter coats and spare bedding. When I reached the last door, his bedroom, I spotted him sitting on the edge of the bed, facing away from the door, head in his hands. In the dark.

With a deep breath, I stepped through the door, but he didn't move. Somehow, I knew this was a big moment and the decision I made mattered more than anything else. I could quietly excuse myself and leave him alone with his feelings. Did he want that? But I realized that I didn't *want* to do that. He needed someone. I wanted to be that person.

With a few quiet steps, I crossed the room to the other side of the bed. I lightly touched his knee and knelt on the floor in front of him.

"Hi," I whispered. Coming out of his trance, he dragged his palm down over his face. The moonlight glinted off his tears. He sniffled, just once, and wiped at his eyes one more time. "Oh, Theo, what's wrong?"

Acting on impulse, I sat on the bed, pulled him to me, and just held him. He didn't fight me, didn't try to get up and put a fake smile on his face—he just settled onto my shoulder and breathed. He wrapped an arm around my waist and held me too. I stroked his hair while he cried silent tears. My heart shattered. And the more my heart ached, the closer I squeezed him to me.

After a few minutes, Theo sat up straight, pulled himself together, and turned to face me. He lifted my hand to his lips and kissed my knuckles softly. I wiped a tear from my own eye and gently placed a hand on his cheek. Theo leaned into it and closed his eyes, letting out a sigh.

"Do you want to talk about it?" I asked, my voice small. Theo shook his head, but after catching my eye, changed his mind. He cleared his throat.

"The last thing Jane did before she died," he spoke slowly. "Was put Oliver to bed. She sang that song... every night, he asked her to sing that song."

"Oh, I—" The blood drained from my face.

Theo took my hand again.

"I didn't—I wouldn't have—"

"It's okay," he whispered. "How would you know? Oliver asked you to sing it—I'm glad you did. It's just that... he hasn't asked anyone to sing that song since. Until you."

Oh.

"I guess it was just too much," he said with a half-hearted shrug. I'd just accidentally subbed myself into a memory of his deceased wife. Anyone would be shaken up by that.

"That makes sense," I sighed. "Do you want me to head out? If you need to be alone, I understand."

"No," said Theo, staring into my eyes. "I think I'm ready. Will you stay?"

"Ready for..." *This could be anything. Do not react until*

you have all the information.

"To tell you what happened," he paused, steadying himself. "Is that okay?"

"Yes, of course." I meant it, but I was terrified. *Big moment, Quinn. Be there for him.*

"It was just this random Wednesday. I left work early that day because Jane called to say she felt ill. I went home to take care of Oliver while she took a nap. Her face was so pale, and said she was dizzy and had a bad headache. Jane never got headaches, so I knew something was wrong. I let her sleep straight through until bedtime, she was so tired. In the middle of the night, she woke up so nauseous that she spent the rest of the night in the bathroom. I had no idea—I slept through the whole thing."

He paused for a breath and I squeezed his hand.

"In the morning, I found her in the bathroom, white as a sheet," Theo slowed down. He cleared his throat again, but I could hear the rising strain on his vocal cords. "I called out from work, dropped Oliver off at school, and drove straight to the hospital. By then, she could barely breathe."

When he paused, we both took a deep breath.

"They did an exam in the ER and couldn't find anything. They did so many tests—blood work, urine test, an ultrasound, a CAT scan—and everything came back normal. They said she was dehydrated, so they gave her saline, and sent her home to rest. That was it." Theo was lost in the memory then, worry etched into his face, lit only by the moon. "I didn't want to bring her home. I fought them. Something was wrong, I sensed it, but Jane just wanted to go home. She wanted to sleep in her own bed, that's what she told me."

Fatigued, Theo lifted his gaze. Until that night, I'd only seen small blips of sadness, never anything like this. His pain all but consumed him. My grief would've consumed me too if I'd let it.

"I gave in. I brought her home," he stopped, lowering his head. He was pulling back again, retreating into that shell.

"It's okay," I whispered. I placed a hand softly on his cheek.

"She tucked Oliver in, sang his song, and went straight to bed. I sat in the bed next to her. We talked about our plans for the next day—she was going to order a cake for Oliver's birthday party, pick up the dry cleaning, then go grocery shopping. We even made a list. Such mundane things that never happened... I kissed her goodnight and she drifted off. I fell asleep still in my clothes. But Jane wouldn't wake up in the morning."

Theo leaned toward me and brushed a tear off my cheek this time, but I hadn't even felt it there. When had I started crying? Because now that I knew there was one tear, I felt the rest of them, hot on my skin.

"I'm sorry," I said, swiping at my face with the back of my hand. Sorry for crying, sorry about Jane, sorry for everything. "Do they know what happened?"

He nodded. "It was a blood clot. It settled into one of her heart valves and she was having a heart attack. No one suspected it because her symptoms didn't fit—but they should have figured it out. She should've had an EKG, but they were so fixated on everything else, they never suspected her heart. I researched it for months after because I just had to understand what happened. Was there something I could have done? I should've helped her. I should've saved her... But heart attacks don't look the same in women as they do in men, and most doctors miss them. It's not studied as much."

"What was the blood clot from? She was only..."

"Thirty."

"Oh, god, Theo," I gasped. I wanted to throw my arms around him and... and what? How did that help?

"Quinn..." He trailed off. His gaze wandered past me, lost in his thoughts. I waited, not sure what to say. When his eyes returned to mine, he spoke again. That usual Theo tenderness was back too.

"I've never talked about this with anyone," he said, shifting his tone. He almost seemed surprised. "I mean, people know the story. My parents, her parents, our friends—they all lived it. I talked about it with my grief counselor a lot for that first year without her. But..."

I pulled him in again. Tightly. If it hurt his ribs, he didn't show it.

"I've just never met anyone I could talk to like this."

"I'm glad you did," I said, releasing him. "I'm glad I know. I wish I could do something to help."

"But you did," he smiled, so close now that I could see every detail of his face in the moonlight. "Right now. This helps. Thank you."

Theo kissed me—but differently this time. It was slow and tender, not the kind that set fire to my skin. It was the kind that pulled at my heart. And... *wow.*

We stayed there together, just holding each other, for a very long time. If I hadn't been concerned about Oliver finding me in the house, I would've stayed there all night. It felt nearly impossible to go home. My stomach flopped upside down when I realized how risky it might be to open up to him. I couldn't tell him about Mom and Dad *now*. Not after that. Theo might think carrying my own grief meant I didn't have room to help him. That night was about him. There'd be a better time to tell him... sometime... eventually.

CHAPTER THIRTY-ONE

I left Theo sleeping, tucked into his bed, and locked the door behind me. When I got home, I was exhausted and emotionally drained. I texted him from the driveway, because I knew he'd be worried about me disappearing, and then I climbed out of the car. I was ready to collapse in my own bed.

But I couldn't do that yet because Franklin was missing from the hallway again. Something like that wasn't unheard of these days, so I didn't panic at first. Usually, he'd trot slowly over after a few minutes, but he hadn't yet repeated that first terrifying episode. That night would make three in a row that I'd have to go find him. The night before, I dragged him out from under the table and to his feet. We hadn't been able to take any walks for several days, but I was doing everything I could not to worry.

"Frankie," I called to him, calmly and cheerfully. I grabbed a few dog treats from the kitchen on the way to the dining room. I crouched down to say hello to him, offering treats as incentive. "Come on out, baby."

I pulled the chairs out slowly, one at a time, until I'd cleared a wide berth for him. One treat got his head up, two treats got him to shimmy forward, three treats got him to his feet, but it took a fourth treat to get him to take a few steps, before slumping back to the floor with a grunt.

I sprinted back to the kitchen to grab the aspirin and gave him the maximum safe dosage, hidden in a spoon of peanut butter. I just couldn't stand watching him in so much pain.

Once he took the meds and ate the fifth treat, I grabbed my phone from my purse and called Dr. Russo's emergency line. My panic level was so high, I didn't even wait for him to say hello.

"It's Franklin, Dr. Russo, he's... he can't... I don't know what to do."

"Deep breaths, Quinn. Tell me what's happening."

I gave him the full rundown, including how this made three days in a row but it was the worst episode yet. Even with the maximum dose of aspirin each day, plus the daily arthritis medication Dr. Russo had prescribed after the last bad episode, Franklin was getting steadily worse from one day to the next.

"Can you bring him in?"

"He's a 180-pound dog who won't move." Ouch, that was snippy.

"We should talk about some of our options." *Our options.* "It's time to discuss Franklin's quality of life."

"No."

"If he's in so much pain—"

"No."

"Please listen to me, Quinn. It doesn't have to be this way, not yet. I could give him an exam, maybe try some other pain meds... but none of those options will give him much more time. Nor will his pain magically go away," he sighed. "Just the trip to the clinic will be stressful for him."

In my heart, I'd felt this moment coming since his first bad episode. A painful lump formed in my throat and I couldn't swallow. My voice was quiet and thick with tears.

"I can't do it. I can't."

"Is Shawn home with you?"

"No. It's just me... and Franklin," I peek into the other room. "He's still on the floor."

"I know this is probably the hardest choice you'll ever make, but you need to consider how Franklin is feeling."

"I don't want to *kill him.*" The lump in my throat throbbed painfully.

Dr. Russo stayed quiet for a minute, giving me time to pull myself together and let the lump shrink a little. When I finally stopped making sobbing sounds, he spoke again.

"I've watched you and Franklin grow up together, Quinn. I want him to be at peace, free from pain. This is always the hardest part of being a pet owner. We almost always outlive them, and sometimes we need to be strong enough to help them when they need us most."

"What if *Franklin* doesn't want to die?"

"We can't speak for him, obviously, and I don't even know if pets understand the concept of life and death. They do, however, understand pain. Dogs are good at hiding it. If Franklin is too tired and in too much pain…"

"I know, I know." At the rate I paced the floor, I was going to leave a worn path across the kitchen.

"Sit with Franklin tonight and think things over. See how he is in the morning. Talk with Shawn and Charlie if you want their help."

"Okay."

"I'll call you tomorrow morning, alright?"

"Yeah, okay."

I ended the call with my back against the wall and slid straight down to the floor. Curled up in a ball, I sobbed until my eyes hurt. Sitting on the floor with that big awkward grown up puppy with giant ears and a heart full of love for me, it was just too much. I grabbed a pillow and blanket and snuggled up on the floor with him again. I wasn't leaving until he was back on his feet.

A few hours later, when the sun was starting to come up, Franklin was still lying on the floor. Shawn sat nearby on the couch, lost in his own thoughts. He must've been scared to find us on the floor like that when he came home in the middle of the night.

"Shawn?"

Startled, he moved to focus his eyes on me. "You okay?"

I nodded quickly. But when that lump swelled in my throat, I shook my head instead.

"Is he…"

"He's still breathing. But he can't stand."

"What can I do?"

My phone rang from underneath my pillow, startling us both. Franklin squinted at me then closed his eyes again. When I touched him, he let out a slow wheeze. *Did that hurt?*

"He didn't get up. He won't," I said quickly, cutting off Dr. Russo's greeting. Shawn wiped a hand across his eyes, leaned over the edge of his seat, and dropped his head in his hands.

"Can you bring him in?"

"Yeah, Shawn can help me now."

We discussed the arrangements and I hung up. I stroked Franklin's neck and shoulders slowly, looking into his eyes. He hurt. He was broken. He needed me to do what he couldn't.

Once Shawn and I had successfully carried Franklin to the car and driven ten minutes to the vet clinic, I called the people who would most want to be there. Uncle Charlie pulled into the parking lot just minutes after we spoke, and Faith was close behind.

Dr. Russo greeted Franklin first, making a big fuss over my sweet boy, who wagged his tail weakly. Even in pain, this dog was full of love and happiness. And... *oh god what am I doing?*

Faith wrapped her arms around me the second she walked through the door. She held me in place, possibly sensing that I wanted to run away. *Take the dog and run. Yeah, sure.* She squeezed me hard and whispered in my ear.

"You don't have to go in, sweetie. You can stay out here if you want."

I stepped back from the hug, shaking my head. "I have to be with him. He needs me."

Faith, her eyes brimming, nodded her head and pulled me closely to her chest again. "I love you so much."

Charlie hugged me next, telling me how strong I was for staying by Frankie's side. There were misty tears in his eyes too.

"Shawn," I said, taking his hand. "Do you want to..."

"If you want me to be there with you, I will—no question."

"I can do it," I said, steeling my jaw. "Just be here for me when I come out."

Shawn, Faith, and Uncle Charlie all nodded, taking seats along the windows. Shawn took Faith's hand when she started to sniffle.

Dr. Russo explained what he was going to do and what I should expect. Normally, I'd have been terrified, but I couldn't think much beyond *My poor baby is hurting. Make the hurting stop.* When he handed me a clipboard with lines to sign, I didn't even read it. While Dr. Russo set up, I stroked Franklin's head.

He was too big for me to hold, so Dr. Russo let me sit on the table with Franklin's head on my lap. I scratched his ears and held his paw. He licked my hand—a thank you for the life we shared. I think he knew. He closed his eyes slowly and he didn't fight.

Underneath the hand I'd placed over his chest, his breaths became smaller and smaller. His pulse slowed until it stopped. And my poor baby was gone.

Even with my brother there to catch me when I nearly collapsed in the lobby. Even after sharing that chocolate cake with Faith. Even after crying for hours. Even after Uncle Charlie told silly stories about him and my dad at summer camp to make me laugh. Even after a long, hot bubble bath and a cozy nap.

All I wanted was Theo.

He answered on the second ring.

"Hey, Quinn, what's up?"

He sounded so happy and carefree and I was about to ruin his day. The first time I talked to him since he told me about Jane and now, here's some more death. Cool. But nothing else could come close to how much I needed him.

Just the sound of his voice was enough—my guard was down, and the tears returned. I was sniffling before I could answer him, which probably made him panic.

"What's wrong? Are you okay?" *Yep, there was the panic.*

"It's okay, I'm okay," I took a deep breath, wiped the tears on my sleeve, and started again. "I'm sorry, I didn't mean to scare you."

"What's going on? Still scared here."

"It's Franklin." More sobs, but more controlled. "He's gone."

"What do you mean, gone? Lost? Do you need my help?"

"No, not lost," I cried desperately. "He died. I killed him. He's dead."

"*Ohhh, Quinn.*" He paused. "Are you home?"

"Mmm-hmm."

"I'll be right there, okay? Twenty minutes." And then he hung up.

I wrapped myself up in the blanket I'd left on the floor and tucked my knees into my chest. A warm, safe little ball on the couch. I caught the vague remnants of Franklin's scent in the fabric and started crying all over again. Theo's knock on the door pulled me from a trance, but I couldn't muster the strength to get up, not even enough to call out to him. He knocked again, paused, then opened the door.

Theo sat on the couch and wrapped his arms around me. He held me closely to his chest while I cried. Under his breath, he muttered reassuring, comforting things. *It's going to be okay. I'm right here. I'm so, so sorry.* Theo stroked my hair slowly until my sobbing slowed and my breathing returned to normal.

That was why I called him. His touch, his voice, his scent, his heartbeat against my ear.

"Thank you," I said, mostly into his chest. "For being here."

"There's nowhere I'd rather be."

"Really?" I looked up at him, blinking. He was sincere—and he didn't try to awkwardly backpedal. Overcome with who-knows-what, I kissed him... like, *really* kissed him. I unwrapped my cocoon and climbed onto his lap. Although he didn't object, Theo flinched. *Bruised ribs.*

"Oh my god, are you okay?"

"Yeah, I'm fine..." He grimaced.

"Liar."

Theo smiled weakly.

"Seriously though, did I hurt you... again?"

He didn't answer right away, so I took it as a *yes, but I don't want to tell you.* Feeling guilty again, I started to move. Theo placed his hands on my hips and pulled me closer.

"Worth it," he whispered, with a sly smile on his face.

A spark had ignited somewhere within him. We were alone and there was nothing to stop us. Theo moved with more fervor than ever before. His kisses trailed down my neck. His hands were everywhere. My hair, my waist, my back. His fingers tingled along my skin as he unhooked my bra. *Oh god this feels good.* He grabbed my hips, pressing me down onto him, and I let out a soft cry of pleasure.

Yes, please yes.

Theo stopped, panting wildly, heart racing, and he spoke. "Shawn?"

"At work."

"Couch?"

"Yes."

Before I even finished the word, Theo's shirt was gone and mine was being pulled over my head. Somehow, I ended up beneath him on the couch, my skin on fire with kisses. I dragged my hands down his back and tucked just a couple of my fingers into the waist of his pants. The sound of his soft, low moan thrilled me. Encouraged, I moved my hands to his belt buckle.

"Wait, Quinn," he said, stopping. "I... *oh my god...* I want to tear off the rest of your clothes right now."

"I'm okay with that."

"But we can't."

"Uhhhh, what?" I frowned. "Why not?"

"Isn't this too fast?" he said quietly. "Too soon?"

"It's okay. I want to, Theo."

"Me too," he groaned. "But I don't want our first time to be rushed and desperate, on a couch in your living room. This should be special. I want this to be perfect."

Overcome with desire, tearing each other's clothes off isn't perfect?

"In four years, I haven't so much as looked at another woman. There's something about you that... I don't know what it is, but I can't stop thinking about you. To me, this feels... special, I guess."

"Oh." *Am I blushing? Yes.*

"Don't you think this should be more romantic, with candles and wine or something?"

"Some soft jazz?" I added, biting my lip to stop the laughter

"Maybe on a real bed?"

"Run a bubble bath and wash each other's hair?"

"No... that's not exactly... Are you making fun of me?"

"Never," I said with a laugh. He kissed me, still smoldering hot, but less hungry. "Fine, let's wait."

"I promise I'll make it worth your while." He sat up, bringing me with him, and then kissed me again with our bodies pressed together, skin to skin.

He was really selling me on the whole romance angle. Still, I didn't want to be alone. I didn't want to be without Theo.

"Can you stay with me? Please?" My voice sounded raw. Sex or no sex, I needed him.

He kissed my forehead and hugged me to his chest, my head over his heart again.

"Of course. Oliver's at my parents' house for a special one-night vacation," he said, and I smiled against him. "Mom demanded I stay with you and volunteered to bring him to school tomorrow."

I was growing to like Lisa more and more.

With popcorn in hand, we moved to my room—so we could have privacy if Shawn came home—and cuddled together watching stand-up comedy specials on Netflix. I needed something funny to watch, but I couldn't concentrate on plots.

After the first show, I reached for him again. More kissing and some light groping ensued. And then when I realized where we were going—where our hands were going—I stopped.

"Sorry, I didn't mean to get us all worked up again. We can go back to snuggling if you want," I said, moving away.

"No, I like it," he said, slowly pulling me back. "I'm okay with frisky snuggling."

"I've waited my whole life for a man to say that to me," I said, rolling my eyes. But we turned off the TV.

At some point, I drifted off to sleep with my head on his chest. When I woke up, I was tucked tightly into the covers, held by a warm, sleeping man. Theo's gentle snores soothed my fraying nerves. I realized, as I watched his eyes flicker with dreams, that it wasn't just tingles that I felt when I was near him. Not anymore.

Suddenly, everything about him, even just thinking about him, pulled at my heart.

CHAPTER THIRTY-TWO

After rehearsal on Saturday, Faith stayed late with me to construct some props. Theo had helped me assemble the platforms and stairs onstage, but hot-gluing flowers wasn't really his area of expertise. There were so many bouquets and corsages to glue together that I needed the help. I'd already burned my fingers on hot glue at least three times before I finally blurted it all out.

"You did *what?*" Faith gaped at me.

"At least try to hide your judgment, Faith." Why did I feel the need to spill my guts to her? And why now? We had a lot of work to do and tech week was *one week* away.

"No, Q," she said, folding her hands. "This isn't judgment. This is pride."

"You're proud of me for mourning the death of my dog by jumping my boyfriend?" I asked incredulously.

"Yes, obviously," she said. "Theo showing up like that, holding you while you cried... Damn, Q, that's sexy. I'm pretty sure *anyone* would be turned on by that."

I crossed my arms but didn't interrupt.

"Plus, combating the devastating emotions of grief with the amazing experience of sex is very smart. Especially when it's with someone *super-hot,* about whom you have strong feelings. Even better when it's the first time."

"But we didn't, so..." I frowned but opted not to argue about the strong feelings bit.

"And I would argue that it isn't a *bad* thing that you didn't," she said pointedly. "For a few reasons..."

"Okay, I'm listening," I sighed.

"First of all, he wants the first time to be *special?* Come on. This proves that romance is not dead. And, honestly, it speaks volumes about how much you matter to him."

I sat with that for a moment, pretending to be super focused on the fake roses that were falling apart in my hands. *I matter to him.* It wasn't news that Theo had feelings for me but phrasing it like that made it sound more serious. A glob of hot glue dripped down onto my pinkie finger. *Oww.*

"Second, it sounds like you guys found plenty of other ways to stay, ahem, entertained."

I could not argue with that. We *did* have a fun night... My face felt warmer just thinking about it.

"And third, it will be mind-blowingly amazing when it finally happens." She paused for effect. When I didn't look at her, Faith took the glue gun out of my hand. "You're blushing. I rest my case."

Faith returned to her project, trimming the fake stems with wire cutters, and sorting the flowers by color. I picked up the glue gun and fought with a pink rose for several seconds before Faith cleared her throat and started talking again.

"What's the problem?"

"These flowers are cheap and crappy, that's the problem." I looked up at her, but that wasn't what she was talking about.

"What. Is the. Problem. Q?"

"With *what?*"

"All of the things I listed, all of that good stuff, what this could mean, how you could look at it, all THAT. And still, you look like a limp dishtowel."

"What does that even mean?" I grimaced. "We don't have time for this."

"You started it. If you didn't want me to cross-examine you, you wouldn't have opened your mouth." She picked up her water bottle and pointed it at me. "You knew what this was."

It's true, *this* is how Faith and I solve problems. And if I couldn't be honest about *this,* I shouldn't even speak about it. I watched her take a sip of water as I contemplated my approach.

"Fine," I groaned. *Talking about it doesn't mean I like talking about it.* "How do I know he's not just stalling because he doesn't want to sleep with me?"

Faith slammed the water bottle on the table and narrowed her eyes. "I'll get the vase, Q."

"Okay, okay," I took a deep breath. "But he's still wearing his wedding ring."

There was a pause, during which my best friend's facial expression softened. Her smile faded and her eyebrows pulled together.

"Ohhh, sweetie," she finally said. "I know I'm not an expert on this, but the ring is part of his grieving process. For some reason—I'm sure an understandable one—he needs to wear it. Maybe the absence of it feels weirder, makes him remember more, scares him. Maybe he needs to fidget with it when he's stressed because her memory gives him comfort. Maybe he doesn't want Oliver to think his father doesn't love his mother anymore."

"You're right, I know all that. But I can't *not* feel how I do. The way he manages his grief isn't wrong. Wearing the ring as he heals isn't wrong either…" I did feel like a limp dishtowel after all. "I don't want him to take off the ring if he isn't ready. The problem is, if he's not taking off the ring, doesn't that mean he's not ready… for me?"

"I don't think it's as black and white as you're making it sound…"

"I just wish I knew where I stood."

"For starters, you could try trusting what he says. It's pretty clear to me where you stand."

"If I tried to numb my grief with him," I had to pause and take a break. Like the extra oxygen could absorb the pain of what was coming next. "Who says he's not using *me* to numb his grief too?"

Faith didn't say anything for a while, watching me. It felt good to get the words out, I had more space to think. But it didn't make the feelings disappear, so I had to go back to my first tactic: distraction. I picked up a different pink rose and tried to make it cooperate.

I barely slept for the next few days. I couldn't concentrate on much, even with constant check-ins of my agenda. The work got done, the things were taken care of, no one even noticed—which was good, because I just needed some time to sort things out. I didn't want this to turn into an issue. Mostly I needed to get some sleep. Without Franklin, though, I wasn't sure how to process it all.

Fortunately for me, it was almost tech week, the last week of rehearsals before the show opened. When you're a techie, you *live for tech week,* so I had plenty of little tasks to occupy my brain. At Tuesday's rehearsal, I was hovering over the lighting board in the tech booth, programming the lighting cues for the show while my eyeballs melted.

My phone buzzed in the pocket of my jeans, startling me enough that I drew a line through the page I was writing on. I sighed. *Now I need a new copy of page 32.*

Leah Lancaster popped up on my phone screen, an unusual occurrence, so I answered the call and snuck out to the lobby where I wouldn't disturb rehearsal.

"Hey," I whispered. "What's going on?"

"Oh Quinn," she said, failing to hide panic from her voice. "Are you sitting down?"

Now there's a trigger phrase…

Are you sitting down? Coach has terminal cancer.
Are you sitting down? Grandma passed away last night.
Are you sitting down? Your parents were in a car accident.

Leah probably wouldn't be calling with that kind of news, so I tried to reassure myself. I sat down on the bench outside the main office and tried to steel my nerves, like I wasn't low-key panicking or anything.

"The Lakeview Hotel is on fire."

"The… what?"

"Lakeview. It's on fire, the entire hotel. Channel 7 is doing a live feed. It's bad."

"The venue for our multi-million-dollar fundraiser in two months is on fire…" I said in disbelief.

"Correct."

"Fuck." Only a curse word could encapsulate how I felt.

"Also, correct."

"Was anyone hurt? Did they get everyone out?"

"Seems like it, but it's still ongoing, so they're not saying anything definite."

"What do we do, Leah?"

"We'll come up with a plan b," she said, with a confidence that I couldn't muster in that moment. "I have a feeling that Neil will call an emergency board meeting about it. I wouldn't be surprised if he already sent an email."

"We'll have to cancel the gala. This is awful."

"No, we will not. We'll find another venue."

"Stupid question, but are we sure Lakeview won't be able to host the gala?"

"Quinn," she said pointedly. "No."

"Okay, plan b it is. I'll be in tomorrow morning."

"Tomorrow's Wednesday. Stick to your routine, don't worry about us. We'll be doing damage control, but there won't be a lot for you to do here until we have the board meeting. I got this, okay?"

I agreed and she hung up, after promising to keep me updated. I've always trusted Leah. Always. And I knew that she was perfectly capable of saving the day on her own. But what if she needed me and I wasn't there?

Theo had parked and walked up to the front door for pickup and I was so distracted, I didn't even see him coming. All the other kids were gone, leaving Oliver and me together. Suddenly, Oliver took off and crashed right into Theo, who winced a teeny bit...

"Hey, Miss Quinn, everything okay?"

"Hey," I said, adding a forced smile. "I'm fine."

"Why don't I believe you?" he asked. "Go ahead, Ollie. Say goodbye and get in the car."

"Bye, Miss Quinn!" Then came my hug, less aggressively. "I love you!"

"I love you too, buddy," I said with a smile.

"There's a real smile," Theo said, after Oliver had skipped off to the car. He watched as his son climbed into the backseat, buckled up, and pulled a book out of his backpack. "So what's wrong?"

"Nothing. I'm just busy." I shrugged, forcing my lips into a bigger smile.

"You're always busy, this is different."

I shook my head a few times, but I couldn't fight off his challenging expression. A tear formed in the corner of my eye, that I was *willing* with all my might to dissolve right back into my tear duct. I'd spent quite enough time crying all over Theo after Franklin died. I did not need him to think I was some sort of basket case.

While I'd been distracted by that one little tear, Theo had pulled me into a hug. And then there were more tears.

"What about Oliver?" I said, pressed into his shoulder. "He doesn't know."

"He knows people hug," he said with a laugh. "You just better keep your hands to yourself. You absolutely cannot throw me down onto the pavement and have your way with me."

I raised my head to look at him, that wry smile on his face. It worked—the tears were drying, and I was grinning.

"To be clear, that behavior would be okay if Oliver knew about us?"

"I'll leave it to your best judgment."

"Noted," I said with a laugh.

"Listen," Theo said as he released me. "How about I cheer you up with dinner on Friday? Maybe we can finally have that date we keep talking about? Alone... while Oliver visits his grandparents."

Oh? *Ohhh.* We stared at each other for a moment, while I fought off every urge to lean into him.

"Yes, that sounds like an excellent idea," I finally said. "And what are we having?"

"Ummmm..." He turned a vivid shade of pink. "For dinner, weirdo."

"Oh," he said, sighing with relief. "I haven't decided. Challenge me."

"The man who can cook anything?"

"I don't know about that," he laughed. "Don't listen to what my mother says. But go for it. What's your favorite thing that you haven't had in a long time? Make it good."

I racked my brain, mentally scrolling through Mom's recipe book for the long-abandoned favorites. Shawn and I were not skilled enough to tackle the tough ones.

"Okay," I said, curating my words carefully. "My... *grandma*, had this amazing recipe for stuffed chicken breast and I can't make it to save my life, so I haven't had it in about... *eight* years. Does that work?"

Deep breaths, Quinn.

"If it's your favorite thing," he said, with a kind smile. "Then I'll make it for you. I can do that."

"I'll send you the recipe when I get home, okay?" I grinned. He nodded.

Another pause.

"I'm gonna go..." Theo said abruptly. "Because all I want to do right now is kiss you until you can't see straight."

"Save it, hot stuff."

"Ooh, I like that..." he said, walking to the car. "Maybe I can—"

"That one's mine, you can't use it," I called after him.

Theo turned around and blew me a kiss before getting into his car.

Seconds later, I got the perfect text message:

Are you a campfire? Because you're hot and I want s'more.

That made me smile for the rest of the day.

CHAPTER THIRTY-THREE

The next morning, I pulled into the foundation parking lot and parked in my reserved space. Leah had told me not to come in, but I couldn't leave this problem for her to solve alone. I needed to help save the day. But then, suddenly, as I removed the keys from the ignition, every horrible memory and emotion came back in a wave. I couldn't get out of the car.

I was frozen in place, sitting in the parking lot of the Mara Davis Foundation, completely stuck. The engine was off, and I was cooking inside the car, but I still couldn't move.

Today was the day. It was eight years ago today. I'd forgotten. How?

Eight years.

Eight years since the day I'd receive that horrible phone call.

"Quinn," the police officer had said over the phone. He'd cleared his throat. "I'm so sorry, but there's been an accident involving your parents. I don't have a lot of information for you right now, but we'd like you to come to the hospital right away."

Although my mind was racing with questions, I couldn't speak. He'd told me where they were and that he'd spoken to Shawn already too.

In the hospital waiting room, we'd sat like two statues, stunned into silence. Twins shocked beyond their wildest nightmares. Mom. Dad. An accident. *What happened? Were they alive?*

Dad had died instantly. They'd told us he hadn't suffered. Mom had made it to the hospital, but they couldn't stop her internal bleeding. They'd run her in on a stretcher, right past us, straight into the emergency operating room. Her face had been badly bruised, her eyes swollen, and her nose broken.

Her airbag had deployed. Dad's hadn't. They'd missed a

recall on their car a year or so before, an easy replacement that might have changed things that day. Might. Given the shape my mother had been in, though, there'd been doubts an airbag could've saved Dad.

She'd been in surgery for four hours while they'd tried to locate and stop the bleeding. There'd been so much damage, they hadn't been able to find the source, according to the surgical resident who'd come out to talk with us. Shawn and I had been sitting in the waiting room the whole time, lamely sharing a Snickers bar that had melted in our hands. We'd sat together, silent, unblinking, and too numb to eat. The nurses had tried to care for us with bottles of water, packs of crackers, blankets, and pillows. But I couldn't sleep that night, or any night for a long time. Neither could Shawn.

Eventually, they'd thought they'd found the bleeding, so they'd stitched it up and hoped for the best. They'd gotten her a room, took out her breathing tube, set her up with plenty of painkillers, and tried to keep her as comfortable as possible. The bleeding hadn't stopped, though, so all they'd been able to do was give us time with her. She'd opened her eyes while we sat next to her bed—still too shocked to speak—and she'd smiled.

"It's okay," she'd said in a raspy voice. The breathing tube had done a hell of a number on her throat. "It's going to be okay."

I'd held her hand and she'd squeezed mine. Shawn had been sitting on her other side, trying to stay in one piece. Mom had pulled our hands in and held them together. She'd looked back and forth between us and sighed, content. How? Painkillers? I've never been able to figure that out.

"I love you, my little bugs. We both love you so much."

My words had gotten caught in the thickness of my throat. Shawn had choked on a sob. I'd looked over to him and watched tears stream down his face. That had been what broke me—Shawn in pain as great as my own, Shawn hurting when I couldn't fix it.

"You'll both be fine," she'd said, now squeezing both of our hands. "Stick together, always. You need each other."

I'd swiped a sleeve across my eyes and nose, wiping away the tears and snot. Pointless.

"I love you, Mom," I'd said, startling even myself. "Don't go."

"Please." Shawn had begged. "Not you too."

We couldn't stop it. The doctors couldn't stop it. She couldn't either.

At 8:32pm that night, only seven hours after the accident, my mother had succumbed to her injuries. She'd been pronounced dead while I watched from the hallway, clutching Shawn in my arms.

Eight years.

Eight years since I'd held Shawn's hand, both of us sobbing, both of us terrified.

Eight years since Uncle Charlie had put aside his own grief to hold us together.

Eight years since Faith had taken a leave of absence from work to stay by my side.

Eight years since those weeks of sleepless nights I'd spent crying on Franklin.

Eight years of trying to pick up where they'd left off. Trying to make them proud.

I wanted to get out of the car and go into that building, sit in that office, and fix the problem Leah was facing. I couldn't do it. I couldn't look at the pictures of Mom and Dad today. I couldn't sit in his office chair.

For eight years, yes, I could. Today? No.

Home wasn't safe without Franklin. At the bar, Shawn and Charlie were probably hanging by a thread too. Faith would just make me talk about it. I couldn't go hunt down Theo on a jobsite and crawl into his arms. He probably wouldn't mind, knowing him, but I'd have to explain. Talking would make this worse. And telling him, after he'd opened up to me, seemed unfair. He'd already done so much to help me recover from Franklin's loss as it was. He didn't need any other emotional luggage dropped on his doorstep.

The only safe place was a puppy corral.

I couldn't be sure if Mary Beth knew that it was the anniversary.

She had no reason to remember, but she was the kind of person to stow away bits of information like that. When I walked through the door, I tried to figure it out. Her expression remained neutral, no pity hiding behind her eyes, no sudden droopy face. Good.

I climbed into the corral with the puppies and tried to zone out. More new puppies, a couple familiar puppies, and then there was Percy, my little love. He'd been here for so long now that we were old buddies. When he saw me, he came over and sat very straight until I said hello. Once I acknowledged him, though, he jumped up to put his little paws on my legs. When I sat down, he climbed back into my lap and batted at my hand until I pet him.

"Hey, good news," Mary Beth said with a huge smile. "Percy's finally ready to get adopted! He got a clean bill of health from the vet. And we already have a family interested. This might be his last Wednesday with you."

Oh? Oh no.

"Good for you, buddy," I said, scratching his chin. I picked him up and held him in front of my face so I could talk to him. He licked my nose. "I told you, didn't I? I bet they have a nice big yard. I bet you'll get to play with little kiddos in a big yard and go for nice walks when it's sunny outside. And I bet they'll get you a nice cozy doggie bed. Right? *Who's a good boy?*"

My voice cracked. Mary Beth stopped cleaning the windows and looked at me. Percy's tail was still wagging as he was suspended in the air. I hugged him to my chest, his little paws on my shoulder, and he playfully chewed on my ear. It's bittersweet—I come in and play with them and we have a great time, but they always leave.

"You... okay?" She asked after a few quiet moments.

"Yeah, yeah, I'm good," I said, recovering. "Sometimes I get a little attached."

"If the family doesn't work out, maybe you could..." she began, studying my face.

"Now's not the time," I said quickly. Getting a new puppy during tech week? Immediately replacing my dog with a new puppy? It wasn't the right time, but it broke my heart.

I helped put the puppies back. The little chihuahua turned in a circle several times, kneading his blanket like he was fluffing a pillow, and then curled up into a little donut and fell asleep. Percy, as usual, tried desperately to chew on my fingers through the metal grid of the cage. I tried to concentrate on my chores and washed the same crate three times accidentally until Mary Beth said something. Once I was finished, I decided to take Percy out of the crate for a proper goodbye.

That had been a terrible idea. As soon as he licked my chin with that little sandpaper tongue, I thought I would crumble. I gave him a few good scratches, told him how much I'd miss him and put him back. He cried as I said my goodbye to Mary Beth and walked out the door.

He would make someone very happy. And I would keep snuggling puppies. We'd both be okay. Eventually.

By Thursday morning, I was refreshed and ready for battle. Yesterday had been a little bit of an emotional stumble for me, but I was back on my feet. It was the day of the emergency board meeting, and Leah was on a mission to save the gala. I paced my office while she talked through her notes. She listed off about a dozen hotels and conference centers, most within the Boston city limits.

My phone buzzed in the pocket of my blazer—a text message from Theo.

> thinking about you xx

I stared at it for a bit, not sure if I was supposed to reply. What could even compare to that cuteness?

> Same, hot stuff. see you at pickup tonight?

> of course, babe

> um, pass

The annual summer gala was only about seven weeks away. Trying to find a big enough venue, during summer wedding season, was as close to impossible as anything I'd ever tried to pull off. As problems go, this one was serious. Our only hope was to convince the board to give us more time to fix it.

> What are the chances you can build an entire hotel in 7 weeks... asking for a foundation...
>
> Umm....
>
> I just need somewhere to host a 500-person gala. You can do that, right?
>
> Your confidence in me is inspiring.

"I've got a cousin who's an event planner," Leah said, interrupting my downward spiral of worry. "I haven't heard back from her yet, but she may have some new leads for us."

> Come on... what kind of contractor are you?
>
> ... not a contractor, snuggle-bunny
>
> barf

"Quinn?" Leah said cautiously. "You okay there? Quinn?"
"Huh? Yes, sorry. All good."
"Your face turned pink."
"I'm totally fine, I promise." I shook out my hands and put my phone back in my pocket. I closed my eyes and filled my lungs. *Time to shift gears.*
"Shall we?"
"Let's just go setup. Whatever happens, we can't let them cancel this. We *cannot.*"
"Understood."
My pocket buzzed again. I hung back to check it and let Leah walk ahead of me.

> Princess?
>
> ewwww

And then I had to put my phone on my desk and walk away so I could focus. Professional Quinn, engage.

The board wasn't particularly excited about "hoping there's a venue out there" to accommodate the gala but they were also not keen on canceling. Dave Jacobs, another longtime friend of my parents, like most of the board, suggested postponing. That, as Leah and I pointed out, would be a logistical nightmare.

"Honestly, Dave," said Leah. "I considered that option, but that's an even bigger headache. In my opinion, we either find a new venue for the same date or we cancel it altogether."

With a gentle nudge from Neil Taylor, the board voted to give us until July 1st to find a new venue.

"We'll let Leah go ahead with her plans and if it doesn't come together, we'll just have to cancel," Neil said, with a tone of finality. *We'll let Leah go ahead... just Leah?*

"Got any Hail Mary passes up your sleeve?" I asked Leah, once everyone had cleared out. "Slam Dunks? Grand Slams? What sports metaphors am I missing?"

She grimaced. "Come on, if we're playing all these sports, then I'm wearing the wrong shoes."

"First, coffee."

"Really?" she said, smiling. "I was thinking whiskey."

At Drama Cares that afternoon, I put away the stress of the gala situation and picked up the lighter stress of the last rehearsal before tech week. I'd prefer a room full of out-of-control kids any day.

Knowing I would see Theo made it easier to compartmentalize things. Our string of random pet-name failures had been entertaining me since the meeting and they were only getting worse. By the time he got to *sexy pants*, I was convinced he was just Googling them. To be honest, he could use whatever name he wanted, but the game was too much fun.

At pickup, he was brave enough to walk up to the door, rather than wait at the car, and I nearly threw myself at him.

"You're really scraping the bottom of the barrel with these

names," I joked. "I hope you've saved some good ones for later."

Theo grinned, "Of course."

Faith exited the theater and groaned when she saw us.

"Ugghhh. Get a room." She chuckled all the way to the car. I exercised some serious restraint.

Theo had the most adorable look on his face, stuck between amusement and embarrassment.

"Don't worry," I said. "Her murder will be quick and painless."

He laughed, then reached out to touch my arm. He wanted to pull me toward him so badly.

"See you tomorrow, muffin."

"Gross," I laughed. "You're out of control."

He shrugged, grinning.

"How are you coming up with these anyway?"

"They just come to me organically."

"You looked at me and thought—wow, Quinn looks like baked goods today?"

He smirked. "There are *so many* dirty jokes I could make right now…"

"Move along, Miller," I said with a fake frown. "Keep trying. I'm sure you'll get it. I believe in you."

With a parting smile, Theo headed back to the car, blew me a kiss, and drove away.

Twenty-four hours. *I can survive that long.*

CHAPTER THIRTY-FOUR

On Friday, Faith helped me via video chat to pick something to wear to Theo's. I wouldn't let her come over and raid my closet again. Eventually, we settled on a pale blue sundress—cut low enough for cleavage but not so low I'd fall out of it. Faith said it was ridiculous to worry about that because I wouldn't be "wearing it for very long anyhow."

That was all I thought about as I stood on Theo's front steps, overwhelmed by the tingly nervousness I felt near him. Theo opened the door in khakis and a button-up shirt with the sleeves rolled up. Simple, casual, delicious.

"Hey baby," he said, with a grin. He moved to let me through the door. "It's almost—"

He didn't finish the sentence because I was already kissing him.

"Is that a yes to *baby*?" Theo asked.

"Oh, hell no," I replied, then found his lips again.

Theo wrapped his arms around my waist and spun around, pinning me to the wall. He kicked the front door closed behind us and the movement knocked my bag off my shoulder. I heard things rattle across the floor. I didn't care.

"That damn bag," Theo said, against my mouth.

"Shut up," I said back.

I kissed him harder so he couldn't talk anymore and ran my hands through his hair. Pulling me closer, his hand traveled down my thigh and lifted it to his hip. I curled my leg around him, pressing against him... *Yes, please.* My hands moved down along his back, searching for the hem of his shirt. I needed to feel the heat of his skin against mine. I needed to...

Beeeeeep. Beeeeeep.

Everything stopped. Theo stepped back.

"Oven timer," he said. All that tension, gone, at the sound of a kitchen appliance.

He headed for the kitchen, dragging me with him by the hand. As he pulled dinner from the oven, I opened the bottle of chardonnay on the counter.

On the table rested a plate of fresh bread, a bowl of salad, a pitcher of water, and two full place settings. One solitary candle, already lit, stood in the center.

He plated us each a stuffed chicken breast with garlic butter sauce, steamed green beans, and mashed potatoes. Setting the dishes down on the table, he took the wine bottle and poured two glasses.

"It looks perfect," I said, truly impressed. Theo smiled, relaxing a little, and pulled out my seat for me. "How did you know about my love of mashed potatoes?"

"Everyone loves mashed potatoes, Quinn."

I closed my eyes and inhaled that familiar scent—the many times I'd sat down at the dinner table with this dish in front of me. I took the first bite and the chicken melted in my mouth. The taste brought me right back to our kitchen at home, watching Mom *try* to teach me how to make it. I'd never really paid attention. I'd never thought I'd need to. Everything around me faded away and I could see her face, hear her voice. *Mom.*

"Quinn?" Theo's voice brought me out of the memory and back to his table. "Are you okay? You zoned out on me for a second."

"Yeah, great," I said, disoriented. I hadn't anticipated how much this would affect me. I could feel a little, hot tear in the corner of my eye, and I hoped he hadn't noticed.

"Is the food okay? If you don't like it—"

"No, it's perfect. This is amazing," I finally said, once I'd sorted that all out in my brain. "I don't know how you did it, but this is exactly right."

"You don't have to pretend," he said.

"I'm not pretending. I'm serious," I said in awe.

"Because it looks like you were about to cry..."

"You're incredible," I said, looking into his eyes. "I was just... overwhelmed, I guess."

"I'm glad you like it." He blushed, which made me want to swipe everything off this table and climb across it. Somehow, I contained myself.

After dinner, Theo refused to let me touch the dishes. He'd cleaned as he cooked, so there wasn't a lot to take care of, but he didn't want to waste a single moment.

"This is a problem for Future Theo," he said, gesturing toward the sink. And then he lifted me onto the counter. "And *you* are a problem for Present Theo."

I wrapped my arms around his neck. All that fire and passion reignited when our eyes connected—but this was different. This time, Theo moved slowly. He tucked a strand of hair behind my ear and leaned in to meet my lips. His kiss was deep but so slow, like a crackling, steady fire. He took his time, gently pulling me in, sliding his arms around the curves of my body. I could feel the urgent need rising in him, but he'd meant what he said. He wanted our first time to be slow, romantic, perfect.

Carefully, Theo scooped me off the counter and I wrapped my legs around his waist. He carried me all the way up the stairs to his bedroom and placed me delicately onto his bed. I pulled him down with me, unbuttoned his shirt, and ran my hands against his chest. I took control of the kissing, and his body relaxed against mine. I dragged my fingertips slowly along his skin to the yellowish, healing bruise and looked back up at him.

"Worth it," Theo whispered, with that mischievous grin on his lips. That look that drove me crazy.

I moved my hands down to the waist of his pants. This time, he helped take them off, leaving just his boxers and *him* beneath them. He stopped me before I reached all the way down.

"Your turn." He sat up and pulled me onto his lap.

His hands slid along my thighs and under my dress, sending tingles up my spine. I exhaled into a long sigh. Theo moaned in response, as he smoothly lifted my dress over my head. His skin against mine. The quickened pace of our heartbeats. The gasping breaths. The sensations of his touch. I pushed down against him. *Please.*

He unclasped my bra and tossed it to the floor.

"God, I hate those damn things," he said, breaking the kiss.

Theo looked deeply into my eyes with such intensity that my insides melted, then he rolled us over onto my back. There was no question on where I stood with him—Theo wanted *me*. He moved down my body, one kiss at a time between my breasts until he reached the waist of my panties. He took them off—leaving me desperate with desire. Every inch of me was alive. *Please.*

But Theo didn't return to my arms like I hoped he would. Instead, his mouth moved *all the way down* until I was writhing and twisting the duvet fabric in my hands. I couldn't stop the wave of sensations as it crashed over me, and he didn't stop until I called his name.

I grabbed for his shoulders and pulled him up, eye to eye with me, and reached down for him. Ready, waiting, and still inside his boxers. But then he broke away and sat up. *Not again.* I moved with him, wrapping my arms around his chest. Quiet, connected, and still. He sighed deeply.

"I want to do this. I want you. Right now."

"And I'm right here," I said playfully. "What's wrong?"

He kissed my forehead tenderly. "It's too... I'm not..."

"Ready?"

He nodded, embarrassed. I leaned forward and kissed him again, but gently this time. No groping, no urgency, just...

Love? Oh dammit. I shook it off. Plenty of time for Future Quinn to work through that one. For now, I focused on Theo.

"I understand. It's okay."

"No... it isn't. You don't deserve to have someone messing around with you like this."

"Trust me," I said with a coy smile. "There are some kinds of messing around that are perfectly fine by me."

"It's just that... before I can... I want to give you my whole heart—not some broken piece of junk," he said, pulling me closer. "The whole thing, intact and full again."

"Oh."

Overwhelmed, I ran a hand through his hair and pulled us into a kiss.

"It's okay if we can't do *everything* tonight, but can I at least say *thank you?"*

He stared into my eyes, considering it. His answer could

reveal how far he was on the path of healing. A no might mean he had a very long way to go.

But then Theo nodded. Thrilled, I pushed him back onto the pillows.

"Good," I said, biting my lip. "Your turn."

We fell asleep on top of the covers, my head on his shoulder and my hand on his chest, Theo had wrapped an arm around my waist and pulled me in close to his side, his other arm resting over mine. Around 3am, I woke up freezing cold. I carefully slipped out of his arms and off the bed, to find something to wear. I picked a t-shirt from one of Theo's drawers. Better.

In the bathroom. I squinted in the light above the mirror until my eyes adjusted and I could see my reflection. I looked like hell—and yet, I was glowing. I tried to contain my hair into an elastic and settled on a messy bun, then washed the mascara from my face.

I tip-toed back into his room, even colder now. I wanted to cuddle up next to Theo again, but I'd freeze if I didn't get under the covers. He was lying in the middle of the bed, so I couldn't climb in without disturbing him. As my eyes re-adjusted to the dark, I found myself frozen, watching him breathe softly. My heart pulled. All I wanted to do was take away his pain. And I never wanted to leave this room.

"You could've woken me up," he whispered, startling me.

"Were you watching me watch you?" I said with a smile. I leaned over and kissed him.

"You creep," he laughed. Theo stood up and lifted the covers for me to climb into. "Come on, let me tuck you in."

"Are you getting in too?" I asked, hopefully.

"Just a couple of minutes," he said, stepping into his boxers. He disappeared through the bedroom door and downstairs. I struggled to keep my eyes open, waiting to curl up with him again, but I drifted off to sleep alone.

In the morning, when the light danced through the curtains of his bedroom, he was back in bed with me. He'd pulled me toward him and curled around me. I didn't want to get up, but I was wide awake. It wasn't quite 6am but I knew I wouldn't fall back to sleep—such is the curse of a morning person. Instead, I listened to his gentle snores as my brain struggled to find a reason why he might've left last night.

Restless, I decided to wander around the house and get some coffee. I padded quietly down the stairs into the kitchen, yawning and stretching on the way. I rustled through the cabinets and found a mug with sharks on it. I placed it on the tray of the Keurig, popped in a new pod, and hit the button. I wandered into the living room, hands tight around the steaming mug, and wrapped myself in an afghan from the couch. Gazing out the window at the early morning sun, my heart was full. I felt at home. I took a few deep breaths with my eyes closed, settling into the feeling.

Last night was *amazing,* even though it had not gone exactly the way either of us had planned. Theo needed time, and I'd give him as much as he needed. I could wait.

Theo was still sleeping, so I decided to explore the house in daylight. Until then, I'd only ever been here at night. Of course, it was all the same furniture, the same decor, and the same pictures on the wall. With the sun shining in through the windows, though, things looked slightly different. The colors in the room came to life. The dark blue couch and armchair looked lighter. The sun shining through the glass coffee table cast little rainbows on the oak floor.

Everything seemed brighter today.

I crossed the room to the massive bookshelf built neatly into one entire wall. The four shelves began at waist-height on top of a long counter. Like any good lover of literature, I was also in love with this wall. This was exactly what happens when a book lover becomes a project manager.

Theo had arranged them by subject matter—a respectable choice—with all the nonfiction books at the top, sorted into work-related topics like engineering, management, and financing. The second shelf contained history books and biographies. But the *fiction* was what I really wanted to see. I thumbed through the shelves, reading the spines, wondering what I could glean from them about Theo. You can learn a lot about a person by the words they surround themselves with and so far, things were looking good for my boyfriend. Plenty of classic titles, some more weathered than others—*1984, The Catcher in the Rye,* and *To Kill a Mockingbird,* especially. I found a pristine, leather-bound edition of the *Lord of the Rings* trilogy and nearly hugged it.

The last shelves were photo albums, neatly arranged and labeled chronologically. They were all lined up perfectly in order, except for one. A large, white, fabric-covered album had been haphazardly shoved onto the bottom shelf, like someone had hurriedly re-shelved it. I reached into the shelf to push one album to the side and fit it back into the right space, but the cover caught my eye. A wedding album, with gold engraved letters on the front: *Theodore & Jane Miller, July 15th*

I froze, not sure what to do. If it had been sticking out like that, so obviously disturbed, did that mean Theo was down here flipping through his wedding photos at 3am? It was late, he would've been tired, and maybe he would've just tossed it up there in his drowsiness. And now that I was holding it, wondering that very thing, what should I do?

I set my coffee down on a coaster on the glass table and climbed into the armchair. Curled up in my blanket, I opened the wedding album to the first page. There they were, standing at the altar of a gorgeous chapel. I'd never seen her before. Her gown was a simple off-the-shoulder sheath dress in ivory silk—pure elegance on her lithe figure. Her brown curls spilled over the back of her dress. She was stunning. And staring into the eyes of a younger Theo.

Then… photos of them posing in front of a beautiful garden, dancing at the reception, cutting the cake, her tossing the bouquet, him hugging a young guy who must've been his best man—one of his cousins, based on the resemblance. I saw Lisa and Henry, about eight years younger, smiling brilliantly on either side of the couple. On the last page, a gorgeous portrait of the newlyweds in a casual embrace, his arms around her waist and their eyes locked. Love. So clear. So beautiful.

Beneath it, that classic wedding shot: the couple's hands together, zoomed in on their rings. Theo's gold band, the one I knew so well, and hers, the one that matched it.

My throat caught. Is this what he was doing last night? Was he sitting here revisiting the happiest day of his life with the woman who should be in this blanket, sipping coffee from the shark mug? In another universe, she was alive, and I would never have stepped foot into this house. He'd probably still be in Chicago and we never would have met. And even if we did, my crush on Theo would've remained a crush. I wouldn't be sitting there like an intruder.

I felt a little nauseous imagining him sitting here with these photos as I snored away, curled up in his bed, wearing one of his t-shirts, from a concert he'd probably attended with *her.* It wasn't jealousy. It was pure guilt. And heartbreak.

I needed to leave.

I carefully slid the album back into its spot, flush with the others, and placed my empty mug into the dishwasher. Then I gathered my things, changed back into my own clothes, and let myself out. I sent a text from the car in his driveway:

Had to leave early—see you at rehearsal! xx

Those were all the words I could manage, because "hey I saw your wedding album and now I can't look at you without feeling like a dirty piece of wet trash" didn't seem appropriate. If I were going to be ready to see him later that morning, I needed to get my brain sorted.

This is all wrong.

CHAPTER THIRTY-FIVE

After a long, hot shower and a change of clothes, I showed up early at the theater, with three coffees and a box of donuts. The moment Faith laid eyes on me, her face fell. And then I burst into tears. She grabbed the stuff out of my hands and pulled me into a hug. After a few minutes, I collected myself and took a very long sip of coffee. Abby came to collect hers and snuck a glazed donut out of the box.

"Thanks, Auntie Quinn," she said, kissing my cheek. Then she wandered off to a corner, eyes on her phone.

"You gonna tell me what happened?" Faith took a bite out of a chocolate frosted donut. "Are we having the post-breakup conversation? Or the one I think it is?"

"Well, I didn't get dumped..."

"Ahh, so it's a no-go still?"

I nodded, swallowing. Then shook my head. Then shrugged my shoulders. And then I faceplanted onto the piano lid.

"We didn't... he said he needed more time. And I'm okay with it... that's not the real problem."

I skipped to the important part about the album he *probably* took out in the middle of the night, while I was snoring away in his bed. It annoyed me that Faith wasn't as scandalized as she should be.

"Of course, you looked at it, didn't you?"

"I panicked."

"Why are you torturing yourself?" She frowned.

"Stop making me feel worse."

"Look, Theo's a good guy," she said. "If he says he wants to give you his whole heart, I believe him. And if he was looking at the album—"

"He was, for sure." The more I thought about, the more

obvious it became. Theo wouldn't leave anything out of place like that under normal circumstances. He was possibly the only person more organized than me. *So sexy.*

"Okay, let's say he did," she continued. "You don't know *why* he had the album out. Maybe it's not as bad as you—"

"Can you think of *one* good reason?"

Faith sighed. "Maybe you should just *talk* to him."

"After tech week?"

"I vote *now,*" she said, shaking her head at me. "But whatever you gotta do, Q. Just get through the show and I won't strangle you."

When Theo walked in, I was still standing at the piano with Faith, but we'd moved on to dealing with show-related tasks. I'd stopped crying, finished my coffee, and refocused my brain power as much as possible.

"Okay," I said under my breath. "Tech Director Quinn, engage."

"You and your *modes*," she said, shaking her head. "You're like a robot."

I scowled at her, wiped my face clean as a slate, and turned around. When I saw him, for the first time since he'd been curled up with me in bed, I was conflicted. Part of me was all dreamy-eyed thinking about him without clothes on and the rest of me felt crushed and confused. Since Oliver was with him now, we were restricted to playing the roles of Oliver's Dad and Miss Quinn for a while. We couldn't greet each other the way we might've wanted to, and that would make it easier.

He'd brought me a coffee—my usual order, from memory, because that's the kind of amazing guy he is. My blank expression faltered for a split second, but he saw it. He smiled, but I couldn't tell what Theo was thinking. After all the time I've spent studying that beautiful face, I could see something was different. Not bad... different.

Oliver gave me a big hug as he delivered my coffee, nearly spilling it. I crouched down for my kiss on the cheek and gave him a good squeeze around the middle. It made him giggle.

"Thank you, sweetie," I said. "It's my favorite."

"Daddy said you would probably need extra coffee today."

"Daddy," I said, looking up at Theo. "Is correct."

Oliver skipped off to join his friends backstage and Theo stepped closer to me as I stood up.

"You know, Quinn," he said, leaning on the piano. "I'm not sure how I feel about you calling me *Daddy*. Father's Day is *next* weekend."

"Not gonna let that one get by, huh?" I stared at him, with my hands on my hips. It was too easy for me to get pulled back into flirting with him. We'd created our own brand of flirtatious awkwardness... and I loved it.

"Absolutely not," Theo said, holding back a laugh. I waved him off, trying not to laugh, and jumped back into Tech Director Quinn mode. So much easier.

"Anyway... Welcome to tech week, the seventh circle of hell," I said with an evil grin.

"You're really selling it," he smiled.

"This'll be fun, don't worry."

Once I gathered up the whole tech team—Abby, Will, and Ethan, another high school drama kid—I gave them my motivational tech speech.

"I'm not going to lie to you—tech week is tough. We're going to be busy, work hard, feel exhausted, and make mistakes. But we are a team, so when you need help, you ask. When you're not sure about something, you ask. Each of you has responsibilities—those come first. When we all do our part, the show runs smoothly. And I promise, when it's all over, we'll have something amazing to be proud of.

"Now, let's talk about those responsibilities," I said, passing out tech scripts. Will and Ethan had one for the tech booth with the light and sound cues. Abby had one for the greenroom, where she'd be responsible for getting the kids on and off stage on time, checking their costumes and props, and keeping them quiet. Theo, the best person on hand to help me move a couch, was going to be positioned stage left for scene changes. I would handle stage right and give Abby some backup when needed... while also calling cues for the whole show.

Back in the workshop, feeling optimistic, I put the finishing touches on a fake floral arrangement. When I was done, I reached for the pen in my hair to check it off my list. But the pen was caught. I pulled it, yanking my hair with it. The harder I tried to free the pen, the more I tangled my hair. *This is why I never use pens with clips on them.*

"Dammit!" I yelled, louder than I meant to. I had given up, face in my hands, when Theo popped into the workshop.

"You okay?" he said cautiously. I looked over to him and held up the pen and all the hair tangled around it. Relieved, he walked over and took the pen from my hand. "I've never heard you swear before. It's... cute."

"This is *not* cute."

"Hold still. Almost got it. Your poor hair..." he said with a laugh.

"It's already trash on its own, it didn't need any help."

"I love your hair," he said, looking me in the eye.

I shrugged, fighting thoughts of Jane's long dark curls. And here's mine, a giant mess of frizz and... writing tools. *Don't do that, Quinn. Do not compare yourself.*

"Got it," he said finally. He unwound the elastic from my hair, and it fell out of the bun onto my shoulders. He handed me the pen and then gently combed through the tangled part of my hair with his fingers. Slow and steady, careful not to pull on the knots.

"Thanks," I said, blushing a little. *Sorta loving it.* He finished combing through the tangled spot, then took my face in his hands. I just stared back into his eyes, not sure what I was hoping would happen.

"You should wear it down more." And then he leaned in and kissed me. When he stepped back, his expression had changed again. "Everything okay this morning? I'm sorry I missed you—"

"You were out cold," I said, forcing a smile. "I didn't want to wake you. And Faith needed my help early today."

Liar.

"I wish you'd stayed," he said, leaning in again. "But I understand."

I froze, completely unprepared to face how I was feeling at that moment. When he kissed me the second time, I didn't fall into it the way I normally would. I didn't pull away, but I didn't really kiss back.

Immediately, Theo knew something was wrong. He stopped and looked into my eyes, wordlessly.

"I've got lots of work to get to today," I said, a lame apology. "And you know how we are.... Once we get started, we just can't stop."

I meant it as a playful explanation, but it was clear, from the way his face pinched together, that he thought it was a dig at him.

"No, I didn't mean—"

"I'll let you get back to work." His tone was neutral, but his body language was anything but. He walked back out of the workshop, leaving me with my hair undone and a pen in my hand. I couldn't even remember what I'd been doing.

The rest of the day was too busy to have a talk. And when rehearsal wasn't in progress, we had Oliver to worry about. I couldn't ask Faith to watch him while Theo and I had a potentially long and uncomfortable conversation. She had stuff to do and her own kid to get home.

I said a quick goodbye, claiming I was needed at the bar. I was too exhausted though, so I just went home and sat in a tub full of scalding water and bubbles. Then I drank a whole bottle of white wine, ate an entire bag of popcorn, and half a package of Oreos. And I fell asleep watching a *Golden Girls* marathon on TV. I managed to keep my mind off all the horrible stuff, but I did look for Franklin a few times... and that was sad.

On Sunday morning, Theo called, and I considered letting it go to voicemail. If we tried to work things out this week, any conversation we had wouldn't go well. Tech week is not the time. The chances of us sorting out a happy ending before the show ended were infinitesimal. And if we were going to break up, I didn't want it to happen *this week.*

But Theo is too important to ignore.

"Hey, Theo," I said, as cheerfully as possible.

"Hey..."

"What's wrong?"

"Oliver spiked a fever this morning and I don't know what's going on. He says he's nauseous, so I'm afraid he's got a stomach bug. I don't think I can bring him to rehearsal today."

"No, of course not! Oh, poor guy," I said, crestfallen. Even when I didn't want to talk to him, I still wanted to see him. "How's he doing?"

"Sleeping, for now, finally," he sighed. "Listen, I'm gonna have my mom come and stay with him so I can—"

"Theo," I said firmly. "Stay home with your son. Dad stuff comes first."

"I can't just ditch you. I'm not sick."

"I'll be fine. Oliver *needs* you."

"Are you sure? Because I can—"

"If you show up, I will be furious with you."

"Okay, okay," he said, clearly amused. Some of the worry was gone from his voice. "Thanks, precious."

"Un-uh. No thanks, Gollum," I scolded. I remembered the leather-bound *Lord of the Rings* trilogy on his bookshelf—and then, that damn photo album.

"Listen..." His tone shifted to something more serious. "I want to talk about something, but in person. It's not a phone or text kind of a thing. I just... it's important and it should be a face to face conversation."

My stomach twisted. All I could think about was Shawn chasing me around to help him break up with Gina. If he *was* going to break up with me, Theo was not the kind of man to shy out of doing it the right way. But if he didn't tell me, I'd just *assume* he was breaking up with me. I felt queasy just imagining sitting there, listening to him break my heart.

"Quinn?" he said after a few moments of silence. "I can *hear* you worrying."

I laughed nervously.

"I'm not breaking up with you. And it's nothing bad, okay?"

"Are you sure?" *Trust no one.*

"Positive," he said. "I would never lie to you."

"Okay..." I was still skeptical, but I'd have to just put it aside for now. I couldn't go to his house if there were stomach virus germs. "Keep me posted on how my little buddy's doing, okay? Tell him Miss Quinn misses him and that she loves him very much."

"I will," he said. Theo paused and then inhaled sharply. I

could picture the look on his face when he did that. "Quinn, I want to... I need... I—"

"Save it, hot stuff," I tried to recover for us both. This was going to get uncomfortable. I just sensed it. "We'll see each other soon, right? Take care of Oliver—and yourself. I don't need you getting sick too."

The following two days, however, showed me just how much I needed Tech Theo. Faith reassured me several times that we'd be fine, but two days of tech rehearsals without my most important stagehand were a disaster.

On Sunday, I left Will in the tech booth alone and brought Ethan backstage to help with set changes. The lighting and sound boards were too complicated for one person to run alone, so that was a complete fail. I sent Ethan back there to help for act two and tried to run the scene changes alone. Nightmare. Plus, I stubbed my toe *really* hard and that just made me cranky.

On Monday, I left Ethan in the booth and pulled Abby from the greenroom to help me. But some of the kids took the opportunity to wander onstage. I didn't stub my toe, but I nearly punched a hole in a flat.

"Positive thinking will not help, Faith," I said impatiently, after her fourth motivational speech in 36 hours. "I don't have enough hands to make these ridiculous scene changes happen."

"Ridiculous?" She was already irritable from her own tech week issues—including an orchestra member with a serious body odor problem. If she didn't say something soon, I would.

"Remember when you told me to stop you if you went overboard? Here we are!"

"It's a little late *now,* Q!"

"Fine, no problem," I replied as I walked backstage. "Quinn Davis will just make all your dreams come true like the amazing magician she is."

"Looovvveeee yoooou!" she yelled after me, fighting her laughter.

Tech week is like one big brewing argument that ends in a party. So, you know, Faith and I were going to be snippy with each other. The beauty of our strong friendship and our long history as partners in theater was that we could do things like this and then forget about it.

Faith wouldn't murder me this week. What might kill me, however, was a performance without Theo backstage.

CHAPTER THIRTY-SIX

Even though I wanted to, I couldn't live in the auditorium all week. I tried to resume some semblance of order to my weekly routine, although I had to cut back a little bit on my time at the bar. And I also couldn't be at the foundation every day in battle mode while we prayed for a building to appear. On Tuesday, I arrived at the foundation as usual and made my rounds, giving everyone a cheery hello along with their orders.

Before I took my first sip of coffee, Leah was in my office with a big smile on her face and a stack of papers in her hand—more pleased than I'd ever seen her before.

"I've been caffeinating since 5 am," she said, anticipating my question. She handed me the packet as I sat in my desk chair. "And I've been here since 6 am, working on this."

I rubbed the bridge of my nose and took a deep breath. I hadn't slept well the night before and a headache was threatening. At the bar after last night's horrific rehearsal, Shawn had bossed me around for hours in this irritating business-like voice. He is *not* the boss of me, which I'd reminded him several times. And then I dreamt about a tequila worm that was still alive and hungry for blood. So... I was tired.

I flipped through the packet, confused, and found an updated gala budget proposal in the back.

"We have a new venue," she said, eagerly.

I flipped back to the first page, a detailed description of the Meadowgreen Manor, a historic landmark used for events and conferences. She'd included photos—a gorgeous lawn, fancy landscaping, a footbridge stretched over a tiny brook, and a white gazebo. A few photos showed wedding guests dancing beneath a huge white tent, trimmed with sparkling white lights.

"Where did you find this place?" I asked, mesmerized. "It's

gorgeous."

"My cousin worked a wedding there last weekend and put me in touch with the owner. It's a little outside our normal area but look at the price. It's 30% less than the Lakeview."

"This is incredible," I said. "Let's get a contract signed today—I love it. Want me to call them?"

"All done. Check page 10," she smiled. "I hope you don't mind. Danny and I went out there yesterday afternoon and signed one. You were busy, so I took care of it. I'm meeting the manager there on Thursday afternoon—do you want to come with me?"

I stared at her blankly for a moment, not quite sure what was happening. My brain was lagging.

"It's tech week, so I don't think I can go with you if it's after lunch," I said, smiling weakly. "This is really great, Leah. I'll give Neil a call to—"

"I talked to him last night. He's scheduled the board to meet on Friday—I cc'd you on the email, but I can resend it." Leah pulled out her phone from her blazer pocket, swiped the screen, and typed rapidly. With a click, she looked up at me again. I realized then that I hadn't checked my work email since last Friday. Oops. "Done! Can you make it?"

"Sure, that's no problem," I smiled thinly and returned my eyes to the paperwork in my hand. I made a mental note to jot that down in my agenda. "So, everything else is—"

"All set," she smiled. "I called the team in early this morning. We've updated the vendor contracts, drafted press releases, letters to the attendants, new mailers to send out... it's all in there. We'll have it all finalized by Friday, possibly tomorrow."

Suddenly her expression changed, and she dropped into the leather armchair across from the desk.

"Sorry, Quinn. I'm overstepping, I can see it all over your face. I knew it was tech week and you didn't need the extra strain."

"This is exactly what you're supposed to do," I said with an even tone. I didn't blame her for the squirmy feeling in my stomach. I should've been *here,* in crisis mode with the team, and I wasn't. "You're the CEO. You don't need my sign-off on anything."

"Okay, I'll get back to it. You can keep that packet, it's a copy. Let me know if there's anything else you need."

And then she was gone. Every to-do item was done without me. Really, Leah should be the one telling *me* if there was anything else *she* needed. I suddenly felt nauseous at the possibility that Shawn had been right all along.

Oliver and Theo returned for Tuesday's rehearsal and I thought I would die from the relief. Oliver's fever and nausea turned out to be the early signs of strep throat, which is quick and easy to treat. Oliver was back to his normal self—*and not contagious, Miss Quinn!*—within 24 hours.

Theo jumped right back in, Abby returned to the greenroom, and absolutely zero children were found wandering onto the stage by accident for the entire rehearsal. Putting that one piece back in the puzzle made everything okay again.

"I'm so glad you're back," I told Theo at the end of the day. I was sweaty and achy but feeling so much better about the show. "It was rough."

"I thought you said you'd be okay without me..." he said with a grin.

"Well, I was *personally* fine," I tried to backpedal. "But the show was definitely suffering."

"Uh huh, whatever you say, boo."

We both reacted immediately to that one.

"Oh, no thank you," I said, wrinkling my nose.

"I regretted it the moment I said it," he agreed, wincing.

"We shall not speak of this again," I said firmly.

"Speak of what?" he said with a wink.

Then it was time for us to say goodbye—in the Oliver-is-watching kind of way. Hugging was okay now, so I could hold him for a moment and just breathe. The way he made me feel, even when we pretended we were just friends, I knew we'd be okay. Eventually.

"We should talk soon," he said, releasing me. "If you have

any time tomo—"

"This week is a wash, Theo. Let's make it through the show and then I'm all yours, okay? Just a few days."

He nodded, though he didn't seem thrilled. But that would have to be okay until Sunday.

Sure, I was busy. Sure, I was stressed. But I was never too busy or stressed to snuggle puppies. This week, we had a lot of new puppies. There was a teacup poodle who acted like he was Franklin's size, bossing everyone around. Several times he came over to bark at my shoes. Apparently, they'd offended him somehow. A couple of labs, a new pug, and three puppies from last week.

Percy, however, was gone. Mary Beth noticed I was looking for him and sighed.

"He went home with a family—two little girls. He'll be okay, Quinn. I made sure."

Saddened, I sat down in the corral and tried to make a new best friend. It seemed even more important now that Franklin was gone. Maybe I should add a second volunteer day to my schedule. Because I certainly wasn't going to be adopting a new dog anytime soon.

Of all the weeks for Percy to be gone, though, did it have to be *tech* week? I could've used some playtime with that little snuggly furball. The yippy poodle just wasn't the same.

I wandered into the back room of the bar, but no one was there. The door had been unlocked though, so someone must've been out front. On the way there, I stopped into the back office to put my things down and my jaw dropped.

The back office was *clean*. I could barely believe my eyes as I surveyed the pristine workspace. Every bit of paperwork was neatly placed in the file sorter, the paper shredder was accessible in its new home beneath the desk, all the junk that had been collected in there was gone—maybe tossed—and there was a dry erase calendar hanging on the wall, filled out for June and July. A brand-new computer sat on the desk, alongside a mousepad with the bar logo on it.

It wasn't just the office that Shawn had cleaned, though. Every shelf of the backroom was even more neatly organized, the floor was immaculate, the sink and counter space were cleared off, and a brand-new dishwasher sat tucked in place of the broken one. Shawn had even replaced the rickety stepstool with a proper, sturdy stepladder. He'd thought of everything.

On cue, Shawn entered from the bar through the swinging door. He stopped, surprised to see me, searching my face—probably to see how angry I might be.

"This looks great, Shawn. Nice job."

Relieved, he smiled. "Thanks. I've been here really late the last couple nights. Charlie is a serious pack rat."

"Where is he today?"

"At home. I'm making him take a day off."

I paused, impressed. "Anything for me to do today? Seems like you've got most things under control."

"Actually, I could use your opinion on something..."

Music to my ears. "What's up?"

Shawn walked me back into the bar, where he'd spread out a mess of legal documents. Are we being sued? What now?

"Calm down, we're not getting sued," he said with a laugh. *He knows how I think.* "This is for the building next door."

"The laundromat?"

"Yeah, that busted-up eyesore that keeps everyone on the street from walking down here?" He frowned. "I'm tired of looking at it. So, I'm buying it."

"You're... what?"

"We're gonna buy it. We've negotiated a decent price—it's been so hard for them to sell; they were willing to listen to our real estate agent."

"We have a real estate agent?"

"It's perfect, really. It's an adjoining building, so we just need to knock down the wall and renovate both buildings together," he said, waiting for my approval. "I thought it was time to give Charlie what he's always wanted."

"A restaurant?" I smiled widely, just imagining how happy

he'd be. "Shawn, that's amazing!"

"Don't tell him, okay? It's a surprise. He'll need to sign the papers with me, but I want to do all the grunt work first." He paused, leaning forward on the counter. "Do you think this is a good idea?"

Swept up in the excitement, I hugged Shawn tightly, brimming with pride—and a couple tears. At first, this seemed like a brilliant solution and I was so happy to know Shawn could come through like that. And then, as I stood there, the doubts bubbled back to the surface. Where was the money coming from? How could I trust that Shawn had truly gotten the best deal—who was this real estate agent, anyway? Was this a wise investment, or would we just be throwing money away? What if the laundromat had never been the real issue and we'd be out of business in a year? How much research had Shawn really done?

It had been such a long time, about seven years, since I'd felt like I could count on Shawn—so it wasn't exactly easy to just blindly trust him again.

When Mom and Dad died, the shock lasted for a long, long time. We'd both walked out of that hospital completely numb. I'm pretty sure I cycled through the Five Stages of Grief more than once in that first year, all while Shawn seemed to be unaffected. Neither one of us had ever been good at processing emotions. I couldn't blame him or criticize him for his coping strategies, whatever they were. For the first year, though, we stuck together and handled all the basic tasks that occur after a loved one dies. We arranged a wake, a funeral, a burial plot. We bought coffins and headstones. We wrote obituaries. We requested that mourners donate to the Mara Davis Foundation "in lieu of flowers."

My parents made sure to leave something for all of us. They'd set up a college fund for Abby and had left a small inheritance for Faith, which she'd used to start Drama Cares. Dad left full ownership of the bar to Charlie. The rest went to Shawn and me, in two equal shares. Neither of us had *any idea* whatsoever that my parents had arranged for us to inherit so much money—the shock of that alone took months to wear off. A magical estate planner appeared out of thin air, provided by the law firm. She ran us through all the options—stocks, bonds, investments, personal savings... My eyes glazed over. I was an English major pursuing a master's degree in education; Shawn left college halfway through a science degree when he was 20. We were out of our depth.

After we took time to sort through our parents' things and sold off or donated whatever we didn't need, it was time to decide what to do with the house. The truth is, when we sat at the kitchen table, staring at each other, neither one of us wanted to stay. But neither of us wanted to leave either. It seemed like the best decision was not to decide—which Faith argued was, itself, a decision. Eight years later, we were still sitting on that decision.

Then came the uncomfortable nothingness. Our lives had been turned upside down and now we were orphans, if one can be an orphan at 25 years old. Shawn and I hadn't decided where our lives were taking us yet, and then when Mom and Dad died, everything just stopped—an engine out of gas, running on fumes. But instead of coping and facing reality together, a wedge developed between Shawn and me.

Shawn, never a man with any plan, took off with all that cash burning holes in his pockets. I'm not even totally sure what he did while he was gone. All I *do* know is that he spent a whole lot of time in Europe with one girlfriend in every country and then came home broke a year later. Within a few weeks back at home, Shawn abandoned his half-hearted job search and started helping Uncle Charlie at the bar.

Meanwhile, I'd left grad school and waltzed into the foundation, ready to do whatever it took to fill Dad's shoes. I audited a few business classes at the community college just to boost my confidence. All I'd wanted to do was preserve their legacies and that had seemed the best way to honor Dad.

For everything that Shawn had run away from, I'd found something to run closer to. And because I had scheduled myself to work part-time at the foundation, I'd left myself plenty of time to dedicate elsewhere—like Drama Cares, the animal shelter, and wherever I could find a need.

Maybe Shawn was finally getting his act together—and maybe he was getting us into even more trouble. More than anything, I wanted to breathe and enjoy that feeling of partnership after so much time. But if eight years had taught me anything, it was only a matter of time before I'd have to save the day. Again.

"Well," he said suddenly. "You *were* happy about this, but you've clearly invented a reason to be mad about something."

"Huh?"

"*Resting Crisis Face,* Quinn…" he said, frowning. "You know, I might've been the screw-up kid who caused all the headaches and drama, but I'm not stupid."

"I know you're not stupid, Shawn," I grumbled.

"Do you?" he asked. His voice was free of anger, but the question still stung. "Because you've made it your life's work to babysit me. I'm not your little brother, Quinn. We are twins. We've been together *literally* our entire lives, and technically, I'm seven minutes older."

"Check the birth certificates, Shawn. I was born first."

"Mom told me once that they mixed us up when we were born and flip-flopped the birth times when they filed for the birth certificates. So there." He said, sticking out his tongue.

"Is now the best time for this?"

"Fine," he huffed. "Don't believe me. But please, can you just trust me for once?"

Yeah sure, but maybe not during tech week.

CHAPTER THIRTY-SEVEN

Every tech week has its own disasters. If it doesn't, you need to worry about opening night. Making a few mistakes during dress rehearsals gets all the bad stuff out of the way so you can have a successful show. That's just science. Things break, actors forget their lines, techies miss their cues. Usually, the problems are a team effort. But every significant *Singin' in the Rain* tech problem was my fault.

After Theo's triumphant return and a smooth rehearsal on Tuesday, I believed my tech-week woes were behind me. Wednesday's run wasn't bad—there were a few issues, all minor, that were easily solved. One of the rain jackets lost a button, so Faith brought that home to fix. Ethan missed a light cue—but it too was minor, so no big deal. A couple of the kids were late for their entrance, but still—nothing big. The only major thing was the headsets running out of batteries because I'd forgotten to replace them. Oops. Headsets were the only way I could communicate with Will and Ethan in the tech booth, Abby in the greenroom with the kids, and Faith in the orchestra pit—so they were important. I put batteries on my shopping list.

Thursday was an eerily uneventful day. I was suspicious. After so many days of disasters, problems, catastrophes, and assorted issues, I wasn't expecting a quiet day of work. I couldn't go with Leah to tour the new gala venue, so that was hard to deal with, but beyond that... nothing happened. I ran my errands, remembered the batteries, and went into the theater early to get myself set up.

I was optimistic that the final dress rehearsal wouldn't be awful. That night, we were running the show from beginning to end in "show conditions," which meant we weren't stopping, no matter what happened. Just like a real performance, the show must go on. But after twenty minutes of desperate searching, I couldn't find the headsets.

"We just had them out yesterday," I said, dumbfounded. Theo had already unloaded and reloaded the entire workshop, helped me dig through the costume closet, and searched the tech booth. We tried retracing my steps.

"We need to start," Faith said, once warmups were over and the kids were getting ready backstage. "There has to be a way to work around it."

"I've got two teenage boys on the *other side* of this auditorium who are responsible for calling their own cues now. I don't know how to work around *that.*"

"They know what they're doing, Q. You trained them yourself. They've been fine all week. Will's not gonna mess up, especially because he lives to impress Abby," she said with a shrug. "What else are we going to do?"

"Running to the store for replacements is…"

"Not gonna happen. Get some for tomorrow."

"Faith, I can't run a tech crew on new headsets *cold* on an opening night. We should use the ones we've rehearsed with all week."

"Where could they have gone between last night and today? Are you absolutely sure they're not at your house?"

I put my hands on my hips. "Yes, I'm sure."

Faith threw up her hands and backed away toward the piano. "Figure it out."

"Five minutes to curtain," I yelled, scowling at Faith. She was right, we needed to start. I'd find a way to deal.

"Thank you, five!" she yelled back, adding a wide grin. "You'll be fine."

After a couple minutes, Theo found me backstage, doing a last prop check.

"Hey, want me to go get new headsets? You don't need me for a set change for at least 20 pages…"

"That's not enough time," I said sharply. I checked everything off the list, then started counting umbrellas. "I can't move a fricking couch by myself. Stay here."

He frowned.

"I'm sorry," I said, dropping the last umbrellas into the stand. "We just need to deal. Two minutes to curtain!"

"Thank you, two," Theo said, still frowning. I heard Faith call from the pit and Abby tell the kids to call from the greenroom. Time calls were the best way to get everyone on the same clock, so we taught the kids early. Theo had learned recently—as of Tuesday—and it annoyed him.

One last thing to do... I jogged up the aisle to the tech booth and popped my head in.

"Okay, guys, you're flying solo tonight. Still no headsets. But I know you'll be fine. Will, you're a pro. You've got this."

Will nodded, with a thin smile on his face. Poor guy looked terrified.

"Get through this and I'll bring cupcakes in tomorrow."

That cheered them up.

"Places!" I yelled as I jogged back down to the stage. The replies came as I muttered obscenities to myself. *This will be fun...*

Thirty pages in, though, I could breathe a little bit. We'd settled into a solid rhythm. Marks were being hit, cues were on time, everything was in its place—even the children. I stubbed my toe on that stupid couch again, but I'd kept my screams to a whisper, and walked away fine. That was it... until the end of act one.

I'd just rushed through the set change before Don Lockwood's big tap number—"Singin' in the Rain," obviously—when I saw Abby waving frantically from the greenroom. Something was wrong, and because we didn't have headsets, she couldn't tell me from where she was. I dropped the set piece I was moving in the wrong spot, planning to come back for it, and booked it over to Abby.

"What's wrong?"

"We're missing umbrellas!"

"What?"

"We only have four of them!"

"But I just counted them... are you sure the kids don't have them already?"

She shook her head. "I looked everywhere. What are we

gonna do?"

"You'll have to tell them to pretend, Abby. We don't have time to figure it out now... they can mime umbrellas, right?" *Where are the damn umbrellas?* I knew I counted them... but I'd been distracted. Had I counted the right number of them?

Abby shrugged her shoulders and headed back inside, where I heard her talking to the kids about it. Add another problem to Future Quinn's list. There was nothing else I could do about it then, so I headed back to the wing and bumped square into Theo.

"Oww!" I nearly yelled, stumbling backwards from the impact. Apparently, I was moving fast. Theo caught me around my waist to keep me upright. *Another good save, Miller. Phew.* "What are you doing over here?"

"Putting this where it goes."

"You're supposed to be on *stage left,* Theo! Did you get confused again?"

"You left the table in the wrong spot. The kids are going to run right into this."

"You can't just walk around back here..."

"I don't have another cue until act two... I'm trying to help."

"It's not helpful if you're in my way."

Not breaking eye contact, Theo picked up the table and walked off. On the way by, I heard him mumble something. No time to figure that out now because the song had just started and my little actor was onstage singing in the rain, without rain.

Dammit! I sprinted over to the pump, grabbed the handle, and pulled... too hard.

Before I could do anything to stop it, the pump was working at double the speed it should have been, pushing too much water too fast through the hose. Within seconds, the trough underneath was overflowing, flooding the stage. The whole thing started to buckle and the more I turned the handle *back* to shut it off, the worse it got. *No no no no no!*

Theo, suddenly reappearing behind me, reached over and unplugged the whole system. I watched in horror as my little dancers tapped and sang around the giant puddle, praying no one would slip. Luckily for me, and our insurance, everyone stayed upright. Some of them were laughing and stomped in some of the puddles on their way offstage.

From the house, I heard Faith yell, *"FIFTEEN!"*

"Thank you, fifteen," came the replies. I, however, was back to muttering obscenities to myself.

Theo, suddenly reappearing behind me again, handed me a pile of folded towels. He followed me out to the stage, carrying his own bundle, and helped me sop up the water.

"Where did you get these?"

"Locker room."

"You made it to the athletic building and back in under four minutes?"

"Yeah," he shrugged. "It's not far. Goalies can sprint too, Davis."

I should've let him get the damn headsets.

"Hey Q, can we talk?"

My head snapped up and I met Faith's eyes, narrowed in something that looked a lot like rage.

"What the hell is going on back there?" she said, once we've walked out to the lobby. "This is a mess!"

"Sorry," I said, crossing my arms. "I can't get my feet under me today."

Faith put her hands on her hips, frowning.

"I'll fix the rain machine, even if I'm here all night."

"And the missing umbrellas?"

"I'll find them."

"And what about the botched set changes?"

"Huh?"

"The cake came out late, and only because Theo ran around to the other side of the stage and pushed it out with Lilly sitting in it. She almost missed her solo…"

"What?"

"You didn't even notice you missed a major cue… what is going on back there?"

I hung my head. What *was* going on back there? Where was my head today? How could I be screwing this up so badly? Everything going on in my life *outside* of this theater didn't belong in here. *Get it together, Quinn.*

"I'm about ten seconds away from canceling your rain

machine and forcing you to rain glitter from the ceiling instead."

"Please... no glitter."

"Fix it," she said, probably angrier than I'd ever seen her. "This isn't the hardest show you've ever teched, Q. And the kids are making this a breeze for you. If it's a problem with Theo..."

"Theo's fine. He's doing my job better than I am, apparently."

"Get your head out of your ass and figure out why you're not on the same page back there."

Back on stage for act two, I was seething with anger... at myself. The glitches were fewer, farther between, and much less serious. Theo had taken care of the puddles and the stage was dry again, at least. But then two of the flower arrangements fell apart on stage, a fedora was completely missing, and a doorknob was locked on set.

Why did I buy doorknobs that lock?

No one was hurt and the actors had a successful rehearsal. Even Will and Ethan were okay in the tech booth without headsets. It was just Miss Quinn who had the problems.

At the end of the rehearsal, Faith ran the cast through her notes and made a nice inspiring speech about how amazing they are and how wonderful the show was going to be. Me? I was sitting on the stage, barely listening to her, making myself a *Things I Screwed Up and Need to Fix* list. It began, of course, with FIX THE DAMN RAIN MACHINE.

I helped get the kids assembled and out the door. Then I helped Abby, Will, Ethan, and Faith pack everything up for the night. Left alone, finally, I gave myself five—or maybe ten—minutes to cry out some of my frustration. And then, I got to work.

"Hey, Quinn," said Theo, startling the ever-living bejesus out of me. "Sorry, I didn't mean to sneak up on you."

"It's fine," I said, pretending I hadn't been crying. "Did you forget something?"

"No, I'm here to help."

"What about Oliver?"

"Mom's staying at my place until we're done here."

"I can't ask you to do that. It could be awhile..."

"Technically, you didn't ask me to," he said with a grin.

Looking at him then, I realized that I hadn't exactly been my nicest over the past couple days... okay, most of the week. I hadn't truly been fair to him, especially since I hadn't let him explain anything. I'd shut him out. I'd been trying so hard not to see the Theo I had feelings for, because Tech Director Quinn needed to focus.

But Tech Director Quinn could shut up for two minutes. I walked over and threw my arms around him. He placed a kiss on my forehead and hugged me to him.

Theo paused, studying me, a puzzled expression on his face. "What?"

"Just checking... Ah, yes. You *are* my girlfriend," he said, before properly kissing me. "Hi, angel."

I batted at him, laughing. It felt good to laugh.

"Is that a no to angel?"

I shook my head, hiding my amusement.

"I brought you a present," he said happily, holding up a shopping bag. "I stopped by my office and grabbed a couple doorknobs that don't lock. I'll even change them for you."

"Amazing," I said, with a genuine smile. "Thank you."

"But I'll make you a deal," he said playfully. "If we can get this thing fixed in two hours, I'm taking you out to dinner."

"Tonight?"

"Yes, tonight," he said with a laugh.

"During tech week?" *Is he nuts?*

"If we finish all the work, you can take a break. If we leave everything perfect here, there's no excuse for you to stay. Be my date."

I looked down at what I was wearing. I was damp, dusty, sweaty, and smelled vaguely like the coffee I'd spilled on my tech shirt four hours ago. *I guess I could change clothes...*

"I'll think about it," I said warily. "I'm *really* tired. Can we play it by ear?"

That seemed good enough for Theo. He followed me to the workshop, where I'd tossed the broken rain machine. With my hands on my hips, I surveyed the damage. I nudged the hose with my toe.

"Fortunately, I have extra materials... because this thing is shot."

We took stock of everything left over, measured the remaining hose and rubber, and decided we didn't need a trip to the hardware store. If the pump needed to be replaced, I'd be able to get one during the day—that was easy. The rebuilding was the most important thing, and the part I *did* need help with. I never would've asked him, but I was glad Theo had decided to come back.

"Are you getting déjà vu?" I asked, laying everything out across the stage. "I feel like we've done this before."

"Ooh, she's making jokes. That's a good sign." He laughed. I *was* feeling better. For a little while.

We fell back into our quiet, comfortable side-by-side work mode. This time, we knew how to build it and what it would look like when we were done, so theoretically, it should've gone faster. But then, Theo started talking.

"Listen, I'm sorry about Friday."

"Oh?" *Do not engage. Now is not the time.*

"I feel terrible about the whole thing."

"You didn't do anything wrong," I said, still looking at my hands as I worked. "I thought we covered that already. *On Friday.*"

"Yeah..." He put the tools down and looked at me. "But after..."

I met his eyes, scowling.

"I just don't want to dance around this anymore," he said. "My wife... she died. I loved her, she loved me, and then one day she was just *gone*."

I couldn't read his expression as he spoke. There was sadness behind his eyes, but his matter-of-fact tone showed a strength that hadn't been there before. The words were presented as facts, almost without feeling. Wait, not without feeling. Without pain.

"I understand all of that," I said, mustering all my patience. "I understand that you still love her and that you're still healing. And I understand that you need me to be patient—I'm okay with it."

Theo smiled, but I could see another thought forming. *We can't do this now.* With another deep breath, I tried to find the rest of my patience—whatever I could scrape together.

"We really have to get back to work," I sighed. "Can we talk at dinner?"

"You'll go with me?"

"Yes, if you promise we can just have a nice, easy conversation. I can't do all this emotional stuff right now, okay? Not this week."

"Can we at least talk about why you snuck off in the morning?" Theo sat there, still not working.

"I told you, I—"

"The real reason."

"Fine. I saw your wedding album sticking out of your bookshelf."

"Did you look at—"

"Of course, I did, Theo. I'm *me.*"

"See, that's what I want to—"

"Not now. Not *today.*"

"Quinn, please listen," he continued. "After you went back to sleep, I went downstairs and got that album out for a reason."

A reason. I'd asked Faith to give me a good reason he might have that album out. *One good reason.* Was I going to get one now? Or just some excuse?

"Stop," I snapped. "I already feel guilty enough when I'm with you…"

"You feel *guilty?*"

"Yes. Well, no… maybe? I don't know." I dropped my head into my hands. "I am not in a good headspace for this conversation right now. *Please. Stop.*"

"You don't need to feel guilty… am I making you feel like that?"

"Think about it for a second," I said, dropping my tools. "If I had a dead husband, how would you feel?"

"What?" he trailed off, stunned. "Are *you* breaking up with *me?*"

"No! For crying out loud," I thought I might scream. "You can't just keep trying to convince me to be patient and wait for you to sort everything out, when I've already told you I *would* be patient and I *will* wait. As long as it takes, I will wait for you. But every time you bring it back up, I want to block my ears and hide."

"I didn't realize…" He picked up the tools and looked away from me.

"What you don't realize, Theo, is that now is not the time for this conversation!"

"Quinn…"

"This is *tech week*. It is the single most stressful week of the *year* for me!"

"Sorry…"

"Can we make a new rule that serious conversations *do not* happen during tech weeks?"

"Sure, I—"

"I just had a *shitty* final dress rehearsal. I'm missing props, I have costumes I need to fix, I may or may not have to buy a new pump tomorrow, and I still don't know where my headsets are. I have to bake cupcakes now, thanks to Will and Ethan, which reminds me that I haven't eaten anything since 2pm—so now I'm hangry."

"We can get back to work. I promise I won't—"

"Outside of this auditorium, the rest of my life is a mess. And I can't seem to compartmentalize it all, so my best friend is pissed off because I'm ruining her show. She threatened to axe the rain machine completely. Then she told me to get my head out of my ass… and she thinks you're distracting me and that's why I can't do my job."

"Am I?"

"YES!"

For a moment, there was silence. We just sat there, staring at each other across a rubber trough, either out of words or afraid to say the ones we had.

"Can we please just…"

"Of course," said Theo. "I'm sorry I pushed you."

"It's okay… I'm sorry I yelled. This will all be over in under 48 hours. That's all I need, okay?"

He nodded and got back to work, but it took me a lot longer

to focus after that.
    Why were we doing this during tech week?

CHAPTER THIRTY-EIGHT

The rain machine was fixed, and the pump still worked, so that was one less thing to squeeze into my Friday. We finished earlier than I expected—well within Theo's two-hour window—but I passed on his dinner invitation anyway. I felt bad about it, but I didn't believe we'd get through dinner without him bringing up serious things. And I didn't trust myself to handle it well.

I did not deserve "a break" until the show was over. I didn't expect him to understand, but he didn't argue.

At home, I shoved food into my mouth and went upstairs to start my bedtime routine. I walked through all the steps and climbed into bed, only to find my insomnia waiting for me.

I got that album out for a reason.
Nope, not now. We're not doing that now.

Even after employing all my anti-insomnia strategies, I was tossing and turning. I used my bedside journal to scribble down all the things on my mind that might've been keeping me awake. *Gee, I wonder why.* I filled up two pages, front and back, before I wrote the word STOP so hard, I ripped the paper. I tried warm milk. I tried listening to the rain sounds app on my phone. I tried meditating. I even took a couple of Tylenol PMs. Nothing helped.

I'd never had a problem with insomnia until after the accident. Sleeping brought horrible nightmares. Sleeping was a waste of time. I knew I needed it, but the little voice in the back of my head wouldn't let me relax. When my insomnia was at its worst, I would sometimes take Franklin for a walk in the middle of the night. Who's gonna mess with a lady walking a giant Great Dane at 2am? I couldn't do that now. Without the dog in the equation, I'd feel much less safe. Even in this neighborhood.

I thought about driving to Theo's and crawling into bed with him. Partly because I wanted everything to go back to how it was.

And partly because I didn't want to be alone. But mostly because sleeping next to him was the most peacefully I'd slept in years. If I went to him, though, he'd insist that we talk through everything before going to sleep. That would probably cure my insomnia, but I still wasn't in the right headspace for another serious conversation. I'd botched the last one spectacularly.

I should've gone to dinner. I should've let him talk. Maybe I would sleep better if he told me the reason. And maybe I wouldn't.

Two days. I will wait. Focus. Go to sleep.

Finally, I gave up, popped some popcorn, and parked my butt on the couch.... Which is where I woke up, two hours after my alarm was supposed to go off. I checked my phone, sitting on the coffee table—dead battery.

How could I have slept so late? I never *sleep in.*

I plugged in my phone, quickly glanced at my agenda for the day—plus the supplemental to-do list for the show. In the shower, I stood under the hot water, planning my day, and failing to mute the words echoing in my brain: *I want to block my ears and hide.*

It was true. I'd already decided to tough it out with him, to wait until he was ready to—how did he put it?—give me his *whole* heart. Not some *broken piece of junk*. It's hard to walk away upset after a line like that. I knew it was sincere. Every bone in my body knew it. But every time I got a mental image of him looking at the album, I doubted it. And every time he talked about needing more time, it eroded my patience. The talk, not the time.

Basically, I could deal without the sex. I could *not* deal with the constant reminders that I was being kept at arm's length until further notice. I didn't need status updates. I just wanted to be with him.

When I turned my phone back on, there was an onslaught of text messages waiting for me. An apology from Faith. A funny meme about tech week from Abby, her way of trying to cheer me up. And a text from Theo.

> I promise tech weeks are now off-limits for all serious conversations. I shouldn't have pushed you tonight. Get some rest. See you tomorrow xx

Maybe he gets it? I answered him.

> I'm sorry I freaked out on you. After the show closes, I'm all yours again. xx

Still, our conversation played as the background noise of my brain as I dressed, ate breakfast, and left the house. The words were there while I ran all my errands. I bought new umbrellas, I replaced the headsets, and then I stopped at the school to find a new fedora in the costume closet and reassemble the props that had fallen apart. I had to borrow a glue gun from the art teacher, because that was missing too, but I got the work done. I tested the rain machine and breathed a sigh of relief that everything was working fine. I even swept the stage.

Back at home, as was typical these days, I got a punch in the gut when Franklin wasn't waiting for me at the door. I still wasn't used to it. *How long would that take?* In fact, that feeling of something forgotten nagged at me while I stirred the cupcake batter, preheated the oven, and cleaned up the kitchen. Franklin was missing—obviously—but that wasn't it. I missed something else. I'd forgotten... *something.* My agenda reassured me that I'd checked off the list. I even texted Faith to be sure she didn't need anything else.

What was it?

It wasn't until I put the second tray of cupcakes into the oven that I remembered.

The board meeting. I never wrote it down!

Frantic, I tore apart the house for my phone, which I found in the pocket of my jeans. The pair I was wearing. The meeting started fifteen minutes ago—I'd never make it. The cupcakes needed at least five more minutes, and there were two more trays to bake, before I could even think about leaving. Add on the driving time to the foundation, and the soonest I could be there was an hour from now. The meeting would be over by then.

Somehow, I hadn't received any calls from Leah. No email reminders. No frantic texts. It was almost like Leah either hadn't noticed or didn't care that I was missing. I knew she wouldn't answer, but I tried calling anyway. Her office phone, her cell phone. I texted. And then I called Janet to make sure the meeting was still going on.

"Yes, they just went in about fifteen minutes ago," Janet said in her naturally snippy voice. "Do you want me to transfer you to the boardroom?"

"Ye—" But I never finished the word because the smell of burnt cupcakes triggered a second wave of panic. *Save the cupcakes.*

I bolted back to the kitchen, phone pressed against my ear, I stuck an oven mitt on one hand—and then picked up the tray with *two* hands. A string of obscenities poured from my mouth and, in the physical reaction to the pain, I dropped the tray of cupcakes and watched in horror as my phone slipped off my shoulder and slid right into the center of the oven.

Dammit.

Two hours later, I was still breathing. My phone turned out to be okay. I saved enough cupcakes for each child to have one. My hand was burned badly enough to be a problem, but not enough to go to the hospital. I put some salve and a bandage on it, then popped a few acetaminophen pills to take the edge off.

Leah called after the meeting to catch me up. It was a success, the board approved, and all was well. It was like the first venue had never burned down. She also said it was no big deal that I missed it—she hadn't expected me to come because I wasn't necessary. *Cool.* With everything approved and all the grunt work done, there truly wasn't anything for me to do. The staff would handle the calls and mailers and press releases. They wouldn't need me again until the night of the gala, where I'd be expected to smile, nod, and say thank you a bunch of times, while also hearing how much I look like my parents. The glamorous stuff.

In other "good" news, I found the headsets in the trunk of my car. How? Apparently, I'd thought it would be better to bring the headsets home to change the batteries… and forgotten all about them. The umbrellas turned up hidden behind the door to the workshop—which I could not explain to save my life. The simple fact that I'd been so distracted and so out of focus was enough to explain just about anything.

I decided to hang onto the extra umbrellas until the show ended—just in case. I was keeping the other headsets, though, because it seemed like backups were a great thing for Future Quinn to have. The hand, however, was not super happy about lifting anything, let alone a couch. With my good hand, I dug through a tote of lighting supplies and pulled out a pair of work gloves. My hand still hurt, but if I could keep the pain from my face, no one needed to know about my cupcake incident... because if they *did* know, nobody was going to let me move anything back here.

Fortunately, I brought the Tylenol.

My busy brain had done a pretty good job keeping me afloat. Now was not the time to indulge my feelings—both the emotional hurt and physical hurt. I had a show to do, and as Faith had said, I needed to get my head out of my ass and focus. *Do the tasks. Keep moving.*

That is... until Theo walked in. When I saw him—and even more when he saw *me*—everything just fell away. Everything that had been on my mind all day dropped at once, including the strain between us. I was standing in a room full of spinning plates with my hands tied behind my back. They were all going to fall and break. But maybe, if he held me tight enough, the shattered glass wouldn't hurt me.

I just wanted to run to him. Instead, I ducked into the workshop, while he got Oliver settled in the greenroom, and pretended to be busy until he walked in.

"Hi, gorgeous."

The next thing Theo said was *oof* as I threw my arms around his neck and knocked the wind out of him.

"Is that a yes to *gorgeous*?"

"Meh." I squeezed him harder and then, tragically, I sniffled.

"Hey, hey," he said soothingly. He hugged me tightly. "What's wrong?"

"Everything?" I said, clenching my eyes shut against the threatening tears. My voice was steady enough to go on. "Things suck right now. I just need to survive until tomorrow night. Can we pause all the drama and just... be together? We can figure out everything else later."

"Of course, we can," he said earnestly. Theo kissed me softly, then pulled me into another hug. If I had him and I knew we were okay and I could stop obsessively worrying about it, then maybe I could focus enough to make it through the show.

"Oh, thank god," I heard a voice whisper behind me. Abby. She grabbed the extra umbrellas off the counter and gave me a wink. "Sorry, Auntie. Carry on."

Just like her mother.

Theo turned his head, but Abby had already ducked out and headed toward the greenroom. He looked concerned.

"Don't worry about her," I said, with a half-smile. "She's *Faith's* daughter. Do you really think she doesn't know already?"

He laughed, light and relaxed. Already, I felt at ease. I knew it wasn't going to last. I knew that he would help me make it through the show, that we could put away the issues between us for a short time, but that we'd have to come back to it at some point.

For now, Davis and Miller were in action, working together through a mistake-free show that we could be proud of. Even Faith forgave me.

Friday night's show was a full house, with the Millers in attendance. They had led the standing ovation from the center of the front aisle and Oliver was just over the moon about it. He kept yelling *Those are my grandparents!* during curtain call. He's just the cutest.

After the show, Lisa came backstage and crushed me with one of her wonderful hugs. My thoughts briefly wandered to a universe in which Lisa became my mother-in-law someday, but I popped that thought bubble almost as soon as it floated from my mind.

"Oh Quinn, that was amazing," she said, smiling ear to ear. "I don't know how you do it, but you and your partner are incredible."

"Theo helped us a lot on this one," I said with a grin. "I gotta give credit where it's due."

"Thank you for getting him involved. I haven't seen Theo so excited about anything in a long time. You know," she said thoughtfully. "All the time that I was pressuring him to get back out there and date, I couldn't have hoped for someone like you to come along. He's so smitten with you."

She hugged me again, but I didn't exactly squeeze back as much this time. *Pressuring him to get back out there and date?* Is that how we got here? *Oh, I guess she'll do...* until he realized he wasn't ready yet. Wouldn't he *be ready* if we were more than a relationship under pressure from his parents? If it was his choice and not one forced on him?

Despite knowing how unlikely that reasoning was—because Faith was right, he did not look at me like I was just some girl—thoughts like that are like thorns. And once you'd pricked your finger on one, it was hard to stop that bleeding.

Like my burned hand, I bandaged that thought up to save for later.

CHAPTER THIRTY-NINE

The show was over, and I'd survived both performances without accidentally burning the building down. That was a close one—quite possibly the worst tech week I'd had since *My Fair Lady* at Yale, when the platforms collapsed and one of the chorus members sprained her ankle. That one wasn't my fault—someone else built those platforms. And once I'd reinforced them, all future tragedies were averted.

The Saturday matinee was an even bigger success than Friday, far surpassing our expected ticket sales. Faith earned enough money to fund Drama Cares for the entire summer and fall. The kids had been abuzz with excitement and pride—there's nothing quite like a post-show high.

Of course, there's also nothing quite like the post-show blues, which would hit them like a ton of bricks in the morning. Especially because Drama Cares was done for the year. Several kids would be back for summer camp in July, and some would come back in September for another school year, but for a handful of kids, this was the end. That night, though, for the hours following the show, they celebrated in the cafeteria together with about 9,000 gummy bears, 10 pounds of popcorn, and a dozen pizzas. Post-show kids are hungry animals.

"Great show, Quinn," said June McEntire, the high school drama teacher. Another alum, she'd graduated a few years ahead of me, Shawn, and Faith before heading to New York City and achieving some moderate success as an off-Broadway actress. She'd moved back around the time my parents died and basically walked into this job. I would've loved to have applied for it too, but I was too busy with the foundation.

"Thanks, June," I smiled. "I'm so glad you came. These little ones worked so hard on this. They deserved a big audience."

"The drama kids and I loved it. I don't know how you do it. My high school kids are hard enough."

I shrugged. "It's fun. And we have plenty of help." My eyes wandered to Theo, talking to another parent. Katie Bennett's mother Christine was also single. The very thought of it made my stomach twist.

"I'm sure you're exhausted," June said. "Go home and get some rest. If you don't mind, I'd like to keep the platforms up for the next show."

"Of course," I said, relieved. Normally after a show, we would've stayed to take apart the set as part of the cleanup. "It would be great to get some sleep tonight."

The set could stay, but everything else needed to be cleaned up and put away. I said goodbye to June and turned up the hallway toward the auditorium, where I ended up face to face with Theo.

"Hey, Miss Quinn," he said with a smile. He held his arms open, almost like he expected to catch me. Relieved, exhausted, grateful, and confused, I hugged Theo tightly.

"Thanks for your help," I said sincerely. "We make a good team, Miller."

"That's what I've been saying." He smiled, then lifted my burnt hand and slid the glove off. He looked into my eyes. "What happened?"

"It's fine... Just a little burn," I said, pulling it back. "How did you—"

"You made a face every time you touched something. Call me observant."

"Why didn't you say—"

"Because I knew you'd just argue with me about it. I know better than that. But why do you think I moved *extra* furniture during the scene changes?"

"And here I thought you were just ignoring my directions," I said with a weak smile.

"But seriously, honey," he said, concern in his eyes. "Is it okay? A real answer, not a *Quinn* answer, please."

"I promise, it's fine. It wasn't a bad burn. And now that I can rest it, I'm sure it will be back to normal in no time." I held out my hand to show him the bandages and he leaned down and placed a soft kiss on my uninjured knuckles. When our eyes connected, Theo leaned toward me for a kiss and stopped abruptly when his son appeared beside him.

At the sound of Oliver's *Miss Quinn!* I knelt and wrapped the little guy in my arms. I gushed over how well he did in the show and how lucky I was that he came to Drama Cares. He threw his arms around my neck and kissed my cheek. Theo, still stuck in place, cleared his throat.

"Go get your backpack, Ollie," Theo said, nudging him toward the greenroom. After the little guy had trotted off obediently, he turned back to me. "I'll tell him, but we really need to—"

"Talk first, right?"

He nodded.

"It's fine," I said, stretching my lips into a thin line. "You know what's best."

Once Oliver had gathered his things, I said goodbye to the Millers for the night. I promised Theo a phone call in the morning—after I'd had time to eat, sleep, and shower. He had a strange, nervous expression on his face as we said goodbye. Usually, when he looked like that, he'd begin spouting all kinds of nonsense. It was eerie how silent he was.

I was immeasurably thankful that I wouldn't need to take apart the platforms. Instead, I did a basic tidy of the greenroom and backstage area. Faith and Abby were staying to put all the props and costumes away and told me to go home.

"You're half dead, Quinn. And I think you've got some other stuff to sort out, right?" Faith asked.

While they took care of that, I disconnected the speakers and tucked them back into the lighting booth, took apart the rain machine, and swept the stage. I half expected Theo to appear out of thin air, as he always seemed to, but he was home with Oliver, exactly where he should be. Most surprising, however, was the fact that he hadn't insisted on staying in the first place. Maybe he was starting to understand my brain and its boundaries.

When I was finished, I hugged Faith and Abby, said goodbye to some of the kids and their parents, and closed the book on *Singin' in the Rain.*

On the way home, I longed for Franklin's company, to clip on his leash and take him for a walk. I desperately wanted to talk things out with someone who would just listen. I needed to scratch my furry baby's head and watch his eyes close in pure bliss. And so, I cried for a few minutes before I even arrived in my driveway. The house was dark, and no one would be waiting to greet me.

I swallowed hard, wiped my eyes with the back of my hand, and climbed out of the car with the tote bag in my arms. And then, I noticed him—Theo, sitting on my porch with a big, brilliant smile on his face.

Startled, I dropped my bag right in the middle of the walkway. I heard the thud and the rattling as things rolled all over the cobblestones, but I didn't care. I saw him get up and walk toward me and I heard him speak.

"Hi, beautiful."

I wanted to be excited to see him. I desperately wanted to let go of everything and just fall into his arms. I wanted the relief I used to feel when I saw him. But something was wrong. There were familiar smells that shouldn't have been there. Mulch. Fresh dirt. Mowed grass. Smells that hadn't been in Mom's garden for eight years. *No, no, no.*

Frantic, I surveyed the front yard, stunned. Mom's garden was *here*—like she'd popped by for a quick visit from the great beyond, done a little weeding and trimming and planting.... Then disappeared.

What happened?

"Theo..." I said, motionless. "What is this?"

"Surprise," he said with a smile.

I spun around in disbelief. Brand new daffodils lined up in a row by the porch. The weeds had been pulled from between the cobblestones and the walkway was pristine. All the broken stones had been replaced. Petunias once again circled the oak tree. Every item on my to-do list that I'd neglected while I sat in the house, staring out the window with regret.

My job. Mine. In just two weeks, everything I was responsible for had been taken from me, every person who'd needed me suddenly didn't, and this last thing—the only way I could honor Mom's memory—was gone. Taken from me. *By Theo.*

"What did you *do?*"

"Listen," he said, stepping toward me. "I know I only made things more stressful for you this week. And even though we've seen each other almost every day, I've missed you. I realized, while I watched you dedicating so much of your time to everyone else, that someone needs to take care of *you.*"

I knew—somewhere deep in the back of my brain—that he had made this huge gesture from the heart. I knew, logically, that he didn't do this to hurt me. But I also knew that I was angrier than I'd ever been. Listening to his heartfelt words wasn't enough to shake it. I exhaled deeply, trying to soothe the fierce blaze of my rage.

"What's wrong? Are you okay?" He reached for me, concern in every line of his face. I didn't move.

"No, I'm not okay." More breathing. "How could you?"

"What? Quinn, what's going on?"

"What's going on?" I repeated, sharply. "Do you have any idea what you've done?"

"Yeah, I tried to help you." The worry had become annoyance. "You worked your ass off for that show and you're *exhausted.* I watched you dealing with that stress, plus everything else, and there wasn't anything I could do about it. I can't help you at the foundation, I can't bring Franklin back, I can't sort out whatever is happening with your family, or magically heal your hand. There isn't a whole lot that I can help you with, but *this* I can do."

"You shouldn't have. This garden was *my* responsibility, Theo."

"It was a jungle, Quinn, not a garden. And it was driving you nuts," he said calmly, trying to appeal to my logic. "You kept saying you didn't want to waste money on it—that you'd do it. I have a full contact list of landscapers at your disposal, most of whom would help me out in a second. All you had to do was *ask.*"

"That's not the point! I was going to fix it. Me!" I pointed to myself, poking my chest hard enough to hurt. And I was yelling. I didn't want to yell. But I needed to yell.

"When? You're so damn busy all the time, when were you going to find the *days* you'd need to do it right? It took five professional landscapers all day to tear out that mess. Imagine how much time that would've taken you."

"That's not your problem. I didn't ask you to send a crew to my house! I can solve my own problems. I always have."

"You don't *need* to solve them alone anymore. Don't you get that? We're a team now."

"A team?" I laughed coldly. "We're not enough of a team for you to tell Oliver."

"Quinn," he said, gritting his teeth. "That's an entirely different conversation. I already told you we would talk first. Just... let me help you for Christ's sake!"

"This isn't *helping*!" My voice grew shrill in my tightening vocal cords. "This is... meddling, Theo."

"*Meddling?*" He scoffed. I hated it. "I can't talk to you like this. Calm down."

I didn't want to be this angry. I didn't want to scream at him. I couldn't stop it. My face was tingling, and I was seeing colors—it was some horrifying out-of-body experience. There was nowhere to put it all, so I exploded.

"Did you just seriously tell me to calm down? *Seriously?*"

"It's just a garden. Why is this turning into such a big deal?" He was on the verge of yelling. I'd never heard Theo yell before.

"It's not *just a garden.* You have no idea. And you shouldn't have messed with *my property.*"

"Well, it looks a hell of a lot better now, so I don't understand what the problem is." He exhaled deeply, getting hold of his anger. He rubbed the back of his neck, frustrated, and turned back to me. "It saved you time and didn't cost a penny. And now there's one less thing for you to worry about. Those are *good* things."

"I could've fixed it," I said again, but this time there were scalding tears in my eyes. "I am not a charity case, Theo! I *run* a charity for crying out loud. I'm so damn busy because I'm helping people. No one needs to help me. *I don't need handouts.*"

"It's not a handout," he said, through his gritted teeth. "Gary owed me a favor—"

"So now I'm a favor?"

"This is ridiculous," he said, growing louder with every sentence. "You know damn well that's not what I mean. I've spent this entire week trying—"

"Why couldn't you just leave this alone?"

"And why can't you just let me show you how I feel?" *There's the yelling.*

"You don't need to make some huge gesture." I'd lost my last ounce of patience and just plowed right over him. I didn't want to hear what he had to say anymore. I just wanted him to stop talking.

"Quinn, I—" He tried.

"You don't owe me anything, okay?"

"Just let me—" He tried louder.

"You ruined everything!"

"Listen to me—"

"Why couldn't you just mind your own business?" I shouted.

"BECAUSE I—"

"I DON'T NEED YOU TO SAVE ME, THEO. I'M NOT YOUR WIFE."

Horrified, I covered my mouth. The moment the words were out, I wanted to take them back. That was too far. The blood rushed from my head. My brain went numb. I'd fallen through the ice and I would drown, trapped in the freezing cold water. My pulse raced. My lungs constricted. I couldn't breathe.

Theo's spine straightened and his arms dropped to his sides, eyes fixed on mine—cold and distant. I reached for his hand and he moved it away. Silently, he turned on his heel and walked back to his car. His expressionless face terrified me.

"Wait," I called. I took a few steps after him. "Theo, stop. Please... I'm sorry, that's not... I don't know why I said that. I didn't.... please don't go."

Theo didn't answer. He didn't even seem to hear a word I said. I watched, sobbing, as he got into the car.

"Please wait," I cried, taking a few more steps toward him.

"I need to tell you som—"

He slammed the door. He slammed it so loud that I jumped. So loud that I was struck silent. There wasn't anything left to say. He was already gone the moment I said those horrible words. That wasn't him that I watched walk away. He was empty, lifeless. I wanted to run after him, to tell him everything so that he'd know... but it wouldn't make any difference now. He didn't deserve to be treated like that. And I didn't deserve the chance to apologize.

What have I done?

CHAPTER FORTY

I stayed in the garden for a long time, curled up on the marble bench that Dad had given Mom as a twentieth anniversary gift. It had been buried here for years, safely hidden in the weeds and overgrown hedges. Now it was exposed, and I needed to protect it.

I laid across it, holding the petunias I'd ripped from the ground. A pile of torn petals lay next to my phone on the grass. My clothes were dirty, my hands were caked in soil, and the bandage on my hand was loose and discolored. My body settled into the marble, seeping into the tiny cracks, solidifying me into this place. I couldn't think of a reason to get up. I'd missed a call from Faith an hour ago. I'd watched the screen, glowing beneath the bench, vibrating into the dirt. I ignored her texts. Then Shawn texted on his way home—looking for a takeout food order—and I couldn't find the strength to reach down and answer.

I wasn't hungry anyhow. The thought of food turned my stomach. Besides, I wouldn't need to eat anymore once I'd become marble. As a statue, I could watch everything in the garden grow back the way it had been before... before...

Theo.

My tears had created a little puddle on the marble. I wiped my palm across my cheek, leaving a streak of mud in place of the tears. He hadn't called. And he wouldn't call. Never, not *ever*. My chest felt tight and empty at the same time.

How did we get here? Things were going to be okay. We were going to figure it out. I would wait, and he'd be ready someday. And then just like that, it was over. He shouldn't have interfered, but I shouldn't have said what I did. As angry as I was, he didn't deserve *that*. Too much. Too far. And way beyond anything I could apologize for. There was nothing I could do to take it back. *I don't need your help, Theo. I'm not your wife.* I'd spoken—no, screamed—the words and still, I didn't know where they had come from.

Shawn's car pulled up, the door closed, and he gasped when he reached the walkway, where my empty bag sat tipped over. Its contents remained strewn about the yard, making a zig-zag trail to my new permanent location.

"Quinn?"

I couldn't answer, but I shuddered with a sob.

"What are you doing over there?" he asked, walking toward me. "What's wrong?"

I sniffled and dragged my hand across my nose.

When he reached me, he crouched down to get a better look. Possibly to check for signs of life.

"Are you okay?"

"No," I said, punctuated with another sob.

"Are you hurt?"

"No..." I paused. "Yes."

Shawn sat down on the grass and leaned on the bench. He held my hand and let me cry. He brushed the wet strands of hair from my face, then wiped away some of the dirt on the cuff of his shirtsleeve.

"Shawn," I finally said, my voice sounded tiny and distant. "He ruined it."

"Ruined what?"

"Everything. And now it's over and he's gone," I said, fighting another sob. "What do I do now?"

"What are you talking about?"

"They did everything. It's all done."

"You gotta give me more than that, Quinn. *What* is done?"

"The garden!" I sat up and gestured wildly around me. Shawn surveyed the yard, now bathed in moonlight, and then nodded.

"I think it looks great," he said. "Everything is where it was... except for the mangled petunias I'm sitting on... What's that about?"

I sniffled and dropped my head into my hands. Shawn handed me a tissue, probably from the packet that fell out of my purse. I blew my nose. He handed me another one.

"He sent landscapers," I said, defeated. "*Landscapers* came here and trampled around the yard, touching everything, yanking plants out of the ground, all over the place."

"Quinn… that's *awesome*," he said, pulling himself off the ground and sitting on the bench. "This whole thing was a death trap. I'm pretty sure there were raccoons living over there. If you stop and think about it, this is one of the coolest, most thoughtful gifts ever."

"No, it's not!" I was nearly back to yelling. "It's rude. He never asked me. He just sent them here, behind my back, while I was at the show. It's sneaky. And it's just *wrong.*"

"What's the real problem?" he asked. I stared at him blankly. "You're not mad about some weeds getting pulled up and the fence getting painted."

"Yes, I am. This was *Mom's* garden. They had no business coming here. This was *hers*. Mom would *never* have hired landscapers."

"Quinn," he said, taking my hand again. "Mom's not coming back."

"I *know* that, Shawn!" I pulled my hand away.

"But that's not how you're acting. You're not offended that Theo helped you."

"Then why am I still furious with him? I didn't *need* help! Theo just took it upon himself to *fix* Mom's garden," I tried not to start yelling again. "I'm tired of everyone stepping in to *help* me all the time. If I need help, I'll ask for it."

"Except that you don't. You never ask for help," Shawn said, handing me the last tissue. "And you're not angry at Theo. Sure, you're a little miffed that he did this without your knowledge, but that's because you're a control freak…"

He's not wrong.

"I know you've got this whole '*I help everyone; I don't need anyone to help me*' thing going on—but why are you pretending to be offended by it? That's not even remotely what you're angry about, and I think you know it."

I hadn't realized I was hanging on his words until he stopped talking. I sat up straighter and looked at him, just watching me.

Was he waiting for me to say something?

"What is it then?" I finally asked.

"You decided it was *your* job to fix Mom's garden years ago, even though no one ever asked you to," he replied. "For eight years, you said you'd take care of it. If you wanted to do it, then you would have—because Quinn Davis always finds a way. But it got out of hand and became this gigantic, insurmountable labyrinth... right?"

He paused, waiting until I nodded.

"And Theo swooped in and solved the problem. You're not angry with him—you feel guilty because someone took away one of your imaginary responsibilities. Now you've pushed him away and turned all of this," Shawn gestured all around us. "Into a reason to be furious."

At the sound of his name, my eyes started tearing up again. Especially now that Shawn was reframing it all, thinking about him hurt even more.

"I know you better than anyone else on earth," Shawn took my hand again. "And I think you need to hear this out loud: you didn't disappoint anyone."

Swallowing the lump in my throat, I nodded again.

"I think it's time to call Theo and apologize."

"I tried. He wouldn't answer," I sniffled. "I'm pretty sure he hates me now."

"He doesn't hate you..."

"Oh, he does, trust me."

"Just call again and apologize," he said indignantly. "You don't want to screw this up. You guys are crazy about each other, right? Even if you haven't introduced us yet..."

"I don't think you're gonna meet him."

"Why not?"

I gave Shawn a summary of why not.

"Oh," he said after a moment. "You're probably right."

"I don't know what to do now, Shawn," I said, my throat still tight, thick. "I ruined the best relationship of my life—I wanted to... I actually wanted to..."

Shawn waited silently while I found the words.

"I think I love him, Shawn." I put my head on my brother's

shoulder and he wrapped an arm around me, pulling me in. "And I destroyed him. If I were him, I'd never want to see me again."

The last words escaped between sobs. When I got enough of my breath back, I kept going.

"And Franklin is *dead* now and it's been too much for me to handle. I don't want to be home. I don't want to open the door to an empty hallway or see his leash hanging on the coat rack. I can't even look out to the backyard without getting punched in the gut. I don't know what to do.

"Then this week was like one big, long bad joke. I spaced on a board meeting, but the foundation went right on ahead without me. The hotel for the gala burned to the ground and Leah didn't need one ounce of my help."

"Leah is the CEO of the foundation, Quinn. She *doesn't* need your help. She is a saint of a woman who understands how much you love your dad and want to be a part of the foundation. She loves having you there, but she doesn't *need* you."

I paused for a moment to really hear those words. After the past few weeks, they seemed more accurate.

"And then I had a *horrible* dress rehearsal, which ended with me breaking the rain machine and flooding the stage. Faith is low-key pissed at me right now, and she should be. I let everything else mess with my head. I spent the whole week stressing out after Theo…"

"What?"

"After he…we… you don't want to know about that part of the story. All you need to know is, we were having trouble."

He made a face.

"The point is, I let everything else get in the way and I almost destroyed Faith's show. She has every right to be angry," I said, defeated. I held up my bandaged hand. "And I did both shows with first degree burns because of some stupid cupcakes, and I thought I would *die* from the pain—or liver poisoning, thanks to all the acetaminophen. Then I came home to this. And now… there's nothing left for me."

"What on earth are you talking about?"

"You and Charlie don't need me, Leah doesn't need me, Drama Cares is closed until camp starts, I killed my dog, and now

I destroyed my relationship. No one needs me anymore, there's no one for me to help…" I stopped for a moment, knowing that there was something else hiding deep down.

"You don't need all of that stuff to have value, Quinn," Shawn said firmly. Then his expression changed to something like compassion. "And because you don't see that, you've been heading toward self-destruction since Mom and Dad died."

"Self-destruction?"

"Oh yeah," he said. "I saw this coming from miles away."

"Then why didn't you—"

"Try to stop you? I did. Many times. But I realized that you were going to keep plowing ahead anyway, so I just had to be ready to catch you."

I stared at him in silence.

"Do you remember how Dad and Uncle Charlie used to call you the Energizer Bunny—because you just kept going and going, marching to the beat of your own drum?"

I nodded, swallowing hard.

"Imagine that bunny wearing a blindfold, riding on a steamroller with a full tank of gas, and an engine so loud, the bunny can't hear anyone above the noise…"

"I'm the bunny?" It would have been hilarious imagery under any other circumstance, but at that moment, it was heavy and uncomfortable.

"Yes, you're still the bunny," Shawn said sincerely. "And you've been rolling along with your blindfold on, ignoring everyone trying to get your attention."

"Everyone?"

"Me, Faith, Uncle Charlie… basically everyone who cares about you. Sometimes even Abby sees it."

I sniffled, wiped my eyes again.

"And now, here you are, out of gas. It's time to pay attention and deal with everything you've been steamrolling past. You've gotta stop running. You need to heal."

Deep inside me somewhere, I felt something crumble. My chest was tight, and I couldn't breathe. I felt dizzy, light-headed. And I wasn't sure if I was ever going to move off that bench. The one thing I truly longed for—more than anything I'd been seeking in those eight years—I couldn't have.

"I miss Mom and Dad. I can't do this. It's too much." My voice was raw. Everything hurt: my throat, my hand, my heart, even my hair. "What am I supposed to do now?"

Shawn stood up and pulled me to my feet, gathering me tightly in his arms. Like a limp dishtowel. I laid my head on his shoulder, leaving mascara and dirt on his shirt.

"Quinn Abigail Davis," he said softly, stroking my hair. "Welcome to rock bottom."

Sobs racked my body again and I nearly collapsed. Shawn held me up, even when my knees had buckled.

"Shhhhh... I promise, it's gonna be okay," he soothed. "Because now you can finally climb up."

Once he'd carried me inside the house, almost literally, Shawn jumped right into action. He turned on the shower, handed me towels, and left me alone. While I stood there, watching the dirty water circle the drain, he was buzzing around the house. He picked up everything from the lawn and put it back in the tote. He laid out my favorite pajamas on the end of my bed. Clean and a little calmer, I put them on and wandered into the kitchen, still feeling a bit woozy and disjointed from reality.

Shawn was standing at the counter with his back to the door, on the phone with someone. Faith?

"...not good, no. I know," he said quietly. "Yeah, she's okay. I got this one."

I coughed quietly to be polite. Shawn mumbled a goodbye and placed his phone on the counter. When he turned around, his expression was a weird mix of calm and concern—something that looked completely foreign on my brother's face. It suited him. He gestured for me to sit at the table, then placed a steaming bowl of soup in front of me.

"You need to eat something," he said, before I could object. "And you're probably dehydrated, so here."

Shawn handed me two bottles of water, then sat down next to me with the first aid kit.

"Let me see that hand." He carefully examined the burn,

applied the salve, and wrapped it securely. Finished, he put everything back in the kit and stood up. He gave me a look. "Good news is, you're not left-handed so you can eat that soup."

I did the best I could. Drank some water. Had enough soup to satisfy him. I didn't taste anything, and my throat still felt raw and dry. I forced a small, pathetic smile.

"In the morning, we're gonna have a chat," he said. "But for now, I want you to get some sleep. We can't work on getting you better if you haven't had a chance to rest. Okay?"

I nodded, still aware that talking could make me cry again. He took my good hand and got me back on my feet, walked me up the stairs, and into my bedroom.

"I promise you're gonna be alright," Shawn said, hugging me tightly. I wrapped my arms around his neck and just buried my face in his shoulder.

"I'm not," I said, my voice muffled in his shirt. "I can't."

"Shhh," he said, stroking my hair. Holding me there, he rocked slowly side to side, the way I'd watched Mom cradle Abby when she was a baby. *Mom.* "I'm here, okay?"

I sobbed again. *Mom.*

"Shawn," I said, as soon as I could manage. "I love you so much."

"I love you too, Quinnie."

Dad.

"Don't leave me, okay?"

"I won't," he said softly. Then he maneuvered me into my bed, tucking me in tightly, and laid on top of the covers and held me until I fell asleep.

CHAPTER FORTY-ONE

I slept for hours, cocooned in my sheets and blanket, too exhausted for dreams—or nightmares, thankfully. But all the same, I woke up alone and looked for Theo, as though he should be in my bed with me. If I hadn't said the most horrible thing ever, he might've been.

That thought wasn't a great way to start my day.

And I cried about it in the shower for a solid half-hour. All this time, my life had been building up momentum, speeding at full force toward this one horrible moment. The morning after I'd broken the heart of a man who was very nearly almost the love of my life. The worst day of my life had snowballed for eight years into something that I couldn't stop, and poor Theo had been a casualty—on the second worst day of my life.

If I'm being honest, it wasn't just Theo either. I'd jeopardized Faith's show. I'd missed the board meeting—whether I was needed or not was moot. I hadn't been there when I said I would. And I'd been *really* unfair to my brother. What else was going to unravel if I couldn't pull it together?

I stared at myself in the bathroom mirror for a long time. My eyes were puffy, outlined with dark circles of dried mascara, even after my shower. I hadn't looked at myself—or truly seen myself—in years. Every day, I'd used the same mirror to put on my makeup, dry my hair, brush my teeth, tweeze my eyebrows. Rush, rush, rush... get out the door. And I never looked.

That morning, I studied the real face of Quinn Davis. She had little lines forming in the corners of her eyes, a freckle I'd never noticed on her cheek, splotchy red marks from tears, and a slightly downturned mouth. Her eyes looked dull, sad. Her lips were pale. Her wet hair looked longer and darker than she remembered. Her nose looked like Mom's.

She looked broken. Me. I looked broken.

When I finally managed to drag my feet down the stairs, dressed in my coziest t-shirt and yoga pants, I found Shawn in the kitchen making pancakes. He handed me a steaming hot cup of coffee in my favorite t-rex mug, my daily vitamin, and a dose of acetaminophen.

"I'm guessing you've got a headache."

I paused, realizing that I did.

"Thanks," I said, popping all the pills with a sip of coffee. I burned my tongue and I knew it should hurt more than it did. I barely flinched.

"Sit," he said firmly, then placed a stack of blueberry pancakes in front of me. *Who is this guy?*

Unlike the night before, I was starving. I shoved several forkfuls into my mouth before I looked up to thank him.

Shawn was leaning against the counter with his arms crossed and his head tilted to one side. Dad would stand just like that when he had something important to say. He'd wait until he had your attention, and then give you some meaningful advice.

When I'd ignored the little stickers on the windshield for too long: *Quinn, oil changes aren't just a suggestion.* When I'd broken curfew for the third night in a row: *Trust is earned, Quinn. Always remember that.* When I'd suffered my first broken heart: *The heart will break but broken live on.*

Yes, Dad could quote Lord Byron at us. It was no wonder I ended up majoring in literature. And that morning, looking at Shawn and thinking about Theo, those words were in the back of my mind.

Although it was unlikely to involve poetry, Shawn's uncanny impression of Dad meant I was in for some serious chat time. *Dad Advice Mode* was no joke around here.

"After Mom and Dad..." he said after several quiet moments. "I didn't run away to Europe like you think I did."

Apparently, we were jumping right in.

"Sure, I went to Europe... and you could say I left quickly, but it wasn't the narrative you created for me. I left to take care of myself, not to escape my problems. At first, I thought I was running away, and I felt bad.

"I mean, during that first year, you just knew what to do, making these huge changes, carrying on the family legacy... You gave up *your life,* Quinn. It terrified me. I felt weak, confused, useless... You were doing things and I was just watching. You were always the one who had the answers. I felt like I was in your way, like I was this useless lump you kept tripping over."

I wanted to reassure him that he shouldn't feel that way. But he didn't pause long enough for me to collect the words.

"My depression scared the shit out of me... and I didn't know what to do. You didn't look depressed, and you convinced all the grief counselors you were fine. You told everyone that therapy would only waste your time. You had all these plans and goals and 'constructive' ways to channel your grief. Not a single person would've believed you were depressed for one second."

If I placed myself back into the body of *that* Quinn, I would've agreed with him. In this version of me, the *new* real version, it all sounded wrong.

"Meanwhile, I was drinking myself into oblivion, partying every night just to feel something—*anything*—and making really terrible choices. I knew I'd get myself in trouble if I didn't change my life. I needed space to think. A friend of mine, his parents owned a home in Spain that they would rent out. For years, he kept offering to let me stay there for free. It seemed like the right time to get myself away from here."

"From me?" I interrupted.

He shrugged. "Not exactly. I was escaping the pressure."

"Why didn't you tell me all this? You could've..."

"I tried. You weren't listening, Quinn. You've never really spent much time listening to me," he said, holding his palms out with a shrug. "What else can I say? It was easier to let you believe I was heading off on some whirlwind bender across the world. It *was* more believable, given my history, and honestly, I was embarrassed to talk about my mental health."

"You'd rather I thought you were abandoning me?"

"You didn't need me. You already thought I was some drunk, high loser with no hope of changing your opinion of me. If I could've gotten you to listen to my feelings, would that have improved anything? I was 25, scared, and really stupid. I didn't want you to think I couldn't handle it, so I left."

"You left me. Mom and Dad were gone. And you left."

"I know. I'm sorry," he said. "I never meant to run away. But if I'd told you the truth, you wouldn't have believed me."

I shook my head. He was probably right. I took another sip of coffee, which was much cooler now, and just considered how I'd let Shawn get so far away from me eight years ago.

"We were *both* 25, scared, and really stupid," I said, after a moment. "What did you do in Spain?"

"Nothing, at first. I spent a lot of time just sitting outside, existing. I was surrounded by trees and plants, sitting at the bottom of a mountain, just being. Just a person, being. It's cheesy, I know."

I shook my head. It wasn't.

"I tried to learn how to paint—bought all the supplies and watched these videos," he said, then paused to think. He snapped his fingers a couple times, trying to jog his memory. "That guy with the hair... what's his name?"

"Bob Ross?"

"Yeah, that guy. I was terrible."

"I'd love to see your work," I said, amused.

He shook his head, grimacing.

"After a couple weeks, I finally felt like I could get out and explore the country. I went to Barcelona, took short trips to Portugal, a weekend in Italy here and there... and I met some girls, made some new friends. I thought there had to be a way that I could hang on to that peacefulness *and* go back to partying. I wasn't ready and the whole thing was a mess."

"All that time you were on your own?"

"Mostly, though my buddy would come by for a few days every once in a while. It was his house, after all. And then there was this one girl..." he said, getting a little pink. "Estella. Gorgeous, long black hair, green eyes, this amazing body—oh my god, Quinn. She was perfect. And she used to do this one thing with her—"

"Shawn. Boundaries."

"Sorry. So, Estella stayed with me for a few days," he said, going starry-eyed again. "It was just this amazing, endless—"

"Keep it up. I'll tell you about my threesome in college."

"What? Quinn, come on!" He gagged.

"You started it."

"Wait... *you?* Are you serious?"

"Do you really want to know?"

He paused, staring at me, and decided to move on.

"Anyway, on this one night, possibly the best..."

I held up three fingers.

"Fine. The best experience of my young life. And I just... broke. I don't know what happened. One minute I was... very happy. And then, I was sobbing in her arms like a baby. I told her everything. My entire life story, literally every painful thing I could ever remember happening to me. And she just held me. You'd think it would be mortifying, but it wasn't at all."

I stared at him, not sure what to say. Or think.

"And then she said the most amazing thing to me," Shawn said wistfully. His eyes focused off into the distance, like he could see this woman across time and space. "*No es hasta que nos perdamos que nos empezamos a encontrar.* Not until we are lost, do we—"

"Begin to find ourselves," I finished the quote. "Thoreau? *Really?*"

He shrugged.

The words settled on me slowly. It wasn't the place I would've gone for a quote right now, and yet... it just made sense. I didn't need to go traipsing through the woods; I'd done a great job getting lost already.

"After that, stuff started making sense again. That was the bottom," he said, frankly. "I came home. Started going to therapy. Went to Uncle Charlie for a job. Stopped partying."

"How did I not know about any of this?" I sat motionless, staring at the wood grain of the table. I traced the swirls with my finger. In a way, not knowing why he left was so much worse than him leaving.

"You were lost. You couldn't see me," Shawn said, sitting down next to me. He took my hand. "And when I was lost, I couldn't see *you.* I don't know how we wandered so far apart, especially after Mom told us to stick together."

"Why didn't you *try?* If you found your way, why couldn't you tell me where to go?" His words were resting heavily on my heart and a new wave of tears formed behind my eyes.

"Quinn, I couldn't," he sighed. "You needed to fall before I could catch you. Would you have really stopped like this because Faith or I told you to? It took *a lot* of really raw emotion and quiet space and... Estella before I fell."

"Straight down into a pit?"

He nodded, squeezing my hand. "When you hit the bottom, you can start climbing up."

"Then what? Where am I supposed to go? What am I supposed to do?"

"I gotcha, kid," Shawn said with a wink. "We'll do it together."

In a well-coordinated changing of the guards, Faith and Abby showed up right around the time Shawn was leaving for work. Faith pulled me into a motherly hug—the tight squeeze, the backrub, and the sweet *shhhhh it's okay.* Abby hit Shawn up for their secret handshake, gave me a kiss on the cheek, and planted herself in her favorite seat on the couch.

"I know what you're doing," I told them all. The more I thought about it, though, the more I appreciated the effort. "You know I don't need a babysitter, right?"

"Quinn..." said Shawn, firmly. "If I find my sister face down in the dirt, covered in mud and tears, holding dead flowers, I'm not going to leave her alone—at least, not for a little while."

It was nice to have the company, so I couldn't complain. I told Faith I wasn't ready to talk about anything and she respected that, so we spent the evening hanging out like the whole thing never happened.

Many episodes of *Buffy the Vampire Slayer* later, which both impressed Abby with its general kick-assery and amused her with its painfully dated technology, I was feeling a little better. I wasn't ready to watch any scenes with Angel in them because a tragic love story wasn't something I could manage at the time. Faith is such a good friend that she fast-forwarded through all of David Boreanaz's scenes.

They stayed until Shawn came home, when I was half asleep

on the couch. He sat down next to me and pulled me into his arms. I'd avoided crying in front of Faith and Abby, but now that Shawn was back, the tears started all over again—silent, steady, and hot on my skin.

"You okay?" he asked, resting his chin on my head. I squeezed him extra hard.

"Mm-hmm," I answered. "As okay as can be expected."

"Here's the plan," he said, letting me go. "You get one more day to cry your eyeballs out if you want it. And then on Tuesday, we talk about how you're climbing out of your pit. But I need you to remember that this isn't another project to bury yourself in without actually confronting anything—"

"Not this time."

"Good," he said, smiling. He placed a fresh notebook and a pen in front of me. "You can, however, make as many lists as your heart desires to keep you on track and focused. Keep that notebook handy. It's now your official guide to cleaning up this mess."

"Shawn…" I said thoughtfully. "When your life explodes, which pieces do you pick up first?"

"I think the first thing is to *identify* your pieces, then decide which ones get picked up and which ones go into the trash bin."

"That's fair," I said with a frown. "Probably most of them are getting binned."

CHAPTER FORTY-TWO

In a bold move, I took the entire week off. From everything. No foundation, no bar, no animal shelter, no library, no senior center. Drama Cares was closed for two weeks, so that was expected, but it still felt weird not to have anywhere to rush off to. The anxiety I experienced from that was overwhelming, but I pushed through it.

Instead, I spent a lot of time staring at my blank agenda, doodling on the empty squares while I thought about where everything went wrong. I thought about why being alone was stressful, why free time scared me, why I could never do *this* before. I started a journal and wrote long, rambling entries about whatever popped into my mind. Many of them were focused on Theo.

I made many lists—all the things I'd set aside, the goals I'd abandoned, the hurts I'd caused, the things I needed to repair—and did absolutely nothing about it for days.

Then on Friday, spontaneously, I climbed the stairs and stood outside my parents' room. My heart raced as I turned the doorknob. It took several minutes of deep breathing before I could push open the door and even longer before I could step into the room.

Inside, everything was exactly the way Mom would've left it. The bed was made and there wasn't a thing out of place. The bureau and dresser were free of dust and the carpet was freshly vacuumed—everything was perfect, like a time capsule. Given how long it had been since I'd been inside their bedroom, I'd expected it to look like one of those old, abandoned houses with the cobwebs and dust everywhere. But it was pristine.

There was a note on the bed with my name on the envelope in Shawn's scrawling handwriting.

UNDER RENOVATION

Welcome back, Quinnie.

I'm proud of you for finally making it inside. Mom and Dad would be proud of you too. I've kept it clean for the day you'd be strong enough to come in. Even the sheets are clean and fresh, in case you want to take a nap. This is a great place to start climbing back up.

Stay in here as long as you need and come back here as often as you like. This room isn't a museum. It can be a refuge. Mom and Dad are here for you and so am I.

Love always, the best brother in the universe,
Shawn (duh)

I climbed into the bed and cried quiet tears into the pillows until I fell asleep. These tears, though, weren't the painful ones I'd cried for Theo. These tears were cathartic, cleansing, peaceful.

Finally, I was ready to talk. Faith and Abby came back with their nail salon supplies once again, which would quickly become a Saturday afternoon tradition. As usual, they barely trusted me to handle my own manicure and subtly took turns helping me—like I wouldn't notice or something.

"This is not an I-told-you-so, but if you didn't tell him about your mom and dad how was he supposed to know?" Faith asked, filing the nail of her left index finger. She'd been making her way through them all, taking great care to examine each nail from every angle and file it to a perfect shape.

Meanwhile, I was just scraping dirt out from under my nails and trimming the sharp edges.

"There was no way he could understand the magnitude of it. Although, to be fair, I don't think even *you* understood it," she continued.

"I know, I know," I sighed. "I knew it in the middle of our argument. But by then I was too riled up to do anything. I couldn't stop myself. It was like some out of body experience, where I was just watching myself do and say things without my permission. It was terrifying."

"Look, he loves you, Q," she said, as though this was a known fact.

"You don't know that."

She raised her eyebrows at me. Abby put down her nail file and gave me a pointed look. Like a mini version of her mother.

"Stop." I dropped my head into my hands. "This wasn't just a regular fight. Do I need to review what happened? I'd prefer to never, ever say those words out loud again."

"Yeah, I think that's best," Faith said with a grimace. "Still... people say things they don't mean all the time. People act out in anger and make horrible mistakes, and they're still forgiven for worse things than that. If he knew what led you to that, maybe—"

"I'm not *people*. Neither is he." I still couldn't say his name out loud. "I'm not exactly sure I *deserve* to be forgiven. Am I the only one who thinks this is the most horrific thing a person could ever say to him?"

"It was pretty bad, but it could've been worse," said Abby, eyes on her hands. She'd gone back to filing her uneven thumb nail.

"Are you telling her to do better?" Faith asked, amused.

"If Auntie Quinn *wanted* to hurt him, she could've done worse," she repeated, looking up. Her mother and I just stared at her. "That was *lashing out,* like a wounded animal or whatever. Do I really have to walk you through this?"

Abby sighed, then picked up her phone. She scrolled for a few seconds and showed me the screen. She'd pulled up a mental health website and an article on depression. *Depression?*

"I'm not a doctor, obvi, but... read it."

I was skeptical, but I took the phone and looked it over anyway. I read through the list of symptoms—it didn't sound like me. Little interest in doing things? If anything, I do *too many* things. Feeling helpless or hopeless? Nope. Loss of energy? Yeah, right. I'm everywhere, all the time. Sleep changes? I've had insomnia for years—well, only since Mom and Dad died. Maybe I should count that one.

But then the back half of the list caught my attention: concentration problems, self-loathing, anxiousness, irritability, anger... avoidance.

Oh.

All those pieces I'm supposed to be picking up? *I think the first piece is mental health.*

On Monday, I decided it was time to resume as much of my routine as I could manage. I spent the morning gathering information on therapists, talked with my general practitioner, and made my first appointment. Maybe I should've listened to the grief counselors I'd pushed away, way back when, but I was ready to take it seriously now.

Then I stopped in at the bar—it felt good to be out driving around again. I gave Charlie the biggest hug I could, without fearing for his safety, and he just held me and patted me on the back.

"Got news for you, sweetheart," he said with a kind smile. He set a Shirley Temple on top of a cocktail napkin—with the bar logo on it. *Okay, that's cool.* "Have a seat."

"Oh hey, Quinn," Shawn said, appearing from the back room. "Charlie, did you fill her in?"

"'Bout to now."

"I hate when you do this, you two. What's up?" I said playfully. Shawn snuck behind Charlie and poured a splash of Grey Goose into it, giving me a wink. I plopped into my favorite stool and stirred the tiny straw in my drink. For the first time in a long time, I didn't feel anxious about getting news.

"Bought the building next door," Charlie said, beaming. "Shawn's turning this place into a restaurant."

"Oh wow! That's awesome, guys!" I pretended not to know this had been in the works. I was glad to know Shawn had closed the deal, but I didn't want to take anything away from Charlie's announcement.

"Really?" My uncle sounded suspicious. I couldn't blame him—this kind of news would've knocked me off the bar stool not so long ago. "We want you to be involved as much as you like, of course. Not tryin' to cut you out, kiddo."

"It's great, really. I'll help where you need me, but honestly," I said, looking at my brother. *Because piece number two is trust.* "I think Shawn can handle this one."

Of course, on Tuesday morning, I cruised into the foundation with my regular tower of coffee trays and *extra* baked goods. I did my usual good morning lap around the office until I finally arrived in the break room, where Leah was waiting for me, tapping her nails on the table.

"When you took your impromptu vacation last week—proud of you, by the way," Leah said, taking her coffee from my hand. "I thought we were making progress on your Quinn-saves-the-world campaign. You gotta stop."

"I am," I grinned, sitting down in the chair across from her. I slid the bag of scones across the table for her to help herself. No need to create my elaborate scone display that day. "This is my last Tuesday."

"No more coffee on Tuesdays? You promise?"

"No more *Tuesdays,* unless you need me," I said, fishing a blueberry scone from the bag. Leah passed me a napkin. "And none of the *of course we need you, Quinn* stuff anymore. You need me, I'm here. But everything I do belongs under *your* job description. And I'm sure that's frustrating."

"Quinn..." she said, dumbfounded. "That's not..."

"You're *the best*, Leah. You don't need me in your way."

"You're not—"

I frowned.

"Okay," she said, leaning back in her chair. "Are you sure?"

"Look, as long as you don't feel like I'm dumping everything on you and running away—"

"I don't."

"Then I'm ready to hand it all over," I said with a smile. *Is this relief?* Shawn had said it would feel good to let some things go. He wasn't kidding.

Back in my office, I sat in my big cozy office chair and just looked around. At everything. At the *stuff* I'd surrounded myself with while I was hiding. Stepping back from the foundation did not mean that I was leaving Dad's work behind or abandoning Mara's cause.

It meant that I wouldn't be hiding anymore, that I would allow myself the room to do what I wanted with my life, to pursue the goals I'd abandoned. No one could take away my name or what I represented to the foundation—and yeah, I was still necessary for events, official appearances, and quarterly board meetings—so I wasn't *leaving*.

Leah and I decided that I would slowly let go of some of the tasks I'd taken on for myself. We planned on a different schedule for the summer—just to transition things over, of course. The summer was the perfect time to clean out some space for myself. *And that's piece number three.*

CHAPTER FORTY-THREE

For the first time in eight years, Shawn and I hosted a Fourth of July cookout in our backyard. It had been a long-standing Davis family tradition before the accident, one of my favorites. I'd missed it.

Even with all the self-care I'd been doing, it was still hard for me to spend time in the front yard and garden. The backyard, though, had never been lost to my sentimentalism. Shawn had been doing a good job of upkeep for a while, so there was no jungle to tear down back there and no powerful feelings to confront.

With the bar closed for renovation, Shawn and Charlie could be with us at the same time. I couldn't remember the last time I'd seen them together outside of the bar.

"Now that you're hiring a real staff," I said, nudging Shawn. We were standing together over the grill, him cooking and me assisting... but mostly just eating pickles directly from the jar. Shawn leaned over and opened his mouth. I shoved a pickle in it. "Maybe you and Charlie could have time off together once in a while, instead of just trading off."

"That'd be nice," Shawn said, his mouth full. He flipped some of the burgers over and placed cheese slices on the finished patties. After he finished eating, he continued. "But the Davises are control freaks, so I'll need someone I *really* trust before I'll leave it."

"When you're ready to confront your control issues, you just let me know."

"A couple sessions of therapy and she's an expert?" he laughed, sliding the burgers onto the tray.

I brought them over to the picnic table, decorated in patriotic colors and covered in too much food. I looked around me, content to be outdoors in the gorgeous summer weather, and happy to be surrounded by people I love.

Faith and Abby came outside with a pitcher of lemonade and a stack of empty glasses. Abby brought a full glass over to Uncle Shawn, who handed her the tongs and put her to work rotating hot dogs. Faith elbowed me, hard, when she realized that Uncle Charlie had cornered Roy under the pretense of casual conversation. Uncle Charlie wasn't much of a talker... until you got him to relax. Fortunately, from the look on his face, Roy seemed to enjoy Charlie's story time.

"I think he's okay," I said with a laugh. "In fact, Roy's been encouraging it. He keeps asking questions to keep him going."

"Yeah... he wants to be a therapist, Q."

"So, let the man practice." I poured myself a lemonade and sat down on the bench. "I didn't realize you and Roy were at the meeting-family stage yet."

"It's been a couple months," she said, thoughtfully. She shrugged and sat next to me, picking grapes from the fruit salad. "Plus, he already knew half of you."

"I don't know, bringing a guy home to meet Shawn is a big deal..."

"Sure..." she laughed.

"Faith," I said carefully. "I'm sorry I haven't been a good friend through this whole... thing. I should've been paying more attention—"

"Yeah, you haven't asked for *any* juicy details..." Faith said, scooping potato salad onto a plate. I noticed she was making a second plate, which I knew was *not* for Abby. My niece loathes potato salad. And that meant... *Aww, Faith.*

"You like him, don't you?" I grinned. "You like, *like* him, like him..."

"Shut up," she scoffed.

"Maybe he'll ask you to prom..."

She rolled her eyes at me.

"Hey," I said, as an idea struck me. "Do you want to come to the gala with us this year? I know you normally sit them out, but if you and Roy want—"

"Oh, that would be awesome!" she said, genuinely excited.

I paused, tilting my head. I'd expected more of a battle. "Really?"

"It sounds fun. You, Shawn, me, and Roy... open bar, formal attire?"

I nodded. "Who doesn't love getting dressed up to get hammered for free?"

Suddenly, Faith put down the spoon and hugged me. "I've missed you, Q."

Piece four? Rebuilding relationships.

Summer camp started that Monday and it was nice to see Oliver every day, even if Theo was nowhere to be found. Lisa had taken over the drop offs and pickups for the summer, as I'd expected. She said it made more sense because summer camp hours were during the day and Theo's schedule didn't line up. And I'm sure that was at least part of it...

The first day had been rough though. Oliver had run right for me, flinging his arms around my waist with such gusto that I nearly fell over. I caught him in my arms and gave him a good hug.

"Hi, sweetie," I said. "How are you?"

"I'm okay," he said, frowning. As much as I'd missed him, I had been dreading what would happen next. The questions. "But I missed you a whole lot. I kept asking Dad if you could come over."

"Oh." *Yup, that hurt. And I'm sure it had hurt his dad too.* But now, I needed to take a cue from Theo, so my story lined up. "What did he say?"

"He told me you were busy getting ready for summer camp, so you said you couldn't visit anymore." Oliver looked totally crestfallen. "Does that mean you're not going to come over again for dinner?"

"You just want more chocolate chip cookies, don't you?" I tried so, so hard to laugh. My weak grin earned a little smile in response, but we were both hurting too much. And Oliver had no idea why.

"I'll tell him you want to come over, okay?"

"I don't think you should, Oliver." I didn't know where to go from there, but Faith came to the rescue.

"Time to play some games!" she said, ushering Oliver to the stage. She turned back to me, concerned. I shrugged. "Go take a minute, okay?"

I wandered into the workshop where I could be alone, but quickly realized it was a mistake. I hadn't been here since the Saturday matinee—the last time I'd seen Theo with a smile on his face.

I should've just stabbed myself in the heart with a flathead screwdriver. It might've hurt less.

Over the next two weeks, however, Oliver and I settled into the new dynamic between us. In a lot of ways, we went right back to the way things were before I'd ever met his dad. And as long as he steered clear of the uncomfortable questions, everything was just fine.

On the other hand, Faith seemed to always have an eye on me. To be fair, I *was* spending more time at drama camp this summer. Normally, I would've only been at camp for two or three days a week. Five days a week of Counselor Quinn was kind of weird for her, I guess.

"Were you planning to be at camp *every* day?" she said after pick-up time one day. "Because you're spending an awful lot of your time here…"

"I'm a volunteer," I said, hands on my hips. "And I am voluntarily coming in every day. What else do I have going on?"

"That's the problem. I just need to make sure you're not…" she trailed off.

"Hiding at drama camp and avoiding the rest of my life again?" I interjected. She hesitated, then nodded. "Allie and I covered that in my last therapy session, don't worry. I *like* being here, so as far as I'm concerned, being at drama camp all day is part of my treatment plan."

Because piece five is joy.

"Good enough for me," she said with a shrug.

STEPHANIE HADDAD

CHAPTER FORTY-FOUR

On Wednesday afternoon, as promised, I headed to the bar to help the guys run interviews for the new staff. I'd come straight from the quarterly board meeting at the foundation, so I was still wearing my skirt suit and heels with my hair in a neat bun. Normally, I'd change out of these clothes into something more practical for working at the bar, but Shawn had asked me not to.

He felt my attire would help separate the serious candidates from the rest of the group.

"You're intimidating when you're dressed like that," he'd said the night before. "I just don't want to hire any idiots who want to goof around all the time. If they think there's a scary lady in charge…"

"*You* could wear a suit," I'd said.

"Sure, but I'm the cool boss. If I start walking around in a suit, they're going to think I'm horrible to work for."

"I just don't think you should deceive people like that," I'd laughed. He'd thrown an olive at me. I'd batted it away. "And I'm not *scary.*"

I'd turned to Uncle Charlie, reading a newspaper at the other end of the bar, pretending to ignore us. He'd looked up at me and shrugged.

So, there I was the next day, trying to be scary enough to keep my brother and uncle happy and frighten off any candidates with a fear of petite women in business attire and heels. My brother's logic wasn't strong, but at least I didn't have to change clothes. I snuck in through the back door to drop my stuff in the office and grab the folder of applications from the desk. I still had twenty minutes until the first interview candidate would arrive. I could hear Charlie's and Shawn's voices in the bar—maybe I could convince one of them to make me a cocktail…

And then Charlie came around the corner from the fridge.

"Hey Uncle Charlie," I said, puzzled. He greeted me with a kiss on the cheek. *If he's back here...* "Who's out there talking to Shawn?"

"Guy from the construction company came by about the renovation."

"Is he gonna be gone before the interviews?"

Charlie shrugged. "Better ask your brother. No one tells me anythin' anymore."

Curious, I pushed the door open and took one step through it before I froze. The blood drained from my face. Because I recognized that other voice, just a split second before I saw him. I'd know it anywhere.

Theo.

"This is where your support beams are, but we'll knock down this part of the wall here and expand into the space," he was telling Shawn, who had spotted me out of the corner of his eye. I knew this because he crossed his arms and a smug smile stretched across his face. *So damn proud of himself.*

The door hadn't even swung closed when I turned right back around and walked out.

"Oh, hey! Come back here!" Shawn called after me. "Hang on, Theo, I need to talk to my sister."

Aww come on, Shawn.

"Come out here, Quinn," said my traitorous brother.

I could only imagine the look of horror on my ex-boyfriend's face. *Ex. Ex-boyfriend. That hurt.* It probably resembled the horror on my own face. I started planning Shawn's brutal murder. At that moment, I assessed that I had two choices.

One, completely bail on my promise to Shawn and Charlie. Just run away and ditch the interviews. That didn't feel right. But if I saw Theo and he looked happy, that would hurt. And if he looked miserable? That would hurt even more because I'd know I caused it.

Two, go out there and get it over with. It wasn't like I could hide from Theo forever; we were going to bump into each other eventually. Just suck it up. Plus, I missed him. If I were completely honest with myself, I would do just about anything to be near him again. Even though it was going to hurt to see him. *I am a glutton for punishment.*

I took a deep breath, wiped my sweaty palms on the sides of my skirt, and relaxed my facial muscles to wipe the slate clean. Clutching tightly to my paperwork, I pushed the door open again and stepped out into the bar.

For a moment, he was the only thing I saw. Everything just as I remembered it—the dark hair I'd run my fingers through so many times; the eyebrow he raised when I amused him; those lips, soft and tender, that I longed for every day. Jeans, trainers, the collared shirt with the rolled-up sleeves—the pale green one I really liked. He had a heavy clipboard under his arm with a neat stack of papers clipped to it, held a rolled blueprint in his hand, and wore a number 2 pencil tucked behind his ear.

I'd never seen Theo at work. He'd always been in the context of *my* world. I'd seen this man paint, drill, build things, move things, hug his child, and blush a bright shade of crimson just talking to me. He'd played with my hair, comforted me in my grief, and touched every inch of my body. I'd watched this man sleep, laugh at a bad joke, cook, clean, and cover a goal. I'd kissed him, caressed him, cared for his injury, and held him while he cried. Yes, I'd even seen him naked.

And yet, Theo had never looked hotter than right then—with a fricking pencil behind his ear.

"Quinn, this is Theo Miller," Shawn said, giving me a pointed look. "He's going to be working with us on the renovations. And Theo, this is my sister Quinn Davis."

"We've met," Theo said emotionlessly, his cold stare fixed on me.

"Oh, how weird... Well, then, you'll be fine while I head to the backroom for an indeterminate amount of time to do... something," he said, with a shrug and a stupid grin. "Quinn, I left you a gift on the bar."

Liquid bribery. That jerk.

And then Shawn disappeared, and I was completely alone with Theo. It took every single fiber of my being not to run to him.

I opened my mouth to talk and quickly snapped it closed. I

pushed through the half door and stepped behind the counter. I tried not to look at him while I spread out the applications on the counter to prepare for the interviews. Maybe we could just coexist in this space until Shawn got back. *If I just keep my mouth shut, I can't make it worse.*

"Did you do this?"

The sound was abrupt, his voice gruff. It startled me.

"What?"

"Did you do this?" he asked again, louder. "Did you set this up?"

"Set what up? I have no idea what you're doing here," I said, frazzled. "I've got nothing to do with the renovation."

"Why do I find this hard to believe?"

"Look," I said, firmly. "I don't work here anymore. I promised to help interview job applicants—that's it. I had no idea anyone else would be here today."

"Someone recommended me to your brother and here I am. *Was it you?*"

I stared at him in disbelief. His face was stone. His tone was cold. A flashback to that horrible night. I wished I'd run far away from the bar when I'd had the chance. Screw the interviews.

"No, it wasn't," I said, growing irritated. The last thing I needed was to have another argument and say another horrible thing. "But why would you even show up? It's not like you've never heard of Shawn Davis in your life. But here you are."

"I don't get to choose where I go…" He hesitated. He didn't want to say my name. I didn't want to hear him say it anyhow. "My company signs a contract and sends me where I'm needed. Your brother claimed someone recommended me. There's not a whole lot I can do about it."

"I didn't tell him to do this, I swear. I wouldn't." *Because this is exactly as awful as I would've thought it would be.*

"There are a lot of things I'd thought you wouldn't do, but I've been wrong before."

Ouch.

And that's when I sort of lost the ability to filter my own speech. Someone helped Shawn set this up—if I know anything about her, I'd bet it was Faith—to give me a chance to say something. Anything.

"Theo…" I said suddenly. His back stiffened at the sound of his name on my lips. I hadn't said his name in weeks—it stung. "I'm sorry. If I could take it back, I—"

He held up a finger. I stopped.

"Don't."

"Please just give me a second to—"

"No."

I leaned forward on the bar, head in my hands.

"I screwed up and I—"

"Yeah, you did."

"But I just want to explain what—"

"I honestly don't give a damn about your explanation."

"Oh."

"Listen," he said coldly. "Because I am a professional, I will treat this job like any other. I will finish it on time, under budget, and without a single nail out of place. I will deal directly with Shawn, *my client*, and treat him with the same respect as anyone else. You'll get your Uncle's dream restaurant, exactly the way you want it to look. *I can do that.* But it would be better for all of us if you just stayed out of my way while I'm working."

"I—"

His icy stare stopped me. I didn't dare say another word.

"I'm going to go now," he said flatly. "I'm sure we can both live our lives without seeing each other."

I nodded, too afraid to speak in case I cried. My throat was tight. I wanted to punch something. At the door, he stopped and turned back to me.

"You know," he spoke quietly. "If Oliver didn't love you so damn much, I'd pull him out of the program. Especially now that it seems Faith wants to meddle in my personal life."

And then he went through the door, out of sight. I downed the entire gin and tonic Shawn had left for me and dropped my head onto the counter.

Shawn came out a few minutes later and found me like that. I lifted my head and held out my empty glass.

"So that went well?"

I flipped him off.

"I'm really not interested in hearing about how you and Faith decided this was a good idea," I said coldly. "Yes, I know she was involved. *He does too.* I'm not an idiot."

Shawn didn't speak—which was wise of him. Instead he handed me another drink, a double this time, and then added the ice cubes as an afterthought. I heard him inhale like he was going to say something.

"Don't, okay? Don't apologize. Just don't try something like that again."

"That's fair."

"And please warn me when he's going to be here—I need to stay out of the way."

He nodded, looking a little bit guilty.

I'm not proud of it, but I drank the second glass in its entirety before my first interview even walked through the door. *This is fun.*

It wasn't until after I'd finished every interview and checked my agenda that I realized the date. The gold letters flashed in my memory. *Theodore & Jane Miller. July 15th*

Their ninth anniversary.

The next morning, I had some choice words for my best friend. I wouldn't call it *rage* but I certainly wasn't happy with her.

"I can't believe you did that," I said, exasperated. She handed me the coffee she'd brought me—after I texted her with a demand. She owed me. "What if he pulls Oliver from camp?"

"Do you think he would?"

I shrugged. "Do you wanna find out?"

"I'm sorry, okay? I didn't think it would go *that* badly."

"Let me reiterate," I said, stabbing the orange straw into the plastic lid of my iced coffee. "We did not just have a *disagreement.* This was not just some *argument.* It wasn't even three fair rounds in the ring. What I did was absolutely inexcusable."

"I thought, if he just saw you again, that maybe…"

"You've got your answer." I took a very long sip of iced coffee and felt the cold hit right between my eyes. Freeze headache. Ugh.

"I'm sorry, Q," she sighed. "Maybe it just hasn't been long enough."

I groaned, throwing my head back. "It's not healthy for me to keep dwelling on this. I know you just want to help, and that you think I can have my happy ending—but that's not possible."

"For now."

"Stop, okay? Just… please." I could feel hot tears forming. "It still hurts. And I don't want to lose Oliver too, okay? Just leave him… Theo alone."

Piece six, forgiving myself, was going to take a little longer.

CHAPTER FORTY-FIVE

Somehow, I'd survived most of July without another huge meltdown. There were speed bumps, but on tough days, I'd open my notebook and look at what I'd accomplished. I journaled my thoughts nearly every day to stay on track. I wasn't *done* and I had a lot of emotional stuff to deal with in therapy, but it was such a relief make progress.

It also helped that I never stopped thinking about Theo. I knew no amount of self-improvement could erase those horrible words. I also knew I was picking up all the pieces for me, not someone else, and that this couldn't be some hopeful ploy to get him back. He served as a constant reminder of *why* I needed to move forward. Next time I got that close to the best thing that ever happened to me, I wouldn't sabotage it.

Meanwhile, it took almost all month just to break my habit of looking for Theo's car at pickup and drop-off times. Until one morning, when it showed up again and my heart leapt into my throat. He pulled up. Oliver hopped out and tackled me with a hug. Theo drove away.

Then my brain picked out a memory from that dinner with Lisa and Henry—*I feel a lot better about us going away this summer, knowing you'll be here for them.* Theo's parents were away for three weeks, so he'd be the one bringing Oliver to and from camp every day. Twice a day for five straight days, over three consecutive weeks. That's thirty times. Well, make it twenty-nine, now. I'd longed to see him, but seeing him like *this*, with that cold and humorless expression, was like being stabbed with that screwdriver. I wasn't ready to be ignored every single day.

This sucks.

"Miss Quinn," Oliver said at pick-up. His face pinched

together. "Why aren't you friends with my dad anymore?"

"Oh, Oliver, I—"

"Cuz he said I should be ready to get in the car quickly. I asked him if he wanted to get out to say hi to you, but..."

"It's okay, buddy," I said quietly. "Sometimes people stop being friends."

"But I still want you to be friends. I think I can help..."

No, no, no. This is duplicitous.

"If your dad wants to be friends again, he'll let me know. You don't need to worry about us."

Us.

Once again... this sucks.

I decided to move on to piece seven—achieving my goals. This was, of course, the reason I was rebuilding my mental health and taking space for myself. I was making the room to move forward with the goals I'd abandoned. Or new goals, as Allie had pointed out. But I knew what I needed to do, because I'd regretted not doing it every day for eight years.

I wanted to teach.

I already knew the steps I needed to take, because I'd done all that grunt work nearly a decade ago. I got to work right away. I had a bachelor's degree in English & Literature, but I still needed a teaching license, so I registered for the exam later in the year. In the meantime, I could be a substitute, so I made an appointment with the principal of the high school and applied.

Finally, I reenrolled in school to finish my master's in Education. When I dropped out eight years ago, I'd been more than halfway through the program. Those credits were still sitting there, waiting for me to return for them. I was finally ready.

When I made it to the last week that Theo was doing pick-ups and drop-offs, and I was proud of myself for keeping it together. I'd created a calendar to check off every day that I survived seeing him. It helped me stay focused. Soon, I stopped feeling the cold panic when I saw his car. I almost mastered the art of pretending Theo wasn't there—although I knew I'd never truly be able to ignore the *very nearly almost* love of my life.

We'd be back to friendly visits from Lisa Miller on Monday. I wasn't sure how much she knew about what happened between her son and me. If she knew, she never showed it. Faith thought she might be my secret ally.

"I bet if you told her," she said to me after one pick-up. "That she'd tell Theo to call you. That woman adores you."

"Yeah... but if she knew what I said, I don't think she'd adore me anymore."

Faith shrugged, unconvinced.

"Q, people in the middle of a nervous breakdown will do and say awful things... he might understand. I guarantee you—if you tell Theo *everything,* he'll forgive you. He has no idea what you were going through. It could change his mind."

"Even if you're right," I replied, growing frustrated. "How would I get his attention? Print a t-shirt? Buy a billboard somewhere? Spray paint the bar counter? And then let's say one of those things works—getting him to listen to *everything* would be impossible. I couldn't even get two words in before he shut me down. It was awful."

"Okay, fair point," she admitted, and then lightened up on me for a bit.

That Thursday morning at camp, I started the day by rehearsing our big group dance number. After the tap dancing in *Singin' in the Rain,* which had been a tad ambitious, I brought us back to simpler jazz squares and step-touches.

Between run-throughs, I gave the kids a ten-minute snack and bathroom break. Little voices calling *Thank you, ten,* always amused me. I grabbed a water from the cooler and sat next to Faith, who'd been having her own stressful day. Abby's dad was in town, causing problems again, and she needed to punch things.

"How're you holding up?" I said quietly. "Do you want to go down to the gym and hit the bag around?"

"Not yet," she sighed. "I'm getting a headache, but I'll live. I've dealt with him before."

Just behind her, Oliver came skipping down the aisle, humming to himself, and caught his foot on someone's backpack strap. I saw it all happen in slow motion, and sprang to my feet, tossing my open water bottle as I ran for him. He careened forward and landed on his outstretched hands before I could get there. He curled up on the floor, sobbing hysterically, clutching his arm to his chest.

"Miss Quinn! Help!" he cried over and over. The other kids meandering around the auditorium froze. All heads turned toward him, lying on the floor, where I was already kneeling at his side.

"Easy, Ollie, easy. Can you sit up?"

He winced, trying to push himself up, but couldn't put any weight on his right wrist. I scooped him up and placed him in a chair in the back row, close to the exit door. I hoped it was just a sprain, but it was already swelling. Oliver clutched his wrist to his chest and blocked me from touching it.

Faith arrived with the first aid kit and tossed me an ice pack. I cracked it to activate the chemicals and shook it around until the whole thing was cold. Oliver's face pinched together when I placed it on his arm, but he didn't fight. Faith cared for his scraped knee with antiseptic and bandages, then took over for me holding the ice on his wrist.

"Ollie, sweetie, I'll be right back." I pulled my cell phone out of my pocket and walked toward the exit. "Abby, Will, could you please bring the kids into the cafeteria for a big game of Zoom?"

Abby nodded and started waving her arms around to herd the kids toward Will and out the door.

I called Theo, and it rang in my ear as I exited the theater into the foyer. The sound of the raindrops pounding on the pavement outside echoed loudly within the space. My heart raced to their beat.

The call went to voicemail. *Damn.* I didn't want him to hear this on a voicemail.

"Theo, it's Quinn. *Oliver is okay.* He tripped and landed hard on his wrist, so I'm bringing him to urgent care for an x-ray. I'm going with him in the ambulance, just meet us there."

After I texted Theo the address, I called 911. Legally, whenever a child was injured badly enough, we had to call an ambulance unless a parent came to collect them. Driving them ourselves was a liability and since I wasn't Theo's *anything* anymore, that meant I was also nothing more than Oliver's teacher. I gave the dispatcher our address and ran back inside, where Oliver's face remained twisted in pain. His cheeks were damp from a new stream of tears.

Faith stood up and followed me to a corner of the auditorium where we could speak quietly. She handed me the consent forms I'd need to accompany Oliver to the hospital.

"Ambulance is on the way," I said, as calmly as I could. "I'll go with him to get the x-ray."

"Poor little guy. It looks bad."

"I called Theo, but he didn't answer. I hope it's not because it was me who called."

"He knows Oliver is here, he'd pick up no matter who called," she said. True. "I'm sure he'll get the message."

"Can you call again anyway?"

"Sure," she answered. "Should I try Lisa?"

"They're not back until this weekend, so we need to find Theo."

Faith nodded, then grabbed my arm.

"Are you sure you're okay to go? I know you don't want to see him right now."

"Of course," I answered. *Oliver needs me.* "This isn't about me. I can handle it."

"Good girl." She gestured toward the door. "Go meet the ambulance out front. The kids and I can manage the rest of the day without you."

"Come on, sweetie," I walked over and helped him up, so he could keep the ice pack on his arm. I leaned down close to whisper in his ear. "You're being so brave. I'm gonna stay right by your side, okay?"

The ambulance arrived just as we made it to the door and the EMTs got Oliver up and into the back within minutes. Strapped into the gurney, Oliver started crying again. He was scared. The paramedic had removed the ice pack to examine his wrist, and it was too much for the little guy. With his good arm, he reached out for me and grabbed my hand.

"Where's Daddy?" he asked, sniffling. The paramedic handed me a ball of tissues and I wiped away Oliver's tears and helped him blow his nose. "Please find my daddy, Miss Quinn. I want *Daddy.*"

I scooted as close to him as I could get and stroked his hair, speaking soothingly to him.

"He'll be here soon, Ollie. Shhhh. I've got you."

At the hospital, I handed the emergency consent forms to the triage nurse, explained the situation, and told her we couldn't reach his dad. I kept my voice down so Oliver wouldn't hear and pushed aside my worries about Theo—a problem for Future Quinn. The nurse promised to call him and allowed me into the ER with Oliver.

Still sobbing quietly, Oliver had finally been given pain meds and a cot in the ER. We watched cartoons on the TV while we waited for the doctor. I checked my phone. Four texts from Faith, saying she couldn't get him on the phone. The last message was from twenty minutes ago. I replied.

> In the ER, Ollie's okay. Waiting for an x-ray. Any update?
>
> Still no answer. Tried Lisa to see if she could help us find him
>
> Maybe she can track him down
>
> Any idea where he might be?

Suddenly, I realized I knew exactly where Theo should be—with Shawn. I texted him next, telling him to have Theo call me immediately. But his response was just as disheartening.

> He's not here today, said he was wrapping up another job
>
> Is there anyone else there who can help find him?
>
> Just the electrician today—only contact he has is his cell

Of course. *Shit.*

As a last resort, I checked in with Lisa. She'd called his office and they said Theo was on an outdoor jobsite, so there wasn't a business line to call. They'd promised to try tracking him down. Now, we were both growing concerned with every text message. I was running out of options and officially worried about the *other* Miller—imagining him dead in a ditch on some jobsite somewhere. Theo *always* had his phone. He *always* answered. Especially if he was separated from Oliver, he was going to answer his damn phone. I just crossed my fingers that we'd find him before Oliver got upset again.

After a painful exam and x-ray, Oliver was diagnosed with a distal radius fracture, the most common type of broken wrist and usually the easiest to treat. The doctor was optimistic that a simple cast would do the job. At least I wouldn't need to explain to Theo that his son was having emergency surgery.

I snuck a quick look at my phone. Still nothing from Theo. *Not good.*

I sat on the cot and held Oliver close while the nurse set the bone and wrapped his wrist and forearm in a blue cast. The poor little guy was on lots of mild painkillers, so he handled it okay.

"Almost done," the nurse said happily. "You're doing so great!"

"Oh, my goodness, I'm so proud of you, Ollie," I said, squeezing him to me.

When it was all over, we waited for Theo to arrive and discharge him. Camp would be ending soon, which meant Theo should *at least* be on his way to the high school. If his phone were lost or the battery dead or something, Faith could send him here.

Oliver hadn't asked for Theo in a while, distracted by the novelty of his cast. Of course, if I didn't keep him occupied, he was going to start asking for daddy and getting upset. Struck by an idea, I rifled around in my tote bag for the perfect thing.

"Okay, Ollie," I said, leaning back onto the pillow. I put one arm around Oliver and held the book in the other. "I'm going to read you my favorite book. It's called *The Hobbit* and it's got dwarves and elves and monsters and magic in it."

"Oooh!"

"Ready?"

He nodded, snuggled up with me, and rested his head on my shoulder. I cleared my throat.

"In a hole in the ground there lived a hobbit. Not a nasty, dirty, wet hole, filled with the ends of worms and an oozy smell, nor yet a dry, bare, sandy hole with nothing in it to sit down on or to eat: it was a hobbit-hole, and that means comfort."

Oliver desperately needed to sleep, his eyelids falling to half-mast, but he fought to stay awake and listen to the story. He yawned several times before I'd finished chapter two. By then, my eyes were tired too.

"Miss Quinn," he said sweetly. "You're the best."

I squeezed him gently. His eyes closed and he drifted off to sleep in my arms, finally. I watched his little chest rise and fall with his breath, until I heard Theo's voice.

"Excuse me, can you help me find my son?" he said, frantically. I sat up straighter and my skin tingled. The sudden effect on me was hard to ignore. "Oliver Miller. Where is he?"

Someone replied but I couldn't hear them.

"Here? This way? Thank you so much." Hurried footsteps echoed down the hall, growing louder, until finally Theo appeared in the doorway. He was panicked, out of breath. But when he spotted his son, the relief was palpable. "Ollie!"

Oliver's eyes shot open. Wide awake, he sat up and stretched his arms out, forgetting about his cast.

"Daddy!"

I slipped out from underneath Oliver, leaving a wide berth for Theo to get by. I watched them for a moment, feeling that little tug on my heart. Theo scooped him into his arms and held him so tightly, kissing his forehead until Ollie tried to wiggle away, laughing. And then Theo made a fuss over his son's cool new cast. In another universe, I belonged here. In a universe where I hadn't said the most hurtful, horrible words possible to a man who'd given me nothing but love.

Tucking the book into my bag, I attempted a quiet escape.

"Don't leave, Miss Quinn," said Oliver, pleading. "Daddy, Miss Quinn came in the ambulance and stayed with me the whole time. She even yelled at the nurses to help me."

I looked at Theo, whose eyes were already on me.

"I didn't *yell*..."

"And she read me a cool book too, with hobbits and a wizard... Can I borrow it, Miss Quinn?"

"Of course, you can," I said with a smile. *Keep it together for the kid.* I took the book out of my bag and handed it to him.

"Ollie, I have that book too," Theo said. "It's one of my favorites. Let Miss Quinn keep her copy. We can read mine, okay?"

"Will you do all the voices like Miss Quinn?" Ollie asked.

I couldn't help laughing—just a little. Oliver giggled, and even Theo seemed amused. When he looked at me again, I couldn't read the expression on his face, but my heart pounded. There were so many things I suddenly wanted to say to him, but I dared not open my mouth. A garbled pile of verbal diarrhea wasn't going to help me then. Especially not in front of Oliver.

"Time for me to go home, guys," I said, forcing a smile. "You heal quickly, mister, and get back to camp as soon as you can, okay?"

Oliver nodded firmly. *It is decided.* "Can I give you a kiss, Miss Quinn?"

I leaned down so he could reach my cheek, and found myself face to face with Theo. There were real emotions in his eyes, no longer cold and blank. He placed his hand on mine and mouthed a *thank you.* Just as I stood to leave, the doctor came in to discharge Ollie. My job was done.

Turning away, I wiped a single tear from my eye, and started walking slowly toward the exit. Not twenty paces down the hall, I heard my name.

"Quinn, wait," Theo called. He caught up to me, with Oliver in his arms and the backpack over his shoulder. "How are you getting home? Didn't you come in the ambulance?"

"I got a Lyft to bring me back to the school. There's a driver two minutes away. No big deal." I showed him my phone, where I'd pulled open the app.

"Cancel it. I'll drive you," he said with a weak grin. "It's the least I can do."

CHAPTER FORTY-SIX

After all the time apart, sitting so close to Theo was unnerving. I didn't know if I wanted to curl up into a ball under the dashboard or throw myself out the window. It might've been wiser to just take the Lyft. At least with Oliver sleeping in his booster seat, nice and cozy, we wouldn't have to pretend to be friends for his benefit. We could talk freely—if we were going to talk at all.

"Quinn," Theo said after several minutes of silence. The sound of my name on his lips gave me a chill. "Thank you. I can't tell you how much—"

"It's no problem. I'm just glad I could help," I replied as cheerfully as possible. Theo had been through enough without feeling obligated to say nice things to me. "Were you okay? What happened?"

"I'm an idiot," he sighed. "I left my phone at home—whole day, no phone—and I was so busy dealing with an angry client that I didn't notice. I never do that. Especially not when Oliver isn't with me. And Mom and Dad aren't even…"

"I talked to your Mom already, they're up to speed on the whole thing. I told them to go back to enjoying their vacation and that they could sign the little guy's cast when they get back."

"You… you did?"

"Of course, I did. I couldn't let them worry," I said easily. "I can't even imagine what my parents would've done in their situation. My mom was the biggest worrier. Dad used to try to get her to calm down—*Shawn's a grown man, Cheryl, he can get a motorcycle if he wants one*—stuff like that. They were a riot when they got going. One of the things I miss most now that they're gone."

And then… silence.

"Quinn, I—" he said, taken aback. "I didn't know."

I stared out the windshield, content to rest in that silence. I blinked, not sure what to say. It was so easy to bring them up like that. Piece eight, opening up, was an incredible relief.

"When?"

"Eight years ago," I dropped my gaze to my feet. Even with all the progress I'd made so far, it was still a struggle. Especially with Theo. "They were hit by a drunk driver going the wrong direction on 95, in broad daylight, on a random Tuesday. And then… gone."

"Why didn't you tell me?" he asked gently. "All this time, when I was opening up and telling you *everything,* you never mentioned that your parents were…"

"Dead?"

"Well, yeah."

"It's not exactly the best conversation starter, you know."

"It's *me*, Quinn. I don't care how you start conversations. You can tell me anything." He waited, silently, for me to continue. He knew it was the only way I'd talk.

I swallowed hard, staring at the sky turning pink as the sun set. If I'd started blurting everything out, where was it going to end? But then again, he'd just used present tense.

"When you met me, I wasn't well. I was just good at faking it. When they died, I dropped out of grad school to work at my dad's foundation. Then I piled on all that volunteering to help me stay distracted—Charlie's, Drama Cares, all the bake sales, everything. If I could be useful, then I'd be okay. The Wednesday before tech week was the anniversary of the accident—and all my coping strategies were failing. I'd relied on Franklin for all eight years and then, he died. I tried to stay out of the house, to avoid the constant reminders that he was gone, but I was running out of places to go. The staff of the foundation—the very thing I'd given up my dreams for—solved the biggest problem we'd ever faced, without me stepping foot in the building. I missed the emergency board meeting and they just kept going without me, like I was optional."

I paused, blinking, and waited. But he didn't move, so I kept talking.

"And then at the bar, Shawn had literally taken care of

everything and had this huge plan to turn things around for Charlie—without my help. He bought the building next door and hired staff to do all the jobs I used to do. He thought he was helping, but we'd been fighting for weeks about it because I wasn't ready to let go. Feeling so distant from Shawn, while dealing with the anniversary, was horrible."

He nodded, eyes still on the road, and let me continue.

"Tech week should've helped, but it was hard, having you there, because of how I was feeling after I found the photo album."

That had been hard to say, but when I paused for him to interject, he kept quiet.

"I tried to compartmentalize, but it was so hard, and everything started falling apart. Faith was furious with me after the final dress rehearsal. It was the absolute worst rehearsal I've ever run, and I was mortified. Then I burned my fricking and before opening night and I had to pretend I was okay for two full shows. My insomnia was out of control. I spent a lot of nights on the couch eating popcorn, watching old episodes of 80s sitcoms until I fell asleep. I slept maybe 25 hours total that entire week and all I wanted—the only thing that could've made it better—was my mom."

We'd made it back to the school and he parked next to my car. I considered making a run for it. I sniffled a few times and tried to discreetly wipe another tear from the corner of my eye.

"I didn't mean to upset you. Are you okay?" he asked softly. I nodded, holding back sobs.

"I'm okay," I said. But my voice cracked, betraying me. I took a deep breath. "The garden—"

The first sob, loud and sudden, snuck out without my permission. Theo rolled down the windows and cut the engine. He unbuckled his seat belt and turned to look at me, then took my hand.

"It's okay," he said softly. "Go ahead."

"The garden," I tried again, averting my eyes from him. *This was the hardest part.* My vocal cords were tight. Every word was a struggle. "Was Mom's. Well, *ours*. We worked on it together—every spring and summer, we'd spent so much time there, talking and laughing while we did all the work. I planted the rose bushes with her when I was nine. I stayed close to my dad's memory at the foundation, but Mom..."

A quiet sob. He squeezed my hand and I kept going.

"When she died, I couldn't go out there anymore. I wanted to—so badly. Every day, I'd walk out the front door and boom, there it was. But every time I tried to do something, I'd just stand there, thinking about Mom in her floppy hat, with a big smile on her face—" I stopped for a big breath. My heart was beating in my throat, but I had to tell him everything. He deserved to know why. "She'd be weeding and pruning and giving me instructions on how to trim a hedge. It got away from me before I had the courage to try, then the job was too big, and I couldn't... I didn't know how to start. But I wanted to do it. It was supposed to help me stay close to her. And then, my chance to fix it was just gone because... well, because..."

That was it. I couldn't keep going. Feeling brave, I made eye contact with Theo. He looked blurry through my tears, but even if my vision had been clear, it would've been hard to make out his expression. When he let go of my hand, another sob escaped. I'd expected him to pull away from me when we got to this part.

Theo got out of the car, peeked into Ollie's open window to check that he was still sleeping soundly, then walked around to the passenger side. He opened the door and pulled me out of my seat, right into his arms. If I closed my eyes hard enough, I could pretend it was Past Theo in the *Before Time*—before I'd ruined everything. My head rested perfectly in the crook of his neck. A few deep breaths, the scent of his cologne, the rhythm of his heartbeat beneath my chin. I'd once expected that telling him would drive a wedge between us—my mourning competing with his mourning, two broken hearts, too much painful baggage to manage. But there I was, wrapped in his arms, wholly supported and accepted, no hesitation and nothing but compassion. I felt guilty for ever selling him short.

Then hurting him and ruining my life.

"I'm so sorry. I didn't..."

Theo tightened his arms around me while I cried, but this was different from the last time I'd sobbed so hard—when Shawn had collected all my broken parts and helped me glue them back together. There with Theo, I cried the tears I'd been saving for this moment. And no matter what happened from here—whether this was the last time I saw him or the first time I'd truly been *myself* with him—it didn't matter. He held me tenderly until my ragged breathing had returned to normal.

I cleared my throat and straightened up, swiping at the tears with my wrist.

"Thank you for the ride and," I said, stepping back. I forced a smile for him, to prove I was okay. "For listening—it means a lot. I'm sorry I cried all over you."

I paused, collecting the rest of my thoughts. He breathed deeply, looking at me.

"I'm not making excuses for my behavior. I just want you to know why I lost it." My voice was raw, and my throat hurt. "I'm so sorry. You didn't deserve that. I wish I could take it back."

"And I wish you'd told me," he said with a sigh. "I never would've—"

"I know, but I couldn't. Past Quinn was hurting too much to see straight. She ruined a lot of things," I stopped to take a breath. "In a weird way, I'm glad you did it. It finally broke me. I completely fell apart... but I was suddenly free, I just didn't see it right away. I'm putting myself back together now. I'm in therapy, I cut back my time at the foundation, and I'm going back to school. I finally have my own goals back. I feel like the real Quinn again."

"Well," he said, pulling me close to his chest again. "I've known the real Quinn all along. And do you know what I think?"

"No?"

"I think she is a beautiful woman with a beautiful heart. Possibly the biggest heart of anyone I've ever known. She is not the kind of person who would hurt someone she cares about on purpose. Even when it happened, I knew it wasn't you. I just couldn't understand why you would say that. I mean, you did say it and that was..."

"Awful?"

"Devastating."

I sniffled and nodded. I owed it to him to listen, no matter how hard it was.

"Past Quinn could've let Past Theo be her partner. That's all he wanted."

"She was an idiot," I said, my voice small. He released me and I took his hands. "Present Quinn wants to fix it."

"She's off to a good start," he said with a kind smile. "Thank you for apologizing. And thank you for telling me everything. I know how hard that is."

"Maybe, if you don't absolutely hate my guts…"

"I don't *absolutely* hate your guts…"

I grinned. "Maybe we can be friends or something."

He lifted my hand to his lips and kissed it. Another wave of emotions hit, but I didn't cry this time.

"Or something sounds good." Theo reached into his car and pulled my tote bag from the passenger seat. He lifted it by the straps and paused when he saw. "New bag? I like it."

"Thanks," I said, as he placed the pale blue straps on my shoulder. No duct tape. No sad memories. But still so much room and so many pockets. "It was time."

With one last smile, Theo opened my car door and shooed me in. "Now get going. And text me when you get home, so I don't worry about you."

As I drove away—which was nearly impossible to do—I checked my rearview mirror for one last look at him. Theo was leaning on the roof of his car with his head resting on his arms. Sadness? Relief? I would've given anything to know what he was thinking.

CHAPTER FORTY-SEVEN

As instructed, I texted Theo when I got home. Picking the right words was tricky though, with that "or something" defining us for the moment. I kept it simple.

> Home safely, thanks again for listening

> I'm glad we talked, get some rest

I decided to follow his lead. It took a lot of bravery to even ask him about being friends again. And while I'd like to get swept up in the idea that we might get back together, I wasn't sure where we were on the road to forgiveness. He hadn't kissed me goodnight, but he had asked me to text. He texted me back but didn't use any pet names or kisses or winking emojis. If we were getting back together, he had to set the speed. I hurt *him*... I needed to be patient.

All I could think about was the night he'd asked me to be his girlfriend in the cheesiest, most adorable, most *Theo* way possible. We were making our own rules. What was the rule for forgiving your maybe-not-ex-girlfriend-or-something after she devastates you?

Oliver was out from camp the next day, as I expected, and then the weekend arrived, so I wouldn't see him again until Monday. I checked in with Theo via text a few times. He always texted back with updates but without any indication of what was happening between us. And that was less than helpful.

Sigh. Mom would've known what to do.

And so, I went to the local garden center and bought fresh soil and purple petunias. Next, I combed through the garage for Mom's gardening tools and gloves. I stood in the middle of the yard for a very long time. Then I sat down on the bench and put the gloves on. I stayed there until there weren't any more tears. I don't know how long that took—I hadn't set myself any timers.

Finally, I pulled together every ounce of mental and emotional strength I had and sat down underneath the oak tree. I poured the soil around the trunk, and created a smooth, rounded flower bed. With a deep breath, I started digging. One by one, I removed the petunias from their little plastic containers and dropped them into the dirt. I covered the roots and patted down the soil.

When I got to the third one, I started talking to Mom. I don't know if she could hear me, but it didn't matter. I'd finally found her again.

Abby doesn't call me often—we saw each other more than most aunts and nieces did as it was—so when she does call, I know it's important. It was a nice surprise to see her name pop up on my phone that Sunday morning.

"Yes, Miss Abigail," I said with a smile. I'd just gotten out of the shower, so I put the phone on speaker while I got dressed and tackled the knots in my wet hair. "How can I help you?"

"Are you busy, Auntie? Will you go to the mall with me?"

Will I to go to the mall?

"Obviously," I said, laughing. "What are we shopping for?"

"New school clothes," she said with a sigh. Abby, who loathes shopping almost as much as her mother does, tolerates it when I go with her. She doesn't like to admit it, but I am a *fun* shopping partner.

"Be ready in twenty minutes, okay? I'll be right over."

Mom had *loved* to go shopping and, aside from working in the garden, it was our favorite thing to do together. Taking Abby out for an afternoon at the mall, even if she didn't love it, brought back a lot of happy memories. I sent her into the dressing room with the maximum number of items, then swapped them out multiple times while she tried them all on.

"Chop, chop, Abigail," I laughed. "We've got a whole store to go through."

"Auntie... stopppp..." she groaned back. But judging from the smile on her face every time she showed off a different outfit, Abby was having a good time.

Once she'd tried everything on, Abby took her time going through all the items that fit to pick the ones she wanted to buy. I watched her check price tags and calculate in her head, holding them out to compare to each other, and growing more frustrated with every choice.

I did the only sensible thing. I took everything out of her hands and put it right on the counter for the cashier to ring up.

"Auntie, I can't," she protested. "I don't think I have enough money for everything. I was trying to..."

"Abigail Marie Anderson," I frowned. "Let your Auntie buy your new school clothes."

She frowned back. "I didn't ask you to bring me shopping so you'd pay."

"I know that, kiddo," I smiled, hugging her tightly. "How about you buy the pretzels today?"

On the way to the food court, both of us laden with her brand-new wardrobe, Abby gasped suddenly and stopped dead in her tracks.

"Look!" she said, placing the bags on the floor. She stood in front of a mannequin wearing the most beautiful dress I'd ever seen. The kind of beautiful dress that might be perfect for, say, *a gala.*

I stepped closer, taking the red satin fabric in my hand. It was a classic strapless ballgown style dress with a skirt slit. The color was a true red, not too orange-y and not too plummy. The fold-over on the neckline was lightly sprinkled with the tiniest little rhinestones. It was, perhaps, the most un-Quinn dress in the entire store—bright red, sparkly, sexy. Yet, there I stood, gawking at it.

"Auntie, you have to try this on!"

"It's beautiful," I said after a few beats. I dropped the fabric and turned back to our bags. "But I have plenty of dresses, Abby. I don't need to get anything new this year. I'm only going with Uncle Shawn."

"So?" she asked with a shrug. "Do you only wear nice

clothes for men, Auntie Quinn?"

I scoffed at her. "You're a stinker."

"Part of my charm," Abby said with a wide, innocent smile. "At least try it on. Pleeeeeeeease? You made me try on like a thousand things. It's just one dress."

I knew I was being manipulated by a teenager, but I took one off the rack in my size and traipsed to the closest dressing room. I left Abby on the bench with all the bags while I tried it on. As soon as I stepped into that gown, I knew. I zipped up the back as far as I could, then popped outside the door for an assist from my niece. And then we stood side by side in front of the mirror and just stared.

Every curve of the dress fit me perfectly, like it was tailored to my exact dimensions.

"Auntie..." said Abby, stunned to a whisper. "You have to buy this."

"Oh, I'm buying it. I might even wear it home."

She laughed and bumped me with her hip.

"Come on," she said, beaming. "I owe you a pretzel."

Ending our shopping trip with a hot pretzel in the food court had been a tradition since I was younger than Abby. Mom had a weakness for them. It runs in the family. Abby found us a table with enough room around it for four shopping bags and an extra chair to lay the garment bag over. Today's wallet damage had been substantial. *Worth it.*

"Auntie, can I ask you a question?"

"Anything, kiddo," I said, between bites. "What's up?"

"Why aren't you going to the gala with Theo? I mean, Oliver's dad. Uh, Mr. Miller?"

"I think you can call him Theo."

"Cool," she said, cataloging that in her mind. "Did you ask him to go with you?"

"Your mother put you up to this, didn't she? You're too young to ask these questions."

Abby shook her head.

"Does your mother tell you *everything,* missy?"

She shrugged. "How would I know if I knew *everything?*"

"That's fair."

"Stop deflecting—why not?"

"It's complicated, kiddo," I said, thinking carefully. "I think we're just friends right now."

She dipped a piece of her pretzel in cheese sauce and popped it into her mouth, considering my answer.

"Ask him to go to the gala. That will help you figure it out," she smiled. "Plus, you've got this amazing dress to wear now. It would be such a shame to waste it on Uncle Shawn."

"Excuse me?" I held back a laugh. "What happened to wearing nice clothes for myself, not for men?"

"With a dress like that? You can do both."

On Monday, Theo was back to his regular work schedule, and Lisa was back on Oliver duty. That first day, she walked to the door to pick up Oliver and just about crushed me with a hug.

"Oh Quinn, sweetheart," she said, getting teary. "Thank you so, so much. Thank you for keeping my boys safe."

Oh.

"I want you to know," Lisa continued, releasing me from her tight embrace. "That I've been pulling for you this whole time."

She winked at me. I just stared at her, dumbfounded.

"You... huh?"

"Theo told me everything," she smiled. I hoped he didn't tell her *everything*. "I know things have been tough between you."

Tough? Yeah, there was no way she knew *everything*.

"But you make him happy, so you hang in there."

"Ummm... thanks, Lisa," I said carefully. With a smile and one last squeeze, she walked her grandson to the car, and they went home.

That was... interesting. But it was also encouraging enough to give me that one last push. And I knew exactly where to find him.

Free from camp, I headed straight to the bar. Or... restaurant? *Sorry Charlie's Bar & Grill,* or that's what I thought they were planning to call it, anyway. No one tells me anything anymore—and I'm okay with it.

I entered through the back door, which had been propped

open to let the crew in and out with building materials. I dodged a couple of guys carrying two-by-fours and wiggled my way around a table saw, finally making it through the door into the bar. They'd taken the swinging door off the hinges to move in and out more easily—and it just looked weird. I gasped when I saw the state of things—the entire wall was missing, except for two columns, and I could see the gutted insides of the laundromat. Minus all the machines and stuff, but there it was—the future restaurant.

All the way across the room, where the front door of the laundromat used to be, Theo and Shawn were standing together, chatting. Shawn was talking animatedly, probably telling a story, and Theo was leaning against the wall, laughing. My brother and my maybe-not-ex-boyfriend-or-something talking together, unsupervised? I didn't love that.

Theo saw me first. He straightened up, smiling. My stomach flipped upside down. He hadn't smiled at me in so long and I'd missed that feeling. Shawn followed his gaze to me and gave me a thumbs up. He leaned over to say something in Theo's ear before they started walking toward me.

"Hey, guys," I said cheerfully—with just a hint of wariness. I had to yell over the drills and hammers. *How does Theo not have an eternal headache?* "What are you two up to over there?"

"Business things, obviously," said Shawn.

"Shawn's been telling me some great stories." Theo answered, overlapping my brother's words. When he realized the difference in their answers, he got nervous. "I mean, stories about him, though. Nothing specifically about *you,* because it would be rude to talk about someone behind—well, I guess you were sorta peripherally in them because they were about your brother, so that—"

"They were all about you, Quinn," Shawn said with an evil grin.

Theo grimaced.

"Well, this is fun…" I said, putting my hands on my hips. "Shawn, I'll talk to you at home."

My brother rolled his eyes at me. I ignored him.

"Theo, do you have a minute to talk now?"

He nodded and followed me out to the backroom, which wasn't any quieter. With all the workers coming in and out—there were maybe a dozen other people there—it was busy everywhere. I navigated the clutter of the backroom, heading for the office, which was full of personal belongings. There wasn't a lot of space, but it would do for the two-minute conversation I needed to have.

"What's up?" he asked, leaning on the doorframe.

"Uhhh..." I froze. *What was I going to say? Oh.* "Next week is the—"

"Hey Theo, got a sec?" A tall man in jeans and a t-shirt, wearing safety goggles on his head and *covered* in sawdust, appeared behind him. He mumbled something to him, but I couldn't make out any of the words over the noise outside. Something about dimensions and counters. Theo flipped through a few pages on the clipboard, took the pencil from behind his ear, and circled something. The other man leaned over to read it, gave him a nod, and walked back to the table saw.

"See?" Theo said, turning back to me. *"Not a contractor."*

The office was, apparently, not private enough, so I took his hand and dragged him toward the back door. *Where can a girl get some privacy around here?*

"Where are we going?" he asked.

"Somewhere quieter," I said, gesturing around me at the mess and the people and the noise. *Ooh, wait!*

I opened the walk-in fridge and he followed me inside. It was cold, but made for a nice, quiet retreat. And given the sweltering August weather, the cold felt nice. I closed the door and leaned against it.

"Don't worry, it doesn't lock from the outside. We won't die in here."

He seemed relieved, but still confused.

"Why have you trapped me in a fridge?"

"It's the only place I can think of with privacy—at least for a few minutes. It's crazy out there."

"Welcome to my average workday," he smiled. "So, what's up?"

I took a deep breath. *Okay, here goes.*

"Do you remember the gala I told you about—"

"The one on fire?" he said, lifting the corner of his mouth. "Yeah, I remember."

"The hotel was on fire, not the gala... sorry, technicality," I said. I shook it off. *Focus, Quinn.* "It's next weekend. The gala. And I was, umm... I'm hoping you will—no, let me try again. I'd like to ask you, if... I need a date. Help?"

"Are you asking me to be your date to the gala?"

I nodded, ready to barf.

"In a building that is *not* on fire, correct?"

I nodded again, feeling less like I might barf.

Theo paused, letting me suffer, with that smoldery, roguish eyebrow and half-smile. I thought I might die. Then he leaned in, placing a palm on the door right next to my shoulder, and moved until his lips were just inches from mine. He stared right into my eyes in silence. I held my breath, praying he would just kiss me.

"Sure." Then he stepped back, a mischievous smile on his face. He placed his hand on the door handle and I stepped aside to let him out. "Sounds fun."

After the door closed behind him, I banged my head against it a few times.

I am being tortured. I deserve it.

CHAPTER FORTY-EIGHT

"Sweet Jesus, Quinn, what are you wearing?"

I looked down at my red satin dress, and back to my brother, tidy and clean shaven in his tuxedo. Even his hair was tamed. He handed me his cufflinks, which once belonged to Dad, then stuck his arms out for me to clip them on.

"It's a dress, Shawn."

"I've seen you wear plenty of dresses before," he said, mouth agape. "That's not a dress. That's—"

"Sweet Jesus, Q! A ballgown? Who even are you right now?" Faith exclaimed, walking through the front door. She wore a floor-length halter gown in sapphire blue satin, with her gorgeous strawberry blonde hair twisted into a loose bun. Roy entered behind her, looking dapper in a classic tuxedo. I noticed that he'd grown a beard since I'd last seen him and I wondered how much Faith had influenced that decision.

"You look gorgeous, Faith. You both look amazing," I said. Roy smiled. Faith waved me off impatiently.

"Thanks, but seriously..." she said, touching the bodice of the dress. I swatted her hand away. "Is this the dress that Abby made you buy?"

"She made me try it on. The *dress* made me buy it."

"I can't believe this," she said, exasperated. "I've spent *decades* trying to get you to wear anything half this sexy. You go out with my daughter one time and come home with that?"

"What time is the limo coming?" Shawn asked, checking his phone.

"Any minute—Leah said six."

"Be right back," he said, then stepped out the front door and walked up the driveway. A moment later, a car pulled into the driveway. Shawn greeted the driver, a woman in a long, black sheath dress. The limo arrived seconds later, and I ushered Faith and Roy down the front steps.

"Can I lock up, Shawn?" I called over to him, still talking to the date I didn't know he was bringing. When he turned back to me, I recognized her. "Mary Beth? Hi!"

"Hang on!" Shawn trotted back to the house and up the steps. "Need my wallet."

"Umm, Shawn? I didn't know you had a *date.*"

"You got one, what was I gonna do? Shawn Davis is not a fifth wheel, Quinnie." He smirked, putting his sunglasses on.

"Ewww."

He dropped the act and shrugged. "It was the weirdest thing—she just stopped by the bar one day to say hi. Just out of the blue."

"She stopped by the *closed* bar?"

"Yeah, she just knocked on the glass and waved. We went for a coffee to catch up," he said nonchalantly. "We hadn't seen each other since high school. I thought it could be fun to bring her. She's nice."

"Wow, I'm impressed..." By Mary Beth especially.

"Where's Theo anyway?"

"He's meeting us there. He wanted to have his car with him," I said, with a shrug. "Hopefully not because he plans to make a quick getaway when this evening crashes and burns."

"After he sees you in this dress, he will never leave."

I laughed, shooed him out the door, and locked up behind us.

The Meadowgreen Manor was every bit as gorgeous as its photos. Rolling green lawns, a huge lighted water fountain at the main entrance, elaborate architecture... a *castle.* I wouldn't be surprised if Leah decided to hold the gala here every year.

The limo pulled right up to the front entrance and the valet opened the door for us. I let Shawn go first, followed by Mary Beth, and then Roy led Faith out. When I scooted across the leather seats to the door, a hand appeared in front of me. I took it and stepped out onto the pavement, face to face with my date.

"Hi," I said, suddenly self-conscious about this dress. Too

flashy? Too risqué? Too... much? But then I watched Theo's face as he took it all in—and I banished all doubts immediately. And as for him? Holy moly. Theo in a tux was some kind of sexy James Bond fantasy, especially with the roguish way he was looking at me. I kinda wanted to slide my arms into that dinner jacket and leave lipstick marks all over the collar of his shirt. That seemed inappropriate in this setting, so I just gawked at him for a moment.

"Hi," he replied, a tad flustered. I was so damn proud of myself. At least we were *both* torturing each other. "You look gorgeous."

His eyes and his voice said one thing, but then Theo leaned in and kissed me... on the cheek. *He's messing with me now. Or something.* He held out his arm and I hooked mine through it, then we followed the others along the pathway to the huge outdoor tent and found our table—all six of us together.

Shawn and I sat next to each other, so we'd be easier for the donors and board members to find. Of course, they interrupted us constantly throughout the night. Still, this was the first time we'd attended a gala with dates and friends, so Shawn and I were already having a better time than we normally did.

Theo sat on my right, then Faith, Roy, Mary Beth, and back to Shawn. Annoyed by the interruptions, Theo and Faith were taking turns saving us whenever we got stuck in a boring conversation. Faith asked me to take her to the bathroom several times. Theo invited Shawn on more than one bar run. I passed the rolls around a couple times. Shawn rescued a contact lens for Theo once—Theo does not wear contacts. It became quite the game. They saved us from several uncomfortable trips down memory lane with someone who knew Dad before we were even born.

"Don't worry," I said to Theo, halfway through dinner. "After they serve dessert, the older guests go home. We're not as popular with the younger donors."

"And then I can have my date back?"

"Hey, this is the price you pay for dating a celebrity," I said, trying not to laugh.

He leaned in close to my ear and whispered. "In that dress?

Worth it."
Oh.

The gala passed in much the same way as any other—the keynote speech was delivered by the parents of a child with cystic fibrosis who had benefited from a treatment the foundation had funded. It was always emotional to hear about the lives we'd changed so, okay, I got a bit teary. After that, we sat through praise from the Governor of Massachusetts and the obligatory address from Neil Taylor, Chairman of the Board. He named Shawn and me during his speech, as usual, so we had to awkwardly stand up at our table and wave while people clapped. At least he didn't make us get on stage like last year.

"I hate that," I muttered as I sat down. Shawn groaned. He hated it too. Theo had the nerve to laugh. "I'm glad my discomfort amuses you."

"Always," he winked. "It's sorta the theme of the night."

"I noticed," I said sweetly, batting my eyelashes. Theo leaned in again, but I wouldn't be fooled this time. I stared at him. "Don't you dare smudge my lipstick, Miller."

He laughed and sat back in his chair.

Much, much later… a three-course meal, dessert and coffee, and several drinks later… The older guests had indeed gone home, and the Davis kids could be normal adult humans again. The evening had been a whirlwind of activity, emotions, chocolate… everything. I was sitting alone at the table, taking it all in, while everyone else was off at the bar or the bathroom.

"Quinn!" Faith suddenly grabbed my arm. Her eyes were wide. She was possibly a teeny bit drunk. Maybe.

"Ow! What?"

She leaned over my shoulder. "Your. Date."

"Yes, my date is Theo. I am *very much* aware."

"And you want to tear that tuxedo off of him?"

"Yes, I very much do. But it's not going to happen," I said, giving her a look. *Who wouldn't?* "He's been messing with my head all night, but we're not back together."

"What if I were to tell you that it's not as unlikely as you might think?" She plopped into the chair beside me.

"No, we're not doing this, Faith."

"Come onnnnn...."

"How much have you had to drink?"

"Not enough, or I'd go talk to him myself," she exclaimed, gesturing toward him. "Just look at him, okay? Do you notice anything, I don't know... missing?"

Annoyed, I decided to humor her. Plus, looking at Theo was never *ever* an inconvenience. He was standing near the bar with Shawn, who handed him a scotch, looking like the casual, relaxed *Before Time* Theo I'd missed so much.

That thick brown hair, the sparkling eyes, that damn dimpled smile... His clean-shaven skin and the way his jaw moved when he talked... the strong shoulders hidden under that tuxedo, and how much I wanted to unbutton that shirt.

I took a long drink of ice water, eyes still on him, just as he turned and caught me checking him out. He winked at me. I choked. On water.

"Don't die," said Faith, laughing. She patted me on the back a few times. "You're so close."

"I'm okay," I said. "But I don't get it. What am I missing?"

"It's what *he's* missing that's important."

I looked back at Theo, still chatting away with Shawn, and then I saw—or didn't see—what Faith was talking about. When Theo raised his glass to his lips, nothing glinted off that finger. *No ring.*

"Ohhhh my god," I said, slapping Faith's arm. "He didn't... we didn't... We're not even back—"

"Deep breaths."

"Together."

"Surprise? Maybe you are." She laughed at me again as I struggled to breathe. "Deeeeeep breaths."

"Hey ladies," said Roy, arriving with a glass of wine for my best friend. Faith didn't even flinch at his words. He sat in the seat next to her and smiled at us both, assessing the situation. "What's going on?"

"Just doing a basic status update on Q's relationship," answered Faith. She took a sip of wine and nudged my arm.

"Shut up," I hissed.

"In fact, my dearest, let's get your take..." Faith began. I nearly slapped her again. She filled Roy in on the details, directing his gaze toward an oblivious Theo. "So, are they dating again or what?"

"He could've just taken the ring off because he was ready to move on... not necessarily with Quinn," Roy said. "Those things aren't mutually contingent."

That's disappointing.

"But..." said Roy, changing tone. "I do think it's likely he wants to get back together."

"Really?" asked Faith, overjoyed. "How do you know?"

"He mentioned Quinn at least ten times at the bar."

"What?" Faith and I said this simultaneously, and it was hard to tell who was more excited.

"As fun as this is..." he said, eyes locked on Faith. "Can I steal you for a dance?"

Faith and Roy drifted off together toward the dance floor, where he demonstrated his ability to waltz. He was just full of surprises. Faith was loving it, laughing as he twirled her around, gracefully avoiding other dancers as he did so. She was in danger of being swept off her feet by this guy—and I approved.

Magically, a new cocktail appeared before my eyes.

"Shawn said you liked the blue things." Theo sat down next to me, placing my new drink and his scotch on the table. "I have no idea what's in that."

"Shawn is correct. It's mostly sugar, alcohol, and potential Quinnsequences."

I took a sip through the teeny cocktail straw and found all the alcohol at the bottom. This bartender does not stir. When I want to drink straight alcohol, I'll order it. I swirled it around while Theo regarded me, strangely.

"Quinnsequences?"

"Yeah...." I said, taking another sip. Better. Now I could pretend it was juice. "That's what Faith calls all the problems I cause when I've been drinking—usually well-meaning things that go awry. Like telling Terry Kearnan he looked like a gerbil when he asked for an opinion on his new winter coat. Or dumping my college roommate's cigarettes down the toilet so she wouldn't get cancer—two cartons of them. Or writing an essay for a college history class about the plight of women in underwire bras. Quinnsequences."

He stared at me for a minute, wordlessly, while I sucked down the rest of my drink. I couldn't read his expression—amusement or judgement? His silence, plus the slight buzz from the cocktail kept me talking.

"I mean, I'm not like this belligerent drunk who robs banks and stuff... I've never done anything dangerous. It's mostly just harmless shenanigans. For what it's worth, my roommate does *not* have cancer and I got an A on that paper. It's not all bad."

He sat motionless. I knew what he was doing, but I couldn't stop talking. I sighed.

"I don't know why I tell you anything, it never—"

Theo leaned forward and kissed me gently.

We paused, looking at each other. "Terry Kearnan really did look like a gerbil though..."

"Shut up," he laughed.

Theo kissed me again, with more intensity. He hooked his foot around the leg of my chair and pulled it toward him, drawing me in closer. With hundreds of people in the room, all I thought about was how much I'd missed him. The softness of his lips. The scent of his skin. Watching his eyes close when he kissed me. And now, here he was.

Theo took my hand and kissed my knuckles, then looked into my eyes.

"Hi, honey."

Oh.

My relief escaped as a tiny gasp, and I threw my arms around him. He laughed lightly as though he might be just as relieved.

"I missed you so much," I said, holding back tears. He squeezed me just a little bit tighter.

"Come on," said Theo, pulling me to my feet. "Let's dance."

CHAPTER FORTY-NINE

Theo was not waltzing circles around the other dancers like Roy, but he was not rocking back and forth in one place like Shawn. Dancing somewhere between those extremes was fine by me. The feeling of his hand around my waist, the warmth between our palms, staring into those beautiful eyes... how did I end up back here?

Just like the *Before Time*... except that everything was different, including one essential detail. Foolishly, I hadn't looked at his hand when we were sitting together—he was too distracting. But now that we were so close like this, I needed to check. Was the ring really gone? I scanned the memory of spotting him so far away—what if we were wrong? What if Faith and I had a little too much to drink—we most certainly did—and imagined it was missing? I had to see. I had to be sure.

Unfortunately, his left hand was busy holding mine as we danced together, which made it hard to get a good look. I tried to casually glance at our hands a few times, just to sneak a look, but the angle was all wrong.

"Hey, Quinn," he said softly. "I'm over here."

I smiled at him, playing it cool.

"Everything okay?"

"Totally," I said, with another smile. After several more seconds of staring lovingly into his eyes, the voice was back—*you need to make sure.*

Theo's several inches taller than me, even with my heels on, so maybe I could duck down and see between our hands from beneath. Not awkward at all. It's not like I could pretend to tie my shoe. What about looking around? I tightened my arm around his shoulders and pulled us close together. If I rested my head and found a way to see around his neck... that angle was all wrong too. Maybe I could try the other shoulder? I was running out of ideas.

Theo started to laugh. I straightened back up, looking him in the eye.

"What's funny?"

"You."

Before I could be offended, he twirled me around and dipped me back onto his right arm. *So maybe he does know how to dance.* He kissed me so tenderly that I melted into him. And then, if I just lifted my head a little bit, I'd be able to see his left hand. But he laughed again.

"What?"

"Yes, I took it off," he replied. He let go of my hand and showed me. I stared at the circular mark where his wedding band had been. "You could've just asked, honey."

"That's not what I—"

He raised a skeptical eyebrow as he lifted me back to my feet.

"Fine. But I didn't want to be... isn't it rude to ask?"

"There's no such thing as rude between us. You can ask me anything."

"Well, I just happened to notice before—actually, *Faith* noticed and then she told me—which is how I noticed," I rambled, screaming internally. *How am I supposed to say this?* "It's just that... well, I guess I just wanted to ask, if you don't mind. Umm... when? Theo? Help."

"Are you trying to ask me when I took it off?"

I nodded, swallowing the rest of my garbled words.

"Before I got back into bed with you that night."

"Wait... *what?* You mean, all this time...?" I was stunned. *"You weren't wearing it during tech week?"*

He shook his head.

"So, when you kept asking to talk—"

"I was trying to tell you," he said, less playfully. "I figured you'd notice eventually. And when you didn't, I wanted to do something big to surprise you."

"Oh, no, I—"

"It's okay," he stopped me. "I'm not saying this to make you feel guilty. We've already talked about what happened to you that week—and we're putting that behind us."

I sighed, unsatisfied. It was going to take a long time for me to be okay with how I'd acted.

The first song had faded into a second, but Theo didn't make any move to stop dancing. He kept me there in his arms, looking into my eyes, and I never wanted him to let go.

"Can I ask... why?" The question was nagging.

"That night, when I tucked you into my bed, it just hit me—all I wanted was to be there with you, but only if I could *completely* be with you. I wanted to wake up next to you and make you breakfast, make you laugh, drink coffee with you in my t-shirt, sitting in my kitchen. I wanted to bring you with me to pick up Oliver, so we could tell him about us—together."

I couldn't move or breathe or blink my eyes. I swallowed, determined not to let go of my hot tears.

"I went downstairs and sat there with that photo album, in the middle of the night, to finally make peace with it all. I was never supposed to be where I was—my life's plan had been completely derailed, and I took all that sadness and grief, and hid it from everyone. I spent my energy raising Oliver, trying to be two parents, and it was easier to stay strong for him than for myself. So that's what I did. But then I met *you* and for the first time, I couldn't avoid those feelings anymore. You held me while I cried, Quinn. I'd never let anyone in so far before. I didn't realize how broken I was until I wanted to heal. For you."

Overwhelmed, I laid my head on his shoulder, burying my face into his neck. He pulled me against him.

"The thing is, I'll always love Jane, and I thought that meant my heart would always be broken and I'd never be able to give it to someone else. But that's not really how hearts work," he said, as his tone shifted. I raised my head from his shoulder, and he was just inches from my lips. But his brows pulled together—he was suddenly nervous. "Now I have this heart, all put back together, and I *can* give it to someone. If you'd like it, Quinn, it's yours."

All that time I'd spent healing my own heart, reassembling the exploded pieces of my life, and it had never occurred to me that he'd faced the same thing. I'd known, of course, that he'd been in pain, but I never saw how similar our paths had been. Faith was right, *loss is loss.*

I moved my hand to the back of his neck and pulled his lips to mine. His arm moved up from my waist to the middle of my back to steady us and he deepened our kiss. Then he broke away and stared into my eyes.

"Is that a yes?"

"Mm-hmm." Laughing, I hugged him tightly.

As we held each other, a third song began, and I realized how dangerously close we were to running out of time. I couldn't stand the thought of watching him drive away, climbing into that limo, and trying to sleep in my lonely bed when my heart was racing like that.

"So..." I began, seductively. I stared into his eyes. "What's your curfew, Miller?"

And then came his own seductive look. It gave me chills.

"Oliver," Theo whispered. "Is visiting his grandparents for the *entire* weekend."

His hand moved from my waist into his pocket for something. He presented a keycard with the logo of the hotel across the street emblazoned on it.

"Room 402."

Ohhhh, yes please.

"Did you have any plans between now and, I don't know," he said playfully. "Monday morning?"

"This is awfully presumptuous," I said, scandalized. It was amazing I could even make words into sentences. "What if I need overnight things?"

"I stole your emergency bag this afternoon," he grinned mischievously. "Shawn unlocked your car for me."

"As in... my *brother* Shawn?" My mouth fell open. "Are you guys like... buds now?"

"At least we know he approves," Theo shrugged, grinning.

"Wow... you know what? I'm not even mad," I said, genuinely impressed. "After all, if you've got the bag, this must be an emergency."

"Yes, it definitely is."

I took the keycard and slid it into the top of my dress. Theo looked like he might pass out.

"There's only one problem..." I said. Theo tilted his head. "My emergency bag does not contain *all* the supplies we might need..."

"Ah, yes," he said, with a sly grin. "But mine does."

"Then it looks like we've solved all the problems."

He winked. "I look forward to the Quinnsequences."

"Oh honey, you have no idea..." I raised my eyebrow. "I just hope you're prepared for *enough* of them."

"Ohh," he grimaced. "More than one box..."

I frowned.

"...of twelve?"

I wrapped my arms around his neck and leaned in so close that our lips nearly touched.

"That's a good start," I whispered.

Judging from the look on his face, it took Theo quite a bit of restraint not to carry me off the dance floor and straight to room 402.

As the gala ended, Shawn and I were stationed near the door, saying goodbye to the remaining donors and members of the board. They said a lot of nice things about Dad, made some patronizing jokes about how big we'd grown, and reminded us that we looked just like our parents, who would be so proud of us... all the usual stuff people say to make themselves feel better. I've been hearing it for eight years now.

Theo stood nearby with an amused smile on his face as I played my role. It was the first time he'd seen me in this context. I wondered what he was thinking. Yes, Quinn Davis can schmooze. Maybe not as well as Shawn, but that wasn't a fair comparison, because he'd gotten most of Dad's charm.

Once the bulk of the attendants had been herded out, I flagged down Leah as she made her final rounds with the vendors. Normally, I'd have been trotting along next to her doing the same, but I realized now that she'd never needed me as much as I'd needed her.

"Hey," I said, meeting her halfway. "This was amazing, Leah."

"Most successful one yet, we nearly doubled last year's donations," she said with a wide smile, revealing her brilliant white teeth. I knew how much Leah had been running around all night and yet, not a single hair was out of place. She'd never broken a sweat.

"Congratulations!" I hugged her.

"To both of us," she said.

"Mostly you this time around—and definitely from here on out. I'll stop getting in your way," I said with a grin. She waved it off politely, pretending she wasn't happy about it. "Starting right now."

"So, I'll see you..."

"Whenever you need me," I smiled. "Just call me and I'm there."

Leah hugged me one more time and we said our goodbyes. It felt good to pass the torch on to someone who deserved to carry it. I think Dad would've been prouder of me for doing *that* and reclaiming my own life than anything else.

Then I returned to my date at our table, where the crew was packing up to go. Faith yawned, stretching her arms out, and landed snuggly against Roy, who held her tightly. She closed her eyes, ready for bed. Mary Beth had been her regular quiet self all night, with an enormous, unwavering smile on her face. Shawn was turned away from me, talking to her, and she was starry-eyed.

Theo offered his arm and we walked everyone to the limo, already waiting out front. The valet opened the door when he saw us, but this was where we'd part ways. I said my goodbyes as they all climbed in.

"Told you so," Faith said with a nudge. Then she pulled me in for a hug, kissed me on the cheek, and whispered in my ear. "Try not to *actually* tear his clothes off..."

I swatted her arm, trying not to laugh.

As they climbed into the limo, I heard her say something excitedly to Roy, who responded with a perfect *yes, dear.*

I told Mary Beth I'd see her on Wednesday, as usual, and

that I wanted to hear all about her night. I decided I could compartmentalize enough to let her gush, if I pretended it wasn't Shawn she was talking about.

And then Shawn, whom I hugged tightest of all.

"Thank you," I said genuinely. "Although I am irritated that you knew about his plans this whole time…"

"I knew nothing," he lied, releasing me. "I'm not allowed to, remember?"

"Uh huh," I laughed. But then I pulled him into another hug. "I wouldn't be here without you, Shawn. Thank you for catching me."

"Mom and Dad would be proud, Quinnie, and I'm not just saying that."

"And even prouder of you."

"Okay, enough sap," he said, pulling away from me. "Time to go get the guy."

"All over it," I said with a wink. "But you better behave yourself."

"And you better not," he answered, then paused to consider what he'd just said. "Just… boundaries, right? Let's pretend you're having a tea party or whatever."

CHAPTER FIFTY

Theo had parked his car at the hotel and walked to the castle for the gala, so we strolled back across the street together and into the lobby. Inside, the hotel was the perfect complement to the elegance and atmosphere of the Meadowgreen Manor. It made excellent business sense—host your wedding at the castle, book your block of rooms here. I noticed right away that some of the Davis Foundation's out-of-town donors had the same idea.

"Okay, here's the deal," I said, trying to use Theo as a shield. "Don't look, but the people behind you..."

He turned and looked.

"Come on! If they see me—or recognize you, which they might because *hello*... you're a stud..."

He chuckled quietly.

"Then they will absolutely come over here to chat with me. We need to get out of here," I said, stepping around him to avoid a couple from Michigan. "I'm not joking."

Still, he seemed skeptical.

"Okay, fine," I said firmly. "Don't take this seriously. Just remember that the longer I'm stuck out here, the longer it will take to get me upstairs and out of this dress..."

That seemed to speed things up a bit, as we deftly navigated the busy lobby. There were donors everywhere and I was wearing a bright red ballgown that I'm positive had stood out all night. It was only a matter of time before I'd get spotted. I didn't go full *Mission Impossible,* but I spent a lot of time hugging the wall of the hallway, until I could duck around the corner and wait for Theo to call the elevator.

After several painful moments, the elevator car arrived. Relieved, I stepped in and hid behind Theo until we were in the clear. The elevator doors closed slowly, and I breathed a deep sigh just as they met in the center. Finally, we were alone, for the first time all night—technically, for the first time in many long weeks. Theo brushed my cheek tenderly, looking into my eyes with such intensity, I thought my knees might buckle. The heat in the space between us crackled.

And then the elevator doors opened again before we'd even left the first floor.

A little old woman entered, walking slowly with a cane, and I recognized her as Phyllis Buckman, one of Dad's oldest and most loyal clients. She and her husband, both in their 80s now, had traveled from their retirement home in Maine for the weekend. At the gala that night, she'd told me how it was the highlight of her year. Of all the donors, she was on the shortlist of those I didn't mind talking to. Except when I was off-duty and trying to make out with Theo in an elevator.

All I wanna do is rip off my date's clothes—is that so wrong? Why can't everyone just leave me alone?

Phyllis looked up once she'd stepped inside and her face lit up at the sight of me. She leaned over and pressed the five, which meant she'd be traveling all the way up with us to four and then some. The door closed again, and she settled against the wall of the elevator, both hands on her cane.

"Hello again, my dear. What a treat to see you twice in one night," she smiled widely. For a moment, she stayed quiet, looking me up and down. Looking Theo up and down.

"Quinn, dear," she continued. "I didn't know you were married."

Oh, sweet lord, no.

"Oh, umm..." I started, positive that my face was the same color as my dress. "I'm actually n—"

"Theo Miller," he said, shaking her hand. He was just ear-to-ear with amusement right now. And I was slumped against the wall with my hand over my face. "It's nice to meet you—"

Oh my god, please no.

"Call me Phyllis, please. My husband and I were clients of Bill Davis's for many years. He built our entire retirement package—brilliant man. Best decision we ever made, trusting him. He was truly one of the good ones."

"Thank you," I said, relaxing. I could do *this*. "And thank you for coming all this way. It would've meant so much to Dad that you and Don have continued your support of Mara's legacy."

"Oh, now, she's just the sweetest, isn't she?" Phyllis, growing a bit teary, was beaming at my definitely-not-husband Theo.

"She is," he answered, with a sideways glance at me. I smiled back.

The elevator dinged, announcing our arrival to the fourth floor.

"That's us," I said, nudging Theo toward the door.

"Quinn, dear," she said, gently touching my arm. "It was so good to see you. I don't think I've ever seen you happier. You're absolutely glowing."

Am I?

"Now... you two have fun tonight," she said, then winked.

Theo interlaced our fingers and tugged my arm. I waved goodbye to Phyllis as I stepped out of the elevator. Just as the doors closed, I heard her mumble to herself, *oh to be so young...*

When the coast was clear, Theo burst into laughter.

"I'm so sorry," I said, turning to him. He shook his head at me, amused.

"Time to go," he said, leading me down the hallway.

Of course, our room was on the exact opposite side of the building. I noticed how much faster he was walking now. We finally arrived at the door and Theo turned to me expectantly. *Oh right... I have the key.* With a coy smile, I pointed to my cleavage and waited for him to retrieve it. I giggled as he reached for it, partly because it tickled but mostly because of the look on his face.

Making Theo lose his cool was my favorite game.

The keycard appeared, the green light flashed as he waved it in front of the lock, and Theo held open the door for me to enter. Room 402 was a gorgeous corner suite with a *very spacious* whirlpool hot tub, a gigantic king size bed, two couches, and a giant tv screen. A bottle of champagne, chilling in an ice bucket, a pair of glass flutes, and a huge bouquet of roses sat on a table near the couches. Behind me, I heard *all* the locks clicking on the door.

Theo turned on a few lights, just enough to create a sultry, romantic atmosphere.

I crossed to the table and leaned down to smell one of the lush, red roses. Theo took my hand, spun me toward him, and caught me around the waist.

"Hi," I said, staring into his eyes.

"Hi, honey," he replied, his lips so close to mine.

"I *do* like that one." It made me tingly when he said it. "I knew you'd get it someday."

"Right under the wire, too," he said, feigning relief.

"Good, I guess I won't have to leave now…"

"Don't you dare." He laughed low in the back of his throat. "I would be absolutely crushed if you left."

"Oh, really?" I said playfully. "Why is that?"

"Because I have fallen completely, ridiculously, desperately in love with you, Quinn Davis," he said, his eyes locked with mine. "Okay?"

"Okay." My voice was low and breathy. I wrapped my arms around his neck. Our lips met. Our bodies pressed together. He lifted me up and pinned me against another wall. Our kiss evolved from desperate and hurried into the most incredible combination of passion and tenderness. He found the slit of my skirt and ran his fingers up my thigh, sending chills along my skin.

"This dress," he said against my mouth. "Was a cruel and dirty trick, Davis. Do you have any idea how hard it was to keep my hands off you all night?"

"Then shut up and take it off."

Theo stopped the kiss to carry me to the bed. There, he slowly unzipped my dress, brushing my skin lightly all the way down. Both hands trailed down my back searching for something.

"No bra," I whispered. And then his hands traveled to my waist and he stopped, looking at me with exactly the right amount of shock on his face. "Nothing."

Theo groaned softly and let my gown drop to the floor. Then he reached up and removed the pins from my hair. It tumbled down, tickling my shoulders. When he looked at me, his eyes were full of lust and he wore a devilish grin.

"Damn, you're gorgeous," he said, breathlessly.

"And you, hot stuff, are still dressed." I pulled off his jacket and tossed it on the floor.

"That's a rental," he said with a grin, while his hands worked swiftly on his shirt buttons.

"I'll pay for it." I untied the bow tie and dropped it on top of the jacket. "Now take off your clothes, before I ruin your new suit."

In seconds, his clothes were piled on top of his jacket—all of them—and he was leading me down to the bed. I felt an instant rush. *It's real this time.* I moved back to the pillows, drawing him along the bed with me, while his kisses traveled the length of my body, along my collarbone, and up the side of my neck, his mouth hot on my skin. When he reached my lips, finally, he paused.

"*Yes,*" I sighed, fighting the urge to speed things up. "*Please.*"

Then he gave me that smoldering look of his that melted my insides. That was what finally did it—the moment I knew, the moment I wanted him to know—the perfect time. I took his face in my hands and held his gaze. My heart was full.

"I am completely, ridiculously, desperately in love with you, too, Theo Miller."

Afterwards, it just made sense to drink the champagne. In the hot tub. I cuddled up to Theo as he leaned back against the wall of the tub, sipping from my glass, perfectly content. I was positive that I was glowing. Now that we'd opened our hearts to each other, every moment was incredible. I settled against his chest, his arm around my shoulders to hold me close, his fingers drawing swirls and circles lazily on my arm. Every inch of me was alive.

Theo was here. With me. And we were truly, wholly together.

I lifted his left hand to my lips and kissed the space where his ring had once been. The very one he'd taken off when his heart was healed and full again. The heart he'd given to me. I lay there, awash with the memories of our reuniting kiss, the longing look in his eyes, the feeling of his arms around me again after so much time apart. The thought of it all and the sensations of our bodies in the hot water, softly brushing against each other—it gave me a buzz stronger than the half bottle of champagne.

Gently, I placed a warm, wet palm on his face and pulled him to me for a soft kiss. When our eyes connected, his were full of love and something else that I couldn't name. Embarrassment?

"Quinn—I just, I have to say, I mean... Four years is a *long time*, honey," he said suddenly, looking away. I'd hoped he wasn't still beating himself up about what happened. He was the only one bothered. "I'm sorry, I—can we call it a warm-up? I can definitely do better—"

"Hey, hot stuff," I said. When he turned back to me, I gave him a coy smile. "Just look at this incredible afterglow—all thanks to you. Do I look unsatisfied?"

He shook his head, a weak smile on his lips.

"You..." I began, wrapping my arms around his neck. I rested my forehead on his. "Are a *very* talented man who would never leave a job unfinished. Are all contractors so good with their hands?"

"Not a contractor," he said, pretending to be annoyed. But the color in his cheeks said otherwise.

"Fine," I said, waving him off. "Then let's say you managed my project very well..."

He laughed suddenly, loudly, and splashed water in my face. I leaned in, laughing with him, and shut him up with a hungry kiss. He slid a hand into my hair, pulling me closer, and kissed me back. I sucked gently on his bottom lip as I broke away, then looked him in the eye again. I could see a fresh wave of lust forming. Much better.

I picked up his champagne glass from the side of the tub and put it in his hand. I clinked mine against his and waited for him to take a sip with me.

"Now that we love each other so damn much, shouldn't we be celebrating?"

"It's still cute when you swear."

"Get used to it," I said in a low, playful tone. "Because if you keep doing stuff like *that* to my body, I will be swearing quite a bit more."

That earned a second, smaller laugh. When both glasses were empty, Theo set them aside and pulled me to his chest again. My hand over his heart, the rhythm of it beating, the scent of his skin, the sound of his breathing. My new happy place.

"Theo," I began, interlacing my fingers with his. "I still can't believe you did all of this—after everything that happened, before we'd even talked about getting back together—"

"Who said we were back together?" he asked with a grin.

"Shut up," I said, splashing water at him. "What if I'd said no? You'd be stuck in this huge, beautiful room, sitting in this hot tub alone. You'd have to drink that whole bottle by yourself."

He raised his eyebrow, giving me that warm tingly feeling all over again.

"You weren't going to say no, honey."

"Again, so presumptuous. How did you know?"

"You leaned in," he said with a smile. "When you asked me to be your date for the gala, in the fridge at the bar. I said I'd go with you, and you leaned in toward me with your eyes closed."

"Did I?" That was true. I definitely had.

"So, I took my chances," he said with a smirk. "And why did *you* come here in that damn dress, wearing nothing underneath it?"

"Wishful thinking. I am ever the optimist."

Theo laughed, letting go of the last of his tension. He kissed me sweetly, but it quickly became something sultry and passionate. He broke away, breathless. As I settled back against his body, I made a sudden realization. I turned to him, my eyebrows raised.

"I think," I said, pressing my body against his. "We're both feeling *very* optimistic right now."

"Definitely," he said, with a mischievous grin. Theo placed his hands on my hips and pulled me onto his lap. I let out a little sigh against his mouth and he groaned deep within his chest.

And neither of us spoke again until we watched the sunrise together, entangled and in love, ready for our new beginning.

EPILOGUE

One Year Later

"I think that's the last of it," Shawn said, carrying out a box marked *Books*. "Unless there are 9,000 more boxes of books hidden somewhere."

"No, that'll do it," I said, hiding a laugh.

"I wouldn't judge you if there were," said Theo, coming up behind me. "After all, you can never have too many books."

"God, I love this man," I sighed, playfully nudging him with my elbow.

Theo laughed lightly as he took the box from my brother and slid it into the back of the moving truck. I checked the last item off our detailed inventory list—the result of the combined organizational skills of Davis and Miller. Moving in with a project manager had its perks—including an *entire room* of built-in bookshelves. Now all our books could intermingle and live a wonderful, happy life together.

"Okay," Shawn said, slamming the truck door shut. "So, we'll meet at your place to unload the boxes, then drop off the rest of the furniture at my apartment, right? What time does Roy's birthday party start?"

"Four," Theo answered, checking the time on his phone. "Plenty of time to make both stops and get to Faith's house."

"You're picking up Charlie, right?" I asked my brother. "His flight gets in at two-thirty."

"All over it," Shawn said with a smile. "I still can't believe we got him to leave the continental United States for an entire week."

"Is Mary Beth coming to the party?" I asked. Shawn nodded, blushing. *"Aww, you really like her."*

"Leave the man alone," Theo laughed. He pulled me in for a hug and kissed me on the forehead. "It's tough to be so in love."

"Now *you're* making fun of me, too?" Shawn said, incredulous. Theo laughed. "And also... eww. Boundaries, guys."

I wiggled free of my boyfriend's arms and grabbed my brother's wrist.

"Come on, let's do one last walk-through."

With a nod, Shawn stepped to the side of the porch stairs to let me pass. Behind me, Theo called for Oliver, who had been running around the backyard with our new puppy.

Inside the house, the shock of the empty rooms and dusty floors took my breath away. Shawn must've heard it because he suddenly took my hand tightly in his own. We'd made this decision together, gone through all the motions together, and now we'd say one last goodbye together.

"I'll check the downstairs," he called over his shoulder. "Are you okay checking the upstairs? Want me to come with you?"

"No, I can do it," I called back. And I could. I knew I could.

I walked up the stairs one last time, took a deep breath, and opened their door. Even though I knew my parents' room was empty, the sight of it was jarring. Their bed was gone, the closets emptied, the vanity sold at the estate sale. The mirror, taken from the wall with great care, was on its way to Theo's—rather, *our*—house. We'd made space on a wall in the living room, alongside the family photos taken after Oliver's birth. There was room for everyone, for all the lost love, and for our new love, too.

After a quick scan of the bedrooms, the upstairs bathroom, and the linen closet in the hall, I was satisfied and ready to say goodbye. I ran my hand slowly over the scuffs on the walls, the remnants of torn stickers on Shawn's door, the chipped paint here and there—things that the painters would cover up before the new owners moved in. The evidence that the Davises had lived here.

I trotted down the stairs and turned the corner into the kitchen, where I spotted Shawn lost in thought. He was leaning back against the counter, staring blankly at the floor where the table and its four chairs once stood. He looked like Dad, more than ever, with the heels of his hands on the rim of the counter, one foot crossed at the ankle over the other, the thoughtful grimace tugging at the corners of his mouth. I walked over to the spot next to him, mimicking his pose, and leaned my head on his shoulder.

We stood in silence for what seemed like a long time and, finally, he took a deep breath.

"You okay?" I asked quietly.

"Yeah," he answered after another pause. "This looks weird."

"It *feels* weird."

Shawn wrapped an arm around my shoulders and squeezed. With my arm around his waist, I squeezed back. My brother had played such a key role in the healing I'd done since my breakdown last year, and although we were both healthy and ready to stand on our own feet again, I would miss having him across the hall every day. Even when he annoyed me.

"Do you think Mom and Dad would be upset?"

"For selling?" he asked, as if there was another option. "Nah."

"They'd understand, right?"

"They've been gone for nine years, Quinn. They didn't want us to stay here forever. If they were alive, they probably would've sold it and downsized by now anyway. Wasn't that Dad's plan?"

"Sure," I said, swallowing hard. We both knew Mom would never have let go of her beautiful garden. Even with Dad pushing to move, she wouldn't have sold it. *Not while I'm alive,* she'd once said. That's why I'd brought the marble bench to the garden I'd built in my new front yard—a garden she would have loved.

That was the thought that brought the tears. I sniffled, squeezing Shawn one last time.

"Come on," Shawn said, standing up straight. "Every minute we stay here will only make it harder to leave. Are you ready?"

I followed his slow steps to the porch, let him trot down the stairs ahead of me, and stopped to close the door. With the doorknob in my hand, I whispered a final goodbye—to Mom and Dad, and Franklin too—and slowly pulled the door shut. When I turned around, Theo was standing at the bottom of the stairs with his hand outstretched.

"Ready to go, honey?" His smile faded at the sight of my

tear-stained cheeks. "Are you okay?"

Go, I heard Mom say. *It's time.*

"Yeah," I said, smiling ear to ear. I took Theo's hand. "I'm ready now."

ABOUT THE AUTHOR

Stephanie Haddad is the author of *A Previous Engagement, Love Regifted, Love Unlisted,* and *Socially Awkward,* as well as the short story collection *Other Kinds of Love* and a collection of essays on motherhood and writing, *My Life in Yoga Pants.* She is an active member of a local community theater group in Somerville, MA, where she often produces plays—the theatrical equivalent of project management. She lives outside Boston with her loving husband, daughter, son, and their unflappably happy dog, Max.

Made in United States
North Haven, CT
16 September 2022

24189091R00192